Prince of Sunland Book 1

The Crown and the Axe

DARCY FORNIER

Stones of Elah Press
Spring Hill, Tennessee

The Crown and the Axe
Copyright © 2019 by Darcy R. Southern

Published by Stones of Elah Press
Spring Hill, TN 37174
darcyfornier.com/stones-of-elah-press/

All rights reserved. No part of this publication may be reproduced, stored in a retrieval system, or transmitted in any form or by any means—for example, electronic, photocopy, recording—without the prior written permission of the publisher. The only exception is brief quotations in printed reviews.

Library of Congress Control Number: 2019913013

ISBN: 9781734002508

Scripture quotations taken from the New King James Version®. Copyright © 1982 by Thomas Nelson. Used by permission. All rights reserved.

This is a work of fiction. Names, characters, incidents, and dialogues are products of the author's imagination and are not to be construed as real. Any resemblance to actual events or persons, living or dead, is entirely coincidental.

Cover design by Molly Southern Photography.
Cover photos © Molly Southern. Used by permission.
Crown graphic from Dreamstime.com; free photo 2012301 © Madartists.

Dedicated with much love …

To Jesus. Always to Jesus.

And to my crazy, wonderful family: Daddy, Mama, Lizzy, and Sunnygirl. I love us!
Thank you for your unfailing support. Without you, there would have been no Sunland.

Table of Contents

1. Quintain 1
2. Fall of the Axe 11
3. The Castle Kitchen 24
4. The Witch's Curse 36
5. The Woodcutter's Son 43
6. Larch Wreaths 52
7. Holding His Own 61
8. Chivalry 68
9. The Healer's Chamber 75
10. The Forester 83
11. Sharpened Shovels and Bitter Tea 88
12. A Hitch in Stride 100
13. Blue Eyes 111
14. His Mother's Son 118
15. Six Small Problems 130
16. Kik 141
17. Firebrands 148
18. That Girl 158
19. Night of Waiting 169
20. The Clearing in the Woods 180
21. Memories 186
22. Fathers and Sons 197
23. Rebellion 208
24. He Knew Better 214
25. No Sight of the Sun 223

26. The Imposter	231
27. Captive	237
28. Lingering Darkness	243
29. The Spy	252
30. Niklas	259
31. Freed	269
32. Questions	275
33. Fredrik	282
34. Shielded	290
35. Allies or Enemies	302
36. Sword on the Snow	313
37. Moritzburg	325
38. No Proof	333
39. Prince on Trial	343
40. The Message	352
41. Footstep in the Shadows	360
42. A True Knight	366
43. A Fist and a Bargain	377
44. The Choice	388
45. The Weapon in His Hands	397
46. At This Hour	404
47. The Coin	415
48. Bound with This Vow	425
Epilogue	433
Glossary	437
Author's Note	439
Acknowledgements	441
Scriptures Referenced	443

Then He said to them all, "If anyone desires to come after Me, let him deny himself, and take up his cross daily, and follow Me.

-Luke 9:23

1

Quintain

Dierk wasn't neglecting his duty, merely postponing it. Meadow grass swished around his knees as he crested a hill. Shouts rose from the large pond below, where his fellow squires had the water churning.

He looked over his shoulder. Duke Ebner's magnificent castle shone in the harsh sunlight. Dierk was supposed to be inside those walls, helping two other squires in the saddle room—inspecting the saddles and bridles, oiling stiff leather, polishing metal fasteners. But the other two would be sure to leave Dierk's portion for him to finish later. He was seventeen, old enough to make a few decisions of his own.

"Ho! Your Highness!"

Only one person called him by that title. Dierk turned back to the pond. From the water, his friend Bastian waved his arm high. Dierk waved back and headed down the hill.

He dropped his clothes in a pile on the bank beside

several others and dove into the pond. Like a living thing, the cool water pushed against him, flowing over him. Now *this* was the way to spend a sunny afternoon.

When his lungs started burning, he shot upward into the warm air, scented with sun-baked grass.

"Hey, watch it." A splash hit the back of Dierk's head.

Dierk spun around. Grinning, he shoved water at his friend. "Is that a challenge, Leonhard?"

"Not yet." Leonhard plunged underwater.

Dierk leaned back and kicked his legs to propel himself. His fellow squires knew not to challenge him unless they wanted all-out war. He could outshoot any of them in a water fight. In other sports too.

Several yards away, a dozen pages and squires played a rowdy game of tackle-ball in the water. One of them jumped an opponent, shoving him under with a terrific splash. Waves rolled toward Dierk, and he swam out of their path. He'd join the next game.

Bastian popped up beside him, shaking his head like a wet hound. "Wish we had time to swim every day in summer, don't you?"

"Aye." Dierk swept his hand underwater, letting the coolness gush between his fingers. "But then Sir Wilhelm wouldn't have as many hours to shout at us for sloppy handling of our weapons."

"He never has to shout at *you* for that." Bastian grimaced. "I almost crushed my own foot with the mace yesterday."

Dierk chuckled. Their training master must've thundered over that. "You'll master it. I could show you a few things to help."

Bastian winked. "Thanks."

"Just come find me Monday."

Though a year younger than Dierk, Bastian had offered genuine friendship from the day Dierk came to Duke Ebner's—when the other squires still weren't sure how to treat a prince in their midst. Dierk had been teaching Bastian things ever since, helping him overcome his natural clumsiness.

"Hey, I can still do the trick you showed me last week." Bastian plunged underwater, balled up, and flipped twice before his head surfaced. "I taught it to a couple of pages before you got here—without half-drowning myself."

Dierk grinned. Small wonder Bastian was the best-liked lad among the squires.

Bastian slung his dark blond hair out of his eyes. "Where's Anton?"

"Finishing his assignment, I guess. He had the armory today."

"Ah. Glad we finished early."

"Mmm." Dierk rolled to his stomach. With powerful strokes, he swam for the pond's far side before Bastian could ask about his assignment. Dierk wouldn't lie outright, and he didn't want Bastian to know he'd taken his leisure before completing his duties.

Duties. As if Dierk Lichtensitz, Crown Prince of Sunland, needed to practice caring for saddles. Kings had other things to occupy their time. Of course, a squire must follow orders, but he'd have time later. Might as well take his swim during the hottest hours with his friends.

But Bastian, with his straightforward ways, wouldn't

understand those reasons.

Leonhard surfaced beside him, spewing water. "Ready for that water fight? Gernot said he and I could take you."

"Ha!" Dierk shoved with his feet and stroked for the deepest end of the pond, overhung by willows. "I'll show you both who's champion."

"DOWN, INGO." DIERK THRUST his palm toward the sleek black-spotted hound jumping around his legs. Ingo settled down and trotted in front of Dierk, almost tripping him twice. Dierk shook his head, a smile tugging at his mouth.

Weaving through the busy courtyard, Dierk caught up with Bastian at the squires' quarters, a long wooden building with small windows just under the eaves. The aroma of roasting meat drifted from the nearby kitchen, and Dierk's mouth watered.

Ahead of Dierk, Bastian paused. He stepped to the side of the doorway and bowed low. "Your Highness's chamber awaits. Unfortunately, it has been overrun by an unseemly mob of youths."

"As usual." Dierk rolled his eyes and grinned. He stepped into the large room lined with beds on one side, and a pillow smacked his face.

"Ha-ha! We caught Prince Dierk!"

He snatched up the pillow and hurled it at the smirking lad, who ducked out of the way. Dierk elbowed Bastian. "Next time you can walk in first."

"I will gladly take any blow for Your Highness." Bastian swept him another bow, his face full of suppressed laughter.

"Except a thrown pillow."

"My thanks." Dierk cuffed Bastian's shoulder and jostled through the noisy crowd of lads toward his bed.

"Anyone seen my shoes?" Gernot called from a few beds away.

"If you wore 'em more than once a week, you mightn't lose 'em so often," someone yelled back.

Dierk laughed. "Maybe one of the hounds mistook them for a choice supper."

"The way his feet smell?" quipped the lad who shared Gernot's bed.

Laughter erupted, filling the large room. Gernot slugged his friend's shoulder and bent to peer under the bed again. Still chuckling, Dierk knelt and reached under his bed for his clothing box. He wanted a dry tunic before he went to work in the dusty stable.

Ingo's tongue slathered Dierk's ear.

"All right, all right." Dierk caught the hound's neck between his hands and rubbed his thumbs in the hollows behind Ingo's ears. He grinned as the long pink tongue stretched toward his face. "Oh, no you don't. Silly hound."

Ingo wriggled with pleasure. Dierk gave the dog a last pat before dragging his clothing box out. He'd had his fun. He ought to get those stupid saddles in order before dinner.

"Attention, lads." The chief squire stood just inside the door, his hands raised for quiet. "Sir Wilhelm has ordered quintain practice. Don your attire and report to the armory to retrieve your lances."

Groans rose from some of the younger lads. Dierk sighed. Not that he minded quintain, but this extra lesson meant he'd have to scrape some time together Monday to tend the saddlery. Or skip it altogether.

"Silence!" Sir Wilhelm's roar shattered the complaints as he stalked into the dormitory. "How many times have I told you, lads? A knight must be prepared for any emergency. Here you are, dawdling, when you ought to leap up to fight at a moment's notice. Make haste! Bastian, Leonhard, saddle the mounts. All of you, to the armory, then to the tiltyard. I want you all ready before the horses."

Mad scrambling for shoes and tunics ensued. Dierk changed into a dry tunic, snatched up his padded vest, and dashed for the door with the others.

THE ASH-WOOD LANCE WAS smooth in Dierk's hand as he awaited his turn at the quintain—a wooden knight holding a shield in one hand. Since Bastian saddled the horse, he got to charge first. "Come on, Bastian. You'll conquer him."

Bastian mounted then grinned at Dierk. "Careful. I'll beat you at it one of these times."

Dierk smirked as Bastian turned the horse to face the quintain. If Bastian's lance struck in the perfect spot, the shield would clatter down. If not, the wooden knight would pivot and smack him with the sandbag in his other hand. With Bastian, that was the usual outcome.

His lance cradled in his right arm, Bastian kicked the charger into a full gallop.

"Bas-tian. Bas-tian." Dierk led the chant, and the others joined.

On the other side of the yard, the second quintain's shield

crashed to the ground. Leonhard raised his lance in triumph, and his team whooped.

Bastian's steed pounded toward the wooden foe. At the last moment, Bastian lowered his lance. It struck with a terrific crash. But the lance missed its precise target, and the wooden knight swung to whack Bastian.

Except Bastian wasn't there. He was falling off the near side of the great warhorse, his lance waving in the air. The sandbag caught the lance, and the horse veered, fighting the rein.

Dierk's stomach plummeted. But squires took blows all the time. Bastian would be fine. Surely.

Bastian fell free of the tangle, crumpled in a heap on the dirt. The horse stamped and snorted, its saddle hanging awry. The wooden knight revolved, creaking, into its normal position. Bastian squirmed, but didn't rise.

"Bastian!" Sir Wilhelm yelled.

No answer.

Dierk dropped his lance and dashed forward, his fellow squires on his heels. He skidded to a stop beside his prostrate friend. Down on one knee, Sir Wilhelm rolled Bastian onto his back.

Bastian gasped, his ashen face convulsing.

"What's wrong, lad?" Sir Wilhelm's gruff tone betrayed unwonted concern.

"My arm." The strangled words gave way to another gasp. "Nothing bad, I guess."

The liar. No healthy arm bent between wrist and elbow. Dierk gave his own arm a shake to dispel the cringe.

"Gernot, fetch the physician," Sir Wilhelm barked. "Try

his shop first. Don't return without him."

Gernot whirled and ran from the tiltyard.

Sweat glistened on Bastian's forehead, and his right heel scraped the ground, back and forth. But no sound escaped his lips.

Dierk turned away. How had this happened? Jaw tight, he surveyed the horse with its drooping saddle. He eased forward, hand outstretched, and caught the bridle. The poor beast whinnied. "Easy, boy." Dierk slipped around the gray nose to the horse's off side.

The cause of the fall glared back at him. Torn stitches left a gaping seam in the saddle's right front quarter. One of the straps had ripped apart.

Someone slipped up beside him, and Dierk glanced over his shoulder.

Anton gazed at the damage. "How'd it happen?"

"Stitches must have been unsound. No way a normal round of quintain could break it otherwise." Dierk's gut clenched. How had the other lads assigned to the saddlery missed this? Or ... was this one *he* should have checked?

But this accident was not his fault. The stableman who put the equipment away should've seen the damage. For that matter, Bastian ought to have noticed himself.

Sir Wilhelm strode around the horse. Dierk edged over to give him a clear view of the saddle. The scent of sweat and onions reached Dierk as Sir Wilhelm fingered the frayed seam. "Who checked the saddles today?"

As if he didn't know. "It was my turn, sir, along with Hans and Erhard."

"How did you miss the flaw in this equipment?"

He could blame it on the others. But they'd be quick to report Dierk's absence. Besides, lying was for children, not knights. "I've had no time yet to tend the saddlery, sir."

"Had no time!" Sir Wilhelm roared, his face turning scarlet. "With your hair still wet from the swimming hole, you have the gall to tell me you had no time?" He seized Dierk's arm with a hand like iron and dragged him back to where Bastian lay.

"Hans, Erhard!" Sir Wilhelm waited until each boy stepped forward. "Did you not inspect Bastian's saddle today?"

The two looked at one another. Hans shuffled his feet. "I think ..." He looked toward the saddle, glanced at Dierk, then bent his head and kicked at the rock-hard dirt. "That's one of our plain training saddles. We left those for Dierk to polish."

"And *Prince Dierk* declares he had no time for his duties." Sir Wilhelm's grip tightened on Dierk's arm. "But he had time to swim. And his neglect brought about this." He jabbed a finger toward Bastian. "Injured his own comrade," he bellowed. "Will he not make a noble knight, lads?"

Waves of white-hot fury seethed through Dierk until the scene in front of him wavered. It took every dram of willpower he possessed not to strike his superior. The man had no right to shame him thus, no right to cast aspersions on his rank, no right to treat him like a child. He twisted free of Sir Wilhelm's grasp, breathing as if he'd run a furlong in record time.

But he kept his chin level. He was Crown Prince. Perhaps he had made a mistake, but others were equally culpable. He had intended no harm, and he would accept no shame. Nor would he deign to argue.

"What will you do about it? We have prayed hard for him, but there must be more we can do."

"Aye, but what it is I am not sure." He expelled a breath of mirthless laughter. "Now I understand how my father felt, praying and doubting himself all the time." He faced his wife and offered a half-smile. "Maybe a peasant's life is the only proper way to raise royalty, after all."

Zorena's lips curved, but she didn't truly smile.

A knock on the large wooden door interrupted them. "Enter," Phillip called.

The door creaked open, and Phillip's Chief of Palace Guard saluted. "You summoned me, Your Majesty?"

"Of course." Phillip frowned. "Dispense with the formality, Fredrik."

Fredrik swung the door shut. "The page was still listening, Phil." He made a deep bow to Zorena. "My lady."

She extended a graceful hand. "'Tis a pleasure to see you, Fredrik."

Fredrik kissed her hand. "And you." He looked toward Phillip. "But what is so urgent it requires a meeting in the Queen's parlor? I confess I feel out of place."

Phillip waved his hand. "Well, don't. I suppose you have heard about Dierk?"

All humor fled Fredrik's face. "I heard he was summoned home unexpectedly."

Phillip paced the length of the thick blue floor rug and back. Dierk had beaten the news home, but the story would soon spread all over the castle. Not that it mattered who knew. The problem lay in the reality of the disgrace.

Phillip turned, met Fredrik's gaze, and relayed the story in the fewest possible words. "This young man now has a broken arm," he finished, "and the fault lies with my son, the Crown Prince." What a blot of shame upon the family.

"I see." Fredrik tugged the end of his mustache. "'Tis a grievous mischance."

"No mischance about it. Disobedience caused this." Phillip marched to Zorena's chair and propped his hands on its back. She slipped her hand up and grasped his arm in a warm caress. He covered her fingers with his own. "Fredrik, I must do something. I cannot let him get to the point I did. I would not have him suffer correction as terrible as mine."

Fredrik's eyes reflected Phillip's concern. Fredrik had endured the "correction" too. He understood.

"Do you have a plan, Phil?"

Phillip glanced down at Zorena's golden hair. "Not a good one. Dierk has heard the stories of his parents all his life, but perhaps if he could hear them from others, from a fresh perspective, he could better receive their instruction. And thus avoid my path."

Fredrik's brows furrowed. "Have you an idea how this might be accomplished?"

"Yes." Phillip rested his hand on his wife's shoulder. He hoped she would approve his plan. He had nothing better to suggest. "Fredrik, I want you to escort Dierk on a tour of the country. I want him to meet someone who saw the curse lifted from Zorena. I want him to see the place where she grew up with the Sisters. To see the town destroyed by Lady Melankardja."

Phillip paused. His next request would demand much of Fredrik. He might refuse the commission, and Phillip would activities for the pure enjoyment of them. But Dierk could find pleasure in his work—always had.

Perhaps Father would forbid him any practice in knightly exercise, confining him to mere book study for a time. That would chafe.

Or maybe Father would sentence him to serve a priest of Sunland's Church for a while, almost like the Roman Catholics and their monks. One of the older squires at Duke Ebner's had served such a penance when he was much younger, so Dierk had heard.

At any rate, this spoiled his hopes of joining the Royal League early. Father would probably make him wait until his nineteenth birthday like any common applicant. Which shouldn't disappoint him as sharply as it did. He'd been anticipating it for five years. What were two more?

A tap on the door brought him to his feet. "Enter."

A servant entered and bowed. "Your Highness, His Majesty requires your presence in the council room."

Here it came at last. The axe would fall, and Dierk would take his punishment without complaint and most certainly without repenting. He had done nothing wrong.

Dierk nodded. "I shall come without delay."

The man bowed himself out.

Dierk squared his shoulders and lifted his chin. Ready to hold his temper and his pride, he left the chamber.

A few yards down the hall, he passed the open door to his younger siblings' playroom, where he'd spent many an hour as a child. He caught the gaze of his five-year-old brother Friedhold but passed on without a word.

"Dierk!"

He turned. The huge doorway dwarfed his little brother as the boy peered out at him.

"Where you going?"

"Father sent for me."

"Will you play with us today?"

"No." He'd long since forgotten how to play, and he was in no mood to relearn.

"But I've waited all day."

"I've been busy, Friedhold." Busy doing nothing because of Father's restrictions.

The nurse appeared behind Friedhold. "Come, lad, don't detain your brother."

Dierk took the opportunity to continue down the hall.

"Tomorrow, then, Dierk?"

He pretended he didn't hear.

DIERK PUSHED OPEN THE council room door. Father stood staring at a banner of Sunland's Crest which covered the far wall with its bright colors. He turned at the creak of the ancient hinges.

"Seat yourself, Dierk."

Dierk shut the door and sat on one of the stools by the cold hearth. He'd expected Mother to be here, with a fresh supply of tears, but the room was empty save for him and Father.

Empty and utterly silent.

Father's footsteps echoed as he crossed the rush-strewn floor. He dropped onto a stool across from Dierk and propped his elbows on his knees. Looking at the floor, he sighed. "I do not think I need to tell you I am disappointed."

Indeed? I would never have guessed. Dierk bit back the sarcasm. "You made yourself quite clear last night."

He thought he'd kept his tone even, but Father lifted his head as if in response to a jibe. "I am not certain I did. Dierk, have you no concept of the enormous responsibility of royalty?"

"You have told me time and again, sir." To put it mildly.

"It is our duty to *protect* our people. To serve them. To always have their interests foremost in our minds. Not our own gain or pleasure."

"I *know* that." Frustration laced Dierk's words despite his earlier resolve. He'd heard all this yesterday. "But I was not so miserably deficient in my duty. If Bastian had not happened to choose the one damaged saddle in the stable, no one would have ever known or cared that I skipped a chore once."

"Which ought to show you the smallest tasks are worth all the attention of the so-called important duties."

Dierk chose not to reply. 'Twas a grievous accident, of course. He took no pleasure in seeing his friend sweating and rigid with pain. But it was an accident caused by a trivial mistake. Not deserving of this disgrace.

Father stood and rested an arm on the mantel. Light from the window glinted off the gold armband on his wrist. "The neglected saddles are not the true source of my distress. Nor is Bastian's broken arm, much as it grieves me." Father glanced at him, then brought his gaze to his fingers, stroking the edge of the mantel. "Your pride concerns me."

Ah, now the lecture would truly begin.

"Pride will destroy you, my son. You know it almost

destroyed me before God saw fit, in His grace, to humble me. You know the Scripture. The Lord abominates pride. Can you not see the need to guard against this sin?"

Dierk fought not to roll his eyes. Last night Father had been angry, and he'd scolded with a loud voice and sharp words. Today he'd fallen into his mood of "sorrow because my child disappointed me." And he tended to start preaching when that mood hit him.

Not that Dierk had anything against God. He had no desire to go around indulging in sin. And he was *not* sinfully proud. The Crown Prince must maintain a certain amount of dignity.

Crisp knocks interrupted the heavy silence. "Enter," Father called.

Fredrik stepped in, carrying a couple axes in one hand. Not battle-axes. The blades were heavy but straighter. "Fine tools, these. Shall I leave them with you?"

"No, stay. I was on the point of explaining the plan to Dierk."

The plan. That meant the punishment.

Fredrik shut the door and leaned against it.

Father dropped into his seat. "Son, your title carries with it a weighty responsibility, requiring strong character. Therefore, I have decided to send you on a journey in the hopes that your character might gain strength."

Dierk took care to keep his expression blank. A journey. Rather soft punishment. Must be a stone in the pie somewhere.

"Fredrik will accompany you. He will take his usual secret identity, a woodcutter called Henrik Holtzer. You will be his son Kik. No one must ever suspect you are anything other than a woodcutter's son."

Take the identity of a woodcutter? A *peasant?* Disgrace enough to boil a man's blood. Dierk set his jaw. He wouldn't let his father see how the punishment stung. "How long is this journey to last?"

"Until Fredrik deems you ready to return to your normal duties."

Alarmingly vague answer. Dierk looked at the man he'd called "Uncle Fredrik" as a child. Dierk hadn't seen much of him since moving to Duke Ebner's.

Fredrik took an axe in his right hand and tossed it upward. It tumbled end-over-end back down, where Fredrik caught the handle. He let the shaft slide through his hand until the head rested on his fist. Then he extended the handle to Dierk. "This one is yours, lad."

Dierk had to stop himself from yanking the tool out of Fredrik's grasp. The wooden handle was smooth in his hand, the weight cumbersome. The steel caught the window light, winking sparks from its sword-sharp edge. "When do we depart?"

"Friday," Father answered.

Two more days at home. "Anything else?" *To add to the humiliation.*

"Three rules." Father caught Dierk's gaze and held it. "Obey Fredrik. Whatever he tells you, obey."

Of course. Be a good little woodcutter's son.

"Take nothing without paying. As Crown Prince, you have a right to commandeer things. As Kik, you must pay your way, even with small things."

As if he needed to be told that.

"And, whatever happens, you must not betray your identity, through anything you say or do, or even the *way* you speak or act. For the duration of this journey, you are Kik, not Dierk. Do not forget."

"I shall remember."

Father laced his fingers, lowered his gaze to Dierk's boots, then looked up. "I do not expect you to fail in any of these rules. But if you do, you will receive three lashes."

"What?" Dierk jumped to his feet, unable to contain his indignation. "You would *lash* a member of the royal family?"

"I want you to know how serious this is."

"So if some peasant with a wild imagination accuses me of being nobility, *I* receive a lashing?"

Father stood. It brought him barely higher than eye-to-eye with Dierk. "See that you give them no cause for such accusations."

Dierk gritted his teeth lest he lose his temper completely. Tension tightened inside him, like a longbow drawn for a shot. "Is that all you have to say to me?"

"One more thing. Remember that I love you."

If Dierk stayed a moment longer, his head would fly off and hit the ceiling. He spun on his heel, marched past Fredrik, and flung himself out of the room. Standing in the hall, heart pounding, he pressed his palm against the stone wall and let the coldness seep into him.

"... I not tell you Dierk is too much like me?" Father's voice filtered through the door.

"He *is* your son, Phil."

Dierk shouldn't be doing this, but he cocked his ear

It took a quarter of an hour to hike to the castle, and Dierk found himself panting a little when they reached the top. Two towers guarded the arch of the gateway, which protruded at least seven yards from the main wall. Impressive fortifications, especially for a seventy-year-old castle.

They stepped into the gateway's shade, and Fredrik approached the gatekeeper. "My name is Henrik Holtzer. Might I be permitted to see the steward?" With a casual movement, Fredrik let something fall into the man's hand.

Not a coin. Some tiny, greenish-pinkish ball.

Not sparing it a glance, the gatekeeper dropped it on the cobblestones and trod upon it. "Of course. If you wait here in the gatehouse, I will send for him."

Dierk followed Fredrik under the raised portcullis to a stone alcove set within the thick walls. He must keep his eyes open. That almost unnoticeable exchange might be the communication of the Royal League.

The gatekeeper made no jest about *waiting* in the gatehouse. Dierk tired of sitting on the wooden bench and rose to wander the room. He peered up the dark staircase in the corner, probably access to the murder holes where castle defenders could rain arrows on anyone attacking the gate. He paused at the bulky wooden table by the door and read the scraps of parchment—insignificant notes about who entered the castle for what reason.

Time dragged on, and still no steward came. A prince, even in disguise, should receive more prompt attention. But Father had likely ordered Fredrik to try Dierk's patience in every manner possible.

Almost an hour had passed before a tall, thin man with a

furrowed brow and an authoritative stride entered the gatehouse. "Herr Holtzer? I heard you wish to see me."

At last. Dierk pinched his tongue between his teeth lest his sarcasm escape. *I suppose it took the messenger this long to find you?*

Fredrik stood and bowed. Suppressing a smirk, Dierk followed suit. Bowing to a castle steward. The man ought to bow to him under normal circumstances.

"Sir, my son and I are woodcutters. If we might be of service, we hoped to earn a meal, perhaps a night's lodging." Fredrik dropped another of those little balls, which bounced across the stone floor.

Ah, 'twas an unripe larch cone, its tiny green scales tipped with red.

The steward didn't seem to notice it. "How fortunate. The castle has a supply of wood which needs splitting, and if you could possibly stay two nights, I have some trees that need felling. Perhaps you could serve us."

"We appreciate the work."

Dierk eyed both men, but their faces betrayed nothing. Still, they must have communicated more than their words indicated.

"Come this way, Herr Holtzer." The steward led them into the main courtyard, which bustled with servants, squires, peddlers, and animals. "The well is at your disposal. The kitchen hall is yonder." He pointed a long finger to indicate. "Take your midday meal there before you commence work. Behind the kitchen you will find the wood, and a whetstone is near the armory. If you need aught else, consult the chief cook."

Of all people. Naturally, the steward couldn't be bothered keeping track of every random worker, but why refer them to the chief cook?

Fredrik bowed. "Thank you."

The steward smiled, nodded, and hurried away. An hour of waiting for three minutes of the man's time. Dierk rolled his eyes. Ridiculous.

"Well, lad." Fredrik slapped his palms together. "We will wash and eat. Then our work awaits."

Dierk stifled a sigh. He would actually be required to swing an axe. He could only hope he didn't betray his disguise with awkward handling.

DIERK WIPED HIS SWEATY forehead with his wrist. Fredrik made it look easy. Feet planted apart in front of the chopping block, Dierk mimicked him again.

Thwack! Wonder of wonders, the blade slammed through the chunk of wood, toppling two halves to the ground. Dierk's jaw went loose. "Fr—Father, I did it."

"Aye, so you did, lad. Only your fiftieth try."

Dierk tried to glare at Fredrik's smile, but a grin slipped out. Finally, he knew how to use the unwieldy tool, after carrying it on his back the last week.

He reached for another piney-scented log and positioned it on the block. With care to maintain proper form, he swung again. The blade fell awry, crooked in the wood. "Ach!" Dierk jerked the axe free. "Why'd it do that?"

Fredrik struck his own log, which split like magic. "Your wrist or your fingers must've slipped."

Dierk huffed. Fredrik already had four times as much wood cut. What a mercy his fellow squires couldn't see him muddling along at servants' work.

Just a few weeks, Dierk. He would pull through this with honor. He was the Prince, and princes didn't fail.

But he didn't have to enjoy it.

THE NEXT MORNING, DIERK trailed behind Fredrik and another man assigned by the steward to show them the trees he wanted cut. The pale sunshine had barely grown warm, but Dierk's brain complained of being tired. He'd never slept in a servants' hall before. If you could call it sleeping, with the men abed beside you snoring like a thunderstorm and the room warm with body heat. Not to mention the hard, knotty mattress.

At least 'twas more comfortable than the last few nights of camping along the roadside. No, on second thought, it wasn't. Outside air provided some coolness.

Witless idea, this working at his own grandparents' palace. This whole journey, in fact.

"Hasten, lad."

At Fredrik's call, Dierk picked up his pace. They reached the woods where the guide pointed out strips of blue cloth on certain trees.

"These are the ones to cut. The townsmen planned to fell them later this summer, but they'll be glad enough to let professionals handle it."

Dierk hid a smirk behind his hand. One professional anyway. Even the most foppish townsman could outwork him at woodcutting.

The guide hitched at his belt. "I shall be off if you need nothing else."

"We're ready. Thank you for guiding us," Fredrik said.

The man gave a nod. "See you at supper." With a wave of his hand, he set off for the castle.

Dierk set his bundle of lunch beside Fredrik's. "Did he know who we are?"

Fredrik shook his head. "No. Very few do. The gatekeeper, the steward, the chief cook, and some of the high-ranking palace guards."

"Why the cook?"

Fredrik slung his axe from his shoulder. "No matter. For now, 'tis time I showed you how to fell a tree."

So they thought to keep him in the dark. He was no child. He'd figure it out.

STANDING IN THE KITCHEN waiting for supper, Dierk wanted to collapse right there. He had thought yesterday painful. He'd even grudged the days of walking. Now that seemed mere play. Unaccustomed work had stiffened his hands, and every muscle complained after his day of felling and stripping trees. They ought to add it to the knight-training program for endurance.

Maybe Father's plan would succeed after all. If Fredrik exhausted him with work, he'd never have the energy for *shockingly delinquent behavior*.

"Lad, your trencher."

Dierk took the piece of hard bread handed him, glancing

at the meat and vegetables it held. 'Twasn't fancy, but he didn't care. Just let him eat it and go to bed.

Fredrik laid a hand on his shoulder. "Come, lad."

Dierk followed him across the huge room, past other servants seated at rough tables. When Fredrik sat, Dierk sank down beside him with a plump, middle-aged woman on his other side. He laid his left arm on the table and focused on his plate. If his eyes would stay open, he could eat better.

But as the hot food filled his stomach, Dierk's head cleared. Sitting rested his muscles, and the ache left his arms. He took notice of the people smiling and talking around him, and even made eye-contact with the young man across from him.

A mistake.

"My name's Enoch. What's yours?"

Dierk swallowed the savory meat in his mouth. "Kik." 'Twas his name for the duration of this trip.

"Never seen you before. Are you new?"

Dierk lifted his fingers in a non-committal gesture. "I'm passing through. Father and I felled some trees for the palace today."

"Ah, yes, I heard a woodcutter came yesterday." Enoch grinned. "Glad to have you. I have to rotate with wood chopping, and your coming puts off my turn."

Dierk mustered half a smile. Maybe the boy would hush.

He didn't. "Have you ever been here before?"

"Uh, no." Well, Kik hadn't anyway. Dierk shoved a piece of turnip into his mouth.

"Nice place. Good pay and good food, and I get to be near my family."

Dierk grunted.

Enoch chewed another bite, and Dierk turned back to his trencher.

"Where does the rest of your family live?"

Dierk looked up. The boy couldn't take a hint for anything. "My mother died at my birth. Father raised me."

"Oh, I'm sorry." Enoch's blue eyes held genuine concern. "So you grew up traveling and working with him?"

"Aye." He felt like such a liar. But he had a part to act. The fictitious Kik had a life far different from Dierk's.

"How long are you staying?"

"Um, I think Father plans to leave after the morning church service tomorrow. We felled nearly all the trees."

"Too bad you can't stay. I would've liked to know you better. All the servants have lighter work on Lord's Day."

A circumstance Dierk often found annoying. The royal castles insisted on it although many of the country's noblemen didn't. Some custom of his great-great-grandfather's.

"I could've shown you the horses."

Judging by Enoch's smell, he kept pretty close company with the beasts. "Father likes to keep moving."

Enoch nodded. "Anyway, you can't go without hearing the castle's story."

"Story?"

"About Queen Zorena's curse."

That. He'd heard it a thousand times, from his parents, and grandparents, and the Sisters who'd raised his mother. "Everyone's heard that story."

Enoch shook his head. "Not by an eyewitness. Lots of the servants here can tell it, but Marta tells it best."

"Who's Marta?"

"The cook sitting next to you."

Dierk jerked his head to look at the woman. She had reddish hair under her kerchief and faded blue eyes. He'd peg her for about fifty.

Marta laughed. "Enoch, you could flatter a pheasant off a clutch of eggs."

"Nonsense, Marta, 'tis true. You tell it better than the chaplain himself. Tell Kik. He'd love to hear you."

Sure he would. If he could keep himself awake.

Enoch gave her the most dazzling smile Dierk had ever seen on a boy. "Besides, I'm dying to hear it again myself."

"And no one can refuse you anything." Marta sighed, a smile touching her lips. "I was younger then, still a maid in the kitchen, not yet a cook. My, but that day was busy. We'd baked bread for days and roasted meat for the townsfolk's festival. But the day of the banquet outdid all the others." She sighed again, and Dierk got the impression the woman's mind had gone a-traveling far away.

He smothered a sigh of his own. Glancing at Fredrik, he found him focused on Marta. Like everyone else seated within earshot.

So he'd be forced to sit through this tale yet again.

4

The Witch's Curse

THIRTY-ODD YEARS HAD PASSED since Marta helped to prepare the feast for Princess Zorena's birth. She never tired of reliving that day. Nor of sharing it with anyone who cared to listen.

MARTA JOINED FIFTEEN OTHER servants who bore the third course to the banquet hall. Amongst platters of meats and vegetables, the dish of peacock crowned this course, crouching on its platter with its tail fanned as if it still lived.

Along with every servant in the castle, she had worked as hard as ever she did in her life to bring about this celebration. But no one minded the heat from the huge ovens or the endless running to and fro. This banquet must be perfect, a celebration befitting a princess's birth.

Not that any of the kitchen servants had seen Princess Zorena, except from a distance at her presentation to the people. But the whole country of Sunrise knew about her three siblings, two girls and a boy, who had lain down to sleep in the palace graveyard within days of their births. Marta had rejoiced when she heard this child would live. At last, Sunrise had an heir to the throne—thus her name, which meant, "dawn." A new sunrise for her country.

Finally, Marta's turn came to enter the banquet hall. Lights from torches and lamps flickered on the tapestries covering the walls. Minstrels filled the room with music. Fresh straw rustled under Marta's feet as she carried her platter to the far table, eyes alert to glimpse the Princess. Ah, there stood her cradle, near her mother's chair. A smile curved Marta's lips. Their sweet Queen Charlotte glowed tonight, smiles lighting her often-sorrowful eyes. How wonderful for her and their noble King Siegbert.

With the other servants, Marta retreated to the corner of the room until the time for removing the dishes should come. The jugglers' performance would have been most diverting, except Marta craned her neck to see the Princess's cradle.

A woman named Frieda bent her head close to Marta's ear. "See King Leberecht and Queen Adelaide of Sunset?"

"Yes." They looked almost as happy as her own monarchs.

"Their son Phillip came, too, though he is abed now, I suppose. The cellarer told me that his brother, who serves in the bed chambers, saw both the queens and kings meeting in the conferring room with their children, His Majesty's secretary, the chaplain, and Lord James."

Marta brought her gaze away from the royal couples and stared at the round-faced woman. "What does that mean?"

"Well, we know nothing for certain, but we hope perhaps

it means a betrothal between our baby Zorena and the young Prince Phillip."

"Prince Phillip. He is what, four years old?"

"Aye."

"If such a thing is true, 'twould reunite Sunrise and Sunset, would it not?"

"Indeed it would." Frieda smiled. "You know the lands were one in the days of the current kings' grandfather, the noble King Phillip."

Marta glanced toward the royal ones at the chief table. "I have heard tales of those days. To think we may live to see it so once again."

"We certainly do not hope without cause. 'Twould be natural, after all."

Marta stared at the cradle. Had its occupant been pledged to wed her cousin before she had yet learned to speak one word? How strange the world of royalty. When a child held the very life of a country entwined with its own, that young life must be planned and protected with extreme measures. Much better to be a servant, so unimportant that it mattered not what one's future brought.

"Do you see those three women seated near the Queen?" Frieda pointed a discreet finger.

Marta followed the direction. The women sat together, dressed in fine but not fancy garments. "Yes. They look like sisters."

"So they are. Those are the Faust sisters. Faith, Hope, and Charity. The prophetesses."

"Oh." Marta took another look. All three had brown hair framing peaceful faces. She'd heard about them before.

Though daughters of nobility, they had chosen to live as near peasants, using their wealth to help others. People whispered that their prayers could truly move mountains if they sought to do so, and they were known to sometimes receive visions when they prayed. Marta leaned toward Frieda. "I believe the King and Queen have great respect for the Faust sisters."

"Indeed they do." Frieda nodded as if she had information from the Queen herself. "The oldest one, Faith, advised the King in a political move five years ago. They say she diverted a war through her advice."

"I see."

"Were you up here when the gifts were presented?"

Marta shook her head. "No, this is my first time serving this evening."

"Ah, you should have seen them. Jewels, silks. The likes of which I never saw in my life." Frieda waved a hand as if words failed her. "The Sisters gave her a Bible."

Marta gasped. "The full Book?"

"Aye. The cover was engraved leather, not jeweled, but the inside made up for that. Even at a distance I could see the colors' richness."

Marta eyed the Sisters again. They must own extraordinary wealth to afford a Bible. Books could cost half a count's fortune.

A commotion at the main entrance claimed her attention.

"Let me through, I say. I *will* deliver this message," a voice proclaimed.

A figure clothed in black garments tore into the center of the room, knocking over a tumbler in his haste. "Silence!" he roared.

The minstrels halted with squeaky notes.

"I bring a message of great import to the King and Queen." In the quiet hall, the man held up a parchment. "Lady Melankardja gives notice that the Princess Zorena is cursed. Before she has completed her sixteenth year, she will die and join her siblings."

The man lowered the parchment and stared straight toward the babe's cradle.

With a cry, Queen Charlotte jumped from her chair and scooped her daughter into her arms.

"Seize him!" King Siegbert shouted.

Palace guards rushed to tackle the man.

Marta stared, scarcely breathing, resting her hand on her collarbone. Lady Melankardja? Hadn't she disappeared years ago, after her curse caused the death of a nobleman who opposed her? The man swearing as the guards hauled him away must be one of her servants. A shiver slid down Marta's spine, like a slimy vegetable peel.

"Oh, my." Frieda's eyes threatened to leap from her head. "Never in my life. What do you suppose it means?"

Marta swallowed. "I don't know."

The Sisters had gathered around the monarchs. One of them marched to the center of the room and picked up the fallen parchment.

"That's Hope," Frieda whispered.

Hope turned to the guests and servants. "Brothers and sisters, you have seen this curse delivered. You know Lady Melankardja's power is strong. But our God is stronger. Through Christ, we do not fight in defeat. We fight assured of victory. Will you join us in prayer?" She tossed the message into the huge fireplace.

Prayer. They would pray this curse away? "How can that undo the curse?" Marta whispered to Frieda.

"Maybe 'tis like a sickness for which we may plead healing. If my prayers can help, I will pray."

The palace chaplain came forward with something in his hand. Ah, 'twas a tiny bottle. He poured a drop of the contents onto his finger and laid it on the babe's forehead. Then his warm voice rose in prayer.

Behind Marta, a manservant whispered, "All who believe in the power of God, let us pray."

Frieda and the other servants bowed their heads. Marta did, too. Murmuring voices surrounded her.

Marta drew a long breath. "Lord God, I do not understand. I am frightened for our little princess. Our land has so long prayed for an heir to the throne. O God, I know I'm not important, not like the Sisters, but I beg You to save our princess. I beg You to break the curse. Don't let Princess Zorena die. The Sisters say You can fight Lady Melankardja's power, and conquer. I beg You to do so."

Time passed, and Marta prayed on with the others. She must have repeated herself several times, for she couldn't find more words. But something charged the air. Something strong and warm and almost tangible. Once she peeked at the room. People, nobles even, knelt by the long benches. Even a few acrobats and minstrels joined in. Others stood, quiet and respectful, watching the proceedings but not participating. Thin smoke filled the room. Odd, because the great hall was well-vented. At any rate, the smoke didn't choke her.

When she had exhausted her words, she stood silent. Her

heart ached as if it were a towel she wrung out on wash-day. Around her, others prayed. Though she spoke their native dialect Sunman, others prayed in German and Latin, languages of nobility. But some whispered indiscernible tongues.

Still they prayed.

Then, for no reason, all words ceased. Marta lifted her head. How much time had passed? Hours, perhaps. The fires and torches burned low.

The chaplain rose from his knees beside the Queen's feet. His kind voice filled the hall. "I heard the voice of my Master say, 'O death, where is your sting? O Hades, where is your victory?'"

Queen Charlotte, her face marred by weeping, smiled. Her lips formed the word, "Hallelujah."

Then Faith stood. "In a vision, I saw Zorena on her eighteenth birthday—she danced with a man whose face I did not see."

Marta's scalp prickled. What had happened? She'd seen naught like this in all her born days. How could the presence of God be so close, so real? For nothing other than the Lord could bring this about.

Charity spoke. "I saw the word 'LIFE' in large, capital letters, sparkling with silver and gold."

"Praise be to God," King Siegbert called.

"He has broken the curse!" someone cried.

"Hallelujah!"

Marta merged her voice with the others. No matter how long she lived, she would never forget this night.

5

The Woodcutter's Son

DIERK BLINKED. THIS WOMAN Marta should have been a minstrel. She'd held his interest throughout the tale as if he had never heard it before. He, the Prince of Sunland, who couldn't remember a time he didn't know the story.

He looked around the kitchen. Every servant had ceased his work. All stared at Marta.

She broke the silence with a laugh. "It does beat all how you listen to me over and over."

Enoch smiled. "No one tells it like you."

"Truly, I've never heard it so powerful before." Dierk startled at the sound of his own voice. He hadn't intended to say anything.

Marta touched his hand. "Thank you, Kik. Now you

youngsters had best finish your duties before bed."

As the kitchen came to life, Fredrik slapped Dierk's shoulder. "We ought to be off to bed, lad." He looked at Marta. "Thank you, Frau Marta, for your story. I shall not soon forget it."

She smiled and gave a nod. "I am honored."

Dierk followed Fredrik to their bunks in the servants' quarters. He wasted no time removing boots and belt before he flopped down on the rough mattress. What had made the story different this time? 'Twasn't graceful language, a cultured voice, or a beautiful story-teller. The story seemed to have some power all its own. Why had he never sensed it before?

Furthermore, what was it?

Fredrik lay awake, waiting for Dierk to stop turning over beside him. He'd not expected that simple woman's story to move Dierk so. The lad actually overcame his proud reserve and complimented her. Maybe Phil's idea wasn't so far-fetched, after all.

Convenient, Enoch's getting Marta to tell the story. Last night, in a few hushed words, the chief cook had named Marta as the best eye-witness to describe the events. Fredrik had planned to coax her into telling them the story, but Enoch beat him to it. A smile stretched Fredrik's face. He would take that as God's blessing on his mission.

At last Dierk's breathing evened. Fredrik pushed himself from the mattress with a silent prayer the lad might sleep well. His eyes well-adjusted to the dim light, he slipped out of the dormitory and wended his way by servant's halls to a room against the castle's outer wall. He rapped a coded rhythm on the door.

Creaking, the door swung open. The steward's smiling face appeared in the opening. "Ah, Fredrik, I wondered if you would come tonight."

"I would have come earlier, but the Prince had difficulty falling asleep." Fredrik entered and shut the door. "Forgive me for keeping you awake."

"Think nothing of it. I always have accounts to tend." The steward indicated a cabinet. "You will find all supplies for the messages in there. Should you need anything, I'll be at my desk."

"Thank you."

"The pleasure is mine, I assure you."

Fredrik sat at a table by the cabinet and wrote a note for Their Highnesses Siegbert and Charlotte. He rolled it, sealed it, and stamped it with his signet, kept hidden in a secret pocket of his tunic. Then he selected a hollow turkey eggshell for the coded message to Phil. Though the person who bore it would be a Royal League member, there was always the slight possibility of highwaymen. One couldn't take too much care about the Crown Prince.

Having filled the eggshell with dried flowers, herbs, and feathers, Fredrik sealed it with an oak leaf and wax. "You will send this tomorrow?" he asked the steward.

"Certainly. And I may deliver your note to His Highness at the noon meal?"

"Aye. We shall leave early in the morning."

The steward grasped Fredrik's forearm. "Your mission

goes well?"

Fredrik returned his gesture. "Aye, thus far."

"God go with you."

DIERK RELISHED THE COOLNESS as the road led into the forest, out of the late morning sunbeams. Leaf shadows dappled the path, dancing with the faint breeze. Sunrise Castle lay at least two miles behind them. Strange to visit and not see his grandparents, but he didn't wish to meet them under the shadow of this disgrace. "Where is our next destination?"

Fredrik smiled. "We're headed to Spatzberg."

Dierk frowned. "Where the Sisters live?"

"Aye."

Dierk thumped his staff against the hard dirt path. They'd have to trek back across the whole country. Spatzberg lay near Sunset Castle in the nation's southwest corner, on the opposite side from Sunrise Castle. And the road Fredrik chose this morning wandered northward, a most indirect route. "This is ridiculous. Why can't we take the main highway through Sun City?"

"This offers some different scenery."

As if Dierk cared about scenery. He wanted this trip done as fast as possible. But, no, he had to meander across his country on foot, lodging in little hamlets and villages, swinging an axe for his bread.

This was too high a fee for an afternoon's swim. Father—his real father—was so unreasonable.

THUNDER CRASHED IN THE distance and lightning ignited the

whole night sky. Dierk tossed within his blanket on the lumpy forest floor. How could Fredrik lie there and snore? If the storm moved in, a tree could crash down on them. Where would that leave Sunland? Less one Crown Prince, that's where. Maybe then Father would think twice about such squirrel-brained schemes.

Dierk woke to rain pounding his face. With a groan, he crawled from under his blanket and dragged it to a nearby tree. Not that the tree offered much shelter with the wind whipping through its leaves. Huddled beneath the woolen blanket, he studied the sky. No lightning, just wind and drenching rain.

Fredrik snorted and sat up. Glancing around, his gaze focused on Dierk. "You all right, lad?"

Aye, the accommodations rivaled his chambers at Sunland Castle. "Fine."

Fredrik stood, gathered their bundles, and joined Dierk under the tree. "At least we got a few hours' sleep."

Maybe.

"My concern is the fire going out in this downpour. I doubt wolves would bother us in the rain, but I prefer to keep a fire."

Oh, great. Now, besides getting soaked, he had to watch out for wolves. He glanced toward the knife lying beside his sleeping place. "What time do you suppose it is?"

"Couldn't say for sure. Based on how often I've fed the fire, I'd guess an hour or so until dawn."

A gust of wind flung raindrops into Dierk's face, and he turned toward Fredrik. "How do you feed the fire if you're asleep?"

Fredrik chuckled. "Lad, years of experience will teach you to wake yourself enough to do what needs doing."

Not Dierk. Kings didn't need to wake up at all hours to perform menial tasks. "Wish we could break camp. Walking would be better than sitting here, even if we do get wet. 'Tis not as if we'll get any more sleep."

Fredrik raised his eyebrows.

What did the man take him for—a whining idiot who couldn't make a rational observation? Just because he loathed his circumstances did not mean he couldn't handle them.

"We'll leave as soon as there's light enough to travel safely."

"All right." Dierk leaned his head against the tree trunk. He'd be wet to the bones by then.

DIERK FROWNED AT THE men gathered in the path ahead. "What do you suppose they're doing—Father?" He added the right name at the last second.

"Let's find out." Fredrik quickened his stride. "Hullo," he called.

Several heads turned toward the voice. Dierk still half-expected respectful recognition to transform them into bowing subjects. Strange to be treated as an average Sunlander.

As they approached, a large fallen tree came into view. The thing had to be over a century old, and its position created an effective road block. The group of men and a few boys carried axes and saws.

When they reached the men, Fredrik sketched a bow.

"Name's Henrik Holtzer. My son Kik."

The name felt odd every time, like a new shirt with its seams still stiff.

A tall man in a red tunic nodded. "I'm Grobel. Pardon the obstruction. We're planning how best to remove it."

"May I offer my services? We happen to be woodcutters by trade."

Dierk smothered a smirk. One of them was, anyway. But what did Fredrik mean, offering to help? 'Twould delay their stupid journey.

Grobel shook his head. "We cannot pay."

Good. They could move on and get this trip finished.

"Food and lodging," Fredrik said, "until the job is done."

Grobel looked at the others.

A tall young man spoke. "They may stay with my wife and me."

Fredrik gave a nod. "Tell us where to start."

Dierk reached for the axe strapped to his back. Here they went again.

"Kik, you help the boys haul the brush out of the way."

Dierk dipped his chin at Grobel. At least it gave him a break from chopping branches into manageable pieces.

Grobel's son Bert, a lad younger than Dierk, bent to grasp a branch at the bottom of a pile. "Grab the other end, and we'll drag it over there. I think we can move this branch without spilling the ones on top."

Dierk wouldn't know, so he obeyed without comment. The rough, damp bark burrowed into his palm. When they reached the appointed location, he dropped his end.

"Ow!" Bert rubbed his arm. "Not so fast. It hit me."

"Sorry. My grip slipped." Not by accident, but he wouldn't show his ignorance if he could help it.

Bert shrugged. "No real harm." He wiped his brow. "'Tis a warm day. Nice to have the shade."

"Aye."

Bert said no more, but led the way to another pile of brush. Dierk followed, skirting a group of men chopping at the trunk near the tree's top. How long would this task hold them up? One day? Two? If Fredrik kept this up, the summer would pass before Dierk returned to Duke Ebner's.

A heavy blow on Dierk's left arm sent him sprawling on the uneven ground. The back of his head struck something hard. Pain stabbed his skull, and he squeezed his eyes shut. What on earth?

"Kik!" Fredrik shouted.

"I didn't see him," someone else said.

Dierk opened his eyes and sat up. The woods spun, and he braced his palms against the leaf-strewn dirt. When the revolving slowed, he glimpsed men staring, horror in their faces. Suddenly Fredrik dropped to his knees beside him. A strong hand gripped his shoulder.

"Kik, are you all right?"

Dierk blinked, and the trees quit swaying. "I'm fine. What happened?"

"I hit you with my axe on the backswing," someone said.

Dierk looked up into a pair of concerned eyes. "Oh."

"Don't you know not to walk so close?" The man's gaze dropped to somewhere near Dierk's boots. "I could've killed you if I'd hit your head."

"I'm sorry." Dierk struggled to his feet, embarrassed.

Fredrik's hand stayed on his shoulder. "Sure you're all right?"

"Aye." If they'd leave him alone.

Fredrik released him, his eyes sharp. Then he turned to the man. "He's unaccustomed to working with anyone but me. I wager he'll be more careful after this."

Cradling his head where it still throbbed, Dierk hurried to join the other boys. Fredrik had apologized. For him.

But then, 'twas his fault. Any woodcutter worth his salt would know to keep out of his partners' way. He'd made an exceptional mess of things.

The boys eyed him askance.

Dierk scowled. "Let's get to work."

Bert issued orders, and, after glancing around to ascertain the workers' positions, Dierk bent to do his part. If he didn't keep his mind focused, one of three things would happen: he'd embarrass himself again, betray his identity through clumsiness, or injure himself or someone else.

None of those options appealed to him.

6

Larch Wreaths

WHEN IT NEARED DUSK, Grobel called a halt to the work. "We'll finish tomorrow."

As the others gathered their tools, chatting amongst themselves, Dierk shouldered his pack and slid his axe into its strap. Their work had progressed well. Along with stripping most of the tree and chopping the largest branches, they'd sawn a section from the trunk. A person could pass on the road, but a team of horses couldn't have squeezed through.

The young man who'd offered to lodge them approached Fredrik and extended his hand. "My name is Karl. I can offer nothing grand, but it will be better than sleeping in the elements, or even a barn." He smiled.

Fredrik grasped his forearm. "Thank you for opening your home."

"'Tis no trouble. We are glad for your help." Karl looked

at Dierk. "You are well since your fall?"

Great thunder. Couldn't they pretend it didn't happen? "I'm fine."

"Good." Karl slapped his leg. "Well, my wife will have supper waiting."

Dierk shadowed Fredrik and Karl as the whole group followed the main road perhaps half a mile before turning into a side path. Dierk flexed his left arm. He'd never mention it, of course, but it was sore. He'd have a nice bruise in the morning.

Not to mention his hands. Though knight-training had toughened them, the rough bark and jagged lengths of wood found any place with the slightest softness left. He inspected his palms. "Two new blisters," he muttered.

"What's the matter?"

Dierk jerked his head around to see a boy the others called Simon. Perhaps a year younger than Dierk, but near the same size.

Dierk hooked his thumb in his belt. "Nothing."

"Sure, nothing." Simon bumped his shoulder into Dierk's. "I've been thinking. You're pretty lousy for a woodcutter's son."

Dierk's jaw went loose before he could stop it. "What?"

"You have to be told to do everything. You got yourself knocked down. Now you're complaining you got two new blisters."

"I did not complain." Knights never complained of physical discomfort, whatever these peasant boys might do.

Simon shook his head. "A skilled woodcutter wouldn't notice a blister, and he sure wouldn't get knocked down by his tonight, Heike. I agreed to lodge two woodcutters who are helping us clear up after the storm."

"Oh, how kind of them." She turned to Fredrik and Dierk and listened to her husband's introductions. Then she smiled. "Do come in and make yourselves comfortable. Supper will be ready in a trice."

Firelight illumined the interior of the tidy cottage. A hole in the roof allowed the smoke to escape, but some of it lingered. Dierk breathed its welcoming fragrance.

"Set your burdens under the window, and sit down at the table." Heike scurried to the fire and stirred something in a pot.

Dierk's shoulders relaxed as he slid his pack off. No chance he'd get soft away from his normal duties. Not on this trip.

Karl whispered something to Heike, strode into the back room, and returned in a moment without his tools. They took seats on the rough benches while Heike laid bread trenchers on the table, talking with Karl about the day's work. She grabbed a wreath of larch cones from a shelf and placed it around the candlestick in the table's center.

"What a pretty decoration," Fredrik remarked.

Heike glanced at him before she lit the half-burned candle with a twig from the fire. "Aye. Karl made it. It takes all of twoscore cones to make the best larch wreaths."

Fredrik stared toward the flickering candle flame. "An exhibition of patience and cunning skill."

Dierk raised an eyebrow. Why all the chit-chat about larch wreaths?

Karl slapped his hand on the table. "I thought so."

Larch Wreaths

Dierk stared at him. The whole bunch of them acted so strange. "Thought what?"

Karl shot a glance at Fredrik.

Fredrik smiled. "He's safe, though not yet a member."

Member of—could it be the Royal League?

Fredrik pulled something from the pouch at his belt. "Seen these, Kik?" He tossed a small brown larch cone across the table.

Dierk caught it. "There's a whole wreath of them right there, as you pointed out. What's with them?"

"Properly used, they are a favorite sign of the Royal League."

So *that* was their significance. "What about the green ones you dropped a few days ago?"

"Ah, you caught that."

"Aye." He wasn't stupid. "What do they mean?"

"It means, 'I am the one you expect.'"

"Expect for what?"

"Depends on previous arrangements," Fredrik said.

"I see." Dierk propped his elbow on the table, nudging a pitcher, which tipped and filled his lap with its contents. He leaped from the bench, grabbing for the pitcher. Which slipped out of his hands and hit the hard-packed dirt floor.

"Oh!" Heike cried. "'Tis the last of the buttermilk."

Dierk stared at his tunic, drenched with whitish liquid. Every time he turned around he made a fool of himself. "I— 'Tis been a long day. Guess I'm clumsy."

"'Tis no matter. Forgive me." Heike waved a hand. "I can lend you Karl's other tunic, and I'll clean yours."

Dierk shook his head. "No, I have a change in my pack."

"Very well. You may go in the other room and change."

Retrieving the tunic from his bundle, he retreated into the room Karl had entered earlier. He unclasped his belt and whisked the wet tunic over his head. Voices drifted from the outer room.

"Poor lad seems nervous," Karl said, "as if he constantly fears he will make a mistake. He did blunder once at work today, but I wish we could set him at ease."

Dierk sighed as he pulled the clean tunic over his head. Everyone would remember him as the woodcutter's son who didn't even know enough to keep out of a swinging axe's range. The exact impression a prince wanted to make.

Fredrik's voice broke in. "He is uncomfortable because he is not truly my son, and he is unaccustomed to this life."

Dierk bound his belt around him, taking longer than necessary. How much would Fredrik tell?

"Who is he, then?" Heike asked.

"Dierk, Crown Prince of Sunland."

A strangled squeak filtered through the door. "Crown Prince! And I scolded him for spilling the buttermilk."

In spite of his day, Dierk smiled.

"Why is he here?" Karl asked.

"His father sent him on a tour of the country, you might say," Fredrik said. "Treat him as any other citizen. I mention his birth only because I could use some help watching out for him while we work."

Right. Dierk mustn't forget his *shockingly delinquent behavior* had sent him on this journey in disguise. And he bungled it at every turn. Glancing around, he spotted a door to the back yard. He opened it and slipped out.

Honestly, this trip was getting old, and he hadn't been gone a fortnight. If he could learn to quit humiliating himself, it might get easier. He let his gaze wander over the yard's contents: a shed that might house some animals, another whose use he couldn't determine, and a pile of large logs near a chopping block.

A chopping block. With Karl's axe leaning against it. Dierk shuffled over and wrapped his fingers around the handle. The tool fit, not as well as his sword or lance, but it found its position. One corner of his mouth curved upward. Maybe he had gained some skill.

He thumped a log onto the block and took the appropriate stance. With a deep breath, he swung the axe high.

Thwack! The blade sliced into the wood, almost to the bottom. He banged the piece on the block until it split in two. Satisfaction rushed through him, like the headiness of wine. Squaring his shoulders, he picked up the pieces to split them smaller still. In two strokes, he divided them. Fredrik himself couldn't have done better. At least he could do something right. Finally.

Yellow light invaded the evening's dusk. Dierk glanced toward the house.

"Kik?" Fredrik called from the doorway.

"Aye?" Dierk snatched up the four pieces and stacked them under the crude shelter nearby.

Fredrik joined him. "How's the day been?"

Dierk shrugged. "I've had worse." The first time he battled using a staff, for instance—he'd lain awake that night with tears oozing from his eyes.

"You did well with your work, lad." Fredrik slapped his back. "Come, let's not delay supper for our hosts."

"Of course." Dierk glanced at the wood pile. Perhaps he could work on it in the morning. He had spilled Heike's buttermilk, after all.

7

Holding His Own

"**Show me again, Kik.**"

Dierk smiled at Simon's enthusiasm. The minute Grobel called a morning break to the work, Simon had begged him to demonstrate the punch he'd delivered last night. Simon caught on well. "Place your feet as I showed you. Pick a spot to hit." Dierk drew a circle in the air with his finger. "Then you swing." He drove his fist through the invisible target he'd marked. "Be sure to turn your body into the punch. You get more power."

Simon mimicked him. "I still feel I'm not moving my arm right."

"Watch me again." Dierk demonstrated twice more. "Hang up a pillow and practice on it tonight. Remember what I've told you about your chin and your shoulder. After a while, it'll be second nature, and you won't even have to worry about your feet. Let me see you do it."

Simon checked his stance, indicated his target, and swung.

"Perfect!" Dierk pumped his fist in the air. "You'll be a regular Squire Franz."

"Who's he?" Bert asked from the circle of boys who stood watching.

Only the most skilled boxer of Duke Ebner's squires. The one Dierk couldn't beat yet. "Uh, one of the squires I watched. He was good."

"Oh."

Best turn the subject before they came up with some other question he'd have to concoct an answer for. "Tell you what, Simon. I'll let you take a swing at me."

"Huh?"

"Aim for my jaw, right here." Dierk pointed to the spot under his left ear. "See if you can topple me. I won't block."

Simon's eyes bulged. "Are you jesting?"

"No." Dierk bounced on the balls of his feet. "Give it to me."

"Uh, all right." Simon took up his stance facing Dierk.

"Now don't hold back. Remember, you want to drive your fist straight through my head." He grinned at Simon's shocked face. "Whenever you're ready."

Simon frowned, his eyes focusing. His body tensed.

"Get him, Simon," someone whispered.

Pain exploded in Dierk's jaw. His head pivoted, and he fought for balance. With no prompting, his fist lunged to retaliate. Just in time, he stopped it. Drawing a long breath, he cradled his offended face. "Good hit, Simon. One of the best I've ever caught." He winked, and the watching boys laughed. "If you'd hit a hair farther back, I'd probably have gone down." He extended his hand, and Simon clasped his forearm.

The boys clapped and whooped, coming forward to pound Simon's back, and Dierk's too. Dierk grinned, exchanging playful slugs with the others. Energy swirled through him, making even the pain in his jaw something to appreciate. Like he was home training with the other squires. Although squires never wore such coarse clothing as these peasant boys.

Grobel approached the group, a smile on his face. "Time to get back to work."

The boys cheered, picking up their tools. Dierk grabbed his own axe. Hard work wasn't so bad once you got used to it. 'Twasn't all that different from knight-training.

BY EVENING, THEY'D CLEARED the road and cut the tree into chunks for oxen or mules to drag to the village tomorrow. The smaller pieces could fit in carts. Dierk smiled as he shouldered his axe and knapsack. Unlike tilting and broadsword practice, woodcutting gave you something to show for your effort besides bruises and cuts.

Or broken arms.

He shook his head and focused on Karl and Fredrik's conversation as he trailed behind them.

At Karl's gate, Grobel stopped to exchange a handclasp with Fredrik. "We appreciate all your help." He glanced at Dierk. "Good work today, lad."

"Thanks." Although Grobel didn't say it, he was probably thinking of yesterday's mishap. Dierk could only hope his work today outweighed his earlier ineptitude.

Grobel shifted the saw resting teeth-up on his shoulder. "Will you stay tomorrow?"

Fredrik gave a quick shake of his head. "We must move on. We thank you for your hospitality."

Grobel dipped his chin. "We'll be sorry to see you go."

Dierk wouldn't. He'd be glad to get on with the journey.

"Hey, Kik."

Dierk turned toward Simon's voice.

The boy grinned. "Thanks for the lessons."

Dierk lifted his hand. "Keep practicing."

"I will." With a salute of his axe, Simon jogged after his father.

Well, it hadn't been complete misery staying here. The boys weren't so bad when he got to know them. If his travels ever took him this way again—

But they wouldn't. The Crown Prince had no reason to visit obscure hamlets of his country unless the King took a notion to send his son on some journey of penance.

Dierk followed Fredrik into the house in time to catch Karl kissing his wife.

Heike blushed and wiped her hands on her apron. "Supper's ready as soon as you've washed."

Dierk shed his axe and knapsack, laying them beside Fredrik's.

Heike scurried to her kitchen, calling over her shoulder, "Kik, I cleaned your tunic. 'Tis airing outside. I'll bring it in."

"Thank you, Frau Heike." Dierk passed his hands through the wash water, then crumpled the hem of his tunic to dry off most of the moisture.

"Karl," Fredrik said, "could I build a message tonight? You needn't send it anytime soon, but whenever the next carrier comes through."

"Of course. Supplies are in here. Chest under the window." Karl ducked into the bedroom, carrying his axe and saw.

Build a message? Why use a code word for "write"? Overcautious, these League members.

Heike entered in Karl's wake, bringing Dierk's tunic. "Here you go, lad. Thank you for chopping the wood this morning."

Ridiculous, how that pleased him. Not that he'd done much, but he'd risen early to accomplish what he could before breakfast, as a sort of apology for the trouble he'd caused her. And she'd noticed. "You're welcome."

"To think I've had a prince chop wood for me." Her eyes sparkled as she handed him the folded tunic. "But if you spill my cottage cheese tonight, I'll swat you."

He had to smile. "I'll be careful, Frau Heike."

She laughed. "You're a dear boy. Your mother must be very proud."

Ha. More like mortified. The day he came back in disgrace from Duke Ebner's, she'd wept as if someone had died. *"Oh, Dierk, how could you neglect your duties that way? This young man's injury is your fault. It is the duty of royalty to protect their subjects, not harm them through neglect. How could you be so careless?"* She hadn't been proud of him since he weeded the rose bed in her garden as a kid.

Maybe he should change that.

DIERK SAT STARING INTO the coals of the fireplace while Karl and Heike talked and Fredrik "built a message" in the other room. Truth be told, he was bone tired. And tomorrow promised a lot of walking. At last Fredrik emerged, and Dierk stood to lay out the mats Heike had provided last night.

"You found all satisfactory?" Karl asked.

Fredrik nodded. "Aye. I left the message in the chest."

"I shall send it on its way as soon as possible." Karl slid his arm around his wife's waist. "We shall bid you good-night, then."

Heike snuffed the lamp before she and Karl retreated. By firelight, Dierk and Fredrik undressed and crawled under their blankets. 'Twasn't the most luxurious bed he'd ever slept in, but Dierk didn't care.

He studied Fredrik's face, wondering what he'd said in that message. Probably some report to Father about the progress of their journey. Had Fredrik had anything favorable to say about him?

Dierk propped himself up on his elbow. "What did the message say, if I may ask?"

Eyes closed, Fredrik smiled. "I requested His Majesty reward Karl and Heike for their kindness."

"Hmm." Dierk flopped down again. "As if we didn't earn our keep."

"Oh, we earned our keep. Even you." Fredrik opened his eyes and winked.

Dierk scowled, but a smile threatened to break out. He resorted to turning his back. "Anyway," he said over his shoulder, "'tis a good message."

"Glad you think so, Your Highness."

Dierk shut his eyes, ready for sleep. He could do this. Just work a little harder, endure a little longer, and Fredrik would deem his punishment sufficient. A couple weeks more at most.

8

Chivalry

THE SUN GLOWED RED-ORANGE above the western horizon as Dierk trudged behind Fredrik along the filthy streets of Habichtheim. They'd left Karl's village yesterday morning only to lodge at a castle and cut trees for the lord's wood supply. And this time Fredrik planned to stay a few days. Their tedious trip wasn't long enough with walking indirect routes. Why not waste time chopping trees someone else could cut better?

'Twould be different if they needed the wages. Fredrik had a liberal supply of silver and copper coins. Dierk stretched his stride to cross a muddy puddle. He didn't mind the work. 'Twasn't hard now that his muscles were accustomed to the movements. He just wanted to return to his life at Duke Ebner's.

As they started up the hill toward the castle, Fredrik clapped Dierk's shoulder. "A good day's work, lad."

"I should say so."

"I mean your skill improves." Fredrik's words were quiet.

"Glad you noticed I didn't get myself knocked down today."

Fredrik slanted him a look and fell silent.

Dierk sighed. Fredrik probably meant to offer sincere encouragement. But what did it matter? Woodcutting was a useless skill for a knight.

DIERK HAD TO WAIT his turn behind two girls at the well. At Duke Ebner's he always enjoyed pouring a cup of water over his head when he finished work. No reason to give up this slight comfort.

Over and over, the girls lowered a leather pail into the well, drew it up, and poured the water into large wooden buckets at their feet. Dierk almost offered to help, but why waste gallantry on a couple of servant girls? Finally, the second girl emptied her pail for the last time and bent to lift her full bucket. Dierk stepped forward. She didn't move away as he expected, and his arm brushed her back.

She whirled to face him, hitting his arm in the process. "Oh, I'm sorry, you startled me." She offered a smile that was a little too bright and brushed back a wisp of blonde hair. "I don't believe we've met. I'm Therese. I work in the dairy."

He almost rolled his eyes, but managed a terse nod. "Kik. Traveling woodcutter."

His brusque tone didn't dim her smile in the least. "A pleasure, Kik. You must have worked hard today. Let me draw your water." She slipped between him and the well's wall and sent the pail down.

A milkmaid was flirting with *him*. The Crown Prince. He smirked behind her back.

Under her vigorous turning, the windlass brought the leather pail back up. She lifted it from the hook and held it out to him. "Will you be staying long?"

Dierk reached for the cup that hung from the little thatch roof over the well. "No." He dipped a cupful, bent his head, and dumped the liquid in his hair. The coolness soaked his scalp, delightfully refreshing.

He lifted his head to repeat the process and found the girl's attention glued to him. Never mind. He returned the cup to its hook. "Thank you for your service."

"Think nothing of it. I hope to see more of you."

Definitely flirting. The way she lowered her head and peered up at him through dark gold lashes. It took all he had not to laugh in her face. "Good evening, Fraulein." He turned his back and hurried through the crowded courtyard to find Fredrik.

SEATED IN THE LARGE kitchen with many other castle workers, Dierk lifted a bite of pork from the bread trencher he shared with Fredrik. The food was decent, but he still disliked eating in a servants' hall. While Fredrik chatted easily with the man beside him, Dierk couldn't make conversation with his neighbors without fearing he'd betray himself through something he said.

"Ah, Kik, we meet again."

He turned to the feminine voice at his right shoulder.

That girl from the well—he couldn't recall her name—slid onto the bench next to him. Just what he needed.

"I hope you're enjoying your stay at Habichtheim." She daintily lifted a bite of stewed parsnip and poked it between her smiling lips.

Dierk grunted. "So far not bad." He shoved a chunk of bread into his mouth and washed it down with weak ale.

"Do your travels take you 'round the whole country?"

He turned to meet her gaze. She looked back, her face expectant, blue eyes coy. She *was* pretty. And obviously aware of that fact. "More or less. Please excuse me, Fraulein. I'm too tired to converse well at the moment."

"Forgive me." She smiled again. "How thoughtless of me."

He gave a negligent wave. "No harm." He turned back to his food.

He finished his portion of the salty, smoked meat and reached for the ale cup. After draining it, he swung one leg over the bench to go in search of the ale jug and refill the cup for Fredrik.

"Is your cup empty? I'll be glad to refill it for you."

That girl stood before him, hand outstretched. She must have flown out of her seat.

Dierk drew a long breath. "Fraulein—"

"Therese."

"Therese, I am perfectly capable of filling this cup. Please return to your meal."

"But I don't mind—"

Dierk stood. "I shall attend to it myself." He strode past her before she could come up with another excuse.

If she weren't a practiced flirt in all her looks and

gazed up at him, hopeful and genuinely apologetic for bothering him. Ach. He couldn't very well leave her to limp up this hill. He sighed. "Let me lighten the load for the pony first."

"Oh, thank you, Kik."

Dierk set the brake on the cart and unloaded three logs, which he stacked on the roadside. 'Twould mean another trip down to retrieve them. But the knight's creed bound him to protect and aid the weak. Chivalry required sacrifice.

Otherwise, he would've let Therese find her own way up.

He straightened from placing the last log. No way Therese could climb into the cart with a twisted ankle. He took her hand and pulled her to her feet. "I'll lift you up."

"Thank you. I am sorry for causing you this trouble."

"Think nothing of it." He helped her hobble to the cart, grasped her waist, and set her on the load of wood. "Hold the side of the cart."

"I will." She tucked her basket between two logs and shifted her position.

Dierk released the brake and tugged the pony into motion. This act of kindness might delay him so much he'd miss supper. But it would be worth it to show Fredrik he *could* be kind and dutiful.

A pity about Therese's pain, of course, but at least Dierk was the one coming to her aid. It meant a good chance of demonstrating his chivalry and thereby ending this journey sooner. Dierk half-smiled. Perhaps flirtatious milkmaids were good for something.

9

The Healer's Chamber

THE PONY TOOK AN age to haul the woodcutter's cart up to the castle. Dierk had no chance of getting winded, plodding along like this. At least Therese held her tongue instead of filling the time with inane chatter.

As they passed under the gate of the castle, Dierk looked over his shoulder. "Where would you like me to take you?"

Gripping the sides of the cart, she offered a timid smile. "To the healer's if you don't mind. I'll send for my father to help me home."

"Very well. If you'll point me toward the healer's chambers."

"In the southwest corner."

The opposite direction of the woodshed. *Of course.* Without a word, Dierk led the pony through the workers hurrying about the courtyard, intent on their own duties.

Outside the healer's door, Dierk lifted Therese from the

cart. As her feet hit the ground, she cried out and clung to his arms. "I'm sorry." Moisture glimmered in her blue eyes. "I let my bad foot take some weight. Would you please carry me inside?" She blinked and ducked her head. "I didn't know such a little thing could hurt this much."

For the first time since he'd seen her, Dierk didn't despise her. Foolish she might be, but she couldn't help spraining her ankle. "Fret not, Therese. The healer will set it to rights." He slipped one arm behind her shoulders. With the other, he lifted her like a child.

Her arms encircled his neck, and she snuggled close to his chest. Hiding her face at his collarbone, she whispered, "Thank you."

She was little more than a child. Her parents ought to warn her against flirtatious behavior, but perhaps she did not truly understand what she was doing. Dierk stepped carefully to the door and knocked with the toe of his boot.

The door swung open, and a young man about Dierk's age grinned at him. "Come in. I'm just leaving, and Frau Olga is pining for another injury to tend." He lifted a bandaged hand. "Mine didn't keep her from supper, and you know a healer never wants to arrive at supper on time. Much more impressive if she arrives late because she had a patient to tend."

"Rodebert, get out of the way and let them in," called a female voice. "They'll be in no mood for your jests."

Dierk half-smiled as he stepped into the chamber, lit by a lamp and a small window. Rodebert burst into laughter, and Dierk startled.

"Therese, I must congratulate you." Rodebert clapped, the

applause muffled by his bandage. "Your ankle trick worked again."

Trick? How did Rodebert know she had a sprained ankle?

Therese's head came up. "Rodebert, don't be cruel." Her voice held tears.

"I'm not being cruel." Rodebert chuckled and met Dierk's eyes. "Don't feel bad, stranger. She once made a fool of me this way. She can act better than an entertainer, can she not?" He slapped Dierk's shoulder. "Well, I must be on my way." He strode out the open door.

A stone grew in Dierk's chest. He could find no words as he looked down at Therese. Red suffused her lightly tanned cheeks.

"You deceived me." His words barely exceeded a whisper.

"Kik, I didn't mean—"

"Didn't mean to lie to me?" he finished, his voice gaining strength. He wanted to drop her right there. Glancing around, he caught sight of a bed. He stomped to it and set her down hard. "You made a fool of me before the whole castle."

He whirled around and headed for the door. Then he spun back. "You are a shameless wench, a disgrace to your family. You ought to be flogged. 'Twill serve you right when some man shreds your reputation. If you have any reputation left. Perhaps you *are* a trollop, and I was the only person in the castle who didn't know it."

Therese hid her face in her hands, choking on sobs. Probably false ones. If she were a man, Dierk would acquaint her with his fists for humiliating him so.

"Young man, I don't know who you are, but you have no right to insult this maiden." The healer scowled at him from under dark eyebrows.

Dierk lifted his chin. "You are mistaken. She has already insulted herself." He turned to leave.

And met Fredrik standing in the doorway. Judging by his face, Fredrik had heard a good deal, and he wasn't pleased.

Dierk clenched his fists and shouldered past. "Don't say a word," he hissed. "Not now." He grabbed the pony's bridle and set out for the wood yard.

He unloaded the cart and hurled the logs into a haphazard pile by the woodshed. He'd broken a fine sweat but lost no energy by the time he started down the hill to retrieve the logs he'd left behind. Left behind because a loose-principled dairymaid tricked him. Heat rushed through his veins all over again.

Stupid girl made him lose his temper in front of her, the healer, and whoever else happened to be passing outside. Including Fredrik. After this, Fredrik would be in no hurry to shorten the journey.

Dierk had to stop himself from yanking the bridle as he brought the eager pony to a halt. It didn't take long to turn the cart and load the wood. Back up he went.

Rage still jangled his nerves. If only he had a sword and a worthy opponent to consume this energy. The pony poked up the hill as if the cart were fully loaded. Ornery beast.

FREDRIK MET HIM IN the wood yard. "You'll miss supper altogether if you don't go to the kitchen now."

"Not hungry." Dierk grabbed a log and threw it next to the others.

"You will be come morning." Fredrik folded his arms on the cart's rim. "The healer told me what happened. I'll save the lecture for later and take the pony down for you."

Dierk glared, not trusting himself to answer. He swiped damp hair off his forehead and reached for another log. "How came you to the healer's?"

"I saw the logs you left by the roadside, so I asked the gatekeeper if he'd seen you. He directed me."

How many had seen Therese on his cart and snickered behind their hands at his gullibility?

"Kik Holtzer."

Dierk turned toward the unfamiliar voice.

A stocky man strode into the wood yard and stopped right in front of Dierk. "So you're the knave who called my daughter a trollop. Have you anything to say for yourself?"

No surprise Therese had whined to her father. Dierk straightened his stance to emphasize his superior height. "Her behavior does her reputation no favors."

A sharp-knuckled fist connected with Dierk's jaw. He staggered back, caught his balance, and lunged to fight.

"Kik!" Fredrik's hand caught his arm.

He twisted around, ready to strike Fredrik.

"Stop it, Kik."

The words cut through his haze of fighting instinct, like Sir Wilhelm's voice during a boxing match. He lowered his fists. "Let me go."

Fredrik released him and looked at Therese's father. "I expected to see you soon, and now you've done what you came for. I can handle my son from here."

The man nodded tersely. "Very well. I don't say Therese

should have lied, but I won't have her honor insulted."

"Your daughter insults her own honor—as well as yours," Dierk snapped.

The man stepped forward, nostrils flared.

"That is enough, Kik." Fredrik's hand clamped hard on the back of Dierk's neck. "I apologize for my son's words, sir. Good evening."

" 'Evening." With a final glare for Dierk, Therese's father walked out.

Dierk drew a long breath, trying to quiet the roiling fury in his chest. "You didn't even rebuke him." He pierced Fredrik with a stare. "He struck the Crown Prince."

"Come." Fredrik heaved the last log from the cart. "I'll return the pony to Jokkel. You chop wood until I return."

THE SUN HAD SET, leaving purplish shadows behind. Dierk glanced at the sky. The first star shone bright in the west. Fredrik hadn't called a halt to the work when he returned. Instead, he'd put his own axe to use.

Dierk had finally calmed enough to drive the axe more or less straight. Darkness would soon force them in.

Fredrik took a seat on his chopping block, resting his axe across his knees. "Join me, lad."

Dierk dropped his axe, planted a foot on his block, and propped his forearm on his knee. Now for the lecture.

Fredrik turned his face toward Dierk, though the darkness left his features indistinct. "From what the healer told me, I gather Therese told you she had a sprained ankle when she did not."

"Aye." Anger flickered to life again. "I learned she's used such a trick before to gain a young man's attention. I unloaded my cart for her, took care of her as if she were my sister, and the little wench was lying the whole time."

"So you called her a trollop?"

Dierk huffed. "I don't remember exactly what I said, but I think I used that word."

"Let me first commend you for taking the time to help her."

As if such a commendation could outweigh the scolding soon to come. "Chivalry lands a person in trouble."

Fredrik chuckled softly then fell silent a moment. "Therese's conduct was wrong, inexcusable. But you lost your temper shamefully, lad."

"Am I supposed to say nothing when a girl deceives me, wastes my time, and makes a fool of me?"

"You are supposed to exercise self-control no matter how others behave."

Sounded like something Father would say. Dierk turned his face toward the blue-black sky. "Well, 'tis the last time I'll go out of my way to show kindness to a stranger."

"Because it injured your pride?"

The quiet words slapped Dierk as hard as the punch he'd received earlier. He jerked his head to face Fredrik. "All you and Father see in me is pride. I could have saved Therese's life and you would only speak to warn me against pride in my accomplishments."

"That is unjust, lad. And mind your words lest someone overhear."

Dierk glanced into the gloom. No one stirred near enough

to hear. "Why must you speak to me? I know I have failed in your eyes. Let that be enough."

"Until your own eyes see your failure and you work to correct it, your character will still suffer."

"Right. And until my character is strong enough to please you, I chop wood. Lesson understood." Dierk slid his foot off the chopping block. "Can we retire, or shall we continue working?"

"We'll retire." Fredrik let out a sigh as he rose. "Kik, there is much good in your character. You must let God help you weed out the bad."

Fredrik's words sounded more like Father's by the minute. Endless preaching. "I'll keep that in mind, *Father*." He picked up his axe and followed Fredrik toward the dormitory.

Of all the rotten days. Worst of all, he'd ruined his chance to present himself as the dutiful, perfect son Father wanted. After such a failure, Fredrik would certainly *add* time to this wretched, demeaning journey.

Unless he decided to abandon the scheme altogether and advise Father to bestow the throne on Anselm.

10

The Forester

DIERK TIPPED HIS HEAD back and filled his lungs with the fresh morning air. The birds twittered as if they competed for the loudest song. Who would've thought he could become as proficient on his feet as on a horse's back? Another week of travel had toughened his feet, steadied his stride.

He'd much rather walk than work at a castle with scheming milkmaids. After the disaster with Therese, they'd stayed two more miserable days in Habichtheim. Dierk was certain Fredrik had dispatched a message to Father, but they hadn't waited for a reply, so perhaps he hadn't lost his chance to prove his character.

Dierk flipped a fallen limb out of the path with his staff. Their route hadn't gotten any more direct. They'd lodged one night in a tavern at a crossroads, taking an even lonelier road north the next morning. Since then they'd slept in farmers' fields and barns, paying sometimes in coin, sometimes in a few hours' work. Last night they camped in the forest again.

Which suited Dierk fine. Easier to play his role in isolation. He'd achieved a rhythm in this woodcutter's-son charade. Even woke up to feed the fire sometimes.

His gaze hitched on something in the woods. Something out of place. A heap of cut stones?

"Fredrik, what's that?" He pointed to the pile a few yards from the path.

Fredrik paused to look. "Ah, we made it. I wasn't sure of its precise location."

"Precise location of what?"

"A village Lady Melankardja destroyed. No one lives here anymore, and I doubt 'twill ever be rebuilt."

Dierk frowned. He'd heard of the Lost Village. Couldn't recall the details, but it savored of intrigue. "Why have we come?"

"Your father wanted you to see it in person. I'm to tell you how its downfall came about."

"Well, get on with it. 'Twill pass the time, anyhow." To be honest, curiosity had thrown down a gauntlet in his brain, demanding satisfaction. But it wouldn't do to admit it.

"No, I shall wait until we've toured the remains of the village."

Dierk shrugged. "Suit yourself."

The path led on through thinning woods, which opened to fields overtaken by brush and weeds. The slender trees hadn't yet reached the lofty heights of the forest residents. Saplings poked up through piles of rubble. Vines crawled over everything, forcing Dierk to watch his step as they wound through the dead village.

His fellow squires sometimes jested of graveyards' eeriness. They ought to see this place. The back of his neck insisted on prickling no matter how often he dismissed it.

He poked his staff into one pile. "Look at this. An old earthenware pitcher."

"Aye. Yonder is the forge." Fredrik pointed with his own staff. "See the mangled iron tools?" Odd shapes of rusty metal protruded from one pile of stone and rubbish, beneath the leaves of a vine.

"What about those walls over there?" Dierk pointed to four stone walls with a short tower built into the front one, the best preserved remnant amongst the destruction. "A church maybe?"

"Likely."

Dierk stirred the dirt by the pitcher, uncovering what looked like ashes. Perhaps a fireplace had stood here.

Shuffles sounded behind them a moment before Fredrik whirled, drawing his knife. Dierk spun, his body tense. He raked the surroundings with his gaze. Nothing. No animal, no human.

There it came again. Footfalls, back up the trail. Dierk clasped his fingers around the hilt of his own hunting knife. The steps moved closer, bold, not muffled like a slinking animal's. But who would be here in this desolate place?

A figure emerged from behind a mound of rubble. He came to an instant halt. "Who goes there?"

"A woodcutter and his son," Fredrik called back.

The man strode toward them. "What brings you this way?"

11

Sharpened Shovels and Bitter Tea

Elbows braced on the table, Pieter stared into his cup as his visitors waited. Thirty years gone, and he could still feel the horror of the village's demise. A mercy he hadn't much opportunity to tell the story, to relive the hated memories. But for the sake of the Truth he'd vowed to fight for all his days, he would tell it again. *Holy Father, grant me grace.*

FINISHED WITH HIS WORK for the day, thirteen-year-old Pieter lost no time making his way to the village. Over the past months, civil unrest had mounted in the village until it reached others outside. Rumors said the Royal House itself, not only the count who ruled this land, might take action against treason.

What a heavy word.

Pieter intended to keep informed of the latest excitement. First stop, the forge.

He found his friend Meine pumping the bellows for his father. "Meine, what's new?"

Meine bore down on the lever, forcing air into the bed of red coals. Waves of heat rolled out. "We're sharpening knives and tools for battle."

"Battle? Why on earth?"

"We've had news the Royal Army is advancing. We'll be ready."

"Ready?" Pieter yelled above the noise of Meine's father pounding a plowshare on the anvil. "How can you hope to fight the Royal Army? You don't even have real weapons."

"We won't surrender." Meine grabbed an armful of knives from a pile on the floor. "We'll fight as long as we can."

"That's stupid." Pieter picked up the remaining knives and followed his friend to the rear of the forge. "You know you'll lose in the end."

Meine threw down the weapons with a clatter next to the whetstone and planted his fists on his hips. "That attitude is the whole problem. No one ever stands up to the Royal House with their religious control and overbearing laws. As long as everyone believes they don't stand a chance, they'll never try."

Pieter scowled. Whence came that nonsense? "I still think 'tis ridiculous because you'll never win. Besides, we have the best king in the civilized world. King Siegbert won't bow to the pope but lets everyone worship God the way they choose. He keeps the serfs free, and he doesn't tax the nobles hard so they don't have to tax us. None of the laws are unreasonable."

Meine took a knife in his left hand and cranked the whetstone with his right. "Lady Melankardja's right. The Royal House has this whole country deceived. I hate them for what they've done to us."

"Lady Melankardja?" A chill zinged down Pieter's spine. He knew the town seethed with discontent over some supposed wrongs, but to make contact with Lady Melankardja? That was going too far. "You mean she's come here?"

Meine bent over the whetstone. "Not yet. Just her man, Demas. The things he says." Meine shook his head. "I didn't realize how blind I was, bound to this endless round of work for someone else's benefit, 'til I heard him speak. We deserve to be our own masters, Pieter, not submitting to some lord or duke or king who thinks he's God's minister. Maybe there isn't even a God. Maybe kings make up stories about him to keep us in their control."

Pieter opened and closed his mouth, his tongue refusing to form words. No God? Then where had the world come from, pray tell? Who kept the stars in the sky and the sun rising every morning? It sure wasn't the king. Meine had lost his mind.

He lifted the blade and thumbed its edge. "Bring me a bucket of water, will you? Need to refill the trough."

"Aye." Pieter carried a bucket to the well in the village center and drew fresh water. He glanced at the people milling about. Too many people. The men should be out working, the women tending their homes. Not conversing in little groups or building what looked like fortifications at the perimeter.

Pieter hurried back to the forge and poured the water into

the trough beneath the whetstone. The screech of stone grinding metal irked him more than usual. He set down the half-full bucket. "Are you serious about following Lady Melankardja, Meine?"

"I am." The stone quit grating as Meine looked up. "You should join us, Pieter. She knows what freedom is."

Pieter shook his head. "I don't know." Anyone who said God wasn't real must be viewed with suspicion.

"A pity you never heard Demas. He can talk better than the priest, even. And I like what he says. Makes sense."

"Well, I need to stay and help my parents. I'm their only son, you know."

"Aye." Meine gave him a calculating look he didn't understand. "Sometimes people have to sacrifice."

Pieter shrugged. "I guess so." But you had to make sure the object of your sacrifice deserved it. "Look, I'll see you around."

Meine waved and started up the crank again.

Pieter walked through the shop to the street. What had gotten into Meine? No God, indeed. Fighting the Royal Army with woodcutting knives and sharpened shovels. This Demas character must be quite a talker.

Pieter strolled to a cottage near the edge of town, eager to see Ilse. She was only eleven, but Pieter had made up his mind. When the time came, Ilse would be his bride. He knocked on the wooden door.

Ilse herself opened it. "Hello, Pieter. Come in."

Pieter strode in. "Where are the others?"

Having shut the door, Ilse walked to the table where she folded a garment and tucked it into a bag. "The others are working on fortifications, even little Fritz. I'm packing for Mitzi. She's going with Lady Melankardja soon."

"She's what?"

Ilse slid a needle case into the bag. "The army is coming."

Pieter nodded. "So Meine said. Why is Mitzi leaving?"

"Lady Melankardja wants all the young people to go with her to join her cause."

Pieter steadied himself with a hand on the table. "What is her cause?"

"I don't really understand." A pucker appeared between Ilse's blonde brows. "She hates King Siegbert and says he's unjust."

He'd gathered that much from Meine. "You aren't going with her, are you?"

"No. I'm too young. Only youth from twelve to twenty-five can go."

Pieter sighed with relief.

"I don't think I want to go anyway. Mother and Father are different since Lady Melankardja's man came and spoke." Ilse's lip trembled. "Home isn't near as nice now. They're always frustrated and worried."

Pieter's heart clenched. "Ilse." He laid a hand on her shoulder. What could he say? "You know if I can do anything for you, you can come to me."

"I know, Pieter." Her small pink lips curved into a smile. "You're a good friend."

"Can I help you with anything now?"

She gave him her adorable smile. "Tell me a story while I work."

So he told her a good, sweet fairy tale where everything

ended "happily ever after." For the moment, it would distract him from the fear creeping into his chest.

When someone pounded on Pieter's cottage door the following day, he leapt to answer. Suppose it were Ilse? It wasn't. "Meine, what are you doing?"

Meine jerked his head. "Come out here a minute."

Something important must've happened. He slipped outside and shut the door. "Well?"

"Guess who's in town. Lady Melankardja herself."

Despite the sun's warmth, cold blanketed Pieter's skin, raising the hair on his scalp. "What's she doing there?"

"Come to gather the young people who are joining her." Meine seemed to swell before Pieter's eyes. "I'm going tomorrow. Here's your chance. Come hear her speak. We're gonna have a good life, Pieter. No silly restrictions, but real freedom. And we'll work to free others. Come with us."

An inexplicable desire to run from his friend flooded Pieter. "No, Meine." His voice carried unusual conviction. "I will not go with Lady Melankardja. You do whatever you want. I'm staying."

"Fine." Meine sneered. "Stay under Papa's roof and follow the old rules. Be a slave if you want. I'm going." He spun on his heel and stalked up the path to the village.

Pieter reached out a hand, wanting to call to his friend. But what would he say? He'd never change his mind. No matter what, he wouldn't serve Lady Melankardja. She didn't believe in God, and she took children from their parents.

Still, 'twas too bad he had to break with Meine. They'd

been friends for a long time.

Pieter's father emerged from the cottage. "What did Meine want?"

Pieter kicked a lump of dirt, which skittered against a rock and crumbled. "He's joining Lady Melankardja. She's in the village getting *recruits*, I guess you could say."

Father drew a sharp breath. "Let's hope the Royal Army arrives in time to catch her. I wish we had some way to send them word."

Pieter did too. He couldn't do anything to stop his friends from joining Lady Melankardja. And he had a dreadful feeling that Ilse needed protection, and, despite his best intentions, he wouldn't be able to help her.

God, please bring the army here in time.

The next afternoon, a man bearing a royal document stopped by the cottage. He talked with Father of his plan to send three men to inspect the village and reason with the inhabitants before they resorted to all-out war on the rebels.

Pieter sat on the hearth, scratching behind his dog's ears. Did the man have any idea of the hatred he would encounter from the townspeople?

Father stroked his beard. "Did you know Lady Melankardja was in the village yesterday?"

"By the bye, no! Did you see her?"

"No, one of the village boys told us. I believe she was recruiting the youth, right, Pieter?" Father turned to look at him.

Pieter nodded. "All from age twelve to twenty-five, boys

and girls."

"Then God help us," the man said. "We should have known she had something to do with this. We must send men to search for her."

Pieter stroked his dog. No one had caught Lady Melankardja before. Why should they now? Her movements were too cunning, her hideouts too clever. If only they could undo her work here.

PIETER DAWDLED NEAR THE cottage until the deputation returned from the village, clothing torn and dirty, swords drawn, eyes wary.

Father hailed them. "No success?"

One of the men spat. "Hardly. They drove us out with rocks and mud and knives. They've asked for battle, and they'll get it."

Pieter's heart leaped up and raced—toward the village. He needed to go. Needed to see Ilse. Get her out if he could.

"Stay away from the village," the man went on. "I doubt you could persuade them to surrender, and they are dangerous. Tomorrow the army moves in."

"Of course." Father gave a sharp nod. "I wish you all success in your conquest."

Pieter dragged his feet as if his shoes were leaden, following Father into the cottage. Tomorrow would bring a battle not three miles from his home. Battles meant bloodshed and death. How could this be happening?

Maybe the sight of the army would bring the village to its senses. He prayed so.

EARLY IN THE MORNING, before the sun's rays softened the darkness, Pieter climbed out of bed. He couldn't stand it any longer. He had to see Ilse. The army would wait for first light. But he was the forester's son. He could creep to the village unseen.

By a roundabout path deer and rabbits traveled, Pieter wove through the woods. Keeping his feet silent, he skirted the fields until he reached the far side of the village. Bobbing lights illuminated figures moving about in the darkness. He'd have to avoid them.

As he slunk closer, the figures materialized as men and women carrying buckets and brushwood. The smell of pitch tainted the air. Pieter reached a break in the crude barrier that encircled most of the town. Crouching and dodging, he found Ilse's back yard and tapped on the rear door of the cottage.

No one answered.

For the first time in his life, Pieter entered a cottage uninvited. A single lamp burned in the center of the broad table. "Ilse?" he whispered.

Something rustled in the corner. He turned. Ilse lay in her little bed, her face toward the light. Pieter moved toward her. "Ilse, are you well?"

Her small hand wormed its way from beneath the covers. "Pieter?"

He clasped her hand and knelt by the bed. She drew a little gasping breath. "Ilse, what's wrong?"

Her eyelids drifted closed, and it took a long time for them to open again. "Mother said she wouldn't let us fall into the hands of the Royal Army. 'Twould be a fate worse than death." She swallowed.

Pieter stroked a strand of blonde hair from her sweaty forehead, his chest aching.

"She made Fritz and me drink bitter tea last night."

Pieter looked at the tiny figure beside Ilse. Fritz's eyes were shut, his face relaxed as if in sleep. But he didn't move, not even to breathe. A harsh gasp scraped Pieter's throat. What had their parents done?

"I wanted you, Pieter." Ilse's fingers curled around his. "I thought if you were here, Mother wouldn't have made me drink it. 'Twas poison, you know."

Oh, why hadn't he come? He could have slipped away without Father's knowledge. Somehow.

"I'm so sorry, Ilse. So sorry. Forgive me."

A hint of a smile touched her lips. "It doesn't matter. You're here now. Will you keep holding my hand? I held Fritz's when he died a little while ago."

"Of course." No matter who came and demanded he leave, he wouldn't. He would stay right here with Ilse. Yet there must be a way to counteract the poison. Mother would know. She understood herbs.

But there was no time.

Ilse drew a jerky breath. "Tell me a story. About Jesus and the five loaves."

Fighting the lump in his throat, Pieter told it as best he could. Ilse's pale face and soft breathing claimed his attention more than the story. Her breaths grew farther apart. He waited, barely speaking, for each successive rise of her chest.

Finally, it didn't come.

But it must. It must. Her hand had been limp for a while, but she must breathe again. He laid a strand of her hair over her nostrils. Everything in him cried out for that hair to flutter. He held his own breath lest he disturb it.

The blonde thread didn't waver.

Tears spilled down Pieter's cheeks. He kissed the hand he held and tucked it under the blanket again. "I love you, Ilse."

Then he rose. He had nothing more to keep him.

Slipping out of the cottage, he eyed the surroundings. Light streaked the sky above the treetops. The Royal Army might be moving now. He must make haste.

Voices came from the side of the house. The smell of pitch burnt his nose. Pieter dashed to the woodpile and hunkered down behind it. Two men appeared and walked straight toward him. If they caught him, they might kill him at once for spying.

Pieter tensed to flee. Had they spotted him? If he ran, they'd see him for sure.

Their movements hurried, the men stacked wood in their arms, then departed without a word.

Thank God. He had to get out of here.

Ducking behind buildings and brush piles, Pieter returned the way he had come. He rounded the corner of a poultry shed and threw himself to the ground. Not five yards away, a woman spread hay and pitch against the wall of a house. Chin in the dirt, Pieter concentrated on inhaling quiet breaths when absolutely necessary. She finished her work, picked up her torch and empty pail, and hurried off.

Muscles taut, twitching at every sound, Pieter regained the break in the barrier. With the increased light, he bent over to run through the fields. No one called to him. The deer path led toward home, and he followed it, gazing at underbrush and tree trunks as if he'd never seen such things before. Halfway home, he turned and looked back.

Ilse, the darling girl he regarded as his, was dead. Her own mother had murdered her.

Pieter doubled over, retching, though he had nothing in his stomach to lose. At last, he knelt in the middle of the path, bending low to rest his fists on the ground, his forehead on his hands. "O God, how could they kill their own children? I hate Lady Melankardja. I *hate* her."

Meine's words echoed in his mind: *I hate them for what they've done to us.* And look where that took him.

To Lady Melankardja. If she liked hatred, Pieter wouldn't have a thing to do with it. "Lord, I won't hate. But I have to fight her. For Ilse's sake and Fritz's, and all the other children who died. And Meine who got more blinded than he thought I was. I'll fight her, Lord Jesus, as best I can. Show me how."

Pieter stood and continued home. Father would have noticed his absence. He might be angry when he found where Pieter had been. Perhaps he shouldn't have gone, but at least Ilse hadn't died alone.

And Father would know how to start fighting Lady Melankardja right now.

12

A Hitch in Stride

DIERK CAUGHT HIMSELF STRANGLING the cup in his hand and forced his fingers to relax. How could people do that? A whole village gone utterly mad. Tears glittered in Pieter's eyes. No wonder, considering his bereavement. Dierk's little sister Adelaide was nine, blonde and blue-eyed like Mother—and Ilse. A nuisance often, but cute as a frolicking hound pup. He'd kill anyone who harmed her. To think Ilse's own mother—

Fredrik cleared his throat. "The people burned down the village, correct?"

"Aye." Pieter brushed a thumb and forefinger over his eyes. "They fired the buildings and fought the Royal Army until every one of the villagers died. Then the army had to fight the fire to keep it from destroying too much land. Father aided them."

Dierk found his tongue. "What were the people

thinking?"

Pieter pushed to his feet. "They weren't. They succumbed to pretty-sounding words. The devil's good at using them."

Dierk frowned. "What do you mean, 'the devil'? You said Lady Melankardja deceived them."

"So she did. Hadn't you heard she was a witch? No fairy-tale witch, either. She didn't go around turning people into toads and love can break the spell or some such nonsense." Pieter ran his fingers through his graying hair. "She tricked them with fear and anger, greed and I don't know what all until they lost their heads and destroyed themselves. But 'twas the devil's doing, really."

"Oh." Not the most profound observation, but Pieter's words would require some mulling over. Maybe that was what his parents had tried to tell him all those times, that Satan gave Lady Melankardja her power. Must be Satan's power to trick a person into killing her own child.

Pieter strode to the cupboard. "Past time for the noon meal. Will you join me?"

Fredrik gave a nod. "Thank you."

"Nonsense. I'm honored to host a loyal Sunlander."

Fredrik smiled. "How long have you been a member?"

Ah, so he was with the Royal League.

"Since as soon as they would have me. I figured 'twould be a good way to fight Lady Melankardja." Pieter pulled some bread and a covered bowl from the cupboard and set them on the table. "When I turned nineteen, I went to Sunrise Castle—'twas the capital then—and applied. They took me after a few weeks, and I spent many years running secret missions, carrying communications and such. Then I ran a few missions in between helping Father with his work. I quit active duty when I took this position."

The more Dierk heard, the more he discovered he didn't know about the League—and the more he desired to join.

Pieter reclaimed his seat. "Will you stay the night with me?"

Dierk glanced at Fredrik. 'Twould be nice to sleep in a house again, even if it were on the floor. Besides, this Pieter intrigued him.

"We had thought to make a few more miles today, but our business is not pressing. If we can be of service, we'll stay."

A genuine smile creased Pieter's face. "To prolong your company, I can invent all manner of work."

DIERK LAY ON THE floor of the cottage, his head pillowed on his arm. A few flames winked at him from among the coals in the fireplace. Fredrik snored beside him, and their host snored in the tiny room at the back. But Pieter's story, not the noisy sleepers, refused to let him rest.

A village in flames, pouring forth smoke. Peasants attacking trained knights and yeoman with staves and knives and farming tools. Children dying in their beds, poisoned by their own parents.

One cunning woman carrying off the town's youth.

The legendary Lady Melankardja. Who was she before she took up witchcraft? More importantly, how had she wreaked such destruction?

Dierk rolled to his back and stared at the smoke-darkened roof timbers.

Pieter said 'twas the devil's deception. And he had witnessed it firsthand.

Maybe that's why Dierk's parents paid to have unadorned, Sunman Bibles in every church they could. Why they insisted on praying so often with the family. Why they harped on a person's individual surrender to Jesus Christ.

Dierk was a Christian. Of course he was. With his parents, he couldn't be anything else, although he wasn't as devoted as his parents would like. He'd gotten out of practice with prayer since he went to Duke Ebner's, and he couldn't remember any sermons from Lord's Day services. But you didn't have to be a fanatic to be a Christian.

Still, perhaps the time had come to take religion more seriously. Not get absurd about it. Great thunder, no. Just behave with more maturity, more responsibility.

Dierk was seventeen. Near a man.

Time to act it.

DIERK KNELT ON THE forest floor to roll up his bed one morning, careful to pick off the twigs stuck to the outer blanket. Nothing interesting had happened in the six weeks since he'd seen Lady Melankardja's Lost Village. Unless he counted the market-fair they'd passed through. Work was plentiful there, and Dierk enjoyed watching the blade-casting competitions, but they'd stayed only two days before moving on.

These days he could walk for hours without a rest and think nothing of it. He could fell a tree within a span of where he wanted it. And he could probably swing an axe in his sleep. Whatever else Father intended to accomplish by this journey, he'd made the Crown Prince into an efficient workhorse.

Dierk cinched the cord around his bedroll and stuffed it into his pack. "Say, Fredrik, when will we reach Spatzberg?"

"Today, God willing. Plenty before dark."

"Good." Shouldering his pack, Dierk grabbed his staff and stood.

Spatzberg, home of the Faust Sisters. He knew them from their visits to Sunland Castle, although he hadn't seen them since he moved to Duke Ebner's. They were kind, and generally soft-spoken until they started talking about God. Which never took long. No telling what it would be like to stay in their home. They probably prayed ten times a day and found all kinds of tedious ways to relate the Bible to everyday life.

Nevertheless, Dierk would be respectful. Mature adults showed respect for other people, even if they privately thought them ridiculous.

But he'd rather not stay over-long.

A LITTLE AFTER NOON, they paused beside a clear, fast-flowing brook lined with moss and tiny blue flowers. Dierk's shoulders rejoiced as he lowered his pack to the ground. Fredrik strode into the underbrush, and Dierk busied himself unpacking their midday meal. They had some raisins left from their last stop at a town. A nice variation on bread and cheese.

He dipped some water from the stream. Its coldness struck his teeth but refreshed his throat. The finest wine couldn't surpass pure mountain water. He set the empty cup aside and plunged his head into the shallow stream. Chilling water rushed into his ears, and he came up gasping, shaking his head like a wet dog. He ran his hands through his hair and grinned.

Something crashed in the woods. Dierk jumped to his feet. *Fredrik?* A sharp groan followed.

Dierk started toward the noise. "Fredrik?"

"Here, lad."

Dierk shoved branches out of his way. A flash of blue drew his attention. Fredrik's cloak. He hurried forward. And stopped.

Fredrik lay on the ground, his elbows propping up his torso. A tight frown knotted his brow.

Dierk dropped on one knee beside him. "What—"

"My ankle. Stepped in some creature's burrow. Sprained it pretty bad, I fear. Maybe I can walk if you help me up."

"Of course." Dierk slid an arm under Fredrik's. He was tall for seventeen, but the man had almost two handbreadths on him. 'Twould be difficult to get him up.

Fredrik curled his good leg beneath him. "Hand me my staff."

Dierk stirred up the musty smell of leaf mold as he reached for the fallen staff. Fredrik braced it in the dirt. Slowly, with Dierk pushing and Fredrik pulling, they stood. Sweat shone on Fredrik's face.

"Put your arm over my shoulders." Dierk wrapped his own arm tightly about Fredrik's back. "Can you make it to the brook?"

"Aye."

Leaning on Dierk, Fredrik hobbled forward. The dozen normal strides took forever. Dierk had broken a sweat himself by the time he helped Fredrik drop to the mossy ground by the brook.

Dierk's knees sank into the soft earth as he tugged on Fredrik's boot.

Fredrik winced.

"Sorry." Dierk's fingers seemed clumsy as he worked the boot off, trying to cause as little pain as possible. Angry red colored the skin of the swollen ankle. Dierk looked up at Fredrik. "You don't think 'tis broken?"

Fredrik shook his head.

"I'll examine it better in a minute." Dierk lifted the injured limb. "Come forward so you can soak it in the brook."

Pushing with the palms of his hands, Fredrik moved forward. Dierk lowered his companion's foot into the ice-cold water.

Fredrik made a hissing noise.

His hand still cupped beneath Fredrik's heel, Dierk looked over his shoulder. "All right?"

Eyes closed, Fredrik nodded. Then the corners of his mustache twitched as if he tried to smile. "Get your hand out of that water, lad. No sense numbing it as well as my foot."

Dierk withdrew his hand and slapped the excess moisture against his breeches leg. "Think you can eat?"

"Aye." Fredrik opened his eyes and sat up straighter. "That cold water's working wonders already."

After they finished eating, Dierk brushed the crumbs from his fingers and knelt by Fredrik's leg. He lifted the injured foot from the water. "Swelling's down some."

"Aye. The pain has lessened as well."

Keeping his movements slow, Dierk twisted Fredrik's foot to see if the ankle was broken. He massaged the joint with his fingertips. "Seems sound."

Fredrik gave a terse nod. "Tear a few strips off my blanket and wrap it up. I should be able to hobble along."

Dierk stood, but he opened his bedroll, not Fredrik's. Fredrik was taller than he; no sense shortening his blanket. It took some muscle to start the tear, but after that the cloth ripped into neat strips.

Amongst all the cuts and scrapes he'd tended for himself and his fellow squires, he'd never bound a sprained ankle. He hoped he could do it aright.

DIERK SIGHED FOR THE hundredth time. With Fredrik limping, it took thrice as long to cover distances. He couldn't put weight on his right foot, and even with the forked limb Dierk had hunted up for him, he couldn't keep their former pace. It didn't help that the terrain required hiking more than walking. Several times they had to stop and let Fredrik rest for a few minutes.

At what must have been their tenth break, Fredrik sank to the ground by the roadside.

Dierk propped his chin on the top of his staff. "Would it help if you leaned on me?"

Fredrik smiled. "Poor lad. Tied down by a crippled old man like myself."

Dierk shrugged. 'Twasn't Fredrik's fault. "How's the ankle?"

"Must be swelling because the bandage pinches. But as long as I don't put much weight on it, I can stand it."

"A pity the path veered away from the brook. We could soak your foot again."

"Aye, well."

"If I wet the bandage, would it be more comfortable, do you think?"

Fredrik gave him a sharp look, as if he'd never heard anything so preposterous.

Dierk held his gaze. The suggestion wasn't that stupid. Everyone knew cool water had a way of soothing pain.

"We haven't over-much water left."

Dierk glared. He was a knight, or would be in a few years. If he offered help to a comrade, he would pay the price without complaining. "I'll use mine. I can do without."

Fredrik gave him half a smile. "Very well, lad. I appreciate it."

Dierk opened his waterskin and poured a trickle of water on the bandage. The dry cloth drank up the moisture.

"Aye, that feels good. Thank you, lad."

Dierk tied the waterskin shut again. "You're welcome."

A FEW MORE HOURS of halting travel made the road feel endless, like an enchanted path from a fairy tale, always leading on but never arriving anywhere. Late in the afternoon, Fredrik sank down under a tree and closed his eyes.

Dierk took a seat himself. He opened his waterskin and tipped several drops into his mouth, just enough to swirl around and moisten his tongue. Then he reached to wet

Fredrik's bandage for the third time.

Fredrik laid a hand on his arm. "Don't bother, lad."

"Why, pray tell? Doesn't it help?"

"Aye, but there's no use wasting your water. I can't walk farther tonight."

Dierk studied the older man, who had shut his eyes again. Sweat glistened on his face and soaked his hair. Dierk thumped a fist into his thigh. How had he not noticed? "We still have about three hours of daylight, and there's no water near, but do you want me to make camp?"

Fredrik shook his head. "Perhaps 'twould be better if you went on to Spatzberg and brought back help."

"Travel by myself?" Before this journey, he'd never gone anywhere without an escort of at least three men. Normally he would welcome the freedom, but with the complication of his assumed identity, he could unwittingly land himself in trouble.

"You're a capable lad. Find the Sisters' home. They'll help you."

Dierk nodded. "Of course. What will I tell them?"

"You're Kik, son of Henrik Holtzer. Your father had an accident and needs help."

"I shouldn't tell them we're the guests they expect? I mean, they do expect us, right?"

"They do." Fredrik drew the words out. "You could give them a green larch cone if you think you can do it inconspicuously. They often have guests, and I daresay most of them aren't League members."

Dierk sat up straight. Communicate within the League, almost like a member? Now that could make a boring errand interesting. "I can do it, I'm sure. I watched you."

"Aye." Fredrik took some tiny cones, both brown and green, from his belt. "This wasn't part of the plan your father and I discussed. But neither was spraining my ankle. Mind you don't misuse these."

"No, sir, of course not." Dierk cupped his hand around the larch cones and stowed them in the leather purse hanging from his belt. He tried to conceal his eagerness. Wouldn't do to let Fredrik know this thrilled him like his first horse ride as a kid. "Do I need to do anything for you before I set off? Build a fire?"

"No, you shouldn't be long. I ought to be fine right here."

"Supposing it takes until dark? You might need a fire to discourage four-legged visitors." Dierk stood. "I'll build a fire. You can light it if you need to."

13

Blue Eyes

MAINTAINING A BRISK PACE, Dierk reached Spatzberg before the sun retired. Dusk had fallen over the little town, and few people moved about the hard dirt streets. One man fastened a wooden shutter over his front window, then reached for its match. Without a word, Dierk stepped up to assist. In a moment they had the shutter hung.

The man looked him over. "Thanks, lad. Who be you?"

"Kik Holtzer, a woodcutter's son." Dierk gave a slight bow. "I am bound for the Sisters' home. Could you direct me?"

"Aye." The man pointed down the wide street that split the village in two. "Second street on the left, last house on the right."

"Thank you."

The man scratched his jaw. "Will you stay with them

long?"

Best not to volunteer too much information. "I know not yet."

"Godspeed, then."

"God bless your home." Dierk passed a slinking striped cat and a few boys chatting by a closed shop. He reached the street the man indicated and turned in. Slivers of light peeked between the shutters of quiet cottages. The last house on the right stood two stories tall, dwarfing its neighbors. Its uncovered windows glowed golden.

Dierk paused before the door and dug a green larch cone from his purse. Now, to do this right. Act as if the cone just happened to fall from his clothes or something. Of course, the Sisters had seen him often enough as a child, though it had been a few years. If they recognized him, 'twould simplify matters.

Dierk knocked on the door and took a step back. In a moment, the door's top half swung inward to reveal a girl. Not an aged woman.

Wisps of gold hair escaped her kerchief, curling like a halo in the lamplight behind her. The candle she held lit her face, glinting off her long, dark-gold eyelashes. And her eyes—deep blue, pulling him. It seemed as if her very soul shone out of them, sweet and bright. He could fall right into her eyes.

What was he thinking?

The girl lifted the candle higher. "May I help you?"

"I—" He swallowed a thickness in his throat. "I am seeking the Sisters' home."

"Then come in." The girl threw the latch and held the door open.

Focusing on the floor to keep his attention off her eyes, Dierk crossed the threshold. Then he dared to examine the room. The Sisters sat near the fire, their hands busy with ... well, with whatever crafts women did in the evenings.

"Do come in," Sister Faith said. "What is your name, lad?"

Dierk walked closer and bowed deeply. "Kik Holtzer, my lady." He let the larch cone fall from his fingers as he straightened.

"You are most welcome, Kik. What can we do for you?"

Had she noticed the signal? Perhaps he should repeat it. Yet that might make it overly obvious, disclosing his lack of skill. "My father, a woodcutter, injured himself on the way. He can walk no farther, and we would beg your assistance if you have aught to give."

"Certainly." Sister Faith glanced at the other two women.

Sister Charity rolled up her wool around a wooden tool and laid them in a basket by her side. "I will ask young Hansel to hitch up the cart."

Sister Faith looked again at Dierk. "How far away is your father?"

"Perhaps four miles, my lady."

"Call me Sister Faith. This is Sister Hope." She smiled at the woman who had yet to speak. "And that is Sister Charity." She nodded toward the woman hurrying out the back door. "Now tell us how your father is injured."

"His ankle is badly sprained, Sister Faith. He came a few miles since the injury, but he cannot walk farther."

"Then he'll be needing rest. Can you drive a cart in the dark?"

"Aye." He'd ridden horseback in the dark and driven a

wagon by daylight. He'd manage.

Faith folded whatever she was knitting and stabbed the needles into a ball of yarn. "Then Hope and I will go with you to your father."

"I thank you." Dierk bowed again. Had they caught the signal or not? Their faces betrayed nothing.

A girlish hand suddenly presented a cup of water to Dierk. His gaze flew to the girl's face. Her eyes. How did they rivet him so?

She stared a moment before her lips parted. "Have you had supper?"

"Uh, yes, thank you." He'd eaten more of the endless bread and cheese on the road.

The girl turned toward the Sisters, breaking eye contact. Dierk blinked and took a drink from the cup she'd handed him. The cool water helped gather his senses.

"I'll fetch your medicine bag, Aunt Faith." The girl disappeared upstairs.

"That is Gertrude, a girl who lives with us for now."

Dierk nodded. The Sisters were known around the country for hosting orphans and destitute children until they found them suitable homes. Which had provided an excellent screen for them to raise Dierk's mother, Queen Zorena. Some crazy notion of her parents' that it would develop better character in a princess to be reared as a peasant.

Gertrude returned and gave a satchel to Sister Faith. Dierk focused on draining his cup. The front door opened, and Sister Charity whisked in. "The cart will be ready soon."

Sister Faith rose. "Good. We will go out to meet Hansel."

The women drew close together, joining hands. Sister

Faith and Sister Hope extended hands to Dierk. "Will you join us in prayer for your father?" asked Sister Faith.

"Uh, yes, of course." Here they went, just as he'd feared. Praying about everything.

Sister Hope, hitherto silent, led the prayer. As her soft voice filled the room, petitioning the Lord for protection, healing, and safety, Dierk couldn't resist peeking. Each woman's face bore the same calm, the same joy. Warmth surrounded him, and he glanced about, half-expecting to see Jesus Himself standing beside them. Sister Hope's prayer was so personal, so trusting.

Kind of like the way Mother used to pray for Dierk before bed. Only stronger.

"In the name of our Lord Jesus Christ, Amen."

Dierk shut his eyes in time to open them with the others.

The women kissed each other's cheeks, and in a moment Dierk found himself opening the door for Sister Faith and Sister Hope. The wooden panels had barely shut when Sister Faith laid her hand on his arm. "You are Prince Dierk, are you not?"

She'd recognized him after all. "I am."

She smiled as her gaze searched his face. "You've grown so tall. Your features are more like a man's. How long has it been—four years?"

Good thing 'twas dark because he had the most disturbing sensation of heat in his face. "Aye."

"I didn't recognize you until you dropped that larch cone, which you did with masterful skill. Have you then joined the League?"

He let a sigh escape. "Not yet. Fredrik taught me that one

signal on this trip."

"I thought so. You omitted the other sign."

Dierk's brain scurried to discover what he'd forgotten. "What other sign?"

"You'll learn in time."

He'd pay more attention next time Fredrik used the signal.

'TWAS LATE WHEN THEY returned and got Fredrik settled in a bedroom at the rear of the house. The minute the Sisters had satisfied themselves they could do no more for Fredrik, Dierk yanked off his boots and collapsed onto the room's other bed. He ought to undress. He'd sleep better.

Pulling himself to his feet, he glanced at Fredrik. In the streaks of moonlight slipping through the shutters, he looked comfortable for the first time since he'd sprained his ankle. Dierk smiled and made short work of readying himself for bed.

And then, though his muscles relaxed, eager to rest, his mind found dozens of things to think about. The Sisters, as sweet as he remembered. Remarkably good health considering they must be in their sixties. Though nobility by birth, they chose to live as commoners. They did have a bigger house than most, no doubt so they could host travelers and others in need. To think Mother had lived here, serving whoever entered the house, like Gertrude had served him this evening.

Gertrude. What a beautiful girl. And what her eyes did to him ... Ridiculous. She was the daughter of some peasant too poor to care for her. He was Crown Prince. The two didn't mix, not even as friends. This journey had led him into unsuitable mingling with the lower classes. What was Father trying to do, corrupt his noble training?

Father. Stern. Angry. Disappointed. Seemed a long time since Father had shown genuine pride in something Dierk had done. Maybe different residences provided little opportunity. But even the last few times he'd visited home, neither of his parents had disguised their disapproval of him.

Mother had even taken him aside a couple years ago to tell him of a character flaw in him which "concerned" her. Always finding fault.

Dierk rolled over, jostling the bed with the force of his movement. Honestly, why couldn't he go to sleep? His first night on a real mattress in days.

"Still awake, lad?" came Fredrik's husky whisper.

"Aye." Unfortunately.

"Thank you for helping me today."

Dierk lifted his head from the pillow.

"You did well tending my ankle and fetching the Sisters."

Satisfaction spread through him, like when the training master declared he'd won a broadsword match with another squire. He settled down again. "Glad I could help, Fredrik."

"Your father will be pleased with the way you handled yourself."

"Think so?" Dierk instantly despised the question, and even more, how he craved an affirming answer.

"Aye, lad, he will."

Dierk burrowed deeper under the covers. He'd have to ignore the emotions swirling in his chest if he wanted any sleep. "Good-night, Fredrik."

"Good-night, lad."

14

His Mother's Son

OF ALL THE TASKS Dierk had pictured himself performing for the Sisters, visiting the sick and elderly had never entered his mind. Yet here he walked down the street beside Sister Charity, his arms laden with bundles of he knew not what. Fredrik had stayed home to rest his ankle with Sister Faith for company while Gertrude accompanied Sister Hope to other homes.

The village was larger than what Dierk had seen last night, almost a real town. The streets bustled with men and women at work and children turning chores into games. Several people greeted Sister Charity as they made their way through the village.

"The place has grown since we settled here thirty-odd years ago," Sister Charity commented. "'Twas much smaller when Princess Zorena stayed with us."

Dierk cast her a sidelong glance. "Did she accompany you

on errands like this?"

"Oh, yes." Sister Charity tucked a lock of graying hair beneath her kerchief, a wistful smile curving her lips. "The invalids loved her for her cheerful disposition."

Funny to think of his mother, Queen of Sunland, carrying bundles like this to visit commoners. Dierk had seen her send food and other necessities to poor families in Sun City, but she never went herself. Too busy with her duties as queen, not to mention raising her children. A responsibility she took too seriously for Dierk's comfort some days.

"Here's our first stop."

Dierk paused while Sister Charity rapped on the door of a run-down cottage. He eyed the shabby thatch. He shouldn't wonder if the rain found its way inside, but there would be no point in repairing such a poor building's roof.

"Come in," called a faint voice.

Dierk ducked under the door frame as he followed Sister Charity inside. Accustomed to the sunshine, his eyes struggled to penetrate the dark interior.

"Good morning, Sara." Sister Charity's light footsteps halted. "Oh, you haven't risen yet."

"Good morning, Charity. My joints pained me so much I couldn't drag myself out of bed today." Sara let out a trembling laugh.

Ah, there was the occupant, lying in a small, plain bed in the room's furthest corner where he couldn't make out her face.

"We'll see if we can't help with that." Sister Charity chattered on about the fine weather today, and a spark flashed near the center of the room as flint clicked against steel. In a moment, a lamp burned on the table, lighting Sister Charity's face. "Kik, will you lay the bundles here?"

Dierk eyed the cottage interior as he emptied his arms. The smoke-blackened walls, sagging roof timbers, and stark furnishings didn't exactly create a welcoming atmosphere.

Sister Charity glided to the bedside. "Sara, this is Kik. A lad who's staying with us for the time being."

At Sister Charity's words, the woman raised her head. "Come where I can see you, lad."

Stifling his discomfort, Dierk shuffled the two steps to the bedside and bowed. Something smelled unclean. "Kik Holtzer at your service."

The wrinkled woman studied him. "Well, you have a pleasant face, Kik Holtzer." She stared as if she expected a response.

"I, uh, thank you." How long must he stand here? Couldn't Sister Charity come up with something for him to do?

"Kik, would you go to the woodpile behind the house and bring some fuel? We'll need a fire."

Dierk strode straight for the back door. Anything to get out of that tiny shack. Probably Sister Charity wanted a fire to cook something, but the heat would only make the room close in more.

The sunshine lit up a small back yard nearly consumed by an ill-tended herb garden. The woodpile could use more efficient stacking, and a few large logs stood waiting for an axe. He should've brought his. 'Twould have excused him from helping in the house, perhaps.

Dierk stacked wood in his arms and returned to the

house, bending to enter the short door frame. Kneeling by the fireplace, Sister Charity coaxed the coals to life. He dropped his burden on the hearth.

"Thank you, Kik. Can you get this fire going for me?"

"Aye." During this trip, he'd learned to make even damp wood burn, and this stuff was dry.

Sister Charity stood. "Get it nice and hot, but make it last a while."

Dierk raised his eyebrows at the orange coals. A grand blaze in midsummer. Well, whatever she asked.

He got the fire going and then stood about, useless, while Sister Charity mixed some kind of bread and chatted with the elderly Sara. He couldn't stand this inactivity much longer. "Sister Charity, I think the woodpile could use restacking. May I attend to it?"

She glanced up with a smile. "Certainly. I'll call you when I need you."

He nodded and retreated.

Within a quarter of an hour, Dierk had the small store of wood snug under the shelter. He brushed crumbs of bark from his fingers. He could stand around out here just as well as inside. If he'd had a better knowledge of herbs, he would've attempted to weed the garden, but he had no desire to pull up a useful plant.

The rear door of the cottage creaked open. "Kik, could you assist me?"

Dierk turned. "Of course."

"Sara doesn't weigh much, and I wondered if you could lift her and carry her to a chair by the fireplace for me."

"C-carry her?" He ran his hand through his hair. After

this, he'd be more careful about agreeing to Sister Charity's requests before he heard them. "I ... but ... how am I supposed to do it?"

"Just pick her up like a child. She's really very small."

Well, of course he could lift the woman. She looked like she weighed less than some of the logs he'd hauled around the last few weeks. But what if he dropped her or hurt her? She'd said she had bad joints.

Oh, Sister Charity waited for his answer. He swallowed. "If you want me to, I'll try."

"Thank you."

Dierk reentered the dismal cottage and approached the bed. He rubbed his sweaty palms against his breeches.

"Sara, Kik is going to carry you to the chair by the fire," Sister Charity said.

"Why, thank you, lad. I can't seem to get the old bones working this morning." Sara gave another tremulous laugh.

"I've told you again and again you ought to let me move the bed closer to the fireplace," Sister Charity chided, her voice gentle.

"Charity, you know as well as I that a woman can't put her bed in her kitchen." Sara shook her head. "It simply won't do."

Dierk glanced around. Looked to him like the kitchen *was* the bedchamber in this tiny hovel, but apparently Sara's opinion differed.

Sister Charity laughed. "Now, Kik, if you'll lift her."

He flexed his fingers. What made him feel so inadequate? He pitied the woman, yet she unnerved him, and he couldn't put his finger on why.

But he was training for knighthood, and knights didn't cower from a challenge. *Like a child*, Sister Charity had said. He'd carried his younger siblings to bed a time or two. Not to mention that scheming Therese, whom he'd rather not remember.

Dierk bent and slid his arm carefully beneath the woman's shoulders. The sour stench from earlier had disappeared. Cradling his other arm under Sara's knees, he straightened. She weighed next to nothing. How was she still alive? He crossed the room and lowered her into the chair before the fire.

Sister Charity wrapped a blanket around her. "Thank you, Kik. 'Tis much easier than when I move her myself, isn't it, Sara?"

"Aye, much easier." Sara snuggled into the blanket. "I declare, Charity, his eyes remind me of some other child you used to bring to visit me, back when I could still support myself. That little blonde girl. The one who turned out to be the Princess. What was her name?"

"Rose." Sister Charity turned and stirred something in a saucepan on the hob.

"Yes, that's it. Rose. I tell you, lad, your eyes look exactly like hers."

Dierk looked to Charity for guidance, but she didn't meet his gaze. Would this little old woman guess who he really was? Surely not. He mustered a smile for her. "Strange, how that happens once in a while, isn't it?"

"Aye, 'tis. Who would guess a woodcutter's son would have the eyes of royalty?"

"Could you bring in some more fuel, Kik? I'd like to leave

Sara a supply in easy reach."

"Yes, Sister Charity." They must be leaving soon. Good. He hurried to fetch the wood.

NEAR AN HOUR PASSED before Sister Charity tied up her bundles and departed. Dierk trudged beside her. Thank heaven they'd finally left that cramped little shack. But midmorning had barely come. How many more such visits could they fit in the day? Far too many, no doubt. To think Mother grew up doing this.

Dierk glanced about to make sure he wouldn't be overheard. "Sister Charity, did my mother enjoy visiting people with you?"

"Oh, yes." Sister Charity shifted her basket to her other hand. "She loved visiting, even if the person needed nothing more than company. She helped Sara with her herbs and cleaning the house. Things like that. Sometimes she went by herself." Sister Charity sighed. "I miss her, Kik. We had her longer than any other child we cared for, and I still miss seeing her every day, even after all these years."

Dierk had never thought about that. Maybe the same wistfulness prompted Mother's excitement whenever the Sisters visited the palace. "I guess the people she visited miss her, too."

Sister Charity smiled. "You mention her to the elderly we visit today, and you'll see how highly they thought of her."

"Why did her parents send her to live with you?" Mother said 'twas to develop good character, but Dierk had long wondered if there wasn't another reason. "To hide her from

Lady Melankardja?"

"No." A breeze caught the cloth on Sister Charity's basket, and she tucked it back in. "I suppose it helped with that. Although with Melankardja's powers, I think 'twas prayer that hid Zorena from her."

"Powers?"

"Aye. What is called divination. Although there is nothing divine about it. Satan can sometimes reveal things to his followers unless the Lord prevents it."

The hairs on Dierk's arms stood erect.

"But to answer your question." Sister Charity grasped his arm for a moment as she stepped over a pile of muck in the street. "Zorena's parents wished her to become a queen who could care for all her people. How could she do so unless she understood their needs?"

He'd always thought it a dangerous scheme. A princess, sole heir of her country, left to grow up in an isolated village with only three women for protectors. "What about the danger? Did she have no guards, no one else nearby who knew who she was?"

"No one but her parents and their priest knew where she was. If urgent need had arisen, however, we could have sent to Sunset Palace, a few miles away. By God's grace, we never needed to."

What a wild scheme. This journey Father had sentenced him to endure didn't even compare.

Sister Charity halted, and Dierk stumbled to bring his stride to a stop. He met her gaze and found her frowning a little. "What's amiss, Sister Charity?"

"You look as if you think Queen Zorena's upbringing

foolhardy."

"Forgive me, but was it not? Something could have gone wrong. She could have ended up dead."

Sister Charity cocked her head to one side. "Christians are not to cower in fear of possible danger. We are to pursue the will of God and leave our safety in His hands."

Dierk's ears grew warm. "Aye. Forgive me."

"Nothing to forgive." She resumed walking. "But I should have thought you would have learned that by now."

The gentle rebuke smarted. Even Sister Charity found him lacking.

THEY TREKKED A COUPLE miles west of town, past lush meadows and neat fields of crops to reach the next house. A middle-aged woman opened the door, but she had no time to say a word.

"Is that one of the Sisters?" a man's voice boomed. "Come in, come in!"

Dierk had to duck under the door frame again. People around here must like short doorways. A robust older man sat in a chair near the fireplace, waving a knife, a friendly grin splitting his beard. Dierk stared for a moment before he caught his mouth half-open and shut it.

Sister Charity smiled at the man. "I've come to pick up your carvings, Herr Alfred. The trader is due to come through town within the week."

"Who's the lad you have with you?" Herr Alfred gestured with the scrap of wood in his left hand. "Don't you have Gertrude anymore?"

The man's voice seemed to vibrate the very walls. If he hadn't had his hands full, Dierk might have covered his ears.

"This is Kik," Sister Charity answered, raising her voice. "Gertrude is helping Hope today."

"Ah, well, I wanted to show the little lady my newest carving. 'Tis a squirrel, and she did say she wanted to see it. 'Tis in the bundle with the others. Make sure she sees it, will you?"

Sister Charity nodded. "Certainly."

The woman who'd answered the door handed a cloth bag to Sister Charity. "We do appreciate your selling Father's carvings for us."

"Believe me, the trader looks forward to Herr Alfred's work." Sister Charity turned to Dierk. "Can you carry this bundle as well?"

Dierk grinned. "Aye, pile it on."

"What did you say the lad's name was?" Herr Alfred bellowed.

"'Tis Kik, Father," the woman of the house shouted.

"Kik, eh? Well, now, who is he, Sister Charity? Royalty, perhaps?"

Dierk's heart leapt right into his head and pounded behind his temple. How had the man guessed?

"You know I've never quite forgiven myself for not breaking my ankle sooner, when you had the little princess living with you. To think I missed the chance to meet royalty." Herr Alfred heaved an exaggerated sigh.

Ah, he was in jest. Dierk's heart eased back into its normal beat. He ought not to be so edgy. Must be Sara's remark about his eyes.

Sister Charity laughed. "Kik is the son of a woodcutter who injured his ankle yesterday. They're staying with us a while."

"His ankle, you say? He didn't break it?"

Dierk almost cringed at the man's shout. 'Twas a wonder he didn't blow the roof off.

"No, only a sprain. He'll be himself in a fortnight or so."

"Aye, aye. Send him my best wishes for his recovery. I know about these ankles. Hurt 'em once and they'll never be sound again."

"I'll be sure to tell him. You have a nice day, Herr Alfred."

"Thank you, thank you! You, too. See you next month. Nice meeting you, lad!"

Dierk's ears still rang as the cottage door closed behind him. "I thought my training master yelled a lot. Herr Alfred has him vanquished like an unhorsed knight."

Sister Charity smiled broadly. "He's nearly deaf. That's why he shouts."

"Well, he's deafening his whole family, too. I hope they put wool in their ears."

A joyful laugh tumbled from Sister Charity. "Oh, Kik, I hadn't thought of that. Perhaps they should."

BY THE TIME DIERK and Sister Charity headed home, he'd lost count of the houses they'd visited. Somewhere around ten. A man laid up with a broken leg, his wife expecting their third child. An elderly couple, bedridden, living with their son and his large family. A little boy so weak and pale Dierk could scarcely believe he still lived. And several widows. He'd even met a young widow who was expecting twins, according to Sister Charity. Dierk had spent that visit chopping firewood for the woman, which suited him fine.

Shifting his bundles, which had shrunk throughout the day, Dierk gazed at the evening sky. He marveled at the things Sister Charity did. She, a noble's daughter. From cooking to emptying chamber pots, she handled each task with a cheerfulness that appeared genuine. But how could a noblewoman possibly *enjoy* such chores?

He'd tried to follow her example, in case she reported his behavior to Fredrik, but he despised much of the work. He could deal with it for a time, but these menial chores were beneath him. Far beneath him.

Dierk shook his head. The Sisters sure had an extreme variety of Christianity.

15

Six Small Problems

*T*HWACK! THE AXE BLADE sliced through the log and stuck in the chopping block. Grinning, Dierk pulled it loose and wiped his face with the hem of his tunic. He hadn't quite tired of the satisfaction a clean stroke brought him. Besides, the work couldn't do any harm for his muscles, which would come in handy at Duke Ebner's.

He placed another log on the block and swung the axe. Perfect. This beat wandering from house to house doing who knew what. When Sister Hope and Sister Charity went out that morning, Dierk had expected to go along to carry packages and lift things. But they let him stay at the house, for which he was grateful.

Gertrude had stayed, too. Frustrating girl. She'd caught his gaze once at supper last night, and that invisible connection had pulled him again. But this morning she wouldn't look at him, even when they exchanged good-mornings.

Not that it mattered. She could please herself.

Dierk leaned his axe against the block and gathered an armful of the wood he'd chopped. Might as well fill the wood boxes before he started stacking. He strode across the yard, and the scratching chickens scattered before him.

At the back door, he twined the latch-string around his little finger and pulled until the door creaked ajar. His boot toe thudded against the wooden panel, and he crossed the kitchen and dumped his load, clattering, into the box by the fireplace.

"Arrange that neatly, Kik." Fredrik's voice, warm with humor, drifted from the living room. "No sloppy work."

Dierk grinned. Fredrik had teased him all morning, no doubt because he had nothing better to do while he rested his ankle. Dierk set the wood on end in the box and switched the pieces' placement until they resembled a mosaic masterpiece.

Sister Faith came down the stairs, mop and bucket in hand. "Ah, thank you, Kik."

Giving her a smile and a nod, he headed out and picked up another load. When he reached the back door again, it opened on its own. He walked in and peered behind the door. Gertrude stood there, studying the floor.

"Thanks," he said.

She raised her head as if she couldn't help herself, but her eyes looked at everything but him. "No trouble."

Whatever. Dierk turned away and walked past Fredrik to pile this armful of wood beside the living room hearth.

Fredrik sighed. "Lad, you're going to outwork me one of these days."

Dierk raised an eyebrow at him. "I already have. You haven't done a lick of work today."

"You impertinent rascal." Fredrik's mustache twitched as he raised his crutch. "I ought to—"

"Ought to what?" Dierk stepped out of reach. "I'm going to have so much wood cut before you recover, you'll never catch up."

"You forget the years of woodcutting I have behind me, lad."

Dierk waved a hand. "Doesn't count. We're counting from the beginning of this journey."

"Oh, we are? Says who?"

"I say." With a taunting grin, Dierk dashed outside, Fredrik's laughter following him.

Truly, he hadn't been idle this morning. 'Twould take a good while to stack what he had cut. He grabbed some logs and arranged them under the shed.

"Kik?"

Dierk turned toward the girlish voice. Gertrude walked toward him, eyes down, carrying something in her hand. He took a couple steps to meet her.

She stopped beside him and raised her gaze to somewhere above his head. "Water?" She held out a leather tankard.

Dierk took it and drank, the liquid refreshing his throat. A trace of wine added flavor and prevented a cold jolt in his stomach. He lowered the cup and licked a few drops from his upper lip.

Gertrude still looked elsewhere, apparently distracted by the birds twittering in the trees behind the yard. Like she could see the tiny things from this distance.

"Nice day, isn't it?" he said.

"Very." She still didn't look at him, preferring those invisible birds of hers.

"I suppose it would be even nicer if I wasn't around for you to avoid looking at."

Sarcasm worked. Her gaze flew to his. And his heart leapt to meet those blue eyes. But that didn't keep him from enjoying the confusion and embarrassment covering her face.

"I didn't mean—That is, I'm sorry, I—" She bit her lip.

She didn't look away, and now Dierk wished she would. Somehow she'd pricked him with guilt for teasing her. "No, no, forget it. I'm jesting." For lack of something to say, he drained the cup. "Thank you for the water."

"Would you like more?"

"No, that suffices." He handed her the cup. "How goes the work inside?"

"It goes well." A tentative smile lit her face. "'Tis satisfying to see the house sparkle."

Sparkle. Didn't seem like dark wood and stone floors could sparkle.

"Anyway, I'll let you return to work. If you get hungry, there's bread and cheese in the kitchen, and we'll have dinner in a couple hours."

"Thanks." He reached for another piece of wood but stopped. "Are you cooking?"

"Yes."

He gave her the kind of grin he gave Duke Ebner's nieces. "I'll look forward to it."

Pink painted her cheeks before she turned back toward the house. Dierk smiled as he gathered more wood. He probably shouldn't flirt with her. She was a peasant who just happened to be pretty—more like beautiful—and kind, sweet, even graceful. With a little training, one might mistake her for nobility.

Nonsense. Dierk slapped a log onto the stack. He had no business thinking any such thing. The less he thought of her, the better.

Would Felizitas have grown up as winsome as Gertrude?

Felizitas. Great thunder. He hadn't thought of her in years. He reached for more wood. *Keep stacking, Dierk. Perhaps 'twill fix your addled head.*

THAT EVENING, DIERK HELPED himself to a drink of water from the well before he stepped inside for a moment. A savory aroma filled the house. Sister Faith and Gertrude whisked about the kitchen, cooking enough to feed about twice as many mouths as currently boarded there. "When do you think supper will be ready?" he whispered to Fredrik.

"Half an hour or so, I'd guess." Fredrik repositioned his propped-up foot.

"Gives me time to finish stacking, I suppose."

"Haven't you worn yourself out yet, lad?"

"Not quite." He rolled his shoulders. "But I think I'll sleep well tonight."

"I imagine so." Fredrik blew a speck of dust off the wooden spoon he was whittling. "I've watched your progress. Any man might be proud of the work you've done today."

Dierk hooked his thumbs in his belt. "Sure my stacking suits you?"

"Well, 'tisn't as good as mine." Fredrik winked. "But it'll do, lad, it'll do."

Dierk rolled his eyes. Fredrik had been so picky the first time he taught him to stack wood. The pieces had to be secure and conserve space. Now Dierk could make a stack as good as Fredrik's, never mind what the older man said.

Someone knocked on the door.

Sister Faith glanced over her shoulder. "Kik, could you answer that?"

Why him? "Aye." He strode over and pulled open the door. A family stood outside: father, mother, babe-in-arms, and more children than he could count at first glance. His mind scrambled for what to say. Ah, the phrase Gertrude had said to him. "May I help you?"

"We're seeking the Sisters' home," the man said.

Dierk stepped back and held the door wide. "Then come in."

The family trooped past, several pairs of small eyes staring at him. Sister Faith entered the living area, wiping her hands on a towel. A warm smile crinkled the fine wrinkles around her eyes. "What may we do for you?"

The man bowed. "I am Jakob Schumer. We hoped we might lodge with you tonight. My wife's father is ill, and we are traveling to see him. We can pay for our board and lodging."

Sister Faith shook her head. "No payment is required for one night. Let me show you to your rooms."

"Thank you," Frau Schumer said, relief evident in her voice. "You cannot know what a blessing this is to us."

While the family followed Sister Faith upstairs, Dierk

headed for the back door. He needed to finish his stacking.

He hadn't been at work five minutes when the back door opened. "Kik?"

'Twas Gertrude. A small boy stood on either side of her. Supper couldn't be ready, and after her reserve all day, she had no reason to speak to him unless she needed something. Whatever she wanted, Dierk had a feeling he wouldn't favor it. "Aye?" he called, placing another piece of wood on his stack.

She beckoned him forward.

Brushing his hands on his tunic, he went to meet her. "What?"

"I hate to bother you, but the children don't want to stay inside—who could blame them?—and I need to help Aunt Faith with supper. Until Aunt Hope and Aunt Charity return, could you keep an eye on these two? They might even be able to help a little." Gertrude smoothed the boys' blond hair off their foreheads. "It shouldn't be long. Please?"

Dierk swiped at a tickle beside his nose. Great. Play nursemaid. Nothing he'd rather do more. He'd never get anything done, trying to keep them from capering around on his pile. Never mind those innocent brown eyes. These two would make mischief, probably worse than his little brother Friedhold.

He looked up to tell Gertrude *no*. A mistake. The minute her eyes caught his, larger than ever, pleading with him, he lost his resolve. "All right," he growled. "If they promise to mind."

"You'll mind Kik, won't you, boys?"

They nodded with all seriousness.

Right. They'd hold to that. Like the squires at Duke Ebner's held to their evening prayers.

"Thank you so much, Kik. I'll call you the minute supper's ready."

The gratitude glowing in Gertrude's eyes might make his trouble worthwhile. Might. He gave her half a smile. "I'll keep 'em in one piece until then."

She smiled and disappeared inside. Dierk looked down at his charges. "Well, what are your names?"

"I'm Guntram." The taller one pointed to his chest, then jabbed a thumb at his younger brother. "He's Jürgen."

"How old are you?"

"I'm seven. He's five."

Dierk nodded. Aye, as bad as he'd feared. "I'm Kik, as Fräulein Gertrude told you. Come over here, and I'll show you how to stack wood."

Dierk demonstrated for them, stressing the importance of keeping the stack tight and level. Before long, they jumped in to help. Such as it was. They could carry but one piece at a time, and Jürgen could barely reach the top of the pile. Again and again, Dierk had to turn a piece over or move it altogether.

Then Jürgen, reaching to stack a piece of wood, dropped it on his toe. "Oww!"

Dierk knelt on one knee beside him. "Let me see your foot."

Jürgen's lips quivered, and his eyes had turned into pools of tears. "It hurts."

Dierk set the kid on his upraised knee and pulled off the tiny, well-worn shoe. The little foot showed no signs of instant bruising. Couldn't be too bad. He wiggled each toe, eyeing Jürgen's face. The kid bit his lip but didn't scream.

Dierk pushed the shoe back on. "Why, that's nothing. A little bump. Nothing to stop a big kid like you." He set Jürgen on his feet and clapped his skinny little back.

Jürgen sniffed and wiped his eyes.

"Tell you what. You two bring me wood, and I'll stack it. That way you don't have to reach so high." And Dierk could maintain the quality of the stack. "See if you can keep me busy."

Eager smiles lit their faces, and they dashed toward the pieces scattered by the chopping block. Dierk shook his head. At least it amused them. And it would save him some steps.

SUPPER PROVED A MOST interesting affair. Wooden spoons clattered to the floor intermittently, requiring the utensil's owner to slide under the table to retrieve it. Guntram and Jürgen insisted on flanking Dierk, pestering him with questions. Their two older sisters chattered like magpies at Gertrude. And the twin two-year-olds across the table sent water flowing in his direction. Twice. The second time he rolled backward off the bench before he got another dousing. The boys cheered.

After supper, the children sat, quiet and still, while Sister Charity read aloud from the Bible. They bowed their heads and folded their hands while the Sisters, Fredrik, and even Herr Schumer took turns praying.

Then the Sisters took out their needlework and Frau Schumer took the babe upstairs to feed it. In a corner,

Gertrude organized some sort of game for the children. Dierk stretched his legs out on the floor, leaning against the wall. He tipped his head back and closed his eyes.

A small body thumped into his lap.

Dierk opened his eyes and discovered Jürgen. "Why aren't you playing with the others?"

"I got outed."

"What?"

"The game. I got outed 'til the next round."

"Ah." Dierk turned his focus toward the circle of children with Gertrude. She offered a smile that seemed to ask whether he would watch the child for a while. He nodded. But what on earth could he say to the kid?

Jürgen tilted his head back and gazed at Dierk. "Do you think I'll be as tall as you when I grow up?"

"Uh, maybe."

"I hope so. Will I stack wood as good as you?"

Dierk shrugged. "Maybe better."

"Nobody could do it better than you. 'Cept Papa."

"Aye, your papa's had much more experience, no doubt."

Across the room, a girl cried, "Ooo, Ivo, you're out. Go sit with Jürgen."

One of the two-year-olds toddled toward Dierk.

Great. The older boys had him way out of his depth. The last thing he needed was a kid barely older than a babe. Shouldn't the children go to bed soon anyway?

Ivo reached them and set to yanking the sleeve of Dierk's tunic. "Wide, wide!"

What had that to do with anything?

"Now, Ivo, say please," Jürgen urged.

Ivo turned enormous blue eyes on Dierk. "Pwease wide?"

Dierk got the "please" but he still couldn't figure out the "wide." He poked Jürgen. "What's he saying?"

"He wants to ride on your back."

Dierk sputtered. "What? No way."

"Papa sometimes does it when we've been good."

Dumping water on your fellow tablemates didn't qualify as "being good."

"And we've been very good today," Jürgen went on. "We didn't complain and we walked for a long, long time."

Dierk rolled his eyes. He wasn't the kid's father, and no one could drag him into crawling around on all fours to entertain some brat.

"Pwease?" Ivo repeated.

What ailed him? Why couldn't he say *no* and mean it?

Jürgen hopped out of his lap. "You be the horsy, and I'll lead you."

No. Not in front of the adults. Although they didn't seem to be paying particular attention.

"Pwease?"

If he heard that word one more time ...

Jürgen watched him with expectant eyes. "It'll be fun."

For whom? He looked toward the other children. Gertrude knelt beside them, smiling and playing with pebbles, no less attractive than ever. And, by all appearances, enjoying herself.

Ivo tugged Dierk's sleeve again. "Pwease?"

"All right, all right." The Crown Prince of Sunland, crawling around to amuse a peasant kid. But he'd already endured plenty on this journey. Why not complete the humiliation?

At least none of his friends could see him.

16

Kik

Something slammed Dierk's gut. He curled forward, gasping.

"Mornin', Kik!" squealed two voices. The thing on his stomach bounced. "Wake up. 'Tis mornin'!"

Dierk got his brain working enough to focus his eyes. Jürgen sat on his abdomen, grinning like the first day of spring. Guntram stood beside the bed, a matching grin plastered on his sleep-marked face.

Clenching his teeth, Dierk flopped back on his pillow. He shouldn't shout at them. They meant no harm. But they had no right to awaken him from a sound sleep by pouncing on his stomach.

"Can we help you stack more wood?" Guntram asked.

Dierk groaned. Aye, he'd walk outside half-dressed, half-asleep, and stack that haphazard pile he'd been obliged to leave unfinished yesterday because of their "help." He dragged a hand down his face.

"Can we, please?" Jürgen bounced again.

"Sit still," Dierk ordered. "Maybe we can after I get dressed. Do your parents know you're awake?"

"They'd have to," Fredrik answered from the other bed, "after their trip down the stairs. I'm surprised you slept through it."

Dierk threw his pillow at Fredrik's head. "I worked harder than you yesterday."

"Aye, that must account for it."

Scowling, Dierk propped himself up on his elbows. "All right, run along and let me dress."

Jürgen climbed down, kicking Guntram's head in the process, and the two ran off squealing. *Honestly.* Dierk rolled out of bed and reached for his clothes.

"By the way," Fredrik said, "you did a great job with those boys yesterday."

"Huh." Dierk wrangled with his tunic. "Kids aren't my thing."

"Those boys look up to you."

Just what he needed: a couple of kids making him into their hero. Him—the Crown Prince under punishment for *shockingly delinquent behavior*. Dierk buckled his belt and ran a hand through his tousled hair. "As long as it doesn't become a regular circumstance."

"You did well, lad."

Dierk grasped the door handle. "Let's see if I can survive until they depart this morning."

GERTRUDE SIGHED WHEN THE children gathered up their things after breakfast. If only more children could stay at the Sisters' cottage. No one had brought them an orphan for several months. Of course, sometimes she played with the village children, but 'twasn't the same as having them in the house.

As everyone gathered to pray for the departing guests, Gertrude joined hands with the two girls.

When they finished, Herr Schumer handed something to Sister Faith. "I know this isn't much, but we hope it might help with your work."

Sister Faith clasped his hand. "We thank you."

Gertrude bent and kissed all the children good-bye. Guntram and Jürgen ran to Kik, who stood a few paces away, and grabbed his hands. "Good-bye, Kik."

He ruffled their hair. "Godspeed, you scalawags. Mind you be good for your parents."

"We will." The two boys scampered away.

Gertrude looked back at Kik. His gaze followed the children out the door of the house, and he shook his head, a half-smile tugging at his mouth. Something warm spread through her chest, and she focused on the departing Schumer family.

The minute they disappeared, she climbed the stairs to her room. She needed to think, and she'd had no time for it last night since she agreed to the girls' pleas to share her bedroom. Closing the door behind her, Gertrude walked to the tiny window overlooking the back yard.

Kik had set to work again, splitting the Sisters' portion of the village wood. Before Kik came, their next-door neighbor

Hansel had chopped their wood every day or two. But at twelve, Hansel couldn't handle some of the big pieces Kik attacked with vigor.

Gertrude turned her back to the window. This wasn't the thinking she needed to do. She sank to the floor and pulled her knees up, leaning her head against the wall. "Lord, why am I attracted to him?"

Her whisper received no answer. No young man had affected her this way before, not even back home. She had no real reason to care for him. She knew little of him. He was handsome and strong, well-spoken and pleasant. A woodcutter's son.

She closed her eyes. Father would never approve. He'd promised not to make her marry for convenience alone, but he had to draw the line somewhere. Even she could see a woodcutter's son wouldn't suit.

When Kik had played with the children last night, her heart had melted like butter on fresh bread. He hadn't wanted to get on all fours and let the children climb on him—his resigned expression told her that—yet he'd allowed every child a turn. Even the girls, who weighed more than the boys and threw him off balance by riding aside.

But she didn't know him to be a genuine Christian. He'd never said a word about it. And still her heart reached for him every time his gaze locked with hers.

She twisted a wisp of loose hair around her finger. "Lord God, letting my emotions jump out of control doesn't display full surrender to You. Please purge my heart. Help me to love Kik as You love all mankind. Let my thoughts, my words, and my actions be pure in Your sight. Give me Your strength, O

Lord, for I have never had to battle something this strong before. Give me Your victory in Jesus Christ my Savior."

Gertrude sat still, waiting for the peace. It came. No doubt she would have to renew her prayer. But she'd returned her heart to the One it belonged to. Where she intended to keep it.

WORD OF A WOODCUTTER lodging with the Sisters must have traveled 'round the village at the speed of a fever. Dierk finished the Sisters' wood within a few days, and then he alternated between chopping for the different widows and working for tradesmen in the village, who paid him. On his thirteenth day at Spatzberg, the butcher counted out coins for his day's work.

Pocketing the money, Dierk bid the man good evening. He'd give his earnings to the Sisters. They'd protested the first time, but Fredrik had sided with him, and they gave in. After all, Father had ordered him to take nothing without payment, and that included food and lodging. Besides, he'd have no use for his earnings after the journey.

Dierk whistled as he walked toward home. The Sisters' house, that is. Tomorrow the blacksmith had engaged his services. A comfortable routine had emerged during his stay. In some ways, life at Duke Ebner's seemed years ago, not weeks.

A shopkeeper called out, "Good evening, Kik."

Dierk waved. "Good evening."

"You're coming day after tomorrow, right?"

"Aye, that I am."

"Give the Sisters my respects."

"I will." Dierk smiled. Some of the townspeople already knew him by name, treated him like one of their own. If he were in truth a woodcutter's son, this would be a good place to call home.

But he was Crown Prince, his home in Sun City. He rested his axe on the back of his neck, gripping the handle at both ends. In another week or so, he could get on his way. Fredrik's foot had mended, and he could hobble without his crutch now. Only the Sisters insisted he not overwork his ankle. Soon they could continue their journey.

Dierk turned down the side street and quickened his pace. The top half of the front door hung open, welcoming him. He reached inside to lift the latch and strode in.

"Ah, Kik, you're home." Fredrik lifted a half-finished wooden spoon in greeting. He'd carved over a dozen of those things since he'd been laid up.

"Evening, Father." That sounded strange every time he said it. He'd gotten used to hearing "Kik" instead of "Dierk," but Fredrik was still Fredrik.

Dierk slipped into the kitchen, where the Sisters were cooking, and dug his wages out of his pocket. "Sister Hope." She seemed the least busy. When she turned, he handed her the money. "I shall wash up for supper."

She nodded, a sweet smile crinkling her eyes.

Dierk propped his axe in the bedroom and went outside to the well. Bending at the waist, he dumped a whole bucket of water over his head. It soaked his hair and coursed down his face, washing away the day's heat and strain. He pressed excess water from his hair before scrubbing the dirt from his hands.

When he went inside, he couldn't keep the smile off his face. But as he closed the back door, his body tensed. He scanned the room to find why. Two men stood at the front door, speaking with Sister Charity. No reason that should unnerve him.

"We shall be glad to give you a meal, but we are unable to lodge you tonight."

Dierk raised an eyebrow. He'd figured the Sisters never turned away any stranger in need. The past days, he'd sat at their table with all manner of travelers, though no one had spent a night since the Schumers' visit.

The men thanked Sister Charity and sat down on a bench in the living room. Fredrik talked to them of the weather and such. Dierk stowed himself in a corner of the room and crossed his arms. Nothing remarkable about their rough brown clothing and bulky peddlers' packs. But an irrational dislike of them made him almost want to forego supper so he wouldn't have to sit at the table with them.

Once before, he'd taken an instant, unexplained dislike to a person. A minstrel who entertained at Duke Ebner's castle for an evening and tried to make off with a valuable gold goblet the next day. These two couldn't get out of here soon enough.

Wise of Sister Charity to refuse them lodging.

17

Firebrands

Dierk woke to someone shaking his shoulder. His eyes cracked open and found darkness.

"Dierk," Fredrik hissed.

Fredrik hadn't called him that since their journey began. He rolled over. "What is it, Fredrik?"

Leaning on his crutch, Fredrik stepped back. "Do you smell that?"

"Smell what?" Dierk sat up. Smoke. Its acrid smell filled his nostrils. "What's afire?"

"I don't know. Could be the house. That window's too light for midnight."

Dierk whipped his head toward the tiny window in the back wall. Orange light glowed through the cracks around the shutters.

Dierk threw back the covers, yanked on his breeches, and shoved his feet into his boots. He snatched up his tunic and pulled it on as he stumbled to the back door. Having thrown the latch, he stuck his head outside.

God have mercy. The lower portion of the rear wall was alive with flames.

"Fire!" he shouted. He dashed inside and met Fredrik, now fully dressed. "Fredrik, the house is afire. That wall, right behind us. Go for help."

Fredrik nodded. "Aye, lad. Go wake the Sisters."

Dierk ran for the winding stairs. He hadn't climbed them since he came, and he had no idea where anyone slept. Banging on the first door he reached, he yelled, "The house is afire! Wake up! The house is afire!"

The door swung open under his fists. Gertrude stood there, a blanket around her shoulders, blue eyes wider than ever.

Dierk grabbed her arm and dragged her into the hall. "Get down the stairs and out of the house. The back door is open. Help Fredrik raise the alarm."

She gave a quick nod.

"Which room is the Sisters'?" he asked.

She pointed across the hall to the second door. "The front room."

He jerked his chin toward the stairs. "Now go."

She turned and started down. Dierk ran to the Sisters' door and pounded. "Wake up! The house is afire! Sister Faith, Sister Hope!"

The door flew open, and smoke gushed into the hall. The front window hung ajar, glowing orange. The fire must be two places.

Sister Charity coughed. "Our window ... let in the

smoke." Another choking cough interrupted her.

He wrapped an arm around her shoulders and pulled her from the room. "Go downstairs and get outside."

She looked over her shoulder. "My sisters—"

"I'll help them." He pushed her toward the stairs and hurried into the room. The smoke clogged his throat, burned his eyes. He bent double, searching for clean air. Murmurs drew him toward the front window.

"Faith, wake up. Come on, sit up." A little cough. "We have to get out. The house is afire."

Dierk found Sister Hope coaxing a drowsy Sister Faith to sit up. "What's wrong?" he demanded.

"The smoke. Her bed is nearest the window."

He'd heard too much smoke could stupefy a person. Right after the drowsiness came suffocation. Dierk grasped Sister Faith's shoulder. "Get downstairs, Sister Hope. I'll carry her if I have to."

"You can't," she said. "Let me help you."

Of all the times for an argument. "I can't carry you both. Take care of yourself, and I'll bring her."

"But ..."

"Go. Please."

She hesitated but a moment. "God bless you, Dierk." She moved toward the door.

Sister Faith sat on the edge of the bed, her head lolling. No point talking to her. Maybe she could walk with his support. He crouched to draw a deep breath. Then he slid his arm around her waist and lifted her. "Come, Sister Faith. Walk."

Her feet shuffled as he dragged her toward the door. Just

let him get out of this smoke. He blinked tears away. They reached the hall, now hazy with smoke as well. *God, help me.* Sister Faith ought to do the praying, but she was incapacitated. *Lord, help me get her out.*

They reached the stairs about the time Sister Faith's knees buckled, putting her whole weight on Dierk's arm. She wasn't as light as Sara, but he'd manage. He pulled his tunic over his nose to filter the air. Then he scooped Sister Faith into his arms and cradled her close. With a shoulder against the wall, he steadied their descent. The smoke wasn't as bad below.

Wavering orange marked the back door. Dierk headed straight for it. At the threshold he tripped. Strong hands caught him before he fell. "Steady, lad." Two neighbors took Sister Faith. Someone else led him away from the heat. A hand pressed a wooden cup rim against his lips, and Dierk gulped the water.

"Don't choke yourself," Gertrude said. The cup moved away. Ah, Gertrude held it. Firelight danced across her flushed face.

"Thank you." He took the cup and tossed the remaining water in his face. The moisture soothed his eyes, just as it had cleansed his throat. "I'm going to help the men."

A few neighbors drew water and filled buckets. Others threw the contents onto the flames. Dierk joined in, carrying buckets back and forth. "What about the fire at the front?" he asked the man operating the well's windlass.

"My son Hansel is spreading the alarm. We'll have a ladder and more men soon."

Dierk nodded and hurried forward with two full buckets. He'd never fought a fire before, but with better heads than his in charge, he could help.

AFTER WHAT SEEMED HALF the night, Dierk stood with the others in front of the Sisters' cottage, an empty bucket dangling from his fingers. The fire in the back had been doused in relatively little time. Hauling water up the ladder cost more time and effort.

But the flames were gone. Charred, wet timbers remained to show what had carved the gaping hole in the front wall.

Dierk wiped his face, covering his palm with soot. At least they'd saved the house. A few repairs would set it to rights.

But how had the fire ignited? Houses didn't sprout random flames halfway between the foundation and the roofline. Chimneys could spread sparks, but no one had a roaring fire this time of year. Lightning couldn't be the culprit. But who in the country would set fire to the Sisters' home?

Lady Melankardja might have, but she was dead. So far as he knew, everyone loved the Sisters because they helped whoever needed it. Why would anyone want to stop their good works?

"Well, fire's out, anyway," said their neighbor. "I don't believe it'll light back up."

Sister Hope nodded. "God has been good to us."

Dierk almost dropped the bucket in his hand. What a thing to say.

"Indeed, God was good tonight." Hansel's father—Dierk still hadn't caught his name—turned to the crowd of men and women. "Thank each of you for your help. I'm sure you all want to get some sleep before the sun comes up. We'll meet here midmorning to start work on repairs."

The crowd gathered 'round the Sisters, the men shaking the Sisters' hands and the women embracing them. Nearly everyone promised to return on the morrow. One thing was certain: these townspeople loved the Sisters. So who started the fire?

Could have been those peddlers. Though 'twas hardly fair to suspect them simply because they were strangers and Dierk took an instant disliking to them.

"'Tis difficult not to be angry at what happened tonight." Gertrude's low voice, close by his shoulder, startled him. "'Twas no accident, of course. The only culprits I can think of are the men who ate supper with us."

His own suspicion grew stronger at her words. Yet ... "Would they really light the house afire just because the Sisters refused to lodge them?"

"Oh, not because of that. I think they planned mischief before they knocked on our door." Gertrude's mouth tightened. "Not everyone likes the Sisters, you know."

"No, I didn't know. Why wouldn't they?"

Gertrude looked at him out of the corners of her eyes. "They proclaim Jesus' teachings with great boldness. Some wish to silence them."

Well, Dierk was no Christian enthusiast, but he didn't care if the Sisters were, or anyone else, for that matter. "That's stupid. If they dislike it, they don't have to listen."

A breath of a laugh slipped from Gertrude. "True. But for some, 'tis not enough. They cannot bear to have others follow the truth."

"You mean people like Lady Melankardja?"

"Yes. Her and others. Her schemes died with her, so they say, but there are others without her cunning and resources who are quite as opposed to anything that builds God's kingdom. The Sisters make a good target." Gertrude's voice was quiet as she watched the Sisters thank their friends.

Dierk caught himself studying Gertrude's profile and the tendrils of hair waving down her cheek. He jerked his mind back to the conversation. "Has this sort of thing happened before?"

"Oh, yes." She turned to face him. "This house has been set afire at least twice before. Someone broke in a window and smashed some of the furniture one night when the Sisters were traveling. And when Princess Zorena stayed with them, she was almost kidnapped once."

"Moth—?" Dierk barely caught himself. Somehow he'd missed that story. "How do you know all this?"

"Oh, the Sisters warned me when I arrived I would be in danger staying with them."

"Huh. I guess you are, considering tonight." Somehow Dierk couldn't recall hearing *these* stories of the Sisters. Perhaps he'd not listened. "Has anyone ever attempted to harm them personally?"

"Once." A peculiar smile quirked Gertrude's soot-streaked face. "He found himself unable to match such seasoned warriors."

"Warriors?" He'd never heard the Sisters employed a bodyguard.

"Prayer warriors. I don't know what they said to the man or how they prayed, but I understand he dropped his weapon and ran."

Dierk stared at the three women with their sweet smiles and gentle touch. What *had* they said to the man? "Did they ever see him again?"

"A couple years later." Gertrude smoothed a lock of hair behind her ear. "He'd become a Christian."

"I see." Actually, he didn't see at all how three gentle women could scare off a bandit, let alone impress him so he later became a Christian. Maybe the anti-Christianity fanatics had reason to fear the Sisters.

"The Lord has given the Sisters strong gifts because they seek His will and do His work. I hope one day I'll be as close to God as they are."

Dierk looked back at Gertrude. Her blue eyes met his gaze, bright in the torchlight, accented by her soot-darkened face. His heart jumped, as usual.

"Kik, are you a Christian?"

That caught him off guard. "What?"

"I mean, is Jesus Christ your Savior?"

He frowned. "Of course." He'd been baptized at the age of thirteen. He believed in God and Jesus. He just wasn't as consumed by it as some people. When he got older, he'd have time for that.

Her gaze didn't leave his eyes, and he had to drop his attention to his feet. Why did he feel like she could look right into him and see his carelessness and rebellion? And why should he care if she did? He'd never been ashamed of it before.

"God was good to us tonight, Kik."

He snapped his head up. "You, too? Why do you say that?"

Her eyebrows arched. "Why would I not?"

He frowned. "If the Sisters are so special, why didn't God keep whoever did it from setting their house afire?"

"I don't know." She shrugged, then pulled the blanket tighter around her shoulders. "But He let Fredrik smell the fire, and He let you be here to warn us. The fire is out, the house is still standing, and no one's hurt." She smiled. "Not even Sister Faith, because the Lord provided you to carry her to safety."

Soot was good for something—'twould hide the heat creeping up his face. A pretty girl's praise would gratify him as a rule, but somehow Gertrude's words didn't stoke his pride.

"Can't you see God took care of us? He doesn't prevent all hardship because then people might serve Him only for what He would do for them. But He gives us grace sufficient to handle whatever comes."

Dierk gave a slow nod. Her words made sense. "I guess you're right." After all, he had escaped the smoky house with Sister Faith. He'd almost forgotten those few, ineloquent words begging God's help to get Sister Faith down those stairs. Maybe God had been with him.

Even though he, of all people, didn't deserve God's aid. He couldn't remember the last time he'd prayed or paid true attention in chapel.

"Gertrude, Kik, are you ready to go?" Sister Charity's voice brought him back to the present. Where were they going?

"Do you want me to gather a few clothes?" Gertrude asked.

Sister Charity tipped her head to one side. "That might be convenient."

Dierk tired of standing there confused. "What are we doing?"

"We are going to rest a few hours at our neighbor's home," Gertrude said.

"Ah." He'd missed that part of the plan.

"I'll run upstairs and gather our clothes."

Dierk laid a hand on her arm. "You're not going in that house."

She frowned at him the way a noble lady might rebuke an insolent attendant. "Why not?"

Stubborn girl. "'Tis unsafe."

"Don't be silly. The men carried water to the upper floor, and no one fell through."

"But there could be weak spots." Dierk released her arm and slapped his hand against his thigh. "I'll go instead."

She let out a merry laugh. "You wouldn't know what to look for."

Dierk appealed to Sister Charity. "Tell her she'd better not risk it."

Sister Charity nodded. "Perhaps it would be wise if you accompanied her."

'Twasn't what he wanted, but if he walked ahead of Gertrude, he might prevent any accidents. "All right. I guess that'll work."

"Come, let us make haste." Gertrude started toward the back yard. "We don't want to keep our neighbors waiting all night."

"Let me get a torch," he called after her. Heedless girl. The last thing they needed was to break a leg falling through the weakened floor. He shook his head. What a night.

18

That Girl

"Hand me that timber, lad."

The hewn-wood beam dug into Dierk's shoulder as he carried it to the carpenter. It rattled the sawhorses when it landed, and Dierk held it steady while the carpenter measured. His planned job of woodcutting had been postponed until the Sisters' house was repaired. In fact, it seemed half the village had dropped their usual work to lend a hand.

The carpenter lifted his saw, and Dierk secured his grip on the timber. Around mid-morning, the men had organized into teams before they set to work cutting away the damaged wood, replacing the supports as they went. A squire's studies didn't include house-building, and the process proved interesting.

Another man came around the side of the house. "Here are more planks."

The carpenter glanced up but kept driving the saw. "Good." With a few more strokes he completed the cut, and the extra wood thumped on the ground. He brushed the sawdust away. "Carry this in, lad."

Dierk replaced the wood on his shoulder and headed for the back door. Pounding hammers and men's voices filled the house. He strode through the living room to where blue sky peered through the front wall and the upper floor.

He tipped his head back. "Next piece."

The hammering quieted. A man's face appeared in the gap above him. "Hand it up."

Dierk lowered the timber to his hands and aimed one end for the ceiling. The man above reached down, grasped the beam, and hauled it up.

"We've got it," the man said as the wood pulled away from Dierk's reaching fingers.

Dierk swiped his hair off his forehead. "Got your next measurement strings?"

"Aye." A little roll of twine dropped into Dierk's waiting hand. "And we've some half-charred scraps to send down."

"Ready." Dierk reached up again as the man lowered a plank to him. Several more followed. He'd grasp one end in his left palm and let the other end swing down and land on his right hand.

"Last one." The man above paused, letting the board hover over Dierk's head. "'Tis longer, barely burned. Just wants a bit of sanding, and it can come back up to its place."

"Aye. I'll tell the carpenter." Dierk took a good hold on the end. "Got it."

The man released it, and Dierk stepped back to let the far

end slide through the hole.

And there stood Gertrude, just inside the front door. Right in the plank's path.

"Look out!" Dierk swung the board hard to his right. The free end crashed to the floor and bounced. Dierk tossed his end aside before it pulled him off balance.

He looked for Gertrude. She'd flattened against the front door post, hands over her head.

The plank had almost hit her. *Great thunder.* He'd almost *hit* her.

"All well down there?" the man called.

Dierk drew a long breath. His heart thudded like the hammers upstairs. "Aye."

Gertrude slowly straightened, lowering her hands. "I ... I didn't know you were passing boards through the floor."

"But you might have known," he snapped. "If you'd bothered to look before you barged in."

"Mercy, Kik." Her blue eyes blazed at him. "I've quite as much right to be here as you have."

He stepped toward her, glaring. "I think not. You almost got knocked out, and if you keep running about so, you'll trip on some tool. Can't you see the place is a mess?"

Her shoulders stiffened. "I was not *running about*. And the mess is precisely what I'm here to observe. I want to see what we'll have to do once you men finish. Heaven knows you take no pains to clean up after yourselves."

Dierk clenched his teeth. "You keep out of this house. You could get hurt."

"I'm not a child, Kik Holtzer." Eyes locked with his, she moved toward the stairs. "I can keep out of the men's way."

Was she related to a mule? She'd almost been knocked unconscious, yet she persisted in her notion of *investigating the mess*, of all things. "There's sawdust and soot everywhere. That's all you need to know until we've put the floor back together."

Gertrude tipped her nose upward. "I don't see what business it is of yours."

A crash rattled the ceiling above their heads. Gertrude jumped. Men's laughter drifted down.

Dierk gave her a pointed look. Had not his argument been proven?

She pinched her skirt and made a great show of lifting her hem above the dusty floor. "As you wish, Your Highness." Sarcasm dripped from her words as she swept toward the back door. "By the way, Fredrik said to tell you to work doubly hard to make up for him."

Of all the messages to send by that girl. Dierk gathered up his charred scraps and stomped from the house in time to see the carpenter and a few others exchange smiles and nods with Gertrude as she passed.

Little princess, putting on airs.

Serve her right if she had to scrub the whole house top to bottom because of the smoke and dust. Scowling, Dierk carried his boards to the pile in the side yard. Calling him *Your Highness*? If she only knew.

But her eyes sure had been pretty, throwing sparks at him.

DIERK WHISTLED AS HE carried his axe home after a day of work. In the week since the fire, the men had repaired the

Sisters' home. Only the glaring newness of the patches against the house's age-darkened wood bore witness to the flames' damage.

The Sisters' life had returned to normal. So normal that Sister Hope and Sister Charity had departed to visit another town, as they had planned for several months. Gertrude and Sister Faith kept the household in order, serving the usual assortment of poor folk and travelers who stopped for a meal or a night's lodging or to ask for prayer.

Entering the house, Dierk almost stepped on a skinny brindled hound-pup in the floor. He lunged forward and staggered to regain his balance. "What is *that*?" He stood on one foot to nurse the ankle which had caught his weight.

Gertrude scurried over and scooped it up. "I'm sorry. She followed me home from my visits today. I haven't yet decided what to do with her."

Looked like a mutt of no consequence. Dierk massaged his ankle once more and returned his foot to the floor. "Drown her," he suggested, no more than half serious.

Gertrude clutched the pup and stared at him, horror flooding her eyes.

Dierk could have kicked himself. Talk about the lowest kind of clod. Why, he *liked* dogs. What ailed him? "No, I don't mean it. She's no purebred hound, but I'm sure you could use her for something." He waited for Gertrude's eyes to relent, to offer forgiveness.

She looked down and fondled the pup's one white ear.

He reached out and tickled its chin. "Truly, she's a fine dog. Forgive me?"

A tiny smile touched the corners of Gertrude's mouth.

"Of course."

He must have lost his mind, begging for forgiveness. He couldn't remember the last time he'd done that.

Fredrik came in the back door, a pail of water in his hand. "Ah, Kik, you're back. Did you finish Herr What's-his-name's wood?"

"Aye, Father. Free to leave tomorrow as we planned." When Fredrik had announced his plans yesterday, Dierk had inwardly rejoiced. Spatzberg Village had been kind of pleasant, but he was ready to move on.

Fredrik set the water on the kitchen table. "The sky says we're in for a storm this evening, but, God willing, it won't delay us."

"Good." Dierk looked back at the pup licking his finger with her little pink tongue. Tomorrow he would leave and never return. Not as a woodcutter's son anyway. He'd never chop wood for the villagers. Never hear the blacksmith call out a "good-evening, Kik," nor receive a cup of water from Gertrude. Part of him would miss it.

Nonsense. Shouldering his axe, he marched toward the bedroom. He was Dierk, Crown Prince of Sunland. He belonged among nobles. Training for knighthood. Preparing for the throne.

"LISTEN TO THAT WIND." Fredrik cocked his head.

Dierk glanced up from their game of nine-men's morrels. A crash of thunder rattled the shutters. "Quite a gale." He moved one of his men on the board.

Fredrik leaned forward. "Let's see." He tugged the end of his mustache. "You know I'm going to win, right?"

Dierk crossed his arms. "I know no such thing."

The front door rattled, and Dierk turned in his seat. Could someone be out in this weather?

Sister Faith arose and opened the door. A man in a dripping cloak blew in with a rush of raindrops. As Sister Faith shut the door, the man pushed back his hood.

Dierk made no habit of reading emotions on people's faces, but this man's countenance fairly shouted his worry.

Sister Faith touched his elbow. "Come near the fire."

He shook his head. "I'll leave water all over your floor. Forgive me for coming so late. My wife." He stopped as if his throat had quit working for a moment. "My wife is ill unto death. I have neither money nor time to fetch a physician, but I have heard you can pray and people are healed. Would you come?"

The man's desperation was pitiful. Dierk averted his face and leaned one elbow on his knee, pretending to study the game board.

"I know the weather is unfavorable."

One way to put it.

"We could wait until morning. But she is so ill. I've left her with no one except our young children. Will you come?"

"Of course I will come," Sister Faith said. "What is your name?"

"Hartwin, my lady. I know it is presumptuous to come tonight, but I knew not what else to do."

"I shall be glad to go with you, Hartwin." Sister Faith's soft voice carried conviction. "How long will it take us to reach your home if we take a cart?"

"We couldn't take a cart. The path from here won't allow

it."

"I see. How long will the walk take?"

Dierk looked over his shoulder. Walk in this weather?

"It took me more than two hours, but I left before the storm came." Hartwin shrugged. "It could take much longer, for the path is rough. Perhaps 'twould be better if you waited until the morning. I can return for you then." Yet the man's eyes belied his words. He needed help now.

"No need to make the trip twice." Sister Faith appeared as unruffled as ever. "The Lord has gone with me on such excursions before. While I gather my things, will you drink some tea?"

He nodded. "Thank you, Sister—?"

"Faith."

Gertrude rose from her seat and headed toward the kitchen.

Sister Faith paused before she ascended the stairs. "Gertrude, will you accompany me?"

"Certainly." Gertrude poured hot tea into a cup and carried it to Hartwin, who still waited by the door. His cloak had shed a sizable puddle.

Fredrik stood. "I'll go with you, too."

Dierk glared up at him. "Indeed not. Your ankle is barely well. We can't risk you twisting it on some slippery path." But this risky mission could use another man. "I'll go."

"But, Kik, you plan to depart tomorrow," Gertrude said. "'Twill tire you to accompany us."

As if such a thing would stop him. "Nevertheless, I will go." Dierk hurried to the bedroom to don his cloak. He also grabbed his walking staff. He'd prefer a sword for traveling at night, but his hunting knife would have to do. In this weather, they'd meet trouble from naught but the storm itself.

He returned to the living room as Sister Faith descended the stairs, carrying a little bundle. Probably medicine.

Gertrude fastened her cloak around her. "Sister Faith, Kik wishes to accompany us."

Was she trying to dare him or something? No matter. "Kik *will* accompany you," he said, not caring that he sounded pompous. He would see they came to no harm he could prevent. Hartwin was all very well and good, but distraught over his wife. The expedition needed a level head.

"Are you sure, Kik?" Sister Faith's brows puckered. "We might be very late."

For answer, Dierk stepped to her side and gently took her bundle. "Let me carry this." He stowed it in the purse which hung from his belt.

Sister Faith smiled. "Let's pray before we go."

DIERK HAD GONE NIGHT-HUNTING before, but never in such formidable weather. The treetops lashed together over their heads, providing scant protection from the deluge. Cold raindrops struck his face and trickled down his throat to soak the neckband of his cloak. The light from Hartwin's lantern hardly illuminated a yard in front of them. But the frequent flashes of lightning made up for that.

Sometimes 'twas difficult not to think the Sisters a little too extreme in their ministry.

This could be some cruel trap. Dierk's heart took off at the speed of a runaway destrier. After the fire last week, one would think Sister Faith would use more caution. Yet she walked beside Hartwin as if it were only natural to traipse through a dark forest in the middle of a terrific storm to go pray for an ailing woman she'd never met.

Dierk was no great woodsman, and the darkness made it almost impossible to keep track of their direction. The trail led upward, doubling back sometimes to make the climb less steep. Poor knowledge, at best, should this journey turn out different than Sister Faith expected. What he wouldn't give for a good sword.

But, if it were a trap, Hartwin could act better than anyone Dierk had ever seen. He let himself relax.

Beside him, Gertrude stumbled on the path. He grasped her elbow. "Are you all right?"

She nodded. "Thank you."

Reluctant, he released her.

"Kik?" The wind almost swept the word away.

"Aye?"

She raised her voice. "I want to apologize for arguing with you last week when you didn't want me in the house. I fear I didn't show a very Christ-like spirit."

"Oh." She'd been a little stiff with him since that altercation, but he'd expected no apology. "No matter. Maybe I came off high-handed."

"Well, yes." A flash of fierce white light exposed her smile.

He grinned, though she couldn't see it. "Friends, then?"

"Aye, friends." Thunder drowned the end of her words.

Friends. The desire to kiss her surged in Dierk. Just grab her hand and pull her to him. The others would never know in this storm.

Had he lost his mind? He yanked his hand back before it touched her arm. He was Crown Prince, miles above her rank. Drawing a hard breath, he tilted his face to the full torrent of raindrops.

He had to get home to Duke Ebner's. Forget the madness of this journey. But first he had to make it through tonight.

With the Crown Prince's self-respect in one piece.

19

Night of Waiting

"HERE WE ARE." HARTWIN'S steps hastened. The path led them 'round a curve of the land, then widened until its edges outran Hartwin's lantern. Ahead, slivers of light outlined what appeared to be shutters. The cottage. Weary, Dierk lengthened his stride. Best he could estimate with no stars, they'd walked for over three hours. At least the rain had slackened.

Hartwin rapped on the door. "Dörthe, 'tis Papa."

A latch scraped back, and the door swung in. A girl maybe six years old stared up at them.

Hartwin ducked into the house and picked her up. "How's Mother, Dörthe?"

The girl wove her small fingers into Hartwin's hair. "Still sick."

"Some friends have come to pray for her, liebchen. Can

you take care of Joachim while we pray for Mother?"

She nodded, and Hartwin set her down. "Please come in," he said.

They entered, and Dierk shut the door behind them. The place looked like every other peasant's home he'd visited. Neater than some, less spotless than others. Glowing coals provided dim light. Dörthe had retreated to a corner where she cuddled a boy who looked half her age.

Hartwin opened a door at the side of the room. "My wife is in here."

Dierk retrieved Sister Faith's bundle from his purse and handed it to her. She took it, giving him a smile before she and Gertrude followed Hartwin into the other room. With no business in there, Dierk turned around. Four enormous eyes confronted him. Kids. Not again.

He shrugged out of his wet cloak and hung it on a peg near the door. Then he stepped to the fire. Here was something he could handle. He grabbed a couple logs from the pile beside the hearth and laid them on the coals. The kids still stared.

Dierk eased into a sitting position on the floor, propping one arm on an upraised knee. "My name's Kik," he said softly. "What are yours?" He already knew, but maybe 'twould get them talking.

"Dörthe." The girl glanced at the round-faced boy in her lap. "This is Joachim."

They volunteered nothing more. He tried again. "We have quite a storm tonight."

Dörthe nodded.

"What do you think of it?"

To Dierk's surprise, Joachim replied. "Scary."

He'd made progress. "Aye, 'tis wild. But I think we're safe in this snug little house."

Dörthe relaxed her hold on Joachim and they both scooted forward. The fire blazed up with yellow flames on the new wood. What was he supposed to say now? "Are you worried about your mother?"

Dörthe nodded again, her expression far too sober for her young features. "She's never been sick before."

"Maybe God will make her well. When people pray, the Lord promises to listen." Who was he to talk so? Sounded like something his mother would say. He'd never seen a miraculous healing although he'd heard plenty about them. He picked a crumb of bark off the floor and tossed it into the fire.

The bedroom door squeaked open and Dierk turned to see Gertrude emerge with cloaks draped over one arm and a little bundle in the other. He got up to help her.

"Will you take the babe, Kik? I need to heat some water."

Babe? But he hadn't held an infant since his little brother—

Too late. Gertrude's arm brushed his chest, and he raised his arms to take the bundle. She slipped her arm free, and he was holding a tiny, sleeping person. What was he supposed to do with it?

"Remember to support her head." Gertrude turned away and hung up three wet cloaks beside Dierk's.

Stepping with great care, Dierk followed her. "What is wrong with the woman?"

Gertrude's gaze darted toward the children. "Childbed

fever," she whispered. "Death is the expected outcome. We will do all we can for her comfort, but we must pray, Kik. I've seen God heal before. Pray he will heal this mother."

Dierk nodded because that's what she expected. Pray for a miraculous healing? Him? He had enough to handle with not dropping this babe. Mindful that his arm supported the little thing's head, he walked to the rear of the room and lowered himself to a bench against the wall. The infant lay so still as if it, too, were ill. It might be, with its mother unable to nurse it.

Dörthe sat down beside him and peered over his arm at the babe.

"What's its name?" he asked.

A pucker appeared between Dörthe's small blonde brows. "*Her* name is Liesa."

"Liesa. Pretty cute, isn't she?"

"Mm-hmm."

Joachim came over and climbed onto the bench.

"What do you think of your little sister, Joachim?"

The boy stared up at him. "She's very little."

Dierk had to smile. That she was.

Gertrude looked up from her pot over the fire. "Can you watch them for a while, Kik?"

"Aye." He mightn't be good at it, but he'd try. Maybe God would accept that instead of prayer.

DIERK SHOOK HIS HEAD and blinked several times. In the darkened room, with the fire barely glowing and rain pattering on the roof, sleep could easily overtake him. Just as it had the youngsters crowded around him. A most inviting bed stood in the corner, but somehow he'd ended up with a curly blonde head leaning on one arm and another blond head pillowed on his leg. Not to mention the tiny sleeper in his arms who didn't move once. She just lay warm and soft against his chest.

The bedroom door creaked open and Gertrude emerged, carrying a basin. She washed her hands in the kitchen and padded across the floor toward Dierk. "Are they all sleeping?"

"More or less." Dierk matched her low tone. "Will this babe ever waken? If she weren't so warm, I would believe her dead."

"She may well die if her mother does not recover. It happens far too often." Gertrude slid her hands beneath the infant and cuddled Liesa against her chest.

Dierk straightened his shoulders and flexed the arm Dörthe hadn't pinned to his side. "How is her mother?"

Gertrude's face was bent toward the babe, but she raised her eyes to look at Dierk. "No change yet. We've done all we can physically. We'll keep praying."

Aye, the others would pray and Dierk would watch the children. He squeezed the stiff muscles on either side of his neck. He needed a good stretch. With a sigh, he glanced down at the little bodies pinning him to the bench. Poor kids. So distraught over their mother's illness that they clung to him, a complete stranger, for comfort. "How could God let the mother of such young children die, Gertrude? They need her."

"Well, in the first place, she hasn't died yet." Gertrude returned her attention to the babe, stroking the tiny head. "And in the second place, 'Will the thing formed say to him who formed it, "Why have you made me like this?"'"

Her words sounded cold as Dierk recognized the quote from the Bible.

She released a sigh so deep it might have come from her toes, though it seemed to snag on something in her throat. "Kik, I don't understand why God chooses to heal sometimes and not to heal other times. I have no idea what would become of this family without their mother. But I know God always helps us through our pain and cares for us if we let Him."

"If we let Him," Dierk repeated. "What do you mean?"

"Well, in one sense, God cares for us whether we want it or not. But He also lets us flounder about in our own will if we insist on it. A very foolish choice on our part." Gertrude smiled. "But why am I telling you all this? You have heard it, of course."

If he had, he'd never absorbed it. "Doesn't matter how many times you hear it," he muttered. "'Tis still hard to understand."

"That I cannot deny. I know the answers in my head, but sometimes it still doesn't make sense."

Dierk moved to cross his arms, but stopped lest he disturb Dörthe. "So why do you still believe it?"

Gertrude kissed Liesa's head. "Does not this newborn child show God's wonderful care? He created a new life, wrapped it in this tiny package, and brought it safely into this family. He created the beauty of this world in which we live. He even sent His Son to redeem us from sin." She gave him half a smile. "I can't say it the way I wish, but if God has proven Himself in so many ways, how can I not trust Him with the things I don't understand? I suppose it may not make sense to anyone else, but it helps me."

No doubt about it. Gertrude knew her God. When she'd asked if he were a Christian, he said yes. But he'd never wrestled with deep questions, never proven his beliefs. He never needed to. He just tended his own business and let God tend His.

He slid his fingers into his hair, giving a pull as he went. What spell had the late night cast over him that he turned his mind to such deep thoughts? Discussing it with a girl, and a peasant girl at that.

Gertrude handed the babe back to him. "Hold her a bit longer, will you? I need to warm some goat's milk for her."

As Dierk settled Liesa against him once more, she squirmed. A sign of life, at last. Dierk ran his finger over Liesa's head as Gertrude had done, and found it downy-soft. She was so small, almost nothing in his arms, yet a real person. He supposed it was a wonder.

Gertrude retrieved a container from a sort of shallow cellar in the floor. Having poured some of its contents into a little bowl, she replaced the pitcher beneath the trapdoor and carried the bowl to the hearth.

She really was beautiful. Not as tanned as most peasant girls, but possessing a creamy, healthy complexion. Her graceful movements would suit a duchess. Light from the red coals glistened on her gold hair and outlined her dainty profile. In some ways, she seemed almost out of place. Yet she stirred the milk like she'd attended to lowly tasks all her life.

As if she felt his scrutiny, she looked up. Her blue eyes caught him, pulling him. He wanted to—

He broke the contact and turned his eyes toward the babe. The late hour must be fogging his brain.

After a little while, Gertrude dipped her finger in the milk and touched it to the tender part of her wrist. "'Tis ready." She picked up the bowl and carried it to the trestle table in the kitchen. "Let me fetch a rag, and we'll see if she takes it."

Gertrude took the babe and settled her in the crook of her arm. She soaked a corner of the rag in the milk, put it in the babe's mouth, and glanced at Dierk. "'Tisn't the best, but it gets a little nourishment in her if she'll take it." She bounced Liesa gently a couple times. "Come, liebchen. Try to suck it a bit."

At Dierk's side, Dörthe shifted and sat up. He stretched his arms in front of him, and his cramped muscles sighed in relief.

Dörthe rubbed her fists in her eyes. "Is Mother better?"

"Not yet, liebchen." Gertrude dipped the rag in the milk again. "We're still praying. Will you pray with us?"

"Right now?" Dörthe blinked.

"Why, yes. You pray first, then I'll say a prayer, and Kik will go last."

Him?

"All right." Dörthe slipped off the bench and knelt beside it, folding her small hands. "God, please make Mother better. She's so sick she can't take care of the baby, and she's never been sick before. Make her better, please, and never let her be sick anymore. Amen." Dörthe lifted her head and looked at Gertrude, who nodded.

Still dipping and holding the rag for the babe, Gertrude prayed aloud. "O Lord, who is also our Father, we thank You for the new life You have brought into this family. We pray You would see fit to spare Dörthe's mother so she might raise her children for You. We know You delight to give good gifts, and You care for the weary and the sick. We beg You would heal Dörthe's mother and let her have many healthy years.

"O Father, nothing is too hard for You, and we trust You will restore this woman's health, according to Your will. We also ask that You give Dörthe and her father and brother peace tonight. In the all-powerful name of Jesus we pray, amen."

Dierk glanced up. Gertrude gave a little nod. He was supposed to follow *that*? He hadn't prayed in years. But he could say something. He'd assuredly listened to enough prayers in his life.

"Lord God, in Your Word, many people came to You for healing, and You healed them. We have nowhere else to go, but we believe You can heal." *Did* he believe God could heal? Well, of course, God could do whatever He wanted. "In Your mercy, touch Dörthe's mother. We know if You are willing, You can make her well." That came straight from one of Jesus' miracles in the Bible. "Please say You are willing and heal her. In Jesus' name, amen."

Like the child beside him, Dierk looked to Gertrude. A beautiful smile lit her face, and she whispered, "Thank you." His prayer must have passed inspection.

What's more, he meant it. Strange. He wanted this woman whom he'd never seen to get well, more than he'd wanted anything in a long time.

DAWN LIT THE SKY when they left the cottage. Despite his

sleepless night, Dierk breathed in the rain-washed air and delight swept through him. Dörthe's mother would get well. Sister Faith said she was improving at an astonishing rate, and within a few days would have the normal energy of a woman who'd just given birth.

"Are you sure you can follow the trail?" Hartwin asked.

"Aye." Dierk clasped Hartwin's forearm. "Your directions were quite clear, and in the daylight, I'm sure we'll be fine." They'd best get out of here before the man started thanking them again. Otherwise, 'twould be half an hour before they departed. "God be with you."

Dörthe stood beside her father, and Gertrude bent to give her one last kiss. "I'll come and visit in a few days. Take care of your brother for your mama, won't you?"

Dörthe nodded. "I will."

"Good-bye, then. I'll see you again."

"Good-bye." Dörthe waved. "Good-bye, Kik."

Dierk had to smile. "Good-bye."

"Thank you once more," Hartwin said.

A radiant smile lit Sister Faith's tired eyes. "To God be the glory. We will come and visit you soon."

Dierk started down the trail before they could get caught in further conversation. Gertrude gave a little skip as she caught up. "Was that not the most wonderful thing you ever saw?"

A smile tugged at his lips. Actually, he had *seen* naught. "Aye, 'twas wonderful indeed." And he meant it.

Gertrude skipped again. "I'm so glad. I don't think I'll have the slightest trouble walking home. To think of the babe getting the care it needs and those children having no need to fear. Oh, God is good, isn't He?"

"God is good," Sister Faith answered. "'Tis easy to believe that now. But even if He hadn't chosen to heal her, God is still good."

"I know." Gertrude paused to let Sister Faith catch up. "Kik and I spoke of it last night. But I'm still glad He did choose to heal her."

"So am I. You don't know how glad."

Dierk glanced over his shoulder at Sister Faith. She looked thoroughly exhausted, now that he took notice. "Sister Faith, I believe you had the hardest job of all. Shall I carry you again?"

She breathed a laugh. "You could never carry me all the way, but I appreciate it."

"Why should you doubt me?" he teased. Then he turned serious. "You let me know if you need to pause and rest."

"I will."

"Come, hold my arm." He crooked his elbow toward her, and she slid her slender, wrinkled hand around his arm. "Do you know? I think I'll miss you when I leave."

She stared up at him. "Is that the honest truth?"

"Aye." Odd as it seemed even to him.

She laid her head for an instant against his shoulder. "Perhaps God will see fit for us to meet again."

Dierk smiled, for the Sisters visited Sunland Castle at least once a year. Maybe he could visit at the same time. "Perhaps."

20

The Clearing in the Woods

"WELL, NOW, THE LAD is alive after all." Dierk grinned at Fredrik as he stepped from the bedroom. "How late is it?"

"Noon."

Dierk swept his hand through his hair. "Then I got about three hours."

"I should say so." Fredrik chuckled. "You slept like one dead, lad. Think you're ready to travel?"

"Of course." Squires often kept night-long vigils, followed by a full day's work. But by tonight, he expected to be exhausted.

"Gather your things, then."

In a minute or two, Dierk had his belongings stashed in his pack and his axe secure in its strap. He'd already bid Sister

Faith and Gertrude good-bye this morning when they all retired to rest. Staff in hand, he glanced once more around the bed chamber. He would remember it. After all, he could have burned to death in that bed.

With a wry smile, he left the room for good. "Ready, Fr— Father?" He corrected himself just in time, for Gertrude stood in the kitchen, speaking with Fredrik.

Fredrik turned and hitched at his pack strap. "Aye."

But Dierk was looking at Gertrude. She made a beautiful picture, dressed in a blue kirtle, her golden hair in a loose, uncovered braid. Her eyes deeper than ever. He'd never known a nicer girl.

But no sense in getting sentimental. "Did you rest well?" he asked.

"Yes, thank you." The pup from yesterday jumped at her feet, drawing Dierk's attention down. Gertrude bent and picked it up.

Dierk stepped forward to scratch behind the mutt's ears. "Have you named her?"

"Not yet. If I name her, 'twill be more difficult to give her away."

Fredrik chuckled softly.

"Call her Inga," Dierk suggested. 'Twas the feminine form of his own hound's name.

"Inga." Her voice tested the name. "Very well. It suits. Thank you."

Dierk cocked a brow. "Now you must keep her."

Gertrude looked up with a smile. "Perhaps I shall if the Sisters don't mind. Then she will always remind me of you."

Just as he would remember her when he called Ingo.

Warm satisfaction spread through his chest. Not good.

Stupid of him to suggest the name. Safer to forget it. Quickly, he took her hand, giving her his "charm the ladies" smile. "It has been a pleasure to know you, Gertrude."

Her blue eyes held sincerity. "I've enjoyed knowing you, Kik."

His charming smile didn't fit. Gertrude deserved more. What exactly, he couldn't tell, especially with Fredrik looking on. "Thank you for teaching me how to take care of children. I never did it before, which I'm sure you guessed, but you made it look effortless." That would have to do.

She let out a gentle laugh. "'Tis a worthy skill, and you mastered it well. God go with you, Kik."

"God be with you, Gertrude." On impulse, he bowed over her soft hand and kissed it. As he straightened, he avoided her gaze, lest her eyes catch him again. He released her hand and strode toward the door.

Fredrik took something from his pocket. "You will give this to Sister Faith for me?" he said to Gertrude.

She took the cloth bag. "Oh, 'tis heavy."

"'Twill help with the work."

She smiled. "Thank you, Herr Holtzer. Godspeed on your travels."

Fredrik bowed, and they were on their way. Dierk glanced back at the house. Gertrude stood at the door with the upper half open. She waved to him, and he turned and saluted with his staff before he went on.

'Twas good he was leaving, of course. A prince had no business there in the first place. Yet, he could summon no disdain for his time spent in the Sisters' home.

Whatever.

AFTER LESS THAN AN hour, gauging by the sun's position, Fredrik left the road and headed into the woods. Dierk shoved a branch aside as he followed him. "Your foot need a rest?"

"No, we're near our next stop."

And here he'd thought they'd walk the whole day, on their way to some other far-flung destination. "Are we meeting someone?"

"Aye."

Dierk frowned. No need to be so secretive about everything. "Who?"

Fredrik's mustache twitched. "Your father."

Father. Why must they meet *him*? 'Twould be painfully awkward. Fredrik would report on their progress, and Father would have something to scold him for, no doubt. "I suppose you sent him a message to meet us?"

"Aye, he'll be here mid-afternoon. We'll arrive first."

After perhaps a quarter mile of pushing through the woods with no trail, the trees gave way to clearing. Sparse grass grew here and there, stunted from light deprivation, but still fresh green.

Fredrik slipped his pack from his shoulders. "Here we are."

Dierk looked around. Wait. The tree across the clearing. An old beech tree. "I've been here before."

"Aye?" Fredrik sank to the ground beneath an oak and removed his right boot. "When?"

"Must've been five years ago." A half-smile pulled at Dierk's lips. "Mother and Father brought me and my siblings for a picnic." He shed his pack and dropped down beside Fredrik. "Have you ever been here?"

"No."

"Then how do you know 'tis the right place?"

"See the branch leaning against that beech tree?"

Dierk nodded. Looked like a dead branch had fallen from the tree. Nothing unusual.

"That's the signal. Just to be safe, there's a marker by the branch."

"Let me guess. A larch cone?"

Fredrik's grin showed his teeth. "Four of them."

Clever. "Is it a common sign?"

Fredrik shrugged. "Variations of it are used. 'Tis all prearranged." He gestured toward the tree. "If Phil fails to come, we'll pick up the cones and leave a larch twig, and he'll know we've been here."

"Phil?"

Fredrik looked at him sideways. "His Majesty."

Dierk laughed. "Never heard you call him that." Except ... had Fredrik called Father "Phil" when Dierk eavesdropped on them at the palace? Not that he'd mention it to Fredrik.

He stood and strode over to examine the signal. Four brown larch cones lay scattered amongst the leaves, as unobtrusive as you please. Tricky stuff, this Royal League.

He started back across the clearing, but detoured to examine another tree. Sure enough, an irregular lump bulged in one side of the trunk. He half-smiled, slapped the rough bark, and sauntered back to Fredrik.

Leaning his shoulder against the oak, Dierk eyed Fredrik's bare foot. "How's the ankle?"

"Not bad. Tired more than pained." Fredrik tilted his head back against the tree. "Tell me, why did your father choose this place for a meeting?"

"How should I know?" Dierk settled himself cross-legged beside Fredrik. "All I know is this is the spot where Father first saw Mother."

"You don't say." Fredrik quit coddling his ankle and stretched his leg out before him. "I've heard him say he fell in love with her instantly."

"'Tis what he says." A smile played with Dierk's mouth. He'd always thought that kind of witless. Now that he'd met Gertrude, he had a bit more sympathy for his father.

But still, as Crown Prince of Sunset, Father should have mastered his feelings. No peasant girl would make a suitable queen. Even Dierk could see that.

"Did Her Majesty share your father's feelings?"

"Mother?" Dierk pictured her face, blushing whenever she told the story. "She says, 'I cannot deny I was attracted to him.' You know Mother. So proper."

"Phil told me the whole story once, but I'd enjoy hearing it again." Fredrik cocked an eyebrow at him. "We have some time until Phil arrives. Care to entertain me?"

Dierk grinned. "All right." The story of his parents' first meeting was a family favorite, told and retold as far back as Dierk could remember.

He picked up a stray stick and pulled out his hunting knife to whittle. "I'll tell you the tale of a picnic, Fredrik, if you promise not to mock my poor story-telling skills."

Fredrik jabbed his elbow into Dierk's ribs. "Quit seeking flattery and begin."

21

Memories

TWELVE-YEAR-OLD DIERK HAD EATEN his fill of the picnic fare: cold roast pheasant, mutton pie, sharp-flavored cheese, bread, and fruit. Dierk sipped the last of his watered-down wine. Weak ale he drank often, but wine was for special occasions. Today he got to drink it for the first time while his younger siblings had buttermilk, and he savored their envious looks.

Across the red woolen picnic blanket, four-year-old Adelaide "shared" her apple with a wooden doll. Baby Friedhold, apparently tired of gnawing bits of bread and smearing them down his smock, started fussing. Mother nursed him while Father fed her bites of pie.

How boring. Father and Mother had talked of this outing for weeks. Where was the promised fun?

Time for some entertainment. Dierk slanted his eyes toward his eight-year-old brother beside him. Anselm stared off into the woods, holding a half-eaten grape before his lips and chewing slowly. Anselm loved to sit and think about all manner of things, heedless of his surroundings. Which left him pitifully vulnerable to pranks.

Dierk snatched the small cluster of purple grapes from his brother's silver trencher.

Anselm flinched and looked from his trencher to Dierk's hand. "Hey, give that back."

Dierk shrugged. "No." He plucked a grape off the cluster and popped it in his mouth.

Anselm grabbed for the fruit, but Dierk swung it out of reach. He bit the grape in his mouth, and its tart sweetness washed his tongue. "Mmm. Anselm, your grapes are better than mine were."

Anselm pounced.

Dierk toppled backward, still holding the grapes high above his head. Anselm scrambled up Dierk's chest, grappling with Dierk's free hand. Anselm stretched his skinny arms, but came nowhere near the fruit.

Dierk grinned. Being tall had its uses, besides looking impressive for a Crown Prince.

Anselm jumped up and dived for the grapes. Dierk rolled over and clutched the fruit beneath him. A few dead leaves crunched between his fingers. He breathed the scent of dirt and waited.

"Oomph!" Dierk grunted as Anselm landed hard on his back. Fingers pinched Dierk's ear and twisted.

"Ow!" Dierk rolled over, leaving the half-squashed grapes behind. Anselm kicked underneath him before Dierk rolled free and landed a light punch in Anselm's ribs.

Anselm jumped on him again, and they tumbled around in the leaves. Anselm slugged him hard, and Dierk grunted again. When did his little brother get big enough to make an almost decent opponent?

Another punch hit Dierk's ribs. Now *this* was a fun picnic.

Dierk flipped the tangle, ready to pin his brother, but Anselm kept them rolling, and Dierk found himself on the bottom. Anselm grabbed Dierk's neck in a mock-chokehold. Aye, his little brother was learning to wrestle. Dierk couldn't let him win, though. Wouldn't want Anselm thinking he could best his older brother. He grasped Anselm's wrists, prepared to toss his brother over his head.

Metal clinked. Was that a trencher under his shoulder?

"Dierk, that is enough."

At Father's voice, Anselm relaxed and climbed off. Dierk sat up, brushed off his tunic, and fingered his hair. Flakes of dead leaves fluttered down onto the picnic blanket.

"Please straighten the cloth," Mother said.

Dierk scooted off the blanket and tugged the corner straight. Anselm sat down again, an angel-child with blond hair and an innocent expression—and a dirt-smudge marring his cheek. Good thing, because Father would never see Anselm's faults if he looked perfectly angelic.

Dierk resumed his seat beside Anselm. He hadn't done anything too rough in their scuffle. Maybe Father wouldn't scold this time.

Aye, Father was sending a smile his way. "I do not mind your play. I only stopped you before you threw Anselm into the remainder of the pie."

Anselm leaned forward and took a fresh bunch of grapes

from the fruit basket. "Dierk started it."

Dierk glared. Little brothers. Just when Father showed no signs of a lecture, Anselm made their game appear to be a quarrel. "Hush, you."

Father's eyebrows rose as he gazed at Anselm. "And did I not tell Dierk it was enough?"

Aye, he'd said Dierk's name, indeed. Not a real rebuke, perhaps, but now it felt like one. Father always held Dierk responsible for the scuffles with his brother. Even when *Saint Anselm* began it.

"Now that we are finished eating, shall we have a story?" Mother held Friedhold against her shoulder and patted his back. "This place is where I first saw your father, you know."

Adelaide straightened, resting her doll in her lap. "Oh, yes, Papa. Tell how you heard Mama singing."

Adelaide loved that story—a favorite for telling before bed. A picture flashed into Dierk's mind, foggy around the edges. Himself, no older than five, holding his sister Felizitas in his arms while they listened. At the end of the story, Felizitas always cried, "Again!"

He could recall little else about that sister. Mother said Felizitas had resembled him—brown hair, blue eyes, strong chin. But Felizitas died seven years ago.

Dierk frowned. No need to spoil the day with that memory. He blinked to clear his head and looked at his siblings.

Adelaide's attention didn't waver from Father. Anselm sat cross-legged, elbows braced on his knees. Even little Friedhold sucked his thumb in contentment. Dierk stretched out on the leaf-strewn grass, propping his head on his palm.

Father always started the story. And he always smiled at Mother before he began.

Pulling his gaze from Mother's face, Father faced his audience. "The one thing I disliked about being Crown Prince was all the people hovering over me. All the time. No privacy, except in the garderobe."

Adelaide giggled.

"Finally, when I turned twenty, my father—your grandfather—agreed to let me go hunting alone sometimes, as long as I informed my squire before I departed. I went as often as I could."

"Will I be able to hunt by myself when I'm twenty?" Anselm asked.

Father winked at him. "Perhaps."

Anselm grinned and stretched out on the ground like Dierk.

"One beautiful, chilly morning, I left the palace a little after dawn. I came here to this clearing and sat down under that old beech." Father pointed across the clearing, and they all craned their necks toward the tree in question.

"'Twas a little smaller then." Father bent one knee up and propped his arm on it. "I sat down to string my bow, and I took off my cloak because the walk had warmed me."

"A red cloak," Adelaide put in.

Father tweaked her nose like he used to Dierk's. "Aye, a crimson cloak with gold embroidery at the hem."

Dierk studied the beech tree reaching for the heavens with its thousands of thin green leaves. He'd heard this story so many times he could almost see his father sitting in its shade working with his bow, the red cloak lying beside him.

"I strung the bow and shot an arrow at that tree to test it." Father pointed to another tree, much smaller than the beech. "The arrow went through, and the head stuck out on the other side."

Anselm sat up. "Is it still there?"

Father shrugged. "I doubt it. It has been fifteen years."

"Let me see." Anselm hopped up and ran to the tree. "'Tis here, Father! The arrowhead sticking out, just as you said."

"'Tis a wonder. I thought surely 'twould have broken off before the tree could engulf it."

Dierk jumped to his feet and jogged over to Anselm.

"See?" Anselm pointed to an uneven lump on the tree trunk's side. "The tip is in there."

Dierk bent over the swell of bark and thrust his finger into the hollow in its center. Something sharp poked him. "Aye, I can feel it."

Anselm pushed Dierk's hand aside and fingered the hollow with its iron barb. "Supposing a woodcutter fells the tree one day and finds Father's arrow in here."

"He'll never know 'twas a royal arrowhead." Dierk rapped his knuckle once more on the lump, then headed back to the blanket before Adelaide could beg Father to go on with the story.

"So," Father said as they sat down again, "I left my cloak and went off to surprise some small game."

Here Mother would take up the story. She kissed the sleeping Friedhold's head and lowered him to the blue velvet cushion beside her. "That morning was the day before my birthday, and the Sisters said they had a special surprise for me that night. They even hinted it involved traveling. But that day Sister Hope wanted beechnuts to flavor a stew, and I walked farther than necessary, partly because this tree had the sweetest nuts." Mother nodded toward the beech tree. "But mostly because I enjoyed singing in the woods."

Friedhold squirmed in his sleep, and Mother rubbed his back.

"And when you got to the tree ..." Adelaide hinted.

"Your father's cloak lay there. I wondered who could have left such a fine garment lying on the ground. But I assumed the owner would return for it, so I moved it to a spot near the tree with the arrow. Strange. I never saw the shaft sticking out."

Anselm spoke around a mouthful of grapes. "You could have hung the cloak on the arrowhead."

Mother laughed. "So I could. But I found a stout stick and beat the lowest branches of the beech tree. The nuts rained down."

"And one hit you right on the head!" Adelaide squealed.

Mother laughed again. "Yes, it did. It hurt, too. One day, perhaps, I'll take you to beat nuts from a beech tree."

Funny to think that Mother grew up beating nuts from beech trees. Only peasants did that, usually to feed their swine.

"Then I knelt to gather the nuts, and I sang with all my heart because there was no one to hear me."

Adelaide hugged her doll. "And that's how Father found you."

"Aye." Father smiled at Mother again.

Dierk had long ago decided that a popular song about a

fierce warrior must have been written about Father.

But with his love, a tender smile spreads full across his face.
With adoration in his eyes, he basks in her sweet grace.

Nothing else could describe the funny look on Father's face other than "adoration in his eyes." Dierk covered his mouth with his hand to hide a smirk.

"I heard her voice at quite a distance when I returned for the cloak."

"With no game," Adelaide added.

"With no game." Father tugged one of her braids. "I do believe you are on the squirrels' side and not your father's."

Adelaide giggled.

"I wished to see the owner of the voice before she saw me, so I hid behind the undergrowth and crept forward until I could see her. Wavy blonde hair flowed down her back, and her voice was even lovelier than my own mother's. Very quietly, I reached for my cloak and fastened it 'round my shoulders. And I decided I wanted to meet this girl."

Anselm leaned forward. "So you stepped on a dry stick."

"Aye." Mother's smile bloomed. "It cracked like ice, and frightened me half out of my wits. I stood up so fast I felt light-headed for a moment." She eyed Father, her brows drawn together in mock-severity. "I still say 'twas ungallant of you to terrify your lady-love on our first meeting."

"And I still have not found heart to feel contrite about it." Father leaned toward Adelaide, lowering his voice to a secretive tone. "Her cheeks turned the prettiest shade of pink you can imagine. Then she promptly compared me to a *cat*, of all animals."

"No, I said your *walk* rivaled a cat's for quietness."

Dierk scoffed in the back of his throat. The idea of Father's authoritative stride being compared to a cat's. His footsteps always announced his coming long before he arrived. Which had saved Dierk from discipline a time or two. Gave him time to *persuade* Anselm not to tattle.

Adelaide bounced. "Then what did you say?"

"I said, 'Pardon my intrusion. I came for my cloak.' I gave her my best smile—the one I saved for ladies at tournaments—and said, 'You have an exquisite voice.' She blushed as red as a cherry."

"As red as your cloak?"

Dierk rolled his eyes. Adelaide couldn't let their parents tell the story for anything.

Would Felizitas have shared Adelaide's enthusiasm?

Dierk shook the thought from his mind. "Aye, as red as his cloak, Adelaide. Let them tell the story."

She pouted, just because she thought she was cute with her bottom lip sticking out. Dierk rolled his eyes again.

Father winked at Mother. "She barely had breath to thank me, and she said nothing else, so I asked her name. And she lie—"

"I did *not* lie." Mother slapped Father's shoulder, pretending to scowl. "I told him my name was Rose—the only name I had ever been called."

"And the Sisters still call you Rose," Adelaide said.

"Yes, they do. And when I asked your father *his* name, he replied, 'Phillip.' Not 'Phillip Lichtensitz' or even 'Phillip Leberechtson.' I knew by his clothes he was no commoner, but he did not tell me he was Crown Prince."

"I feared your mother would feel uncomfortable if I disclosed my rank." Father reached over and captured Mother's hand in his.

"What did you say next?" Adelaide again.

"Oh, I asked if I might help her fill her basket."

"No, no." Adelaide frowned and shook her head, setting her blonde braids to swinging. "Mother asked about your hunting."

Dierk sighed. Adelaide had to have *all* the details. As if omitting one would disturb the story. Father backtracked to recite the entire conversation for Adelaide's benefit. The truly important detail was Father's learning Mother lived with the Sisters in Spatzberg.

"I had never met such a charming girl, especially not a peasant girl," Father finished. "Not to mention her angelic voice. As I watched her walk away, I decided to visit her soon."

Anselm leaned back on his elbows. "But you didn't get to."

"No, because the very next day, the Sisters took your mother to meet her parents."

"What did you think of Papa, Mama?"

As if Adelaide didn't know. Dierk had caught her reciting the whole tale to her doll one day.

Mother gave Adelaide a fond smile. "I thought him a fine young man, although perhaps a bit arrogant. I suppose I was suspicious of him—"

"Suspicious of *me*?" Father splayed a hand over his heart, pretending to take offense.

Mother shook her head at Father's antics, laughing softly. "You were a stranger. What reason had I to trust you?" She turned her attention to Adelaide again. "I cannot deny I was attracted to him. I thought about him most of my walk home. But that night the Sisters told me I was Princess of Sunrise. My astonishment banished all thought of your father from my mind."

Adelaide clapped her hands. "But you never quite forgot him, and Father never forgot you. It took a long time, but Father *finally* found out you were his betrothed, and you wed and lived happily ever after."

Dierk quirked his mouth. Adelaide's favorite part of the story. She always had to say that line. Yet Father and Mother had not lived "happily ever after." Felizitas had died. But Adelaide, though she'd heard of her dead sister, knew only happy days.

Mother looked at Father and almost whispered, "We have lived joyfully ever after."

Father leaned in to give Mother a quick kiss on the lips. Adelaide beamed. Anselm gagged.

Dierk shook his head. When he had a wife, he would never be that silly.

22

Fathers and Sons

FREDRIK'S LAUGHTER RANG THROUGH the woods. "So you weren't going to be that silly when you had a wife?"

A grudging smile pulled at Dierk's mouth. It did sound funny coming from his twelve-year-old self.

Fredrik slapped his leg, still chuckling. "And do you still hold by that resolution?"

Dierk shaved a bit of wood from the stick in his hand and thumbed the smooth surface. "I think it unlikely that I will feel for my wife the same love Father feels for Mother."

"Indeed? Why is that?"

He turned the stick and hacked at one end. "I'm Crown Prince. When I marry, I must choose the woman best suited to be queen of my country and mother of my heir."

"I see."

Dierk glanced up to find Fredrik's eyebrows soaring above their normal position. "What?"

Fredrik wiped the surprise from his expression. "Merely seems strange, coming from the son of your parents."

"They were fortunate." Dierk had seen many noble couples at Duke Ebner's, and few had what his parents did. Father had just happened to fall in love with his betrothed because he met her under unusual circumstances. Had they met as planned, like as not they'd have felt indifference for one another.

Similar to the attraction Dierk had toward Gertrude—a foolish fascination inspired by the novelty of their strange meeting. But he had more sense than to fall as his father had.

"Of course my wife and I must have mutual respect and amiability." He'd given thought to this matter a year ago and decided on his course of action. "But foremost, the woman I wed must further my plans for Sunland. To expect love as well ... A man can't have everything." He blew a speck of sawdust off his stick and shot a teasing grin at his companion. "Anyway. Since when are you an expert on the subject? You never married."

Fredrik drew a sharp breath. "I was married once. My wife died."

Dierk froze. How rude he'd been, albeit unintentional. He kept his attention on his hands. "Forgive me. I ... did not know."

Fredrik waved his hand. "'Tis not your fault. I've told no one but your father about her."

Then it must've happened before Fredrik met Father. And Fredrik never spoke of those days in Dierk's hearing.

"Her name was Annelisa." Fredrik's voice held unwonted tenderness. "She was beautiful—dark hair and eyes. We wed when she was fifteen and I was nineteen."

Dierk stole a look at Fredrik, who faced the sky, his body very still.

"She was small, Dierk. Very small-framed. Our first child came too early. Annelisa died soon after the delivery."

Dierk swallowed. What did a person say to that? "I am sorry, Fredrik." What inadequate words.

"Thank you, lad." Fredrik breathed deeply and settled closer against the tree. "I was not myself after her death. Lady Melankardja took me about a week later. I like to think I would have withstood her if Annelisa and my daughter had lived."

Dierk rubbed the wood in his hand, trying to fit this new information into his mental picture of this man he'd known all his life. *Fredrik had a child.* In truth, he scarce knew Fredrik at all. "Did you ... did you name your daughter?"

"Aye. We named her Felizitas."

Dierk's gaze shot to Fredrik's face.

"Your father asked me if he might name his first daughter after mine. I was honored."

But then Dierk's sister Felizitas had died too.

"I'd never heard you mention your sister before today." Fredrik glanced at him. "Do you think of her often?"

"No. I barely remember her." He best remembered her funeral. When she took ill, the physician exiled Dierk to the castle's far side, lest he catch the illness as well. So when she died, Dierk had begged to see her once more. Her tiny white face burned itself into his memory, and he could never recall a picture of her face alive. "I remember Mother wept for days when Felizitas died."

"Aye. So did your father. So much that I feared for him, knowing the grief. But he still had his wife, and you and Anselm."

The picture of his strong father sobbing uncontrolled filled Dierk with a strange horror. Great thunder. Why under the sun did he need to know any of this? Fredrik's sorrow, his parents' grief. What business had he with any of it?

None. None at all. He would shove it away and forget it. He inhaled a long breath.

Fredrik reached for his boot, nodding toward the woods in front of them. "Looks like our friends are coming."

Excellent timing. Dierk jumped up. Sure enough, two figures moved through the trees. Father, dressed as a common yeoman in breeches, a long-sleeved shirt, and a rough jerkin over it. And with him—Grandfather?

Fredrik got to his feet in time to greet them. "Your Majesty. Your Highness." He bowed.

"Dispense with the formality, Fredrik." Father extended his hand. "How is your ankle?"

Fredrik grasped Father's forearm. "Good as new."

"Hmph." Father winked as he slid a pack from his shoulders. "I hope so, anyway." He turned to Dierk, and his brown eyes grew solemn. "How has the journey been for you, son?"

The weight of Father's disappointment the last time they met descended on Dierk's shoulders. He gave a careless shrug. "Not bad. Sir."

"'Twas not the easiest task I set you, but Fredrik tells me you have acquitted yourself well. I commend you."

Dierk gave a quick nod. "Thank you, sir." He *would not*

show how much Father's praise mattered. Besides, he had yet to complete the journey.

"Well, Phil, I don't recall the arrangements including a visit from the former King of Sunset," Fredrik said.

"That is because I was not sure I could convince him to come." Father smiled. "But I have persuaded him to tell Dierk what happened before I ran away."

That tale? Dierk had heard it more times than he could count. Father had displayed atrocious disrespect, which led to his running away and getting caught by Lady Melankardja. Father always ended the story with a subtle or not-so-subtle warning against disobeying authority. Reminiscent of the fairy tales where fantastical curses befell all the bad children. Unrealistic.

"Meanwhile, Fredrik can inform me of all the details too small to include in the messages." Phillip turned to his father. "Remember, no lenience."

Grandfather nodded. "I remember."

Dierk eyed them both. This might prove more interesting than he'd thought.

FREDRIK WALKED BESIDE PHIL into the woods, far enough to give Dierk and His Highness some privacy. "How have you been these past weeks, Phil?"

Phil ran a hand through his hair. "Trying not to worry. Praying a great deal." He faced Fredrik, hands resting lightly on his hips. "How has it been with you and Dierk? In truth, Fredrik."

Fredrik arched his eyebrows. "In truth? I'm glad I never

had a son to follow in my footsteps."

Phil sighed. "That bad."

Fredrik blew out a dry laugh. "I think I received the brunt of Dierk's punishment. I'm tasked with attempting to guide a young man who desires no guidance at all. A lad who, by your own admission, cares more for his own importance than anything else. And I have to accompany him on a journey to make him fit for the throne." Fredrik crossed his arms, half in jest, half in earnest. He was ill-equipped for his role the past weeks, and it had taxed him more than he cared to admit. "All you had to do was stay home and worry." He flashed a grin.

"All I had to do?" Phil half-smiled, studying him with the experience of an old friendship. "You are right. I can only thank you and hope you guess the depth of my gratitude. Tell me: Do you wish I had asked someone else?"

"Certainly not. You know I love your children as if they were my own."

"Which is why I could trust Dierk with you." Phil's quiet smile faded. "But do you think I shirked my duty by not going myself?"

Ah, that was half Phil's torment. Yet Fredrik had asked himself the same question more than once. "No. Firstly, the kingdom couldn't spare you that long."

"The kingdom could spare me any length of time for my son's sake."

"And, secondly, you were right—he needed some distance from you."

Phil turned his head to the side. Aye, that must have pained him.

Fredrik stepped forward and clapped his hands on Phil's

drooping shoulders. "Though I complained a bit in jest, Phil, Dierk has done well. I have not lied in my messages."

"Outside he has done well, but has any of this reached his heart?" Phil touched Fredrik's arms and pulled away from his grip to stare at the silent woods. "You know as well as I that outward show means nothing without inward transformation."

"Aye, I know it."

"Fredrik, my son needs strength for his own sake, but also for his country's sake. Though we are small, the Holy Roman Empire would like nothing better than to annex our land." Phil paced as he spoke, crushing hapless ground-plants beneath his boots. "I must pass my crown to a man staunch in Sunland's principles, namely reliance on God and His Word alone. What if Dierk decides not to accept that mantle?" He stopped and speared Fredrik with his gaze. "What then?"

"I don't know, Phil."

"Ach, who could?" Phil turned away, planted his fists on his hips, and tilted his head upward.

Fredrik's heart ached for his friend. Phil was the man of faith, the man who trusted God to work out all things for good. The man who reminded Fredrik to pray when he forgot. Yet his son's struggles had upset him deeply. He'd drive himself half-mad if he fretted much longer. He needed a good ribbing to lighten the situation. And Fredrik had just the barb to use. "By the way, there is one difficulty I've not yet told you of," he remarked to Phil's back.

Phil whirled around. "Another injury you forgot to mention?"

"No, rather more serious."

Phil stared at him, his mouth a grim line. "Tell me."

"A girl."

Phil raised one eyebrow. "A girl?"

"Aye, a beautiful, blue-eyed blonde living with the Sisters, who has unquestionably captured Dierk's fancy."

Phil's eyes grew wide. Then he bowed his head and pinched the bridge of his nose. "Tell me Dierk isn't following in his father's footsteps."

"I couldn't say that with certainty, Phil." Fredrik delighted in the solemnity of his tone.

Phil groaned. "Does she sing, too?"

Fredrik nearly laughed aloud. "Not like Her Majesty. She's a kind girl, and a strong Christian."

"Well, that is something." Phil dragged his hand down the side of his face. "I should have foreseen something like this. After my experience, I hate to seem proud, but my father had a point all those years ago. It takes a knowledgeable mind to govern a country, and royalty needs to be well-educated." He let his hand drop to slap his thigh. "Not that it is impossible to rectify a neglected education ..." He looked at Fredrik. "How did Dierk take it?"

Ah, this was working beautifully. "I don't think he entertains any thoughts of marrying a peasant."

"Then perhaps he will not hatch some wild scheme as his father did." Phil shook his head. "Did you happen to ask the Sisters who she is?"

"I did. She goes by Gertrude, but her name is Crescentia." Fredrik grinned. "Daughter of Lord Sonnenburg."

"Lord Sonnenburg!"

"Don't yell, Phil." Fredrik maintained impeccable calm for the sole purpose of aggravation. "They'll overhear you."

Phil shot him a mock scowl. "Fredrik, explain yourself."

Fredrik didn't try to bar the smugness from his voice. "It seems ever since Her Majesty's sojourn with the Sisters, other nobles have thought it prudent to send their children to spend a few months or even years at the Sisters' home. Gertrude, that is, Crescentia, has been there a year and will remain two more."

Phil turned his head away and drew a deep breath. "And here I thought there might be cause for real concern." He shifted his gaze back to Fredrik, his lips twitching. "That was uncharitable of you."

Fredrik smirked. "'Twas too good a jest to pass up. But truly, she is a worthy girl. You haven't betrothed Dierk to anyone, have you?"

Phil smiled wryly. "No. Zorena and I did not feel the Lord leading us to take that step. I will keep this maiden in mind when the time comes for such things. Lord Sonnenburg is an honorable man." He took a seat on the leaf-strewn ground and clapped his palms together. "Now that you've enjoyed great entertainment at my expense, perhaps you would like to tell me more interesting details."

Fredrik chuckled as he dropped down beside his friend. His wildest dreams—and he'd had wild ones—could never have hinted at such a friendship. Bantering the King of Sunland, indeed. Yet he wouldn't trade it for the world. God had extended boundless mercy to him.

DIERK HADN'T SEEN HIS grandfather since a Christmas celebration almost two years ago where there had been little time for personal conversation. What did Father mean by bringing Grandfather today? Awkward. Well, he must carry it off as best he could.

Employing his court manners, Dierk bowed as he would to any noble stranger. "I hope you have been well, sir."

"Thank you, lad, I have. And you?"

"Ah, yes, I've been well." If one could call traipsing around the country in disgrace *being well*.

"I am glad to hear it. Shall we sit down?"

"Of course." Odd to see his grandfather sit on the ground beneath a tree, bending one knee up to support his arm. Dierk lowered himself to the leaves beside him.

"Your father has instructed me to tell you of his worst rebellious outburst."

"You mean there were more than one?" Dierk said, half in jest.

"Oh, yes. The time he lamed his charger when the stableman had warned him the animal's foot was unsound. It took the horse weeks to recover."

Dierk hadn't heard about that.

"The time he took a falcon out hunting against the falconer's orders, and a young squire was punished because the bird was thought to have escaped."

Another new one.

"The time he deceived some of his tutors and bribed the rest into giving him a week's respite from his studies."

And Father had scolded *him* for *shockingly delinquent behavior*. Dierk had never deliberately plotted mischief.

"Phillip kept me on my knees in prayer, that is certain." Grandfather smiled without humor. "Dierk, it takes courage for a man to admit his faults to his son. I would ask that you not despise him for what he bade me tell you today."

"No, sir. Certainly not." He'd never thought it courageous of his father to tell them of his faults. But maybe it was. After all, Dierk wouldn't care for Guntram and Jürgen to discover he was in fact a disgraced prince instead of a respectable woodcutter's son. And those boys were no special relation to him.

Grandfather drew a deep breath. "Forgive an old man if he rambles."

23

Rebellion

Leberecht rubbed his left knee, its slight ache a protest against his mounting a horse today. He still did not quite understand why Phillip wished him to share this story with Dierk, but if Phillip thought 'twould benefit the lad, Leberecht would gladly oblige.

Strange how, as a man grew older, so many memories dimmed or disappeared, yet others remained as fresh as if they had happened the previous week. This one ... this one had scarce faded enough to dull its pain.

Leberecht glanced at the young man beside him. His eldest grandchild. Yet he barely knew the lad these days.

And wasn't that feeling as familiar as the rhythm of his own heart?

Relaxed in his cushioned chair before the fire, King Leberecht stared at his son. He and Adelaide had prayed for years before the Lord gave them an heir. Phillip was now twenty, and many times Leberecht wondered what passed through his firstborn's mind. He couldn't hope to guess.

When Phillip was a child, Leberecht had tried to make time for him. But governing a country demanded so much attention. How many days had he exchanged a few words with Phillip at the evening meal and told himself that would suffice? Far too many.

He should have done better for his only son. The heir to his throne.

"Papa, look." Six-year-old Rosaline clung to the arm of his chair, thrusting her sampler toward him.

Leberecht smiled. "'Tis lovely, Rosaline."

She laid the bit of colorful embroidery on his knee and climbed onto his armrest. She slid her small arm around his neck. "Are you tired, Papa?"

"A little, liebchen." He lifted her into his lap and kissed her temple where the soft brown hair curled. "I need to talk with your brother tonight. Go with Nurse now, and I'll come pray with you, hopefully before you fall asleep."

Rosaline sighed. "Yes, Papa." She slipped from his lap and skipped to Phillip's chair. "'Night, Phillip."

Phillip looked up from his book. "Good-night, Rosaline." He leaned down, and Rosaline kissed his cheek. A slight smile crossed his face before he returned to his reading.

Leberecht stifled a sigh as Rosaline left the room with her nurse. He beckoned to the chamberlain who stood in the corner. "Please give us some privacy."

The man bowed. "Of course, Sire."

In a minute, all attendants had departed from the

chamber. Leberecht straightened in his chair. *Lord, let me speak aright.* "Phillip?"

"Yes, Father?" Phillip kept his nose in the book.

"Please look at me, son."

Phillip shut the book, placing it on the ebony-inlaid table beside him. Then he turned his gaze to Leberecht, albeit with a bored expression. "Yes?"

"You have heard of your cousin Zorena, have you not?"

"Of course." Phillip glanced at his fingernails.

Perhaps he should demand Phillip's attention, but 'twould only rile him. "Tomorrow is Zorena's sixteenth birthday and a momentous day for her. For fourteen years she has lived in ignorance of her royal birth, but tomorrow that comes to an end. Sunrise Castle hosts a grand celebration in two weeks, and we must leave the day after tomorrow to attend."

Phillip raised a languid eyebrow. "Is that all?"

"No." Leberecht held his son's gaze. Perhaps it had been unwise to withhold this news for so long. But he and his cousin King Siegbert had planned it so, years ago. He could only hope Phillip took it well. "We will also celebrate your betrothal to her."

Phillip blinked. Twice. "Betrothal? I am to marry her?"

"Yes, you have been betrothed since her infancy. You will wed on her eighteenth birthday."

"You have things well-planned, I see," Phillip snapped. "I would have thought you might give me a choice as to whom *I* must marry."

There it came. The displeasure he'd feared. "From all reports she is a beautiful girl with a pleasant personality."

"From all reports," Phillip scoffed.

"Come, Phillip. It can do no harm to meet her." Leberecht attempted to laugh. "Surely you have no one else in mind."

"You think not?" Phillip's jaw tensed, and he stared toward the dark window. Then he looked back, challenge blazing in his eyes. "Suppose I did?"

Leberecht drew a long breath. "The fact is you are legally betrothed to your cousin."

"Exactly." Phillip's low tone held steel. "Of all the controlling, political schemes. I wouldn't have thought it of you. To trap me before I was old enough to know what was against me."

"Phillip, no—"

"This is a political marriage to consolidate land. You had no thought for my wishes when you arranged this."

"Phillip, that is not true!" Leberecht broke off before he said something he would regret. He must not let his temper bungle this.

"So you think I couldn't choose a decent wife for myself?" Phillip jumped up and paced to the fire. Then he spun around. "Well, perhaps you are right. I met a girl today—a peasant—and, yes, I like her. Possibly enough to marry her. What do you think of that?"

Leberecht leaned his head back and stared at the ceiling. *Lord, please help me.* "Phillip, you are legally bound to your cousin. No one would grant a divorce except perhaps the Roman Church, and you know they have no power in this land." Leberecht's grandfather had broken with the Roman Church decades ago.

"More's the pity," Phillip muttered.

Leberecht met his son's gaze. The fury in Phillip's brown eyes struck his chest like a physical blow. He swallowed before he could speak. "Your mother and I prayed before taking this step, and we felt it was the right one."

"I'm sure that's very comforting."

"You know my marriage with your mother was arranged. Such alliances have flourished for centuries, my son. You will have two years to learn to know, and even love, your cousin."

Phillip flashed him a smile that looked more like a snarl.

"As for the peasant girl you mentioned, I do not doubt she is an honest, pretty maiden." Leberecht tried to keep condemnation from his tone. "But without proper education, I think you would find her to be somewhat of a burden as your queen."

Phillip scowled at the tapestry over the mantelpiece. "I think I am better suited to decide that myself. You are too blinded by your political customs."

Leberecht clamped his jaw shut and stood. Nothing could be gained by addressing that remark. "Come, son. Be reasonable. All I ask now is that you meet your cousin at her celebration. We need not publicly announce your betrothal yet."

Phillip lifted his chin and looked Leberecht in the eyes. "I will not." With that, he stomped from the room. The heavy wooden door slammed, and a decorative gold shield which hung above it hit the stone floor with a jarring clatter.

Leberecht sank into his chair and rested his forehead on his palms. Why did it have to turn out this way?

Adelaide should have been here. She could have gotten through to their son. She'd always had a closer relationship with him.

But Adelaide had died six years ago, her body unable to handle the strain of Rosaline's difficult birth. Phillip had only grown more distant since.

Leberecht pressed his fingertips into his temples. What now? Forcing the issue would drive Phillip to deeper stubbornness. Perhaps if Leberecht gave him some time, he would come around. "Lord, give me wisdom," he whispered. "Phillip's pride has been evident for years. But to give me such blatant defiance ... I feel I must have failed somewhere. O Lord, I beg You to repair what I have left undone. Bring my son to You. I love him. I give him to You, once again, for I simply do not know what to do."

Leberecht prayed a few minutes longer before he trudged out of the room to bid Rosaline good-night. He passed Phillip's chamber on the way. If only he dared knock and enter to pray with his son. But he'd never had time for that when Phillip was a boy. Phillip certainly would not appreciate it tonight.

Leberecht walked on. He must have faith. God could handle this.

But his regret remained.

24

He Knew Better

DIERK STARED AT THE leafy treetops. Wow. He'd never mouthed off to his father that way, not even when Father sentenced him to this journey. Half a smile pulled his lips. No wonder Grandfather hadn't wanted to tell him.

He looked at the older man sitting beside him. "That *was* bad."

"Aye, it gave me much grief." Grandfather's voice thickened. He blinked hard, and the corners of his mouth twitched downward.

Great thunder. Dierk jerked his attention back to the treetops. No way he'd watch his grandfather fight tears.

"Phillip was twenty years old, and he knew better, of course." Grandfather's tone had steadied. "But you cannot know how much I regret letting the affairs of my kingdom come before my son when he was younger. Maybe I could have spared him what he suffered afterward."

Dierk shrugged. "Maybe." *His* parents' involvement hadn't kept him from disappointing them.

Grandfather clapped a wrinkled hand on his knee. "Well, I believe my part is done, Dierk. I need to take these old bones back to the comfort of the palace."

Dierk jumped up and offered his hand to help his grandfather rise.

Grandfather stood. "Thank you, lad."

"You won't walk back alone, surely?"

Grandfather smiled. "No, a man-at-arms and a good steed await me but a furlong or two off." He grasped Dierk's shoulder, his eyes keen but gentle. "My prayers will be with you."

"Uh, thank you, sir." Dierk stared after the old man whose erect walk contrasted with his white hair. Grandfather Leberecht admitted he hadn't been a perfect parent. Somehow, Father made it sound like Grandfather had been cursed with an especial miscreant for a son. Hmm.

Snapping twigs and rustling leaves announced Father and Fredrik's return. Father gave Dierk half a smile. "What do you think of me now, son?"

Ha. As if he'd answer that. He'd get himself in trouble quicker than Fredrik could swing that axe of his.

"I asked you, Dierk," Father said. "You are free to answer."

Dierk crossed his arms. "Do you think Grandfather's neglect of you in your youth contributed to your rebellion?"

Father's eyebrows shot up.

Dierk held back a smile. He'd caught Father off guard with that one.

"I fear your grandfather may not have been as forthright about me as I hoped."

"No need to worry. He fully explained your *shockingly delinquent behavior*." Dierk got great satisfaction from throwing that phrase back at his father. "But I want to know whether you think Grandfather was partly to blame."

Father squeezed the back of his neck. "'Tis difficult to say, Dierk. I was never close to him. Perhaps if I had been, I might have behaved differently. But I still take entire responsibility for my actions."

"Hm." Father was no simpleton. He'd circumvented the next question—whether Dierk's behavior could be blamed in part on *him*. "So you think he was perfect?"

"No-o." Father dragged the word out. "Not perfect."

Dierk lifted his chin a tiny bit. He might get in trouble for this later, but a reckless mood had struck him. "Do you think you're a perfect father?"

"Dierk, I have never claimed to be a perfect father. I have made mistakes."

"But you still hold me responsible for my behavior?"

"Of course. You are seventeen, and you have been taught well in spite of my failings."

True. Heaven knew Mother and Father had harped on Christianity and noble behavior as long as he could remember. Well, *harped* might be a bit harsh. They'd made their expectations clear, anyway.

"Dierk, after a certain point, a child can no longer blame his parents for his choices. 'Tis part of becoming an adult."

Dierk cocked an eyebrow. "Are you saying I am an adult?"

Father smiled. "I am saying you should be *becoming* an adult."

Dierk sighed. When it came down to it, Father was probably right.

"Do you understand what I mean, Dierk?"

"Aye."

Fredrik, who'd kept still through the discussion, reached for his pack. "Then shall we set up camp?"

DIERK STRETCHED OUT ON his blanket, elbow bent, head propped on his hand. They'd eaten roasted rabbit, snared by Fredrik, while stars accumulated in the darkening sky. A yawn stretched Dierk's face. Sleeping under the stars again. Kind of nice, now that he was used to it.

He reached for a dead leaf and crumbled it in his fingers. "So, where do we go in the morning?"

Father looked at him across the crackling fire. "Lady Melankardja's fortress."

Now that would be a sight worth seeing. "I can't remember—how did she capture you?"

Two deep lines appeared between Father's brows. "I still am not certain how she knew an opportune time had come. I can only surmise she had spied on me for years, possibly through servants in our palace." Father stood and laid another limb on the fire, then brushed his hands together above the flames. "In any case, I left the palace early the morning after I quarreled with your grandfather. I spent the day fuming, and I refused to speak with my father that evening. The next morning I slipped away to this place and ate breakfast. I was determined to visit your mother."

Ah, yes, Dierk remembered that part. Funny to think if Father had succeeded in reaching Spatzberg Village, he would have found Mother and the Sisters gone.

Father sat down again and leaned against his pack. "A peasant came up and asked my destination. I told him, and he offered to take me by a shortcut. I accepted." Father gestured over his shoulder. "There is a thicket of underbrush not far from here. As he led me through it, two other men met us. Between the three of them, they got me tied up." A wry smile twisted Father's mouth. "One of them received a black eye and a close encounter with the dirt for his pains."

Dierk grinned, and Father winked. Then he sobered. "But black eye or not, they caught me. We walked most of the day, avoiding roads. After the first few hours, I swallowed my pride and asked where they were taking me. They said, 'Lady Melankardja bid us capture the Prince of Sunset. We obeyed.' You can believe I was scared then."

"With good reason," Fredrik mumbled.

Dierk glanced at him. Fredrik would know. He'd worked for her for two years. "Tell me, Father. How bad was it at Lady Melankardja's fortress?"

Father drew a long breath, picking up a twig from the ground beside him. "I will tell you more of it later. I have no wish to recall those days more often than necessary."

Leaves rustled as Fredrik pushed himself to his feet. "You will forgive me, I hope, if I walk and pray for a while. Considering tomorrow's destination, I need some mental fortification."

Father nodded, the firelight illuminating deep lines in his

face. "I will be praying too, you may be certain."

With a curt nod, Fredrik strode into the woods, escaping the ring of orange light.

Staring after him, Father spun the little twig between his thumb and forefinger. "The next day or two might be more difficult for him than for me, and that is saying something."

Dierk frowned. What had the place been like? Hitherto, Father must have whitewashed his experiences for his young children.

But Dierk was a child no longer. He was ready to know the truth.

"Get some sleep, Dierk. We have a long walk in the morning."

"That will likely be harder on you than me." Dierk gave him a sly grin. "I've acquired a great deal of experience the last few weeks."

Father smiled, tossing his twig into the fire. "So you have. Good rest to you, my son."

"You too, Father."

MID-AFTERNOON OF THE NEXT day, Fredrik paused and leaned on his staff. "We're nearly there."

Dierk studied the woods around them. They'd left the road a couple hours ago, and the forest had grown denser through the past furlong. In fact, if it weren't for the path, a person would have to cut his way through the underbrush.

Father took a drink from his waterskin. "How's the ankle, Fredrik?"

"Holding up. You have the pass?"

"Of course." Father slapped his pocket. Then his face grew somber. "Are you ready?"

"As I'll ever be. Let us go."

With occasional branches tugging their clothing, they maintained single file down the winding trail. More paths intersected with bewildering frequency, yet Fredrik chose his route without hesitation. The farther they went, the more uneasiness crept up Dierk's spine and settled on his shoulders. If he had to flee for some reason, pure chance alone could lead him out of this maze.

They rounded another of the everlasting corners and met a man wearing a mail tunic. The royal crest gleamed on his jerkin. "What is your business here?" he demanded.

Father stepped forward and slid a parchment from his pocket. "We have come to inspect the fortress."

"'Tis an unusual time." The man took the parchment and read it, then looked up with new respect in his face. "Your Majesty. Forgive me for not recognizing you at once in your unusual attire."

Father smiled. "Perhaps you will recognize this?" He rolled back his left sleeve, exposing his gold wristband set with jewels depicting the Royal Crest. Dierk had never seen him without it. He hadn't even thought to wonder if Father had it hidden under his long sleeves.

The guard briefly touched his chest, moved his hand to his forehead, and then let his arm drop as he gave a slight bow. The salute reserved for royalty. Been a while since Dierk had seen it.

"We expect you will find all in order, Your Majesty."

"I have no doubt we will. Thank you, Sir Knight."

They passed on, and Dierk shot a glance over his shoulder at the knight. "Why the guards, Father?"

"Lady Melankardja was the last person to use this fortress, but not the first. 'Twould bode ill for the country should another like her take up residence here."

Reasonable. "How many guards are there?"

"Eight at a time, stationed in this thicket which surrounds the fortress. We have four teams who rotate throughout the year."

"Are they all knights?"

"Aye. League members, too. Besides Fredrik and a few others, they are the only ones who understand the intricacies of these paths."

"You mean you don't?"

Father turned to smile at him as they walked. "I visit in person once a year. I know but one route through this maze."

By the tone of his voice, Father didn't care to expand his knowledge. But it might be advantageous for a member of the Royal House to navigate the paths without relying on a guide. Dierk might learn them some day. "If the route is kept so secret, why have so many teams?"

"Three months at a time is all anyone can be expected to handle," Fredrik said from the front of their group.

Dierk frowned. What meaning did that remark hide?

"I ought to dismantle the fortress," Father said. "I have never taken the trouble to do it since this has worked so well."

That suited Dierk fine. The more he reflected on this place, the more his curiosity demanded satisfaction.

"Here we are." Fredrik stopped.

The path opened into a grassy clearing. About a stone's

throw away, a stone hut squatted in the center of the open area. A garden occupied one side of the clearing, and a large wooden building stretched along the other edge of the thicket.

Dierk's chest clenched. He sucked in a deep breath, trying to relax from this inexplicable ... whatever it was. His heart beat hard against the tightness.

So this was Lady Melankardja's fortress.

25

No Sight of the Sun

DIERK SCANNED THE CLEARING, searching for he knew not what. The source of the strange oppression hanging in the very air, perhaps. He clenched his fist and discovered his fingers wrapped around his knife hilt. Half-ashamed, he released the cool metal.

Father pointed to the wooden building on their right. "Those sleeping quarters were built for our guards. When I came, there was only the stone hut, the entrance to the fortress."

A young man emerged from the guardhouse and strode toward them, his mail tunic clinking. "I must see your identification." As he neared them, his scowl changed to a look of respect. "Oh, Your Majesty." He delivered the Royal Salute. "I did not expect to see you, Sire."

"I am early for my inspection," Father said.

"You will find all in order. The ceiling in the far north

chamber continues to fall in. Otherwise no change. I inspected it myself last week." The man's face cringed as if the memory sickened him.

"My sympathies," Fredrik said.

The guard looked at him. "Sir Fredrik?"

"Aye."

The guard grasped Fredrik's forearm. "I haven't seen you in forever. Why didn't you greet me when you were here last month?"

What was the man talking of? A month ago, Dierk and Fredrik hadn't even reached Spatzberg yet.

Fredrik frowned. "I was not here last month."

"But ... Sir Ortwin said he met you inspecting the paths."

"Georg, I *never* come to this place," Fredrik said.

"Never?"

"Not since I first led King Leberecht's army here almost two decades ago."

Dierk glanced at Father, who gave unswerving attention to Sir Georg. If not Fredrik, who had Sir Ortwin seen?

Sir Georg fiddled with his sword hilt. "Ortwin said he met a man whose pass identified him as you."

"Where is Sir Ortwin?" Fredrik snapped.

"Somewhere on the north side."

"Find him. At once."

"Yes, sir." Georg saluted and hurried away toward the opposite end of the clearing.

Fredrik paced a few yards, then marched back. "I don't know Sir Ortwin well. Do you remember him, Phil?"

"Of course. I chose all the guards myself."

"And you trust him?"

"I have no reason not to."

Fredrik nodded. "Of course." He turned around and surveyed the clearing as if some clue lay hidden in plain sight.

Dierk glanced over his own shoulder. In case the place hadn't enough horror, add an unknown intruder.

"If Sir Ortwin were in league with this stranger," Fredrik said slowly, "'twould seem likely he would never mention he saw the man."

Father nodded. "True."

Something rustled in the underbrush a few feet away. Dierk grabbed his knife hilt. *Stop it.* It couldn't be anything bigger than a rabbit. No one else appeared to notice it. And if any immediate danger lurked, which it didn't, he would need a cool head to deal with it.

"Could take a while to find Ortwin," Fredrik said. "Shall we tour the dungeon and get it done with?"

Father sighed. "Might as well. We can lay our packs in the guardhouse."

When they had dropped their burdens inside the door of the building, Father drew a deep breath. "Fredrik, will you pray for us?"

"Gladly." Fredrik bowed his head. "Dear Lord, I thank You for a safe journey today. I thank You for Your unending mercy toward me. Seeing this place again, I can't help thanking You for bringing me out. Lord, I'm concerned about this man who impersonated me. I pray You would bring forth the truth. And as we enter this fortress, help us learn the lessons it would teach, and protect us from its darkness. In the name of Jesus, amen."

Dierk studied the grass by his boots. *"Learn the lessons it would teach.*" Doubtless, that part was for his benefit.

Father placed his hand on Dierk's shoulder. "Let us go."

When they reached the stone hut, Father touched Fredrik's arm. They exchanged looks, and Fredrik gave a sharp nod.

Fredrik lifted the latch, and the thick wooden door swung open with a screech. "We used to keep the hinges oiled." The inside was empty. Stone steps descended through a hole in the floor. Fredrik lit a torch on the wall, slipped it from its bracket, and gave it a moment to catch well. "Come on."

Dierk waited for Father to go first, but Father gestured him ahead. He stepped into the hut and followed Fredrik down the stairs. The half-dozen steps emptied onto a landing.

Fredrik flashed the torch to the right, illuminating another descending staircase. "That leads to Her Ladyship's residence and the guards' quarters. We won't explore it. She filled it with lavish furnishings. Horrible place."

Dierk frowned. The lavish furnishings made it horrible? Or perhaps Fredrik meant no luxury could compensate for dwelling underground. "What is this place, anyway?"

"Old castle dungeon. Fortress fell decades ago. Lady Melankardja and her predecessors fortified and expanded the dungeon with materials from the old building."

Dierk peered at Fredrik's face in the unsteady torchlight. His voice had never sounded so flat, so crisp, as if he'd become some sort of longbow that fired scraps of information instead of arrows.

Fredrik led the way down another staircase on the left. "This takes us to the prison."

As Dierk glanced back to see that Father followed, his

foot stumbled on an uneven stone. Lurching, he waved his arm to regain balance.

"Try taking these steps with your hands tied behind your back." Father's voice had acquired an unusual tightness as well. No wonder, considering his imprisonment. Even empty, this place closed in on a person. The deeper they descended, the heavier the air seemed.

The staircase emptied into what looked like a wide hallway. Nothing was distinguishable beyond the wavering torchlight. A faint musty smell filled Dierk's nostrils and stuck in the back of his throat.

Fredrik tapped on a door in the right-hand wall. "This is where Lady Melankardja worked much of her witchcraft."

A chill shot up Dierk's spine. He drew a deep breath. *Take control of yourself, Dierk. 'Tis nothing.* They continued down the hall, passing doors Fredrik didn't stop to identify.

Their footsteps echoed off the stone floors and walls. Damp coldness blanketed Dierk's skin. He wanted to look over his shoulder to make sure nothing followed them. But he didn't—just in case some black apparition truly lurked there.

Which, of course, it couldn't.

A spot of dim light glowed on the stone ceiling. "What's that?" He pointed.

Father looked up. "'Tis a tiny tunnel to the surface of the ground. A vent for the torches that used to hang on these walls."

The torchlight splashed against the end of the hall. Fredrik pushed open the door on the left. "Here is the cell formerly occupied by the Crown Prince of Sunset."

Father stared at that doorway like it led to the pits of

Hades. He shook his head. "In all these years, I have never inspected this chamber. But I did not expect it to be this hard. Of course, I know Fredrik will not shut the door and bar me in, but you do not know how much I want to run."

Dierk bent his head. He didn't need to be here. For Father and Fredrik this place meant something—something terrible, but something important. Dierk was just touring a hair-raising relic he'd heard tales of all his life.

Father stepped past them into the cell. "Nothing much changed." He turned around slowly in the middle of the cramped floor space. "'Tis not a pleasant place, but I surrendered to Jesus here and His Spirit met with me time and again." Father looked at Fredrik. "God came here, even amidst the vileness."

"Aye, that He did." Fredrik smiled a little.

Father beckoned. "Come in, Dierk."

Dierk entered. The floor sloped under him, slanting to a deep hollow in the far left corner. Father pointed to the circle of light in the ceiling. "My skylight. I was so grateful for it, even when it let in the rain."

Dierk walked over and looked up. A tiny scene of green leaves filled the opening.

Joining him, Father examined the view. "'Twas blue sky when I stayed here. A gift from God."

Mighty small gift.

"A man might go mad imprisoned underground with no sight of the sun." Fredrik's voice, hard and bitter, carried from the doorway. "If only that could excuse me."

In a moment, Father stood in front of Fredrik, gripping his shoulders. "Fredrik, you are forgiven. You are not to revisit sins that God has cast behind His back."

"I know." Fredrik nodded.

"You know, but nevertheless you do it."

"I can't help it, Phil."

If Fredrik had betrayed no emotion before, his voice overflowed with it now. Dierk turned away and stared through the skylight. He definitely shouldn't be here. He glanced over his shoulder. Judging by their bowed heads, Father and Fredrik were praying.

Why did this place upset them so? Fredrik, who could command the Palace Guard or fell trees all day with equal competence. Father, who faced everything from disgruntled vassals to threatening enemies without hesitation. What had happened to them here? How much power had Lady Melankardja possessed?

"Dierk, come see one more room."

He turned and followed his father across the hall. Father pushed open a door, and Fredrik handed him the torch. The light couldn't reach the farthest edges of this chamber, which must be three times the size of Father's cell. And what were those queer contraptions in the corner? His flesh cringed just looking at them.

"This is the torture room," Father said, his voice as matter-of-fact as a servant saying, *This is your bedchamber.* "Many a beating I received here."

Dierk's heart pounded against a sudden weight. His neck prickled as if someone were breathing on it. He glanced behind him, but Fredrik still stood in the hallway.

Gooseflesh spread down his arms. Sweat coated his palms. A strange smell of death—like blood—washed over him, and he locked his knees against the urge to run.

Father turned away. "Come, let us leave."

Dierk didn't argue. Fredrik led them out with long strides, but not fast enough for Dierk. No wonder Father loathed the place. Dierk had seen enough to satisfy his curiosity as long as he lived.

When they emerged from the hut, he sucked in a deep breath of clean air. The door screeched shut behind him, closing in whatever thing had—or hadn't—stalked them through the tour.

Dierk had never been so glad to see the sunlight.

26

The Imposter

"Sounds like someone's coming."

At Father's words, Dierk tossed aside the stick he'd whittled on. Must be Sir Georg with Ortwin. At least it better be. He jammed his knife into its sheath.

Father straightened from leaning against the guardhouse wall. "Fredrik," he called.

Dierk had never seen Fredrik so nervous. He'd paced the clearing's perimeter since they exited the dungeon. A moment ago, his route had taken him behind the guardhouse and now he rounded the corner of the building. "Aye?"

Father tipped his head toward the far side of the clearing. "Someone's coming."

Sir Georg and another knight emerged from one of the path entrances. Father moved to meet them, and Dierk followed. So that was Sir Ortwin, a broad, stocky man, not as tall as Dierk, but no one to challenge without good cause.

Both men delivered the Royal Salute, but Sir Ortwin bowed deeper. "What can I do for Your Majesty? My colleague told me nothing specific."

Father acknowledged it with a nod. "Sir Georg tells me you met my Chief of Palace Guard in the paths a month ago."

"Yes, Your Majesty."

Dierk studied Sir Ortwin's face. He looked neither surprised nor embarrassed, merely ready to serve. Either he was innocent or a marvelous actor.

"Are you certain it was Fredrik?" Father asked.

Sir Ortwin's thick eyebrows pinched together. "Of course. That is, I have no reason to think otherwise. I've seen Sir Fredrik only twice before, but it looked like him. Tall. Tawny hair. Blue eyes, I think." He shrugged. "He carried a pass that identified him."

"The pass bore the Royal Seal?"

"Yes, Sire."

"I see." Father drew a deep breath. "Fredrik is with me today. Will you tell me whether he is the same man you saw?"

"Of course."

Father beckoned to Fredrik, who waited by the guardhouse as they had planned. Fredrik strode close, his expression hard. If he'd worn that look throughout their journey, Dierk would have scarce spoken to him.

Sir Ortwin's eyes grew round. "Sire, 'twas not the same man." He looked at Father. "A very close resemblance, but not the same. Your Majesty, I crave your pardon. He had the appropriate document. I had no suspicion he was not who he claimed." He shot a frightened glance toward Fredrik, then focused again on Father. "Forgive me, I beg you, for this grievous error."

Father clasped Sir Ortwin's shoulder for a moment. "I do not hold you responsible. You had no reason to mistrust him."

"If only Georg had met him." Sir Ortwin slammed the butt of his spear into the dirt. "He could have recognized the fraud."

"It can't be changed now." Fredrik spoke for the first time. "What matters is that we find this man if possible. You say he resembled me. How was he different?"

Sir Ortwin's gaze locked on Fredrik's face. "Thinner, I think. He had a beard. His eyes were different somehow. Perhaps farther apart." Sir Ortwin slapped his thigh and turned his gaze toward the woods. "Ach, I don't know."

Dierk felt sorry for the man. He'd have a hard time describing his own father's face, and he knew it as well as he knew anyone's. Never mind describing features he'd seen but once.

"Wait, his nose. It had a little lump on the bridge as if it had been broken in a fight."

"Ah, something definite to go on." One corner of Fredrik's mouth curved up. "He looks like me with a broken nose."

"I'm sorry. 'Tis the best I can do."

"I didn't intend to be facetious," Fredrik said. "'Tis much better than nothing."

Father crossed his arms. "I wonder if the man passed himself off as Fredrik to anyone else. We might track him that way—find out if anyone else nearby saw 'Fredrik' last month."

Sir Georg nodded. "You could send a message to your contacts in the area."

"Who are the contacts?" Dierk asked.

Everyone looked at him. He should've kept his mouth shut. Engrossed in the conversation, he forgot to play the silent, trustworthy servant, a League member who would know the answer to the question he'd just asked.

"Our contacts are League members in direct communication with the palace," Father told him. He turned to the knights. "This is my son, Prince Dierk. He has not yet joined the League."

Now that he'd made a fine show of his ignorance, Father had to explain, right in the midst of their discussion.

They both saluted. "Honored to meet you, Your Highness," Sir Georg said.

Odd, after all these weeks, to receive the Royal Salute. He returned a military salute, touching his left shoulder with his right hand. "Forgive my interruption."

Sir Ortwin struck the ground with his spear again. "*My* concern is how the man got that seal."

"Aye, 'tis another problem." Fredrik's frown deepened.

Father stroked his chin. "Obviously, we must devise more secure measures for identification if people can steal the seal. 'Twas a wax imprint, correct?"

"Yes, Sire."

How could someone get possession of a signet? Only four existed: one for Mother, one for Father, and one for each of his grandfathers. And Father would know if one went missing. This stranger must have considerable skill to carve the Royal Seal's imprint so that it aroused no suspicion.

"I suspect someone melted a seal off some old document, perhaps a royal proclamation. Although how they acquired even that is cause for concern." Father clapped his hands. "I will take measures against this as soon as I return to the palace. Meanwhile, accept no one who does not bear a royal armband." Father turned back his sleeve to expose his. "Except your suppliers, of course. Otherwise, even coded messages shall not be acceptable for a time. I will inform you in person when I have formulated a new plan for identification."

UNDER SIR GEORG'S DIRECTION, Dierk and the others stowed their packs in the guardroom's storehouse.

"We have six bunks, but we never use more than four at a time unless someone is ill." He waved a hand toward the four sleeping men in the bunks. "Perhaps Your Majesty and Your Highness would be comfortable in the extra ones."

Dierk shook his head. "Not I."

Sir Georg raised an eyebrow. "'Tis the best we can offer, Your Highness."

Great. That hadn't come out right. He'd styled himself as some supercilious child of royalty. After guarding his tongue so well on this trip too. "I mean, I'll take the floor. I prefer it." And Fredrik ought to have the bed. Today had been rough on him.

Father smiled. "With that settled, we have some private conversing to do."

Sir Georg saluted. "I will be in the barn if you need me."

"Thank you."

Sir Georg disappeared through a door which led to the other half of the building, and Father opened the outer door. "Let us go out lest we further disturb these men's rest."

The late afternoon light cast a faint golden glow over the clearing as Father took a seat against the guardhouse. Dierk dropped down beside him, but Fredrik remained standing. "Do you need me now, Phil? I thought I'd take a walk through the paths."

"Go ahead." Father grinned. "But take this, in case Ortwin has already alerted the other guards." He handed Fredrik his armband.

Fredrik stowed it in his tunic pocket. "God guide you, Phil."

"Thanks, Fredrik. And you."

Dierk picked at a blade of grass. Strange conversation. Both of them so grave.

Fredrik strode into the thicket, and Father sighed. "I have demanded much of him."

"Why?"

Father breathed a mirthless laugh. "Because I could not do it alone. Thank you for giving him the bunk. Perhaps it will help him sleep, and he needs all the help he can get."

Dierk shrugged to hide his pleasure. "I don't mind."

"I know." Father sighed again. "I may as well get on with the story. I know you've heard much of it before, but—"

"I want to hear it all, Father. I'm old enough."

Father looked at him, his face sober. "So you are."

27

Captive

WHENEVER PHILLIP HAD TOLD his children this story before, he always left out the darkest parts—the pain and terror that had haunted his nightmares for years after the ordeal.

This time he needed to tell all but the very worst.

O Lord, help me to do this for my son.

AFTER HIS CAPTORS HAD forced him to walk most of the day with no food and little water, Prince Phillip was almost too tired to fear anything. Almost.

By all reports, Lady Melankardja was ruthless. If she had ordered his capture, it boded no good. In fact, he might as well get accustomed to the idea of dying soon. He could only hope she'd make it quick.

His captors guided him into a thicket of underbrush that had to be cultivated to keep it so impenetrable. After fifteen minutes of apparent wandering along narrow paths, they emerged into a clearing. A stone hut stood in the center with two men guarding it.

This was the fortress of Lady Melankardja? He'd expected something grander.

One of the guards disappeared into the hut. In a few moments he returned and announced, "Lady Melankardja."

A graceful woman stepped from the hut and scanned the men before her. She had to be near forty, but her beautiful features could still turn a man's head. Long, glossy black hair streamed loose down her back, held away from her face by delicate gold bands. Her kirtle of fine purple silk flowed to the grass at her feet. A naked, double-edged sword hung from her plain leather belt.

Her green gaze settled on Phillip and bored into him. "So this is the Crown Prince of Sunset." Her cold smile sent shivers racing up and down his spine. "Welcome to my fortress. I will speak with you soon." She turned to the guard at the door. "Show our guest to his room."

The guard grasped Phillip's arm and pulled him into the hut. Weapons hung on the walls, but Phillip had no time to count them before the guard dragged him down the stairs leading underground. Phillip struggled to keep his balance on the uneven stone. They reached a hallway, deep underground, which glowed with reddish torchlight.

A sickening smell assaulted him. The dark, heavy, overpowering stench of … evil. He'd never thought evil could have a smell.

The guard led Phillip to the end of the hall and shoved him inside a tiny room. "Make yourself comfortable." He closed the door, and a bolt grated into place.

Phillip looked around. Comfortable, indeed. Torchlight reached through the barred window in the door, making a crisscross pattern on the floor. A pile of dingy straw lay against the right wall. In the corner of the ceiling, a bit of daylight beckoned to him.

He crossed the floor and tipped his head back. A narrow tunnel opened to the sky, letting in the evening light. His shoulder pressed against the stone wall, and he quickly pulled back. Slime drew a streak down the rough stones, likely from rain leaking through the tiny skylight.

Moving back from the circle of light, he found a dry place to lean. His body screamed for rest, but with his hands tied behind him, he didn't want to attempt sitting down.

What did Lady Melankardja want with him? Would she hold him for ransom or ... something worse?

The bolt grated again, and another guard opened the door. He jerked his head toward the hall. Phillip walked past him into the torchlight.

Lady Melankardja faced him, flanked by two strong men.

"Bow to Her Ladyship," his guard hissed.

Phillip remained erect. She could do what she wished, but he would never bow to her. He was Crown Prince of Sunset.

Something slammed the backs of his knees. His legs buckled, and his kneecaps met the stone floor. Pain shot through the joints. He gritted his teeth and stood tall on his knees.

Lady Melankardja lifted her eyebrows, seeming amused. "I hope you find your quarters comfortable."

"Very."

"You can see you are my prisoner." Her eyes grew colder. "You will one day be King of Sunset, and I see no reason to waste that power. I want you to swear fealty to me and participate in an initiation ceremony."

Phillip raised his chin a notch. "And why would I do that?"

Her smile would have been beautiful if her eyes weren't so sinister. "To make your stay here more comfortable, Your Highness. Also, to ensure your departure. The life I live is pleasant, perhaps even more than yours. I have power, wealth, no restrictions. You can have it, too, if you merely swear fealty to me."

Phillip squared his shoulders. Let her kill him if she wished. "I will not submit to you or anyone else when I am king."

"You have a night to think on my offer," she said, as if he had not spoken. "You are in my power, but you choose your treatment." She nodded to the guard who stood next to him. "Unbind him. Give him bread and water for supper."

A LOUD CRASH WOKE Phillip. He sat bolt upright on his pile of straw. A guard held a torch in the open doorway, a cruel grin on his face. "Sleep well, Your Highness?"

No, he'd had nightmares.

"Get up. Her Ladyship wishes to see you."

Phillip pushed aside his red cloak and stood. Fitful though it was, sleep had refreshed him. He would meet Lady Melankardja with his head up. Running his hands through his hair, he stepped from the cell. Her Ladyship stood in the hallway as she had last night, with four men this time. Phillip gave her a haughty prince's smile.

She arched an eyebrow. "Have you thought over my offer?"

"I have."

"And your conclusion?"

"What makes you think I would keep my word if I said yes?"

She fingered her sword hilt. "You would die if you didn't."

"I might outsmart you," he taunted.

"I think not. No one outsmarts me."

"No?" He matched her aloof expression. "What of the curse you cast on my cousin at her birth? Someone outsmarted you there, for nothing came of it."

Her eyes blazed. "How would you know? You have heard naught since you came, and the curse was to bear fruit but two days ago. Zorena is dead, as dead as if she had been stillborn like her sisters."

She must be lying. For the first time she'd thrown off her cold indifference. Besides, she couldn't have received news from Sunrise Castle so soon.

She drew a deep breath and smiled. "Perhaps my men can help you make up your mind." She turned and swept up the corridor.

The guard at Phillip's side grabbed his arm and hauled him through the door across the hallway. The man thrust his torch into a holder on the wall, slightly illuminating the large room. "We'll see what kind of fighter you are."

Before the words registered, pain stabbed Phillip's ribs. He gasped and swung at the man, making contact with his jaw.

"Now this will be interesting," said a voice at the door. The other four men entered. "Let him have it, Meine."

Phillip took his fighting stance. His training master had always advocated offense when possible. So Phillip launched in.

Meine fought well, but at last he collapsed on the stone floor. Bruised, Phillip stepped back, trying to catch up on the breathing he'd missed. Meine might stand up in a minute.

Another guard shoved away from the wall. "My turn."

Phillip stared at him, his chest heaving. If he had to fight every one of them, he wouldn't last. Not if they were as good as Meine. But he would show them what a prince could do. If he had to go down, he'd make them pay dearly for it.

28

Lingering Darkness

FATHER STARED STRAIGHT AHEAD as he spoke. "Against so many, of course I went down, unable to resist any longer. They continued beating me until I was unconscious."

Dierk swallowed. He knew the bruising of a fistfight, but his matches always followed the rules.

"When I regained my senses, they had left me on the floor of my cell. I saw no one else all day." Father drew a long, shuddering breath, rubbing the back of his neck. "I guess 'tis enough for today."

Not quite. Dierk still had a question. "When you came to, did you consider submitting to her?"

Father glanced at him and shook his head. "No, too stubborn."

"Guess it served you well that time."

Father raised skeptical eyebrows. "Maybe. Had I not been

him. In the dark, Dierk couldn't make out his face, but he'd met all the knights at supper. This would be the sentinel assigned to guard the inner part of the maze, including the clearing. "Sir Burckhardt?"

"'Tis I. How came you to work at this hour?"

Dierk leaned the mallet against the woodshed. "Couldn't sleep."

"Nightmares?"

Dierk frowned, positioning one of the halves to greet his axe. "What makes you ask?"

"I have 'em sometimes. Have to pray hard."

Pray over nightmares? Now that sounded strange. Dierk swung the axe into the wood, then yanked the tool free. "Does it really work?"

"'Tis the only thing that works."

Likely story. "How so?"

Sir Burckhardt came nearer and sat on one of the largest logs. "Some nightmares are from our brain's foolishness while we sleep. And some are caused by worry over something."

Dierk struck the log again, hitting his previous cut dead-on.

"But some of them are the devil tormenting you."

Dierk froze with the axe in the wood. "You jest. Satan wouldn't trouble himself to send a person nightmares."

Sir Burckhardt snorted. "He'll do anything to keep you from serving the Lord valiantly. Fear is one of his favorite weapons."

Dierk banged the wood against the block to drive the axe further. He'd expected these knights to be loyal, of course, but not so devout. Still, 'twas kind of interesting talk. "So how does one go about praying against nightmares?"

Sir Burckhardt tapped his spearhead against his palm. "Well, you surrender yourself to the Lord, make sure you're not giving the enemy an unwatched gate into your fortress, and you pray God will defend you against Satan."

"And it works?" Dierk tossed aside the piece he'd sliced off and started a new cut.

"Sometimes you have to pray harder and longer. Often I quote Scripture, too. 'Tis much better than doing naught, let me tell you."

Sir Burckhardt fell silent while Dierk whacked off another piece. One more split, and he'd be ready to start the other half of the log. But he didn't want the conversation to die yet. "What did you mean by not letting the enemy find an unwatched gate?"

"Any kind of sin leaves an unguarded gate, even the things that seem insignificant. Once I quarreled with another knight over some little thing—can't remember what. But I stayed angry, and when I slept I had dreams that left me sweating." Sir Burckhardt propped one ankle on his knee. "It took three such times for me to understand the connection. 'Tis but one example, but whenever something's amiss in your heart, the devil has room to work. And he uses different attacks on different people."

"Such as?"

"Most of the knights here experience an inexplicable, crippling sorrow at times. Hard to describe. Sometimes our most even-tempered men succumb to unreasonable, explosive anger. And there are ... other things. The devil will twist up your mind if you give him half an opportunity." He shrugged and stood up. "But we always make it. This is no easy place to work because of the darkness, but it keeps you dependent on Christ."

Dierk blinked and turned to his neglected wood. Who would guess? He brought the axe down with a thud. Father ought to destroy this fortress. Then they wouldn't need guards to live in such an oppressive place.

"Hist."

Dierk let his axe swing past the wood without striking. "What?"

Sir Burckhardt faced the woods, his body tense. Dierk strained to listen. A low whistle floated through the darkness. Might have been a bird. Sir Burckhardt whistled back, low and haunting. A shrill whistle like a hawk's cry stabbed the quiet. Sir Burckhardt made three squeaky sounds that carried well. Two more of those hawk's cries replied.

"Great thunder, they've caught an intruder."

Dierk propped his axe against the chopping block. "The guards?"

"Aye." Sir Burckhardt turned to Dierk. "Wake the others while I see what else they know."

Leaving Sir Burckhardt to his whistles, Dierk ran to the front of the building, and shoved the door open. It bumped the wall, but no one moved. These knights slept like dead men. He stomped across the floor and grabbed Fredrik's shoulder. "Fredrik, wake up."

Fredrik's snore broke, and he twisted under his blanket. "What, lad?"

"Sir Burckhardt said to wake everyone. The outer guards have caught an intruder." Dierk climbed on the edge of

Fredrik's bunk to reach Father's bed above. He gave Father's shoulder a firm shake.

Father's body jerked, and he grabbed Dierk's wrist.

"Father." Dierk tugged against his grip. "'Tis I."

At once Father released him. "Forgive me. Nightmare."

Interesting.

The upper bunk beside Father's creaked as Sir Georg sat up. "Did you say the guards caught an intruder, Your Highness?"

"Aye." Dierk leaned back to face Sir Georg, though he could see no more than his outline in the dark. "Sir Burckhardt bade me wake you while he got more information."

Sir Georg kicked the wall beside his bed. "Up, men!" he bellowed.

Dierk jumped off his perch. The bunks came to life with men rolling out and crawling down. So that's how 'twas done.

Sir Georg lit a lamp with a coal from the hearth, and the knights reached for clothing and armor in a sort of organized mayhem. Within two minutes, they stood at the ready.

Sir Burckhardt strode in. "The north guard caught a man sneaking about in the maze. They will need reinforcements to scour the paths for signs of others. I need three volunteers."

Sir Ortwin and two others saluted.

"Good." Sir Burckhardt gave a crisp nod. "God go with you."

The three volunteers gathered their weapons and headed out. Sir Burckhardt finally looked at Father. "I'm sorry your sleep was disturbed, Your Majesty, but I'd just as lief have you here. In view of the unwelcome visitors lately, may I summon another team for reinforcement?"

"Of course." Father nodded. "Use your judgment." He crossed his arms. "Refresh my memory. Have we ever caught intruders in the thicket?"

"Once in a long while, we catch a boy sneaking around the perimeter. 'Tis always in daylight. Idle curiosity, I believe."

Half a smile touched Dierk's mouth. Easy to imagine boys who lived nearby daring one another to explore the dense woods. They might not even know what the thicket hid.

"'Tis understandable." Father frowned. "But this concerns me. Two intruders in—what is it? Six weeks?"

"Thereabouts."

Father shook his head. "I must get to the root of this. As soon as I return to the palace, I will notify the League. And we will, as you suggest, double the guard. Have your suppliers mentioned anything unusual of late?"

"No, Sire."

Father ran his fingers through his tousled hair. "'Tis a difficult matter."

"Aye." Sir Burckhardt sighed. "We'll question the prisoner, but 'tis doubtful he'll talk."

"He can be made to talk," Fredrik muttered.

Dierk looked at the man beside him. His eyes were hard in the flickering lamplight. What ailed him?

"Fredrik, you know we cannot—" Father began.

"Aye, I know, and I wouldn't." Fredrik slapped the side of his fist against the wall. "It frustrates me to see such a thing happen."

"We will pray. Shall we do so now?" Father looked around at the men.

One by one, they knelt on the wooden floor. Masking his surprise, Dierk joined them. Odd to see knights in their tunics of mail kneeling to pray.

"Fredrik, will you lead us?"

Planting his fists on the floorboards, Fredrik bowed his head.

29

The Spy

AFTER SEVERAL MINUTES OF prayer, Dierk arose with the others. Calm had settled over the room. The men stood tall, but relaxed. The tension had left their faces. They were once again confident soldiers.

And their prayers ... Having listened to each of these knights pray aloud in turn, he had to dismiss his fellow squires' arguments that prayer could offer nothing to strong men.

Sir Burckhardt grasped the door handle. "I must return to my rounds. Signal me when the prisoner arrives, Georg. I'll be alert lest he happen to break away."

Sir Georg lifted a hand, and Sir Burckhardt headed out.

Drawing a deep breath, Dierk glanced at the window. This time he didn't imagine the faint light filtering through the darkness. Sir Georg moved to a chest along the far wall and drew out what looked like herbs and eggs. A bit early to cook breakfast, and what a strange place to keep the stuff.

Sir Georg took a candle from the shelf above him and lit it. "I'll build a message to send to the next team, Your Majesty, and when full daylight comes, I'll carry it to our nearest communicant."

There it was again. *Build* a message.

"Good." Father wore his thinking frown once more. "You will also tell your communicant of the situation here so he might keep his ears open?"

"Of course, Sire." In the dim light, Sir Georg took up an herb and poked it into an eggshell. At least, so it appeared.

Dierk crossed the room to stand beside him. Sure enough, Sir Georg slid a little dried flower into a hole in the bottom of the eggshell. A tiny puddle of wax hovered in the taper, and Sir Georg spilled the hot liquid onto a small beech leaf. He pressed the waxy leaf against the eggshell to cover the hole, then repeated the process at the other end to stop an even smaller hole.

Dierk folded his arms. "So this is what you League members mean when you say you'll build a message?"

Sir Georg glanced at him as he blew out the candle. "Aye. 'Tis safer, in case the messenger should fall into trouble."

"I should say so." The highwayman who waylaid the messenger and took his belongings would likely think he'd robbed some pitiful idiot who collected herbs in eggshells. "When will it arrive?"

"Within two days, God willing."

Dierk knew better than to ask what each herb represented. Probably if he weren't the Prince, destined to join the League at some point, Sir Georg would never have let him see the message at all. What he'd seen on this journey made him more eager to prove himself ready to join the Royal League.

The door swung open, and one of the night guards, Sir Albert, stuck his head inside. "I have brought the prisoner."

Sir Georg thrust the message into the chest, and everyone hurried to the door. Dierk stifled his curiosity enough to let the older men go first. Finally, he emerged into the semi-darkness. In the splash of light from Sir Georg's lamp, a lad younger than Dierk stared at them, eyes defiant.

A boy, not a man. Interesting.

"He won't tell me anything." Sir Albert glared at the boy. "I'm tempted to throw him in the dungeon for a while. I wager 'twould loosen his tongue."

The dungeon at night? A shiver tingled between Dierk's shoulder blades. Of course, Father would never allow such punishment.

The skinny, dirty boy exuded rebellion from every angle of his posture. Looked close to Anselm's age, which made Dierk old enough to inspire respect, but young enough to qualify as a friend.

Aye, he could get this kid to talk sooner or later. Much better than the others could. He stepped forward. "So you caused the alarm that roused everyone and sent extra men searching the maze for your partner." He raised an eyebrow. "Impressive feat."

The boy's gray eyes locked on him, then shifted to look at all the other men.

Dierk kept his focus on the boy. If the men would just keep silent, Dierk could make headway. "Not sure I'd enjoy creeping around this maze at night myself." Understatement. "That makes you either brave or foolish." He winked, letting a smile slip onto his face. "I'm Kik, by the way. What's your name?"

The boy's gaze slid to somewhere around Dierk's boots.

Sir Albert shook the kid's shoulder, and Dierk flicked a hand to stop him. With a questioning frown, Sir Albert stilled.

Adults. They thought they knew everything. They'd ruin this yet. Dierk weighed his tone before he spoke. He needed both sympathy and casualness to undo Sir Albert's interference. "'Tis in your best interest to talk, my friend."

"Ha!" The syllable was sharp as an arrowhead. "Friend."

"Or enemy, depending on how you want it." Dierk shrugged. This was his territory. He'd won friendship from his fellow squires even when they were jealous of his rank. He could build an understanding with this boy. "I'd guess you're about fifteen. Am I right?" Actually, he'd say a year younger, but flattery wouldn't hurt his cause.

With a scornful smile, the boy shook his head.

Dierk raised his eyebrows. "Sixteen?"

"Fourteen."

He'd guessed right. And what's more, he got a straight answer. Progress. "What's your name?"

The boy's gaze focused behind Dierk again, and Dierk turned his head to look at the men. All of them frowned more or less, maybe in surprise, maybe in displeasure. But he hadn't time to explain.

He turned to the boy again.

For a moment, the kid studied Dierk. Then he dropped

his gaze. "Thomas."

Dierk smiled, giving him a friendly cuff on the shoulder. "You're lying." He drew a deep breath. "Anyway, I was chopping wood when your capture interrupted me. We can chat while I work." He grasped the boy's arm and tugged him free from Sir Albert's hold. With his skinny arms bound behind him and his feet hobbled by a short rope stretched between them, the kid couldn't cause much trouble.

The looks on the men's faces didn't share Dierk's certainty, but he grinned and saluted with his left hand. "See you at breakfast."

He led the boy toward the woodshed, ears alert to any movement behind him. *Don't follow me. Give me a chance to see what I can do.* He guided the boy to the same log Sir Burckhardt had occupied. "Have a seat."

He scanned the area for anything the boy could use as a weapon. Nothing. With that, he grabbed his axe and split the chunk on the block into two neat halves. "So, what's your real name, Thomas?"

"Why would I tell you?"

"Because it can't hurt and it might help." Dierk wrestled another log onto the block. "You're a prisoner anyway. Might as well make the best of it."

"Niklas."

Dierk looked at him. The boy looked back, defiant. Aye, 'twas his real name. "Niklas. What brought you to explore the thicket at night?"

"Curiosity."

Too quick an answer, too succinct. "Then why not come in broad daylight? You could see better." Dierk raised an eyebrow in challenge, even though Niklas might not see it in the dimness.

Niklas looked at his feet.

Dierk slammed his axe into the wood and added the wedge. "Do you know what this place is?"

"How would I?"

Dierk pulled his axe free and pounded the mallet on the wedge. Irritating rascal. "I'm sure I don't know." Taking his time, he finished the log and hauled another onto the block before he tried again. "Been here before?"

"Wouldn't you like to know?"

Dierk straightened, propping his fist on his hip. No, now wasn't the time to plow that fist into Niklas's face. He forced carelessness into his voice. "I guess I would, but it doesn't matter as much as the fact that you'll never be coming back. 'Tis a shame to lock up a person so young, but when it comes to something like this, we can't take chances."

Niklas lifted his chin. "What's so special about this fortress? What do you hide here that you have to guard it?"

So he did know about the fortress, and probably that it had belonged to Lady Melankardja. "Wouldn't you like to know?" he copied Niklas.

Niklas looked down at his feet again, scratching one ankle with his bare toes.

Dierk relented, hoping to draw Niklas to speak more. "In fact, we don't hide anything here. A long time ago, a wicked person held people captive here. The Royal House wants to make sure that doesn't happen again."

Niklas didn't look up. "I'm not some Lady Melankardja. Why punish a person for just looking around?"

"They don't." Dierk paused to drive the wedge into the wood. "But the best way to make sure no wicked person finds and uses this place is to keep it a secret."

"Whatever."

"So, who put you up to this? Your father?"

"I told you. I was curious to see what was back here, so I came to look. Any harm in that?"

Stubborn peasant. "No, except I don't doubt you knew it was forbidden to wander around in here. Which means you broke the law."

"Well, aren't you smart? No need for me to tell my side. To you I'm already guilty."

Dierk clobbered the wedge with the mallet until the log split and the wedge started to bite the chopping block. He banged the piece of iron loose. Niklas might never talk. If he were nearer Dierk's size, Dierk would probably thrash the kid to convince him to speak. But he couldn't beat this boy. A knight didn't abuse those weaker than himself.

Maybe he should turn Niklas over to Father and the others. But the way they talked, they would let the kid sit there, sullen, without even trying to worm the truth out of him.

Dierk replaced part of the log on the block. He had to keep trying. There had to be some way—

Niklas sprang to his feet and dashed for the woods.

30

Niklas

DIERK DROPPED HIS AXE and raced after Niklas. With his shorter height, the kid didn't stand a chance. Dierk leaped and landed flat on top of him, pinning him to the damp ground. The scent of moist dirt filled Dierk's nose as Niklas kicked beneath him.

Dierk hooked his arm around the boy's neck and squeezed. "Lie still," he hissed. "I tried to give you a chance to come clean. Thought maybe this wasn't your fault. But there are other ways to make people talk. Spit it out before I choke it out of you."

Niklas coughed, his throat rippling against Dierk's forearm. "I can't breathe."

"Of course you can," Dierk snapped, but he eased his hold. If the kid wanted to talk, he'd let him. "Who put you up to this?"

Silence.

With his left hand, Dierk found Niklas's arm and gave it a twist.

"My uncle." Pain raised the pitch of the kid's voice. "He wanted me to figure out how the maze worked, that's all. I swear it."

True, or mostly true. Dierk released the boy's arm. "Why does he want to understand the maze?"

"Curios—"

Dierk tightened his grip on Niklas's neck. "Don't give me that. Decent men have more important things to tend to than idle curiosity. Why does he want to understand the maze?"

Niklas gasped. "He didn't tell me."

As if he would give up at such a stupid excuse, although he did loosen his grip. "You're a smart lad. What do you suspect?"

"He wants to get in and out without someone catching him."

Anyone could guess that. "You're trying my patience, Niklas. *Why* does he want to get in here unobserved?"

Niklas swallowed, his Adam's apple pressing into Dierk's arm. "If you didn't act so suspicious, maybe people wouldn't think you stored treasure here."

"So your uncle wants to rob the fortress, and he figured you could learn the maze and teach him."

Niklas didn't answer, but Dierk didn't need him to. "Has your uncle ever tried the maze himself?"

Silence for several heartbeats.

Great thunder, he'd end up punching this waif yet. He squeezed the kid's throat again. "Has he?"

"Once," Niklas sputtered. "He went in disguise. The guards saw him, and he didn't dare come back."

The guards saw him, but didn't capture him? Could it be the man posing as Fredrik? "What was his disguise?"

"I don't know."

Dierk filled his fist with Niklas's hair and yanked the kid's head back.

"I don't know!" Niklas started kicking again. "He didn't tell me."

Dierk let the boy's hair slide out of his grasp. "All right, I'll believe you. But the Royal House stores nothing of value here. No weapons, no treasure." What other information did they need? He had to make the best of this chance. "What's your uncle's name?"

Niklas's hands balled into fists under Dierk's stomach.

Dierk almost sighed. The kid was preparing to hold on to that secret, and choking him might not work. Dierk couldn't give him the wallop he deserved. Why couldn't the kid cooperate? "Just tell me, Niklas. Shielding him will do you no service."

Niklas's fists didn't relax, and the quiet stretched long. "Veit Nagel," he whispered.

A reply he didn't have to squeeze out of the kid? Could be a lie. "Is that his name or his false name?"

"His real name. He's my father's brother. If he has another name, I don't know it."

Could still be trickery, of course, but on the chance it was sincere, Dierk gentled his tone. "Is your father part of this, too?"

"My parents are dead."

"I see. One more question. Is this your first time in the maze?"

"No. 'Tis my fourth."

Dierk winced. Niklas could learn a lot in four trips, no doubt. "How well do you know it?"

Niklas turned his face toward Dierk's for the first time. "But that's another question."

Dierk chuckled. "Aye, I know. Answer it." He shifted some of his weight off his prisoner, landing his hip in the dewy grass.

"I know the outer edges pretty well. The inner parts are still foggy."

"And I suppose you reported to your uncle as you learned." Dierk smiled. Not technically another question, although he did expect an answer.

"As best I could." Niklas's shoulders hitched beneath Dierk in a motion probably meant to be a shrug. "But I'm not sure what good 'twill do."

True. What Veit could do with partial maps was anyone's guess. "I suppose that's enough for now." Dierk got up, brushing at his damp tunic. He bent and gripped Niklas's arm. "Will you run again if I leave your feet untied?"

"Would you believe me if I said no?"

"I would." He couldn't gain the kid's trust unless he offered a little in return.

Niklas sighed. "I won't run."

"Good." Dierk hauled Niklas to his feet, then released his hold on the boy's arm. "How'd you get your feet free, by the way?"

Niklas squared his shoulders, his smile proud. "Untied the rope with my toes."

Dierk laughed. "Impressive, and no jest." Had to respect

the kid's determination. "Tell me, Niklas. If spying is your uncle's idea, what's in it for you? A share of the treasure?"

Niklas looked away, breathing a bitter laugh. "Fewer beatings."

Dierk's heart surged, pumping liquid fire through him. He'd like to personally beat this Veit Nagel. "'Tis not our intention to hurt you, Niklas. But we can't have people breaking the law."

Niklas shrugged.

"Sorry I had to tackle you. You gave me no choice when you ran."

"I know. I had to try."

Dierk couldn't say he wouldn't have done the same thing. "Look, we can't let you go, of course, but the more information you give us, the easier it will go with you."

Niklas looked down and shuffled his feet. "If I tell you everything ..." He glanced at Dierk. "What will happen to me?"

Dierk kept silent until Niklas met his gaze, and he held it man to man. "Niklas, if you tell us everything you know about your uncle's schemes, I give you my word no harm will come to you."

Niklas gave a tentative nod.

"Come on. I want to tell the others what you told me." Dierk turned toward the guardhouse and waited until Niklas fell into step beside him, but he didn't touch the boy. 'Twould shatter their new truce if Niklas felt coerced. They rounded the corner of the guardhouse and almost ran into Fredrik and Sir Georg.

Of course. They'd spied the whole time. They couldn't

trust Dierk for anything. "Is there any need to tell you what I learned, or did you hear it all?"

Fredrik smiled. "We couldn't hear from this distance, lad."

Sir Georg lifted a lantern from behind his feet. "I confess I had my doubts when His Majesty forbade us to interfere, especially when the boy ran, but you did well, Your Highness."

What? Father had let him handle this, even kept the others back?

Niklas let out a little gasp. Round-eyed, he stared at Fredrik. "I swear you could be my uncle's twin. You look so much like him."

So Veit *had* impersonated Fredrik.

Fredrik's hand shot out and grabbed Niklas's shoulder. "Who is your uncle?"

Niklas flinched.

"His uncle is Veit Nagel." Dierk reached behind Niklas and jabbed his finger into Fredrik's hand. The last thing they needed was Niklas getting frightened and turning defiant again. "Let's go inside where we can untie this lad, and we'll tell you about it."

Fredrik withdrew his hand and ran it through his hair. "Aye."

Dierk clapped Niklas's shoulder. "Come."

As he and Niklas followed Sir Georg, Dierk glanced back at Fredrik. This business sure had him worked up. They reached the front of the building and met Father and Sir Albert.

Father grasped Dierk's shoulder as he might have done to Fredrik.

By lantern light, Dierk caught the look in Father's brown eyes. *He's not displeased with me.* Dare he say paternal pride shone in Father's eyes?

No, he didn't dare. But whatever it was, it flowed through Dierk like sweet wine.

EARLY SUNSHINE STREAMED THROUGH the open door of the guardhouse. Dierk spooned a mouthful of warm porridge and meat, and chewed slowly to enjoy the savory flavor. Across the table from him, Niklas ate like one starved. Which he might be, considering the way his shoulder blades jutted out and his arms resembled knotty sticks. Poor kid.

Niklas shoveled in his last bite, and Sir Georg reached for the boy's bowl. He scooped more porridge into it, and handed it back with a smile.

Dierk smiled himself as he swallowed another bite. Father, Fredrik, Sir Georg, Sir Albert—they'd all looked skeptical when he insisted on unbinding Niklas earlier. But all of them had softened as Dierk related the information about Veit Nagel with Niklas adding details, unprompted.

Sir Georg scraped his bowl and set it down with a thump. "Well, I'm off to deliver that message."

Sir Albert nodded. "Godspeed, brother."

Fredrik crossed his arms on the table. "Have you an extra mail tunic and a spear? I'll join the guard today."

Sir Georg stood. "We don't keep extra armor, but I'll leave you mine. Should fit you. More weapons are in the storeroom."

Sir Albert pushed his bowl away. "Your Majesty, you said

you and Prince Dierk have business to discuss today. Would it be possible for you to watch the lad?"

Niklas's head jerked up. He stared across the table, first at Father, then at Dierk. "You're the Prince?"

Dierk shrugged, giving him a half-smile. "Aye."

"But you ... you chopped wood, and—" His eyes narrowed. "Your name isn't really Kik."

"'Tis what I go by these days. Long story." One he didn't care to air in front of the knights—or even Niklas himself. How they would despise him if they knew the truth.

Father smiled at Sir Albert. "I am sure Niklas will give us no trouble. Is there anything else we can do to help?"

Sir Albert opened his mouth, but shut it again.

"Just because I am King does not mean I cannot serve alongside you."

"Well, if you should have time, the horses will want care, perhaps exercise. Sir Georg will take one, of course, but the other two ought to be staked out to graze in the clearing." Sir Albert shrugged his mail-clad shoulders. "But, ah. I can do it before I go."

"Do not give it another thought," Father said. "I think we can manage."

A smirk crept across Dierk's face. Now this would be fun: watching Father muck out a horse's stall.

DIERK HUNG TWO PITCHFORKS on their hooks in the barn and turned to watch his father empty the wheelbarrow full of manure and dirty straw. Father tipped it forward and kicked the bottom. The smelly contents flopped out at the base of the muck heap.

Dierk grinned. "For a king, I think you handle a pitchfork tolerably well, Father. Except for spilling its load on your feet once in a while."

Father glanced over his shoulder as he kicked the barrow once more. "I believe you bumped into me, lad."

"Indeed not. *You* backed into *me*." Dierk nudged Niklas with his elbow. "Did he not, Niklas?"

Niklas smiled faintly. He'd said little since breakfast.

"Perhaps next time I shall spill my load on *your* foot for that impudence." Father turned the barrow around, a smile on his face. "Let me park this thing, and we shall go outside for the storytelling."

Dierk stepped out of the way so Father could push the barrow into the empty stall that served as the tool room.

Father brushed his palms together and cocked his head toward the back door. "Come."

Bright sunshine greeted them. Father led them to the front of the guardhouse and sat down in its shade. Dierk sank down beside him and leaned against the weathered wood at his back. On his other side Niklas sat cross-legged, bony fingers picking at his tunic.

Dierk sighed. He had nothing against the kid, but he might hinder Father's storytelling. And Dierk wanted no whitewashed version. Not this time.

"Well, to pick up where I left off." Father crossed his arms. "During my second day in the dungeon, guards brought meals in the morning and evening—such as they were. The men asked if I wanted to see Lady Melankardja, and of course I said no." Father's brows drew together. "The darkness was very heavy that day. You cannot understand, Dierk, no matter how much I tell you."

Dierk nodded. "Felt bad enough yesterday."

Father looked at him a moment. "Magnify that ten times. 'Twill give you an idea."

Dierk's peripheral vision caught Niklas leaning forward. He glanced at the kid, who looked away.

Well, he couldn't fault Niklas for being there. "Father is telling me of his imprisonment at this fortress in his youth."

Niklas nodded. Unasked questions filled his face.

Dierk turned back to Father. "Go on, please, sir."

31

Freed

PHILLIP AWOKE AND SCANNED the dark room, eyes blurry. Where was he? A faint light glowed above his head. The skylight.

Right. Lady Melankardja's dungeon. His third morning here, if he could call it morning in this darkness. If he somehow managed to live through this, he feared his eyes would suffer permanent damage from the lack of light.

He moved his arm, and soreness flared through his muscles. Gritting his teeth, he sat up. His whole body ached. A strange heaviness filled his chest, and he sucked in a deep breath. His ribs protested with stabs of pain.

When would that madwoman give up and kill him? Not that dying was a pleasant prospect, but neither was living in this cell.

His nose had almost become accustomed to the stench of his own waste in the corner, but he could not get used to the grime covering everything. Or the clammy, underground feeling that made his flesh cringe.

Ugh. He rubbed his arms, as if 'twould do any good. Along the far wall, a small creature's toenails skittered across the floor. A ferret, he hoped. He'd seen no rats yet, only the weasel-like ferrets that darted through cracks between the stones and stared at him with sharp, beady eyes.

Leaning against the cold wall, Phillip flexed his arms until the stiffness eased. Then he pushed to his feet and walked the few steps across his cell, stretching his stride as much as the tight muscles would allow. After three trips, the sharp pain faded to soreness.

He walked to the skylight and gazed up at the tiny circle of gray sky. How long could he endure this?

Of course, he could always acquiesce to Her Ladyship's demands.

Phillip cursed under his breath. He would never surrender. What satisfaction could the throne offer if he had to submit to some fanatical witch?

A breath fanned the back of his neck, and he whirled around.

Nothing. Or was that a shape in the corner? No, of course not. Just darkness. And his own overactive imagination. He breathed deeply to calm his pounding heart.

Soft orange light filtered through the barred window in his door. It grew stronger, then halted. Footsteps thumped, and a man's silhouette appeared in the window.

Another beating about to commence? Phillip widened his stance and folded his arms. He could endure this. He could.

The bolt scraped, and the door screeched open. The guard

barely glanced at Phillip as he poured water into the empty bucket by the door and laid something on the floor beside it. Then he shut and bolted the door.

Phillip waited for the guard's footsteps to fade before he went to pick up his breakfast. A cup of lumpy, lukewarm gruel that smelled like dirt, a sure sign of spoilage. And a piece of brom bread—dark, dry, tasteless stuff fit only for hounds. Had she no decency whatsoever? He was human, after all, never mind being a prince. But he had to eat to live. To minimize the flavor, he swallowed the meal at a rate which would have horrified his courtiers.

His stomach still cramping with hunger, Phillip lay back on his pile of dirty straw. Why did he feel as if someone were watching him? He searched the room's corners as best he could in the low light. This darkness ... it seemed able to creep into his bones. It slithered through his veins like cold poison.

Ridiculous notion. Was he losing his mind in this wretched place?

He forced air into his lungs, but he couldn't lift the invisible weight from his chest. As if something had a hold of him, squeezing tighter and tighter, determined to stop his breathing. And he couldn't prevent it.

Cold sweat drenched his skin. He gasped for air. His heart raced as if fleeing from—what? Nothing. Anything. Everything. Just unidentifiable fear.

Shaking, Phillip sat up and pressed his back against the wall. Lying down made him vulnerable. Whence came this terror? How could he stop it? He had to stop it. He would go mad. Or die. Or both.

He who dwells in the secret place of the Most High shall abide under the shadow of the Almighty.

Mother had loved that psalm. The memory broke through his confusion, and he sank his head onto his palms. "God," he whispered, his voice faint in the cold cell, "I am terrified, more than I have ever been in my life. I do not know what to do. There is nothing I *can* do. So if you're real, will You do something? In the name of Jesus, amen."

An almost tangible *something* encompassed him, breaking the grip of the vise around his chest. He swallowed, waiting for the pain to return.

It didn't.

"O Lord," he breathed with new reverence, "You *are* real, and You care. I—" A sharp lump swelled in his throat, and he swallowed again.

Able to breathe once more, Phillip flopped back on his bed. God was here in this dreadful place. And He had helped him even though Phillip cared nothing for Him. Another verse from the Psalms invaded his head.

If I ascend into heaven, You are there. If I make my bed in hell, behold, You are there.

This was as close to hell as Phillip cared to get.

How had he gotten here anyway? By flouting Father's request. 'Twasn't such an unreasonable demand—merely meet his cousin. Phillip had played the fool with unmatched skill.

Mother would have been horrified. And Father. Tears stung Phillip's eyes. If Father's countenance could be trusted, he had been devastated. Phillip closed his eyes and tears spilled down his cheeks. He brushed them away, and more came.

What kind of man had he become, to land himself in such a place?

With a groan, Phillip rolled over and buried his face in his arms. "O God!" His voice caught in his throat. "I am so sorry. I resisted You, hated You, because You took my mother and I thought You did not care. Can You forgive me?"

If we confess our sin, He is faithful and just to forgive us our sin and to cleanse us from all unrighteousness.

"Lord, I have been rebellious toward both You and my father. I have been selfish, proud, arrogant. I am sorry, desperately sorry." His shoulders heaved. "Please forgive me," he whispered, "for the sake of Jesus Christ."

For I will be merciful to their unrighteousness, and their sins and their lawless deeds I will remember no more.

Phillip drew several long, shaky breaths. Never had he been so grateful for all the Scripture Mother drilled into his mind. "Thank you, Lord, for Your mercy. I am Yours now, and I will do whatever You want me to do, no matter what happens." It promised to be a long, hard fight in this place. "Keep me, Lord, for You."

Phillip rolled to his back and wiped his eyes. What other Scripture could he recall?

For you did not receive the spirit of bondage again to fear, but you received the Spirit of adoption by whom we cry out, "Abba, Father." The Spirit Himself bears witness with our spirit that we are children of God, and if children, then heirs—heirs of God and joint heirs with Christ, if indeed we suffer with Him, that we may also be glorified together.

Well, if he stayed here much longer, he'd have ample opportunity to suffer with Christ. But God was his Father, and no one could snatch him out of God's care. Tears sprang into Phillip's eyes again. This time he smiled.

The heaviness, the terror had been replaced with deep joy, unbelievable peace, and, yes, hope. Even in this place. He felt *free*. Nothing could touch him, not the darkness of the dungeon, nor the guilt of his past behavior.

Lady Melankardja wouldn't be overjoyed when she found out about this. But it didn't matter. Phillip was content with no observable reason to be so.

He laughed aloud. "O Lord God, thank You."

32

Questions

DIERK SPUN A BLADE of grass between his thumb and forefinger as he eyed his father. In truth, Father had never told the story that way before. "Did you ever figure out where the fear came from?"

"Of course. 'Twas demonic."

What had Sir Burckhardt said this morning? Something about the devil using fear often. "What did Lady Melankardja do when she found out?"

Father smiled an odd smile. "She raged. Mocked me. Called my salvation an illusion. Declared it useless. And then had her men beat me to prove her point. I did not attempt to fight when five of them attacked at once. Melankardja said the beating would end if I renounced Christ, yet all I could think of was the honor to suffer for the Lord."

Dierk started. "What?"

Father chuckled. "The first joy of a new believer defies reason."

"Did it last?"

Father tipped his head back against the guardhouse. "The Lord renewed it. But the following day proved much harder. She tried witchcraft on me."

Coldness skittered up Dierk's spine.

"She took me into that room Fredrik pointed out to you. It had shelves with human and animal skulls and I know not what else. She chanted curses and prayed to Satan. She killed a chicken." Father glanced at him. "She even—"

Dierk leaned forward, frowning at the hesitation. "Tell me, Father."

Father drew a long breath, and his voice grew quiet. "She had two men hold me down and forced me to drink blood."

Dierk recoiled, his stomach twisting. "Why?"

"She wanted to control me, so she tried every demonic rite she could." Father met Dierk's gaze and held it. "The power of Satan is not to be scorned, but God's power makes Satan's weak." A slight smile touched Father's eyes. "I prayed as I never knew a person could pray. 'Twas like learning to swim in a wind-whipped lake, but God kept me from sinking."

What could a person say to that?

"She left me alone for a few days then, but the demons did not." Father rubbed the back of his neck. "So I kept praying."

Dierk twisted the grass blade through his fingers until it broke in two. "I guess I thought most of your ordeal was physical."

"'Twas a large part of it. She beat me and starved me, but I had to fight discouragement and fear the hardest."

Much as he'd wanted to hear this story, Dierk didn't care to linger over-long. His insides were tensing too much. But he had one more question. "When did you meet Fredrik?"

"About two weeks after my arrival." Father sighed. "He gave me my first lashing."

Fredrik? *Lashing* Father? Great thunder. Why, everyone at Sunland Castle knew the Chief of Palace Guard was the King's closest friend. And Father had sent the Crown Prince traipsing around the country with Fredrik alone for escort.

"'Tis a skill he does not exhibit these days, but he can lay a whip lash exactly where he wants it. They tied me to a pillory, and he lit my back on fire."

Dierk's muscles tensed at the image Father's words painted.

With a grunt, Father pushed to his feet. "Let's walk. I need to clear my head. Besides, it tires a certain member of the body to sit too long." He smiled. "How are you, Niklas?"

Dierk turned toward the boy. He'd forgotten his presence.

Niklas's round eyes all but engulfed his face. "F-fine, Your Majesty."

Dierk stood and gave Niklas a hand up. A hundred questions he didn't know how to ask tangled in his mind.

Foremost, what would happen if he found himself in a situation so physically and mentally demanding? Would he crack under the pressure? Because if prayer was required to survive ... Well, Dierk was sorely out of practice.

Father was right: they needed to walk.

DIERK BROUGHT THE AXE down, dividing a log with a crash. The wood's piney scent, as familiar now as the smell of a hearth-fire, spiced the air. While Father continued his walk around the clearing's perimeter, it hadn't taken long for the woodpile to call to Dierk. He needed the physical exertion.

Niklas picked up the fallen pieces and laid them on the stack.

As he watched Niklas work, a half-smile pulled at Dierk's mouth. "Might want to turn that piece over." Fredrik must have rubbed off on him.

"This one?" Niklas rotated the one under his right hand. It fit, snug, into the pieces beneath it.

Dierk gave a nod as he positioned his next log. "Aye."

"Kik, what's going to happen to me?"

Axe poised mid-air, Dierk looked up. "What do you mean?"

Niklas shifted his gaze to his feet. "After you catch my uncle. Will I stay a prisoner?"

"I doubt it, unless you prove refractory." Dierk slammed the axe into the wood and yanked it free for another stroke. "Father will arrange something. Have you any other relatives?"

"No." Niklas tucked another piece into the stack.

Thwack! Maybe the Sisters would take him. Gertrude would like that.

"What if they never catch my uncle?"

"I don't know." Dierk gave up work and propped one foot on the chopping block, resting his axe atop his other boot. "But with the information you gave us, I'm near-certain we'll catch him. The Royal League rarely fails."

Niklas looked away. "Wish I could join the League."

Dierk shrugged. "Who says you can't?"

"Really?" Even Dierk couldn't mistake the hopefulness in

Niklas's face. Which quickly died. "But after I spied like this."

Dierk straightened and planted his feet for another swing. "I have a feeling Father could overlook it if you met his main requirement."

"What's that?"

Crash! The log split apart. "'Tis a secret." So secret even Dierk didn't know it. Though he'd never admit that.

"I didn't know His Majesty was a prisoner of Lady Melankardja in his youth."

Dierk gritted his teeth. Of course Niklas had to bring up that subject. He'd rather let it rest a while. "I thought the whole country had heard of it."

"Not me. How did he get away?"

"You might get to hear if you stick around." He forced a smile. "Come on. Let's see how much we can accomplish before Father's ready to tell the next part."

THE RING OF AN axe greeted Fredrik as he strode toward the inner clearing. Must be a break in the story-telling. He emerged from the thicket to see Phil a few yards to his right.

Phil's pace quickened. "Anything new, Fredrik?"

"Nothing. No sign of the boy's uncle, nor of aught else amiss." Fredrik spun the smooth spear-shaft between his hands. "How goes it with you, Phil?"

Phil let out a heavy sigh. "Pray for me. It has been years since I remembered some of this."

"Aye." Fredrik understood. He'd guarded these paths when he served Lady Melankardja, and walking along them today summoned memories he'd tried to keep dead ever since.

Phil ran his hand through his hair. "Deciding what to tell and what to omit is delicate business. Also, I have no wish to lecture him."

Fredrik clapped Phil's shoulder. His turn had come to encourage Phil for a change. "With God's help, you can do this, my brother. My prayers are with you."

Phil nodded. "I thank you."

"How's Niklas doing?"

"Seems fine. He and Dierk are chopping wood at the moment."

Fredrik smiled, trying to lighten Phil's despondent mood. "So I guessed, by the sound of it. You should try it. Do you a world of good."

Phil laughed as if against his will. "Perhaps I shall."

GASPS OF LAUGHTER BURST from Dierk's chest. He bent double, hands braced on his knees.

Father looked up with a mock-scowl. "Impertinent lad. What am I doing wrong?"

Dierk shook his head, barely able to speak. "I don't know." He couldn't explain things like Fredrik. All he knew was the knights would need a new chopping block by the time Father learned to swing an axe straight. The blade kept bouncing off the target, sending some awkward chip of wood flying.

Father raised the tool over his shoulder again.

"Keep your feet apart," Dierk reminded him. Fredrik was particular about that. No need for a gashed leg if you missed the wood altogether. "And stand farther back."

Father followed his directions.

"Grip the shaft with both hands and don't let your wrist get loose."

Father checked his grip with careful attention.

Dierk couldn't resist. "Now rub your nose three times and swing."

Father glared.

Dierk shouted with laughter. This was more fun than winning a sword fight. "Come on. Swing it."

With a deep breath, Father swung. The blade bit straight into the center of the log, driving halfway down.

"Hurrah!" Dierk punched the air. "Only your fortieth try."

"And on that successful stroke, I believe I shall withdraw." Father left the axe stuck in the wood and brushed his palms together. "Ready to continue the story?"

Dierk sobered. "Aye."

"Sir Georg said there's bread and cheese in the guardhouse. Let us take our midday meal early, so we need not interrupt the story again."

33

Fredrik

PHILLIP WOKE TO THE bolt scraping back. At once, he sat up and rubbed his eyes. Ever since a guard had roused him with a bucketful of water in the face, he tried to stay aware of their movements. He shot a glance at the skylight. Still pretty dim.

The door swung open, and the guard named Fredrik set down the usual brom bread and water. A dish of meat this morning too, or what passed for meat. Bits of gristle and mushy stuff that used to gag him. Hunger had long since conquered his revulsion.

Fredrik straightened and swept back the hair that had fallen over his forehead. "I thought to inform you: you'll get some exercise this afternoon."

Phillip's stomach twisted. That meant a beating. "Thanks for the warning. Will you be directing it?" Not that it mattered. A beating was a beating.

"No, not I."

At least his back wouldn't burn with bleeding lash-strokes. "Well, thanks for breakfast."

A frown creased Fredrik's face. "How do you stand it? Why don't you give up?"

Phillip narrowed his eyes. Fredrik never taunted him. He delivered lashings in stone-faced silence and rarely spoke otherwise. So whence came this question? If Phillip answered, what would happen?

Fredrik shrugged and started to turn away.

"'I can do all things through Christ who strengthens me.'" Phillip's voice surprised his own ears. "And 'I consider that the sufferings of this present time are not worthy to be compared with the glory which shall be revealed in me.'"

Fredrik breathed a bitter laugh. "You're lucky to have such strong faith."

It was Phillip's turn to frown. "What makes you say that?"

Crossing his arms, Fredrik cocked his head. "Once upon a time I was you."

"I don't understand."

Fredrik leaned his shoulder against the doorjamb. "I was thirteen when I became a believer, and—"

"What?" He must have misheard.

"Strange, isn't it?" Fredrik stared at the skylight as he spoke. "Maybe I was never a true Christian at all. I thought I was. A friend of mine had connections to Lady Melankardja. Didn't know it at the time. One day I went out to fell trees, and three men kidnapped me."

Three men in the woods. An eerie similarity to Phillip's story. "How old were you?"

Fredrik gave him the briefest glance. "Your age. They brought me here, and Lady Melankardja tortured me as bad as she does you. The difference is you've been here eight weeks. I lasted only three." His voice grew softer. "I couldn't sense God. I couldn't stand the pain, the oppression, the fear. I had to get the demons off my back. So I caved. Threw away my faith and recanted. God!" Passion speared his voice. "What I wouldn't give to go back."

From all appearances, Fredrik had forgotten his audience.

Phillip broke the pause. "I think you could."

Fredrik looked at him, his eyes haughty. "Go back? No, you don't understand." He returned his attention to the hint of light in the corner. "I don't know if you believe in spells, but I do. Not turn you into a toad or something, but change you. Since I joined Her Ladyship, I've committed every sin in the book, from drunkenness to fornication to murder. Things I never thought myself capable of. 'Tis easier to live for Satan—less fighting yourself—but I've found no real reward."

He gave Phillip a sideways look. "Don't know why I'm telling you this except maybe to warn you. You make me think of what I could have had if I hadn't been so weak. I almost wish—" He stopped.

Phillip waited a moment. "What do you wish?"

Fredrik sighed. "Sometimes I wish she'd just kill you so I wouldn't have to see you all the time. Be better for you anyway."

Phillip blinked. How could a person reply to that?

Fredrik straightened. "Keep your faith, kid. My life's no better than yours. I've been both places." He turned to go.

"Fredrik." Phillip stood and limped on a sprained knee

toward the door. He couldn't let Fredrik walk away after sharing such a tale, but he hardly knew what to say. "How old are you?"

Fredrik turned back, an ironic smile twisting half his mouth. "Twenty-two."

Barely older than him. Phillip extended his hand. After a moment, Fredrik clasped his forearm.

Phillip finally found words. "I'll pray for you."

"Thanks. 'Twill do no good, but 'twill be nice to think of the Prince of Sunset taking my name before the King of Heaven." He clapped Phillip's shoulder. "I'll try to bring some liniment tonight." He strode out and bolted the door.

Phillip gulped down his breakfast as fast as possible so it might have time to digest before they gave him his "exercise."

So ... Fredrik had not set out to join Lady Melankardja.

Or had he? Could Fredrik's story, told with such conviction, actually be a lie, some trick to infiltrate his guard and defeat him? Her Ladyship was clever enough to devise such a scheme.

But no. Fredrik was too blunt for subtlety. And he'd always been different from the other guards. Not like Meine, for instance, who exuded the same cruelty as Her Ladyship.

And if Fredrik wanted to return to the Lord, surely the Holy Spirit was drawing him. If God could show mercy to Phillip, He could show mercy to Fredrik. Phillip bowed his head to pray.

PHILLIP'S WHOLE BODY screamed for relief, and he couldn't prevent the tears from leaking out. Facedown on his straw-pile, he focused on drawing gentle breaths. His back burned and throbbed. His abdomen ached with the blows he'd received.

And his mind kept repeating the men's chant as they beat him. *"Your faith is useless. Your God is powerless. You can never withstand. Give up! Give up! Give up! Your faith—"*

He would not believe them. He could do all things through Christ.

This is the victory that has overcome the world—our faith ...

The Lord reigns, He is clothed with majesty. God is our refuge ... we will not fear.

Take up the whole armor of God, that you may be able to withstand in the evil day.

I will not give up. I will cling to Christ. I will not give up.

He. Would. Not. Give. Up.

THE BOLT SLID BACK, and Phillip opened his eyes. Orange torchlight from the hall splashed into the cell. Phillip slid his stiff arms forward to push himself up.

"Don't rise."

At Fredrik's voice, Phillip sank back into his half-rotten straw. A different guard would have kicked him for lying down, but not Fredrik. Thank God Fredrik had come tonight. At least Phillip need not sit up and risk fainting from the pain when he moved.

Near the door, something thumped on the stone floor. Footsteps drew near, and Fredrik knelt beside Phillip. "Came as soon as I could. 'Twould bode ill for both of us if someone suspected—" He broke into a low whistle as he pulled the cloak from Phillip's back, exposing the welts and ripping off scabs. "The rods today, was it?"

"Aye." The cold air stung his bruised flesh. "At least not all the stripes bled." No more than half, based on the amount of blood crusted on his skin and on the straw around him.

Fredrik didn't answer. He touched Phillip's back, and Phillip jumped.

"Easy. 'Tis only water on a rag."

Phillip focused on breathing again. After a minute, the coolness soaked into the stripes, soothing them. "Good of you to do this." He craned his neck to see Fredrik's face. "What if someone finds out?"

"No one will find out." Fredrik scowled down at his work. After he finished washing, he pulled a small clay flask from inside his tunic. "This will hurt, but it should help." He poured some of the liquid into his hand.

Phillip braced himself for the pain. Fredrik's hand touched him a second before fire hit his shoulder blade. Phillip sucked air through his teeth.

"Sorry, Phil," Fredrik murmured.

Phillip barked a laugh. "Phil, is it?"

"Oh, I beg your pardon, *Your Highness*."

"Don't stand on ceremony," Phillip said through a tense jaw. "Nicknaming the Prince—isn't fashionable around the palace. But I don't mind."

Fredrik chuckled. "'Twas an accident. I nickname all my friends."

Phillip smiled, and breathed long, in and out. He had a friend. Here in the horror of Lady Melankardja's dungeon. God was good.

Fredrik poured more liniment into his hand. "How's it feel?"

"Burns like fury, but feels good in a painful sort of way."

Nodding, Fredrik continued to massage the bruised muscles. Who would have thought a servant of Lady Melankardja could be so kind?

They fell silent, and it seemed a pity to waste his first friendly human interaction in two months. "Fredrik, could you talk to me? I get tired of my own voice." He clenched his teeth until another stab of pain passed. "And this place is painfully eerie."

"I can tell you why that is." Fredrik refilled his palm and set down the flask with a *clink*. "'Tis overrun with demons."

The perfect topic to put a person at ease. But Phillip wouldn't complain. "Indeed?"

"Infested with them. I see them once in a while."

"See them?" Thank the Lord he'd never *seen* one of them.

"They're dark and hideous." Fredrik cringed. "Some of them look like birds of prey. 'Tis the most frightening thing I've ever seen, but I think Her Ladyship arranges for us to see them now and then, in case we harbor thoughts of insubordination."

Phillip's scalp prickled like a target full of arrows. "You certainly have a talent for hair-raising conversation."

"'Tisn't near as bad in here. I know you hate your cell, but for me 'tis a respite." Fredrik cocked his chin toward the door. "Out there, demons swarm over everything."

Phillip frowned. "But not so in my cell?" Some days the spiritual darkness almost crushed him, yet Fredrik called this chamber a respite?

Fredrik glanced around as if he expected to spot an evil spirit somewhere. "They're here, but they hide in the corners, I think. They can only get so close to you most of the time because your light drives them back a little."

He'd hate to be at their mercy without Jesus' light. 'Twas bad enough with it. "That is some comfort, I guess."

"It should be. Never forget, no matter what you feel, God is stronger than the devil."

Phillip gazed up at his lecturer. "Then why on earth don't you quit working for Lady Melankardja?"

"I told you this morning." Fredrik corked the flask. "I turned my back on Jesus."

"But don't you want to come back?"

"Aye, but 'tis too late." He wiped his hands on the rag. "Try to keep off your back for a couple days, but exercise some tomorrow. Her Ladyship said you could have an apple—can't have you too weak to entertain her during your torture." Fredrik scowled. "Anyway, 'tis a choice piece of fruit. Picked it out myself."

Phillip had to roll on his side a little to meet Fredrik's gaze. "Thank you for being kind to me."

Fredrik shrugged. "I like to think if someone had done this for me, maybe I'd still be on the right path." He stood, stowing the liniment in his tunic. "Hope you sleep well."

"You, too, Fredrik."

The door clanged shut, and the bolt grated into place. "Good-night, *Phil*." The whisper floated through the grating.

Despite his pain, Phillip smiled. *Thank You, Lord, for Fredrik. Please let him know he can come back to You.*

34

Shielded

THE COLD STONE OF the torture-room floor dug into Phillip's bare back, still tender from the rods last week. It galled him to lie there, stripped to the waist, arms pinned above his head, a guard sitting on his legs. But if he fought, they'd strike him, and he didn't need another blow. Not with what was coming.

In the corner, a man stoked a small forge with a powerful *whoosh* of the bellows. The man turned and stalked toward him, an iron rod in his hand. The tip glowed orange in the dim room. Lady Melankardja's soft, cruel laughter mingled with the hazy air, and Phillip writhed. His guards grinned.

God, help me please. I'm Yours. Jesus, help me.

The man with the rod sneered down at him. "Recant, Your Highness?"

Phillip closed his eyes. "No."

The man laughed, and Phillip braced himself.

Hot iron seared his chest. A scream built in his throat until he could hold it no longer. It tore free and echoed against the stone walls.

THE CELL DOOR CREAKED open, and Phillip turned his head to look. A smile pulled at his split lip. "Fredrik." He sat up, and pain stabbed in the five burns on his chest and abdomen. He inhaled with a hiss.

"Lie down." Fredrik scowled. "Brought some salve for those burns." He deposited the bread and water by the door and came forward. "This stuff has a strong smell. You just pray no one catches it." He pulled a small crock from inside his tunic.

Phillip held up a hand. "You should not risk it. You'll get punished worse than I if they find out."

"*I* don't care. Lie down. I haven't got all evening."

Phillip obeyed, and Fredrik knelt on one knee beside him. He dug some brownish salve from the jar and smeared it on the top burn.

The touch chafed the wound to flaming agony again, but then the salve's coolness soaked into his flesh. As the pungent odor filled his nostrils, Phillip tried to smile. "It is quite strong."

"Let's hope it helps." With a half-smile, Fredrik moved on to the next wound.

Phillip gritted his teeth at the fresh wave of pain, waiting for the slight relief. "Fredrik, why doesn't she kill me?"

Fredrik met his gaze for a moment. "'Tis my opinion she's a bit intimidated."

"By what?" Phillip breathed a jerky laugh. "My incomparable defense skills?"

"By the fact you became a believer while in her dungeon. That's never happened before. She's had Christians who wouldn't cave and she killed them. She's had Christians who caved, like me. And she's had non-believers who just needed a little *persuasion*. Never had a non-believer who converted." Fredrik gently spread salve over the last wound. "I think she wants to prove to herself that your faith isn't real. That she can make you admit defeat."

"I see." At least his life testified to the power of God even in this place. But part of him wished he could die and get it over with. He had no other hope of escape.

"Well, there you are." Fredrik capped the salve. "I dared not bring bandages. Someone might see them."

"Of course. Thank you for this." Phillip glanced down at his throbbing wounds. "I'll try to keep them clean." Which would be a near-miracle in this place.

Fredrik stood. "And don't get your tunic stuck to them."

"I won't." Which promised a cold night. The dungeon stayed cool even in the daytime.

As Fredrik walked to the door, Phillip remembered something. "Fredrik?"

"Aye?"

"Is my cousin Zorena dead? Lady Melankardja said she was when I first came."

Fredrik snorted. "Princess Zorena isn't even a little sickly from what we've heard. Her Ladyship is furious."

"Ah." Good to know. Not that he'd ever have a chance to wed Zorena. But after this ordeal, he'd marry his betrothed tomorrow, and make her a good husband, if it meant freedom from this dungeon. Notwithstanding his attraction to the pretty peasant girl. "Thank you, again, Fredrik."

"Don't mention it. Good-night, Phil."

TWO WEEKS LATER, PHILLIP sprawled in the middle of his cell where the guards had thrown him. Blood oozed from his nose and a cut on his cheek. His entire body throbbed with pain from the blows.

He couldn't drag himself to his pile of straw. Couldn't even lift his head. Later. He would move later.

Phillip blinked. How long had he lain here? He gently reached up and touched his cheek. Long enough for the blood on his face to dry. Biting back a groan, he pushed himself to his knees and glanced at the skylight. A few hours had passed. Too bad Fredrik hadn't come. 'Twould be nice to see his friend's face and show him how the burns were healing. But Fredrik hadn't visited in a fortnight.

Phillip crawled to the door and found the usual water bucket. He took a long drink and washed the blood from his face. He wasn't hungry—at all—but he forced down the hard bread and unappetizing pottage.

At last he dragged himself to his pallet and shifted until he found a position that hurt less than the others. Closing the eye that wasn't swollen shut, he whispered, "Lord, I'm not complaining. You have done so much for me, and I am Yours, come what may. But I do not think my body can take much more of this."

PHILLIP HAD BEEN AWAKE for about half an hour, praying, when the bolt slid back. He waited to see which guard would enter. The door swung in, and familiar tawny hair poked through the opening.

"Fredrik." Phillip struggled to stand and greet his friend. "I haven't seen you in three weeks."

"Aye, been laid up with a fever. Just started improving last week." Fredrik set down his burdens by the door.

"You do look thinner." Although compared to Phillip's emaciated frame, Fredrik was a paragon of health. "How are you?"

"I've recovered enough strength that they let me deliver your breakfast alone."

Phillip rolled his eyes. "As if I'm any threat to a grasshopper."

Fredrik's gaze met his. "How are you faring, Phil?"

Phillip couldn't summon even half a smile. "I'm still breathing, no thanks to Her Ladyship."

"I thought so." Fredrik glanced toward the door, shuffling his feet. "Can we talk a little?"

"'Twould be a pleasure." Phillip spread his cloak over the pile of filthy straw and took a seat. "Sit down if you can stand the dirt."

Fredrik did. "We'll have to hurry."

"What's on your mind?"

Fredrik drew a long breath. "When I was sick, I had awful dreams—darkness, demons, fire. I couldn't get away. I was terrified I'd die and go to hell. Tell me why you think I could come back to God."

Phillip had prayed for such an opportunity. *O Lord, give*

me Your wisdom. "Fredrik, the mercy of the Lord endures forever. And 'whoever calls on the name of the Lord shall be saved.'"

"But there's a passage in Hebrews, I think, that says if someone has tasted the heavenly gift and turns away, it is impossible for him to return and be forgiven. And if a man sins willingly, he cannot be forgiven because he crucifies again the Son of God and puts Him to an open shame. At least, that's how I remember it."

Phillip blinked. He hadn't expected that. Fredrik must have paid attention in church years ago. "But you said you didn't want to give up. You felt helpless."

"I did it with my eyes open." Fredrik picked up a stray straw and pinched off a tiny piece.

Phillip laced his fingers, thinking hard. "Don't dwell on the obscure passages at the moment. Look at Peter, Jesus' disciple. Peter denied his Master publicly when he was under pressure. But he repented, and Jesus forgave him."

"But Peter was ... he was—"

"No different from you, except he didn't go and serve the devil."

"'Tis a huge difference." Fredrik scowled and tossed the straw across the cell. "Besides, I enjoyed sinning at first."

"Do you now?" Phillip asked.

"No."

"Then think about this. Jesus once told his disciples that if their brother sinned against them *seven times in a day*, and seven times in a day came to them saying, 'I repent,' they must forgive their brother. Do you think God would ask more from His servants than He would do himself?"

Fredrik let out a heavy sigh. "No."

Phillip smiled a little. "Neither do I."

"But I sinned more than seven times."

Once again, Fredrik had missed the point. Frustration rose in Phillip, until a glance at Fredrik's tormented countenance smothered it. "My friend, the number matters not. In another place, Jesus instructed us to forgive seventy-times-seven offenses. Remember?"

Fredrik nodded, dragging his hands down his face. "I want to believe. I just can't."

"Think about the prodigal son. He left his father and sinned *deliberately* for years, but his father received him home again. Fredrik, you are the son, and God is your Father. He longs for you to come home."

Phillip laid his hand on Fredrik's shoulder, but could think of nothing more to convince him. He bowed his head. "Holy Father, I bring You my friend, one of Your prodigal sons. He has come to himself. He wants to believe; help his unbelief. Convince him, Lord, that You have no pleasure in the death of one who dies. Therefore, he may turn and live."

With a sudden gasp, Fredrik spoke, praying. His words came fast, his sentences disjointed. He poured out his shame and fear and begged for another chance.

Phillip prayed in silence as the presence of the Holy Spirit surrounded them. He found himself praying in a language he did not understand.

Fredrik slipped from under his hand, and Phillip looked up to see his friend on his knees in the filthy cell, hands lifted, head bowed, tears streaming down his face.

Thank You, Lord. Thank You, thank You!

Fredrik turned and grabbed Phillip's arm. "You were right. He could save me. He did." The joy shining in his face almost blinded Phillip. "I haven't felt like this *ever*, Phil. I think I could fly."

With his free hand, Phillip pulled Fredrik into a hearty embrace. "Welcome home, brother."

As they sat back, Fredrik rubbed the nape of his neck. "Lady Melankardja will notice as soon as she sees me, you know."

"Of course." No way could someone so dark miss something as bright as a new believer.

"She will kill me," Fredrik said, his voice matter-of-fact.

"Perhaps. But she'll probably kill me for causing so much trouble. She can't have Christianity infecting her other men, can she?" Phillip grinned.

Fredrik offered a wry smile. "Aye."

Quiet returned.

"We could try to run away."

Phillip's heart jumped with excitement, despite the fact he knew 'twas useless. "I thought she had the place well-guarded."

"Aye, but we might as well die trying to get away as not."

"Why don't you run, Fredrik? You could bring back help."

"No, Her Ladyship might kill you when she found me gone tomorrow."

Lady Melankardja must keep a close eye on her men. "At least one of us would escape."

"I escape without you?" Fredrik glared. "Fine way of showing gratitude. Besides, you're the Prince. I ought to try to get you out of here." He scratched his jaw. "We could switch clothes, but I'm a little taller than you and my hair's lighter. Think you could pull it off?"

"And leave you to face Lady Melankardja's wrath?" Phillip took his turn glaring. "Fine way of showing gratitude."

Fredrik sighed. "There must be something we can do."

"Let's pray." Phillip placed his hand on Fredrik's shoulder again. "Lord God, You know our circumstances, and You see what we need to do. Should we stay, or should we try to go?"

In the quiet after he stopped, the answer came.

"Did you say something?" Fredrik demanded.

"No, why?"

"I heard something, as clear as if you said it."

"What was it?"

"'Fear not, for I will go before you.'"

The hair on Phillip's arms stood up, and he smiled. "That is what I heard, too."

"You ... you're not serious." Fredrik's eyes were wide.

"I would not jest on such a matter."

"Then what are we waiting for?" Fredrik stood and gave Phillip a hand up.

Phillip wrapped his filthy cloak around his shoulders.

Fredrik handed him the bread he'd brought for Phillip's breakfast. "You can eat this on the road." He looked up the hall. "Clear so far." He bolted the cell door behind them, and they crept toward the staircase.

Fredrik climbed the stone steps first. Phillip waited below, his heart pounding like the hooves of a steed in the jousts. Fredrik waved a hand, and Phillip ascended.

In the alcove of the landing, two guards slumped on the floor, a dicebox between them. They were sound asleep.

"So that's what they do all day," Phillip whispered.

"Play dice, not sleep." Fredrik eyed him. "Wait until I see if the hut is empty."

Phillip waited at the convergence of the three stairways, one leading up, two leading down, in plain view of the unusually negligent guards. What if one of them awoke? Or what if someone came up from the side of the fortress he'd never seen? He reached for the wall to steady himself. A fine time to get dizzy.

"Come."

At Fredrik's whisper, Phillip climbed the steps, careful to make no sound. His leg muscles quivered in protest, but he hadn't time to heed them.

By the time he reached the top, Fredrik had selected a sword from the weapons in the room and tied it to his belt. "You want one?"

He did, but ... "I think I'd be too weak to use it."

"A dagger, then?"

"Aye." Better than nothing.

Fredrik handed him a dagger with a span-long blade, and Phillip tied the sheath-thongs to his belt.

Fredrik grasped the door handle. "Here's the real risk. You hide behind the door. I'll send one of the guards down on a pretense, and then try to overpower the other. You slip out and run. I'll follow as soon as I can."

Run blind through that maze? But he had no better idea. And truth be told, he was near to bursting with excitement. "God goes before us, remember."

With a smile, Fredrik pulled open the door, letting in a blast of icy air.

Phillip shivered and fisted his hands against the cold. Winter had set in with a vengeance during his imprisonment. Flat against the wall behind the door, he waited for one of the guards to come in.

Silence.

What was going on?

Fredrik's hand appeared around the door and motioned him out.

Sudden terror struck Phillip. His stomach knotted, his pulse pounded through his head, and clammy sweat moistened his palms.

Nonsense! He could trust Fredrik. And he could trust God. Drawing a long breath, Phillip crossed the threshold and shut the door behind him. Two guards flanked him, yet neither turned to look at him. Their gazes drifted over the clearing, not even pausing on Fredrik, who stood but three paces away.

Fredrik tipped his head to gesture Phillip on. They left footprints in the shallow snow, and soon the thicket enclosed them. In silence they walked on until Fredrik stopped and looked back.

"If this is a dream, 'tis the best I've ever had."

Phillip smiled. "'Tis no dream, Fredrik." But 'twas no ordinary occurrence, either. When God said He would go before them, Phillip hadn't dared to hope for such a miracle. He gazed about him at the falling snowflakes, snow-crusted tree limbs, and heavy green-and-white boughs of spruce and fir. He filled his lungs with the frosty air. Could anything be more beautiful?

Fredrik turned toward him. "You all right?"

"I'm *fine.*" Despite the trembling inside his body, Phillip hadn't felt so well since the day he surrendered to Christ.

Fredrik rested his hand on his sword hilt. "There will be a few guards in the thicket, but I think we can avoid them."

Phillip nodded. "Lead on."

Fredrik walked fast, but Phillip kept up with no difficulty. Must be joy that stoked his flagging strength. And the pace warmed his blood. When they had left the dense thicket behind, Fredrik paused again. "Let's kneel and pray. I must thank God for bringing us this far."

Phillip couldn't agree more.

35

Allies or Enemies

DIERK BARELY BREATHED WHEN Father paused. The story had never engrossed him so strongly before, and he wanted nothing to break Father's momentum. They had a confrontation with Lady Melankardja still to come, if Dierk's memory served him.

Perhaps such eagerness was beneath him, a squire of seventeen years. But didn't minstrels entertain nobility with their sagas? And those tales were no more than half true. Father had lived this story.

Father drew a deep breath, but still did not speak.

"Well." Dierk kept his voice low. "Go on."

Father sighed as he curled one leg under him. "I cannot."

Break off the story at such a moment? "Why not?"

"I am too weary." Father braced his hand on the grass and stood. "Perhaps I can finish tomorrow, but I cannot tell any more today. Not as it should be told."

Dierk stood as well, holding back a sigh. Childish to be so disappointed, of course. "I suppose 'tis as good a place as any to pause."

A wan smile curved Father's mouth. "But before we find some work to do, I need to show you my scars." He started unbuckling his belt.

Dierk glanced at Niklas standing beside him. His gut told him he was about to get some practice with hiding embarrassment. Why did he, the Crown Prince, have to have such an unconventional father?

Father's brown woolen jerkin landed on the grass beside his belt. Then he peeled off the tan long-sleeved shirt beneath.

Five purplish pink spots marred the pale skin of Father's chest and abdomen. Two were small knobs, like the bumps on an unhealthy tree. The other three spread wider, perhaps a handbreadth long, stretching and pinching the surrounding skin. Their surfaces bubbled like congealed porridge.

Father covered one of the spots with his palm. "Burns."

"Aye." Dierk swallowed. His gaze traveled to Father's shoulders. Licks of white scar tissue curled around the shoulders and even down the arms. No wonder Father always wore long sleeves.

Father turned slowly.

Dierk stepped back without meaning to. Did Father's back have any normal skin at all? Thick white ropes of scars wove all over the muscles. They wrapped around his ribs at the sides and disappeared under the waistband of his breeches.

And why did he need to see this?

Footsteps rustled the grass behind Dierk. He glanced back

to see which knight would be bowing himself away as fast as possible.

Fredrik stared at Father's back, his face carved into an expression of horror.

Father turned then. His eyes opened wide, and he yanked his shirt over his head.

Dierk grasped Niklas's arm and backed up until his shoulders touched the guardhouse. Father scrambled to don his jerkin and fasten his belt. Fredrik's face still resembled graven stone, including the grayish color.

Dierk glanced to his right. He and Niklas needed to get out of here. Slinking along the guardhouse wall would be least obtrusive.

"Phil." Fredrik's voice was hoarse. "What are you doing?"

"Showing them my scars." Father's tone was gentle, tentative, like a man calming a spooked horse.

"Warn me next time." Fredrik gasped as if he'd been punched in the gut. "I'll make myself scarce." He spun around and headed across the clearing.

Father strode after him without a glance for Dierk and Niklas.

Which suited Dierk fine. "Come, let's chop more wood." He pulled Niklas along beside him, stretching his stride.

"There isn't much more to split, Kik."

Pity. Dierk needed the distraction. Desperately.

"Why did His Majesty do that?"

"Show us his scars? How should I know?" Dierk marched Niklas around the corner of the guardhouse. Perhaps Father felt 'twould make the story stronger. Unforgettable. If so, it succeeded.

Always, from Dierk's earliest memory to the beginning of this journey, his father had epitomized strength. He was kind enough, but invincible. The scars cast him in a different light. Damaged. Hurt. Vulnerable.

Niklas stopped walking, and Dierk jerked to a stop.

He scowled. "What's amiss?"

Niklas crossed his arms. "Why did that knight act so ... strange?"

"Because he's Sir Fredrik, the same Fredrik who worked for Lady Melankardja. He gave Father some of those scars."

Niklas's frown morphed into wide-eyed surprise. "Oh."

"Exactly." Dierk released Niklas's arm and jabbed a thumb toward the woodpile. "Can we speak of something else while we work?"

"Aye." Niklas fell into step beside him.

Dierk wrestled the largest log he could find onto its end. Too tall for the chopping block and thick enough to require all Dierk's energy to split it. He'd prefer a sword fight, but this would be decent distraction.

DIERK ROLLED FROM HIS back to his side. Fredrik and a couple other knights snored, but he'd gotten used to that. He hadn't worked enough today. He had no exhaustion to force his mind to sleep. Aggravating.

"Kik?"

At Niklas's whisper, Dierk opened his eyes, though he could see nothing. "Aye?"

"I've been thinking about what your father told us."

Hadn't they both? "Me, too."

"How did Lady Melankardja get to be a witch?"

Dierk sighed. "No one knows. She wasn't a native Sunlander. I guess at some point she sold herself to Satan."

"What does that mean—sold herself to Satan?"

"Well." Great. He'd have to recall a long way back to explain this. "See, a person either serves God or serves Satan. There are only two sides. But some people choose to serve more ... devotedly, I guess. Lady Melankardja chose the wrong side and devoted all her life to it."

"Which side are you on?"

Dierk frowned, lifting his head from the pillow. "Which do you think?" He huffed. "Of course I'm not on Satan's side."

"Well, I think my uncle is." Niklas moved around, and the chain linking his ankle to a bedpost clanked under his blanket. "But I don't want to be. How do you join the other side?"

Ach. Where were the Sisters when you needed them? "Well, you confess your sin to God and turn away from it. He will forgive you because Jesus died to pay for your sin. And then you follow God's laws instead of Satan's or your own."

"Is that it?"

"That's it." As best he remembered. And he'd heard it enough times as a kid.

"So could I do it—right now?"

"Aye. You don't even have to pray out loud if you don't want to." *And please don't.* 'Twould be too embarrassing.

"All right. I'm gonna do it."

Dierk forced a smile into his voice. "Good for you." He rolled away from Niklas and punched his balled-up cloak that served as a pillow. Who was he to lead someone to Jesus? He wasn't a follower of Satan, not really, but he was no devoted servant of God.

In fact, he was pretty good at serving himself.

And he'd just told Niklas there were only two sides. Did that make him an unknowing servant of Satan?

No, a thousand times no! Was he? The harsh possibility galled Dierk's heart like someone grinding salt into an open wound.

Dierk believed Jesus was God's Son, the Savior of the world. He'd known that since childhood. He'd even been baptized into Sunland's Church four years ago.

Yet he had never done what he'd just told Niklas to do. Never renounced his own sin and selfishness. Never committed his entire life to Jesus Christ and His kingdom.

What a way to show gratitude to a God who died to save him from slavery to sin and Satan.

Lord, I'm sorry. When I was a kid, 'twas easy to say I wanted to obey You. To say I loved You. 'Tis different now. Don't know why. But I'm sick of playing at being a Christian. Please forgive me for counting Your sacrifice a light thing. If You'll take me, here I am. I'll fight for You and obey You. In Your strength, I'll quit putting myself first. I'll put You first. In the name of Christ I pray.

He squeezed his eyelids tight, and pressure built behind the bridge of his nose. He drew a long breath and discovered his throat had closed up. He swallowed. What if God wouldn't have him? After he'd known the truth so long and still not heeded it ...

For God is not willing that any should perish, but that all should come to repentance.

He couldn't remember the exact location, but the Bible said that somewhere. It must include him. The pain burning behind Dierk's breastbone eased.

"Kik?"

Dierk turned over again so his whisper would carry better. "Aye?"

"I did it." Even the quiet voice couldn't conceal Niklas's eagerness.

Dierk swallowed again. "Me, too."

"You, too? But I thought you said—"

"I know. But I had deceived myself. Now I am truly on God's side."

"Oh." Niklas's chain chattered a bit in the quiet. "Well, thanks for telling me how to do it."

"Don't mention it."

"Good-night, Kik."

"Good-night, brother." Dierk shut his eyes. He had much to set right tomorrow. But now he could sleep.

MORNING SUNLIGHT GLINTED OFF the dewdrops as Dierk leaned against the guardhouse, whittling a stick. Father was giving the knights last-minute instructions regarding messages and precautions. After Sir Georg had come back with one of the reinforcements yesterday evening, Father had decided to go to Sunset Castle and alert the League to Veit Nagel and his mischief before returning to Sun City.

Dierk shaved a curl of wood from the end of his stick. He must speak to Father privately before he left. He didn't want to, but he had to. There had been no time yet.

The knights saluted, and Father turned away.

Dierk sheathed his knife and stepped up beside him. "I'll

walk you a little way out."

Father smiled. "I wish I need not leave so soon. I had hoped to tell you the rest of the story myself. But Fredrik can handle it from here."

On Father's other side, Fredrik nodded.

"The plan is for you to travel with Fredrik back to Duke Ebner's. Unless I visit, we will not meet until your Christmas journey to Sunland Castle."

"Sounds good." Dierk picked a splinter of wood from his tunic. "I need to see how Bastian's arm is coming along." He didn't look up, but his peripheral vision told him Father was staring at him.

They entered the thicket, and Dierk trailed behind Father and Fredrik until they reached the first intersection of paths. Father turned. "God be with you, my son."

Dierk drew a deep breath of sweet morning air. Then he met Father's gaze. "Give Mother my love, and greet the children for me."

"I will." Father blinked a time or two, as if trying to mask surprise.

Well, now or never. "Father, I surrendered to Jesus last night. And ... I ask your forgiveness for my disrespectful and rebellious behavior these past years."

"Dierk." Father moved as if he would step forward, hands lifted slightly. But he never took the step.

Dierk shifted his weight from one foot to the other. Would Father embrace him? *Please don't.*

"Of course I forgive you."

Dierk called up a smile. "I thank you." Then he saluted as if he were one of the knights. "Godspeed, Father." He turned and ran.

His heart thudded when he halted before the entrance to the clearing. He'd done it. Now to demonstrate his sincerity by his behavior.

DIERK SETTLED HIS PACK straps on his shoulders and grabbed his axe. He glanced at Fredrik, who was still rolling his blanket. "I'll be in the barn, Fredrik." He opened the door from the knight's quarters and slipped into the stable's half of the building.

Thumps and scrapes led him to the far stall where he found Niklas clearing the muck. The lad was to stay at the fortress for now, until Father secured him an apprenticeship in Sun City.

Niklas held his pitchfork upright. "You leaving?"

"We'll head out soon."

The boy nodded. "Safe journey."

"Thanks." Dierk idly swung his axe in a circle. "You won't forget about last night, will you?"

"No." Niklas shook his head, jaw set. "Never, not even if my uncle gets me again."

"Good. He won't get you, by the way. You heard Father promise he'd see to that."

"Aye."

Dierk smiled. "I'll keep track of you. One day I expect to see you apply to join the League."

Niklas drove his pitchfork under the soiled straw again. "You really think they'd take me?"

"I think they would as long as you keep straight."

Niklas dumped his forkful in a barrow. "Look for me the

minute I turn nineteen."

"I will." Dierk held out his hand. "God be with you, Niklas."

Niklas grasped his forearm. "And with you, Prince Dierk." He grinned. "Overheard the knights say your real name."

Dierk grinned back. "Just so you don't blab it about."

As FREDRIK LED THE way out the thicket's eastern side, Dierk tried to note the paths' twists and crossings. 'Twould take a long time to memorize this place. Once out of the dense woods, Fredrik set a northeasterly course.

Dierk stepped over the burrow of some animal. Wouldn't want to sprain his ankle this close to the journey's end. "When will we reach the road?"

"Less than an hour, God willing." Fredrik glanced up through the trees. "Not the earliest start we've made, but we'll reach our destination by nightfall."

"Which is?"

"Moritzburg."

Moritzburg. "Isn't that one of the places Niklas said his uncle frequents?"

"Aye. If we see him, I'll drop my disguise to arrest him."

Dierk would relish the opportunity to see the snake conquered by the very man he'd impersonated. "I'll be right behind you. As your loyal squire, of course."

Fredrik winked and adjusted the pack strap on his right shoulder. "Meantime, shall I pick up the story where Phil left off?"

Dierk couldn't stop his smile at the nickname. "Aye.

Father stopped at a most interesting moment. You two had just escaped the maze."

Fredrik smiled, an odd sadness in his face. "That part of the tale I can handle."

36

Sword on the Snow

As he and Dierk walked away from Lady Melankardja's fortress, Fredrik's heart beat more easily. Twenty years had passed since he escaped, and still he shrank from remembering his two years there—two years on the brink of hell.

But the day God delivered him ... Fredrik allowed himself a smile. Many a night when shame crushed him, he called to mind that day and how God had led him since.

Aye, he would be glad to tell Dierk this part of the tale.

Moisture burned behind Fredrik's eyelids as Phil closed their prayer. Blinking it back, he rose and slapped snow from the knees of his breeches. He gave Phil a hand up. "The nearest village is about an hour and a half away, but I wouldn't feel safe stopping so close to Her Ladyship's fortress."

"Nor would I."

"The next town is maybe five hours away, longer if the snow gets deep." Fredrik eyed Phil. He'd need a miracle to walk so far after his imprisonment. "Or I know of another place, tiny, out of the way, three or four hours up a rough trail. What do you say?"

"I like the sound of that out-of-the-way place."

Fredrik frowned. His estimates stemmed from a healthy man's pace. "Are you sure you can make it?"

Phil looked him in the eye. "I am willing to try."

Well, 'twas a risk any way you looked at it. "Let's go."

The snow kept falling, and Fredrik thanked the Lord. 'Twould cover their tracks soon. They reached the road and followed it south, walking in the track of a wagon wheel. Phil ate the bread he'd brought from the dungeon. A poor breakfast for such exertion. Fredrik had had no time to snatch more food. *Lord, please give him strength.*

After a couple hours, Fredrik spotted the path he sought. Still looked like a seldom-used hunting trail. Good.

"You made no jest this place was obscure," Phil said, breaking a long silence.

"Aye. There may be twelve households." Fredrik tugged his round knitted cap further over his ears. "Ran across the place when I ran a secret mission for Her Ladyship. I think they call it Sweet-Air Glen. You'll like it."

"Snow's deepening," Phil commented after a moment.

"Aye." Fredrik rubbed his cold-numbed face as he eyed his friend. That threadbare cloak, riddled with holes from the dungeon's damp, could offer scant warmth. His calfskin boots weren't built for winter walking. And he looked as if a stiff wind could knock him flat. "You making out all right?"

"Not so bad." Phil coughed. "I wonder if they've missed us yet."

Fredrik didn't miss the swift change of topic. Phil was struggling. But neither of them could do anything about it. "They didn't plan on giving you any exercise today, and everyone will probably think I'm with someone else. They might not notice our departure until they take you supper."

"Supper. Ha. Something I won't miss." Phil gave a dry laugh, which turned into another cough. "I don't even want to know what happens to that stuff."

"'Tis certainly not what *she* eats."

The path sloped upward. As they gained altitude, the snow grew deeper. Fredrik walked ahead to break the path, and he kept his pace slower than normal. They had to make it before nightfall, but Phil could only go so fast.

At last Fredrik paused for a rest. He scooped a handful of clean snow and ate it. The icy fluff melted instantly, refreshing his dry mouth. "We've crested the ridge. Mostly downhill from here."

Phil nodded, breathing hard. "Good." A shiver shook his frame as he reached for a handful of snow.

Lord, help him make it. Fredrik's own body had reminded him of his not-too-distant illness, but it had to be ten times worse for Phil. He was too thin to combat this cold. A pity Fredrik hadn't been able to grab his own cloak before they left. Phil could have used the warmth.

Phil shivered again as he ate more snow.

"Don't eat too much. It can chill you from the inside out." Fredrik worked the hem of his woolen jerkin from under his belt and hauled the garment over his head.

"What are you doing?" Phil asked.

A wave of cold slapped Fredrik's chest, but he still had a linen undershirt and a thick woolen tunic, both long-sleeved. He'd survive. He held out the jerkin. "Put this on."

"No." Phil backed up a step. "You need it."

Stubborn man. "No, I don't." Fredrik reached for the ties of Phil's cloak. "My clothes are thicker." He got the cloak off and shoved the jerkin into Phil's hands. "Put this on, and let's get moving."

"Thank you." Phil broke into a cough as he slid his arms into the garment and pulled it over his head. "I shouldn't let you do this, but I'm too exhausted to argue."

Fredrik flung the cloak around Phil's shoulders again.

"You could at least wear the cloak, for what it's worth."

Fredrik knotted the ties at Phil's throat. "Quit arguing. You need its hood. What I need is to keep walking."

"If I live through this, I'll thank you properly, Fredrik."

If? The word hit like a blow to Fredrik's breastbone. Phil had to live. "You'll live." *Please, Lord God, let him make it.*

The long descent led toward a small valley. Noon had passed long ago when the path widened enough to be called a road. Fredrik halted for what seemed the hundredth time to let Phil catch his breath.

"Put your arm over my shoulder, Phil. 'Tisn't far now."

Phil complied. "I'm sorry."

"Nonsense." Fredrik scowled. "Not your fault."

Phil's weight bore on Fredrik more with each furlong. At least the exertion kept him warm. They passed cleared spots in the woods, and then snow-covered fields stretched away from the road. Fredrik glanced at the smooth gray sky. The short winter day would soon end.

Shouts reached through the frosty quiet. Children's voices. Laughter. Fredrik helped Phil around the next curve of the road. In the field on the left, more than a dozen children hurled snowballs at one another.

Until they caught sight of the strangers. Wide eyes darted between Fredrik and Phil. Hands poised for a throw lowered. No wonder. Phil made a startling sight with his emaciated face, filthy clothing, and a twenty-year-old's straggly beard. Fredrik smiled at them, hoping to set them at ease.

The children blinked, except one boy, maybe twelve or thirteen years of age. He returned Fredrik's smile and stepped forward. "Ho, strangers. Lost your way?"

"No, we're on the way to your village. Could you point me to the home of your priest? I guess you have one."

"Aye, Brother Bonhoeffer. Fifth house on the left. Can't miss it."

"Thanks." Fredrik gestured to Phil. "My friend's pretty done in."

The boy nodded. "You're almost there."

"Thank you."

BY THE TIME THEY reached the hamlet, Fredrik had to support most of Phil's weight. Poor fellow dragged his feet forward with obvious effort. The few villagers working in this weather stared, but Fredrik paid them no mind. He went straight to the fifth house on the left.

A slim, middle-aged woman with graying hair answered his knock. Her eyebrows climbed her forehead.

Fredrik braced Phil against him. "Is this the priest's home?"

"Why, yes. I'm his wife. What can I do for you?"

"My friend is exhausted. We seek shelter for a few days. I can pay in coin and in work." Mostly work, but he always carried a little money.

The woman smiled and pulled the door wide. "Come in. My name is Frau Bonhoeffer."

"Thank you, Frau Bonhoeffer. I'm Fredrik Holzmann." He helped Phil inside the house.

Frau Bonhoeffer shut the door. "You two sit down at the table, near the fire."

Fredrik helped Phil across the small room. Warmth washed over them, and Fredrik's throat constricted with sheer relief. Phil sank down on the bench, whispering his thanks, but his eyes drifted closed.

"Poor boy." Frau Bonhoeffer glided to a cupboard and took down wooden trenchers. "Where do you two come from, and what brings you here this time of year?"

"You will perhaps find this difficult to believe," Fredrik said, choosing words with care, "but we've escaped from Lady Melankardja's fortress. This was the closest place I knew we could hide."

"Lady Melankardja!" Wide-eyed, Frau Bonhoeffer caught Fredrik's gaze. "You mean the witch?"

"Aye. She'll be furious when she finds out"—an understatement—"so if you'd rather not risk shielding us, I understand." Although Phil would likely die tonight if no one took them in.

"Mercy. You could go nowhere else even if I were afraid to

keep you, which I am not. Nor will my husband be." Frau Bonhoeffer resumed placing the trenchers around the broad trestle table. "But how long have you been there?"

"I was there a couple years, but I ..." *Admit it, Fredrik.* "I was one of her men. I surrendered to Christ today. My friend, Phillip is his name, she held prisoner for nearly three months."

A concerned frown creased Frau Bonhoeffer's brow. "And you walked how far?"

"Couldn't say exactly. Hours."

She clucked her tongue. "No wonder he looks half-dead. He must go straight to bed." She took some blankets from a chest and began making a bed on the floor beside the hearth.

Fredrik would have helped, except he feared he'd end up in the way. "Thank you more than I can say for taking us in."

She glanced up with a warm smile. "Very glad to."

Phil slumped, then toppled.

Fredrik launched forward and caught him. "Phil." He shook his friend's shoulders. "Phil!"

Frau Bonhoeffer hurried to them. She pushed up one of Phil's eyelids. "Unconscious. Get him to bed."

Fredrik half-carried, half-dragged Phil to the pallet. Then he helped Frau Bonhoeffer pull off the jerkin and filthy tunic, exposing the still-oozing burns on Phil's chest.

Frau Bonhoeffer cried out.

"Lady Melankardja was cruel to him." Fredrik fisted his hands.

Two tears slid unchecked down Frau Bonhoeffer's cheeks as she covered Phil with blankets. Then she brought water and sponged his face. He didn't rouse, but his lips drank in the water. Several times she dipped a clean rag in water and let him suck it.

Phil lay there so pale, so helpless. Fredrik swallowed to unclog his throat. "Think he'll live?"

"If the Lord wills," she murmured, washing Phil's face and neck. "Was he healthy before?"

"Aye."

"I daresay he has a good chance, then. Pray he doesn't get a dreadful fever."

"I will." Fredrik grasped Phil's bony shoulder through the blankets. *Lord, please don't let him die.*

FREDRIK DROVE AN AXE into the wood and extracted it for another stroke. The familiar movements kept him from running stark mad with worry over Phil, who hadn't awakened since he passed out two nights ago.

Please, Lord, he's the Prince. The kingdom needs him. Please let him live. I'm trying to trust You.

He brought the tool down again, dividing the chunk of wood. By now Lady Melankardja had men out hunting for them. *Lord, defend us against her spies. And her powers of divination.*

He sure had a lot of requests these days. But it was for Phil. He'd do whatever it took to keep Phil safe from Her Ladyship. Even die if he must. Thank the Lord he had no reason to dread death anymore. His eyes moistened as he struck another log. God was good.

"Fredrik?"

He dropped his axe and started for the back door. "Is Phil worse?"

Frau Bonhoeffer smiled. "No, he's awake."

Fredrik snatched off his cap and dashed past her to drop on one knee beside the pallet. Phil gazed up at him, looking tired, aye, but alert and healthy. Fredrik sighed. "Ach. 'Tis good to see you awake. I almost went crazy. How do you feel?"

"Tired, but much better than I was." Phil slid his hand from beneath the covers, and reached for Fredrik's. "Did I really sleep through yesterday?"

"Either that or you were passed out." Fredrik grasped Phil's hand, rejoicing in the steady grip of fingers which had lain limp all of yesterday.

Frau Bonhoeffer smiled down at them. "No fever this morning. Are you hungry, Phillip?"

Phil smiled. "Very."

She gave a gentle laugh. "He'll get well, Fredrik. Praise the Lord."

As Frau Bonhoeffer turned to stir the broth over the fire, Phil's handclasp tightened. "Thank you, Fredrik. I would have died without you."

"Don't speak of it," Fredrik growled. He deserved no thanks after all he'd done. "If not for you, I'd still be Her Ladyship's slave."

Phil half-smiled. "God has shown mercy to both of us."

Fredrik would be the last to deny that. "Aye."

WHEEL TRACKS STRETCHED BEFORE them through the trampled snow and mud of the road. Fredrik rolled his shoulders against a creeping stiffness and glanced at Phil walking beside him. "How are you doing?"

Phil smiled at him. "I am fine. After three weeks of Frau Bonhoeffer's care, I will not faint on the short journey to Sunset Castle."

A couple days' walk was nothing for a healthy man, but Phil should've waited at least another week. He was over-eager to see his father again.

"We're almost there." Phil looked around. "I can't stop marveling at the sunshine reflecting off the snow, Fredrik. There is so much *light*."

Fredrik smiled. Lady Melankardja's dungeon instilled a new appreciation for that commodity. He glanced at the sun. "Will we be late, do you think?"

"I doubt it. Throne Days last until dark. I used to find them rather tiresome. My perspective has changed." Phil winked.

"Aye." Fredrik imagined Phil's perspective had changed on a lot of things. Another effect of Her Ladyship's fortress.

Phil breathed deeply. "Smell those evergreens."

Grinning, Fredrik drew a long breath of the frosty air, giving heed to the spiciness that tickled his nose. Ever since his escape, Phil had taken a childlike delight in the simplest things. But Fredrik couldn't blame him. Freedom was sweet.

A figure in a black cloak streaked out of the woods and stopped in the midst of the road, not ten feet away. Phil halted, and Fredrik froze beside him, his stomach twisting into a rock-hard knot. He knew that silhouette. The person whirled toward them, tossing off her hood.

Lady Melankardja.

She drew her long sword. Its razor edges winked in the sunlight. "I suppose you two thought you got away. You did not think I would guess your destination?" She smiled as a cat might smile over a trapped mouse. "Now you will reckon with me."

Fredrik grasped his sword hilt as he glanced into the woods. Aye, she had reinforcements lurking back there, though he couldn't see them.

"Fredrik." Her voice, like ice cracking, snared his attention. "I will deal with you later."

He hadn't thought his gut could grow tighter, but it did. He would be dead before day's end. If he was lucky. He might just be praying for death.

Lady Melankardja lifted her chin. "The Prince first. If you interfere, traitor, my men will also interfere. Step away."

He obeyed. *Lord, show me what to do. Show me how to protect Phil.*

"Now, Your Highness, we'll see what kind of swordsman you are." Lady Melankardja pulled a sheathed broadsword from beneath her cloak and tossed it at Phil's feet. "Or you can surrender to me and save yourself the humiliation—and pain."

Phil would never surrender. He'd die fighting first. And die he would. Fredrik had seen Lady Melankardja's swordplay with her men. She beat them every time. Every time.

Phil bent slowly, one hand reaching for the weapon. But his fingers hadn't touched it when he straightened and held his head high. He looked Lady Melankardja full in the face.

Fredrik shuddered for him.

Phil's voice rang through the cold air. "The Lord rebuke you, in Jesus' name."

Lady Melankardja's green eyes widened. The hand

brandishing the sword lowered, and the weapon fell into the half-frozen sludge of the road. She opened her mouth, but said nothing. She turned and fled into the woods.

As she ran, stumbling, Fredrik waited for her men to attack.

They didn't.

Stunned, Fredrik turned to Phil, who drew a shuddering breath and sighed. "Let's go on, Fredrik. I want to see my father."

37

Moritzburg

Dierk swung his staff at a roadside thistle. "Was it really that simple?"

"Simple, aye." Fredrik glanced at him. "If you think it easy to look that maniac in the face and not take up a weapon, you misunderstand." He struck a weed on his side of the road. "Phil had stronger faith than I to do such a thing."

Well, Fredrik would know if anyone did. "What happened to her after that?" He couldn't remember the details.

"King Leberecht lost no time." A frown carved deep lines between Fredrik's brows. "I led his army to her fortress two days after Phil's return. We captured her guards and laid siege. In three days her men surrendered."

Her men, not her. "You mean they mutinied?"

"In a way. Half her men forced the others to surrender because Lady Melankardja had died. They told us she refused to eat or drink, and she died."

Dierk frowned. "Why did she starve herself? I mean—" He broke off to get his thoughts in order. "Did what Father said actually do that to her?"

Fredrik shook his head. "Dierk, I don't understand any more than you do. All I know is God promises to judge wickedness, and I guess she'd had her last chance." He rubbed the back of his neck. "For all I know, she may have surrendered to Christ before she died. But I doubt it."

Dierk stopped walking. "Do you think God would ... well, forgive her after all she did?"

Fredrik turned to face him, eyes somber. "God forgave me."

But ... it seemed worse with Lady Melankardja.

As if he'd read Dierk's thoughts, Fredrik said, "Sin is sin, Dierk."

True. Couldn't argue with that. He resumed walking. "Are you certain she died and didn't escape before you came?"

"Her men showed us her body. She was dead."

Dierk grimaced. Conclusive evidence for sure. "What became of her men?"

"Death for some, prison for others."

"How did they decide which men received death?"

"Trial, how else?"

Dierk cast Fredrik a sideways glance. No need to get sharp.

Fredrik sighed and rubbed his face. "Forgive me. Men lived or died largely on my testimony at those trials. I hated it. Can we turn the subject, lad?"

"Of course." By now, Fredrik's unsettled moods around this topic were familiar. 'Twas a wonder he'd told what he had. Dierk tipped his head toward the sky, dappled with fluttering leaves. "Nice weather today, is it not?"

Fredrik shot him a dry look, then broke into a low chuckle.

THE SUN HAD SUNK low and tradesmen were closing their shops as Dierk and Fredrik entered the southern side of Moritzburg. To the town's north rose a steep hill crowned by the sun-gilded castle of the Count of Moritzburg.

As they wove through the crowds of the main thoroughfare, Dierk searched faces for one resembling Fredrik. Chances were slim they'd just happen to catch Niklas's uncle, but if God willed it, Dierk would be ready. 'Twould give him more satisfaction than anything to catch Veit Nagel.

Above the door of a large building, a wooden sign jutted out into the street. Its crude engraving of a table and a fire marked it an inn. Rich smells of food wafted from the open doorway.

"Hope it has good food," Fredrik remarked.

"I hope it doesn't have fleas," Dierk muttered.

Fredrik's mustache twitched as they walked inside. The hum of voices greeted them. Men and boys clustered around tables and in groups near the hearth. A few glanced up to see who entered, but their attention went no further. Dierk had seen it before on this journey. At least half these people were locals, swapping bits of news over cups of ale. Come full dark, the inn would empty of all but the overnight lodgers.

Following Fredrik, Dierk edged around a knot of loud

men who gesticulated with gusto. No one here looked like Fredrik with a broken nose. Hard to know if Veit would hide himself, or if he had a spotless reputation and could move about without arousing suspicion.

After Fredrik located the innkeeper and paid him for their meals and a night's lodging, he led the way to the table. Dierk slid onto a long bench between Fredrik and a burly man who smelled like a barn. The savory brown venison stew tasted good after a day of walking, but not as delicious as what Gertrude cooked, spiced with juniper berries.

Who sat around the Sisters' table this evening? Maybe a family with children Gertrude could enjoy.

Too bad their route home couldn't take them through Spatzberg. He'd like to see Gertrude again, maybe tell her he'd rectified things between him and God. She would be glad without condescension.

A shadow momentarily blocked the light from the doorway, and Dierk glanced up. He froze, a bite of meat halfway to his mouth. The peddlers. The ones who set fire to the Sisters' home. When one of them glanced his way, he ducked his head over his bowl and kicked Fredrik under the table.

Fredrik grunted, his mouth full. He leaned closer. "Wha's wrong?"

"Two men at the door," Dierk hissed, and stuffed the chunk of venison into his mouth.

Fredrik's gaze darted that way, his body stiffened, and he bent over his stew as Dierk had done. "Our bed is in the corner," he whispered. "Hasten your meal. 'Tis best they don't see us."

Dierk licked his fingers and pushed his near-empty trencher away. Careful to keep his back to the men, he stood and lifted his pack from the floor. Trying to watch the peddlers from the corners of his eyes, he shouldered his way through the crowd and sank down on the wide, padded bench that served for a bed.

The shadows hid him here. He kept an eye on the men as they paid the innkeeper and Fredrik slipped to the corner.

"Good job, lad." Fredrik set his pack on the floor as he joined Dierk. "We will watch them."

"Can't you arrest them for setting fire to the Sisters' home?" Dierk whispered, still eyeing the men.

"No, I haven't enough proof."

Dierk pounded his fist against his thigh. Where would they get proof? Must they let these men traipse wherever they wished, wreaking whatever havoc struck their fancy?

"Patience, lad. We will watch them. Keep yourself out of notice."

He could do that. He'd shadow these men until they showed their guilt, and then he'd make it a personal duty to see them brought to justice.

'TWAS DIFFICULT TO LIE down and pretend sleep without dropping off. Dierk blinked and rubbed his eyes. Fredrik had watched the first few hours. Now Dierk's turn had come, and he'd lain awake for perhaps an hour. The peddlers would not work mischief unnoticed this time.

Something thudded, and Dierk's brain jumped to attention.

There, across the room. The peddlers shouldered their packs and moved toward the door. And the night had not passed far enough to dismiss their departure as "an early start."

Dierk drove his elbow into Fredrik's ribs, breaking a loud snore.

Fredrik shifted on the bench and mumbled, "What's wrong, lad?"

"The peddlers," he hissed. "Leaving."

Fredrik's breath caught, and his instant tension mirrored Dierk's.

The inn's heavy wooden door swung open so slowly it divulged no sound. Two shadows glided through the opening. As the door eked shut, Fredrik sat up. "We'll follow them."

Dierk pulled on his boots and slid his knife into his belt. No drowsiness fogged his mind now. Every nerve stood alert.

It took far too long to get outside without rousing anyone. Dierk looked up and down the dark street. Starlight offered little aid in finding the peddlers. They could be hiding between the buildings.

"We split here," Fredrik said. "If we find no one in five minutes, come back the other way, or go to the church."

"The church?"

"Aye. Keep quiet." Fredrik set off to the right.

Dierk crept down the street. Every shadow moved. Every breeze sounded like footfalls. Every chirping insect communicated a secret signal.

Nonsense. The peddlers had no reason to expect company in the sleeping streets. Nonetheless, Dierk kept his fingers on his knife-hilt.

The longer he searched, the less he worried. The men

must have taken the other way. But Fredrik would have to catch them alone. If he found them at all.

Dierk gritted his teeth. If the men got away ... Why didn't God help him catch these snakes?

Maybe because you forgot to ask, Dierk.

Half a smile emerged at the thought. *Forgive my impatience, Lord. If it be Your will, I ask You to help us find these men and bring them to justice.*

There. He drew a long breath. Surely five minutes had passed. By now, he was nearer the church than the inn. So he turned down an alley leading toward the church's spire.

A shadow crouched at the end of the alley, blending into the blackness of the building. Dierk pressed against the wall and slowed his steps as his heartbeat sped. The shadow turned its head and brought a profile into view.

Ah, Fredrik. With a grin, Dierk hurried to join him. "Fredrik?"

Fredrik flicked his hand in a quick gesture for silence. "I found them. They entered the church."

Across the street from the alley, the church stood dark and silent. How had Fredrik guessed? "What are they doing?"

"I intend to find out. When they come out, can you handle one of them?"

Dierk rubbed his palms on his thighs. "With pleasure."

"If these men are indeed making mischief, they won't fight with honor as you're used to. Can you keep your head?"

Dierk nodded, sober. "God helping me, I can."

Fredrik gave Dierk's shoulder a quick squeeze. "I'll sneak around, see if there's another door. If I find one, I'll watch it. If not, I'll return. You watch the front."

Dierk saluted. "God be with you."

"And with you." With a glance along the street, Fredrik slunk across to the church and disappeared behind it.

Dierk waited, counting. He got to one hundred. Fredrik must be guarding a back door. What were the peddlers up to? Why didn't they come out?

A glint of light flashed through the church window, then held steady, as if someone had lit a lantern. Another glow sprang up. What were they doing?

"Lord, let me be wise," Dierk prayed under his breath.

He waited. The light burned on, grew stronger. Where was Fredrik? Why didn't he move on the men?

"Kik!"

At Fredrik's shout, Dierk launched from his hiding place. He ran for the rear of the church and rounded the corner. Light from the building illuminated Fredrik on the ground, straddling a man who fought him.

With a superb blow to the chin, Fredrik stilled the man. "His friend escaped, lad, and I'm going after him." Fredrik stripped the peddler of his belt and bound his wrists behind his back, working so fast Dierk couldn't follow the movements. "They've set the church afire. Wake the village. I'll return soon, God-willing."

But ... Dierk blinked.

Fredrik stood. "Go, lad."

With a quick nod, Dierk turned and dashed for the inn, yelling, "Fire in the church!"

38

No Proof

BY THE TIME THE men organized a bucket line from the nearest well to the church, the flames had gained a strong hold. Dierk found a position near the church itself, passing full buckets up the line. The scoundrels had lit the inside of the building, using pitch if the pungent smell indicated anything. Even some of the rafters blazed.

Heat fanned Dierk's face. The men dousing the flames in the church had to be parched. He grabbed the next full bucket and handed it on. Had Fredrik caught the other peddler yet? How could he even track him in the dark? Maybe they should have waited for the fugitive to try to rescue his friend.

Dierk glanced across the street. The prisoner had regained consciousness, and now he slumped against the wall of a house. Better keep an eye on him. The townsfolk had no attention to spare for him, and he mustn't escape in the confusion.

A man leapt out the church door, something clutched to his chest. "The Scripture Book!" he shouted. "'Tis not destroyed."

Cheers rose from the workers, and the bucket lines picked up speed.

"Who is that?" Dierk asked the man beside him.

"Our priest." The man swiped his forehead in the pause between buckets. "'Tis good he saved the Bible."

"Aye." The Royal House could not afford to place copies of the Scripture in all the churches. 'Twould be a pity to lose even one.

THE SMELL OF SMOKE tainted the air as Dierk stood with the men and women in front of the church. At least they'd saved much of the wooden furniture, and the flames couldn't destroy the stone walls. The building needed a new roof, but the unharmed Scripture Book outweighed the loss. Altogether, he counted it a victory.

The priest mounted the church steps and surveyed the crowd. "The damage could have been much worse. Thank you all for coming to aid in the middle of the night. I also want to recognize our young friend who spread the alarm." He pointed to Dierk. "Forgive me, lad, I don't know your name."

"Kik Holtzer." Dierk swept his sweaty hair from his forehead and stepped forward. "The praise belongs to my father. He caught the men trying to burn the church. There's one of them." He jabbed a thumb over his shoulder toward the prisoner. "Father pursued the other man and has not yet returned."

"He lies!" the peddler yelled.

Heads turned in his direction.

"Who are you?" the priest demanded.

Seated where Dierk had dragged him, hands still behind his back, the man kept his chin up. "I am Torben, a peddler by trade. My comrade Ottmar and I came to the church to pray this night. We discovered that boy and his father setting the fire. They tried to capture us, but my comrade escaped."

"You filthy cur." Dierk stomped through the crowd, which parted for him. He glared down at Torben. "If I set that fire, then why did I stay to put it out? Why didn't I escape in the confusion?"

"Because your father bade you stay," Torben snarled. "He was frightened lest my comrade return and report your crime, so he bade you give aid to divert suspicion."

"That makes no sense." Dierk whirled toward the crowd and searched the faces. "You!" He pointed at the man who had worked beside him. "Did I not exert as much effort to quench that fire as any man in this town?"

The man hesitated, looking at the others in the crowd. At last he gave Dierk a crisp nod. "You did."

Torben scoffed. "That proves nothing."

Dierk spun to face Torben again, clenching his fists. "It proves I had no desire to see the church burn."

A hand came down on Dierk's shoulder. He flinched away.

"Easy, lad," said the priest. "Tell me your side of the story." The man's gold pendant depicting a cross above a rising sun winked in the torchlight, marking him a priest of Sunland's Church.

Dierk drew a long breath. Hopefully, the priest could see reason. "Father and I lodged at the inn where these two also stayed. We saw them leave in the middle of the night, and we thought it seemed suspicious, so we followed them and caught them setting the church afire."

"'Tis a lie!"

The priest held his palm toward Torben. "Hush, man."

Dierk relaxed enough to uncurl his fingers. "Father caught this man Torben, but the other escaped, and Father pursued him into the woods. I ran to the inn to raise the alarm. Haven't seen Father since."

Which was another cause for worry. Fredrik ought to have returned by now, with or without the fugitive.

"I tell you, he lies!" Torben shouted again.

Dierk's pulse pounded in his head, muddling his thinking. *God, show me what to do.* He locked his gaze on the priest's eyes. "With God as my witness, I have told the truth."

The priest turned to the gathered men. "I think this lad's actions speak for him."

"But the peddler has had no chance to tell his story," someone objected. Dierk tried to search out the voice's owner, but people blocked his view. "Perhaps the lad *is* following his father's orders. He might sneak away to join him the minute we turn our backs."

"If Fr—" Dierk broke off just in time. He dared not let his temper bungle this. "If Father and I had wanted to burn this church, then why did we leave our belongings at the inn? Go see. Our packs, our axes, all at the inn. You will find this man's bundle lying on the ground behind the church."

Someone ran behind the soot-blackened building. In a

moment he returned with a bulky bundle. "It holds peddlers' wares," he announced.

Dierk flashed a triumphant look at Torben.

"We always carry our goods with us," he protested. "To protect from theft. I tell you, I heard the man Holtzer bid his son raise the alarm lest my comrade return and betray their guilt."

The liar. He'd been unconscious before Fredrik spoke to Dierk at all.

Torben lifted his gaze piously toward heaven. "I pray my friend escapes. But if he doesn't, this Holtzer will drag him back, bound. Then he will claim he caught the other malefactor, and no one will believe in our innocence."

Dierk snorted. Innocence, indeed. Sir Wilhelm had a long list of unsavory adjectives which applied perfectly to this knave.

The innkeeper came forward. "'Tis unlikely the lad's father can catch the other man in the darkness. If the peddler returns tomorrow, bold as a champion knight, we'll know he is innocent. If he is guilty, fear will hold him back."

"Perhaps not," called another voice in the crowd. "Perhaps the lad's father will kill the other peddler, and then who will speak for this man?"

"Or perhaps the peddler will kill my father, and then who will speak for me?" Dierk snapped.

"'Tis the lad's word against the man's," someone said. "Who knows who lies?"

"If I had wished to burn the church," Dierk said, raising his voice like a prince addressing his subjects, "do you not think I would have killed this man, the only other witness to my crime? He is bound, as you see. If I were guilty, do you not think I could have slain him with this knife I carry?"

The rippling murmurs ceased. The people looked at one another, exchanging thoughtful frowns. His words made sense to them. Perhaps he had cleared himself in their minds.

"The only reason he did not kill me," Torben called, "is he feared my comrade would escape Holtzer and tell the truth. Otherwise my dead body would lie burning in that church now."

Dierk could have kicked the man if 'twould do any good. Torben's falsehoods had just enough plausibility to make them dangerous.

"'Tis possible these two are in league with one another," someone said. "Whoever we release will try to free the other."

Dierk gaped and stood on his toes to search out the source of the voice. Of all the absurd notions. Then he assumed his haughtiest air, shoulders back, chin elevated, gaze unrelenting as he faced the priest. "I would never stoop to associate with one who would burn a church."

"Then how came these four to arrive on the same night?" This time Dierk caught sight of the speaker, a man from the inn.

Dierk clenched his teeth until his jaw hurt. If only Fredrik were here. People listened to Fredrik. Besides, he could reveal his identity and provide proof. That would silence these ignorant peasants.

"Listen." The priest's voice cut off the growing murmurs. "Let you all return to your homes now. We will deliver these two into the bailiff's custody. Lord Moritzburg shall call a council to pass judgment when he sees fit."

The bailiff. Lord Moritzburg. A council. Dierk sucked in a hard breath, for the scene before him had suddenly lost focus. He was going to prison. He, Dierk Lichtensitz.

But Fredrik would return tomorrow. Then all would be well.

A man with a barrel of a chest pushed through the crowd. "Brother Marwin's plan is good. Go home for the night, citizens. Let two men keep an eye on the church lest a coal blaze up." The man grabbed Torben's arm and hauled him to his feet. "You and the lad will come with me and my brother to the castle."

Dierk gathered his wits and turned to the innkeeper. "Sir, you will keep our belongings safe until my father returns?"

The man nodded. "Aye."

Dierk unbound his knife sheath from his belt and handed it over. "My thanks. We will settle payment when we have cleared our names."

"Fret not, lad."

Another barrel-chested man grasped Dierk's arm. "Come."

Dierk fell into step beside him. The first man followed with Torben.

This tangle would work itself out as soon as Fredrik returned. He must return. Because Dierk had no chance without him.

BY TORCHLIGHT, THE CASTLE'S gaoler led Dierk down winding stone stairs. A dungeon. He, the Crown Prince, trudging to confinement like a common criminal. This could not be real. Surely he was dreaming.

His skin, still sweaty from the fire, pebbled in the cool air. Two steps in front of him, a rat scurried away from the light, its claws scratching on the stone.

The gaoler halted and unlocked a thick, metal-plated door. His assistant shoved Torben into the cell. As the lock screeched into place under the gaoler's key, the man looked at Dierk. "'Twill not suit to confine you with him, nor with the men in the other cells. They might abuse you, as you're so young. I'll chain you at the end of the hall."

Dierk nodded. Why couldn't he wake from this nightmare? Their shadows preceded them, wavering in the torchlight borne by the assistant.

When they reached the wall, the gaoler picked up the fetter lying on the floor. "You must remove your boot."

Dierk bent, unlaced his right boot, and tugged it off. The gaoler knelt and fitted the iron above his ankle, twisting a small key in its lock. The metal's coldness seeped into Dierk's skin and shattered the dream-haze.

He was imprisoned for a severe crime. No one believed his innocence, and he had no way to defend himself.

Humiliation engulfed him, like a swollen river dragging him down. He gasped for air.

"Take heart, lad." The gaoler's voice was kind. "Perhaps the count will hear your case on the morrow. He is not greatly preoccupied this time of year."

More humiliating still that he could not control his reactions. Dierk summoned his wits and met the man's gaze full-on. "I thank you for your gracious consideration, sir."

The gaoler smiled. "Rest if you can. Dawn comes soon."

The torchlight retreated up the hall and halted

somewhere after the stairway's first bend. Better than pure darkness. Dierk's chain clattered as he curled up on the hard stone floor. Not that he'd sleep. But he couldn't stay on his feet forever.

He drew a long breath. The air down here was rank with the stench of filth. The cold chilled him. But he could endure it. At least this wasn't Lady Melankardja's dungeon. A shiver tingled across Dierk's shoulders.

O Lord, help me to bear this well. You know I am innocent. And please, O God, protect Fredrik. In Christ's name I ask it.

WISPS OF MORNING LIGHT filtered through the barred windows in the cell doors and mingled with the warmer torchlight. Little enough light, but better than none. Steps on the staircase drew Dierk's attention. He halted the physical exercises he'd commenced to pass the time and scrambled to his feet. Might be Fredrik.

There came the gaoler. Behind him—the priest, Brother Marwin. Disappointing.

"Kik Holtzer?"

Dierk brushed a hand through his hair, hoping he looked respectable. "Sir?"

Brother Marwin crossed the stone hall until he stood but a yard in front of Dierk. "May I speak with you a moment?"

"Of course. Has my father returned?"

"No, lad." Brother Marwin looked solemn. "Kik, if your father is indeed the culprit, you must confess. You are yet young, and he is your father. You will not be punished harshly."

Dierk clenched his teeth. *Don't explode.* He fingered his belt a few moments until he was sure he could answer with proper respect. "Brother Marwin, I appreciate your concern. But my father is not the culprit. He is innocent."

"Lad, there is no need to shield him. If he—"

"You are right." Dierk cut him off. "There is no need to shield him because he is not guilty. When he returns, he will set all your fears at rest." *And give you a surprise to remember all your days.*

Brother Marwin opened his mouth, but Dierk held up a hand. "I know you mean well. But you do not believe me, and I don't fault you. So we have no more to say to one another."

The priest's brown eyes studied him.

Dierk returned his look. He had nothing more to say.

At last Brother Marwin sighed. "I hope your father returns soon."

"Thank you, Brother Marwin." Dierk dipped his chin. "God be with you."

"And with you, lad." The priest walked away, glancing once over his shoulder. He and the gaoler disappeared up the staircase.

No help to be had from that quarter. Dierk picked a crumb of dirt from his tunic and flicked it to the floor. What would he do if the count decided to try his case today? Father would probably—probably—forgive him for revealing his identity in this situation. But he had no proof except he could speak German, French, and Latin. Not good enough.

Where under the sun was Fredrik?

39

Prince on Trial

A PERSON CHAINED TO the wall couldn't invent exercises all day. Eventually Dierk resorted to studying the dungeon's architecture, finding patterns of animals outlined by the irregular floor stones, and praying off and on. He tried to pray for others: Mother, Father, his siblings, Bastian, not just himself and Fredrik.

By noon, or so it must have been, though 'twas hard to tell in this dungeon, he was near ready to take up mental exercises in arithmetic, despite his hatred of the subject.

Footsteps padded on the stairs again. Dierk's heart leapt with hope. Stupid thing. Fredrik should have returned by now. Something bad had befallen him. Must have. *O Lord, please release me that I might aid Fredrik.*

The gaoler and his assistant rounded the curve of the staircase, fiddling with their keys. The gaoler went to Torben's cell, and the assistant walked straight toward Dierk.

Dierk scrambled to his feet. "Any news?"

"Aye, the count has called a court for you and the peddler." The young man dropped on one knee and fitted a key into Dierk's fetter.

Court. *O God, let the council listen to reason.* If he could clear his name, 'twould be a start toward helping Fredrik.

The iron shackle fell from Dierk's ankle and clanged on the stone. Dierk crammed his foot back into his boot and pulled the laces tight. He'd washed his face with some of his breakfast water, but last night's soot and the damp of this place left his clothing in a pathetic state. Ah, well. He straightened his tunic and combed his hair with his fingers.

"At least your eyes aren't bloodshot from drunkenness," the assistant remarked. "That never makes a favorable impression."

Dierk grunted a laugh. "I suppose not."

"Come. The day does not grow younger."

THE COUNCIL ROOM STRETCHED long and narrow, its walls hung with thick tapestries depicting battles in vibrant color. Dierk followed his escort across the rush-strewn floor to stand at the end of a long table. At the far end sat Lord Moritzburg. As the law of Sunland prescribed, four men of noble birth chosen by the count lined one side of the table. Five commoners selected by the townsmen sat on the other side.

Brother Marwin and the innkeeper had been elected. Interesting. Last night they had seemed to show him favor. But whether they could—or would—help him now was another matter.

Whispers behind Dierk brought his head around. A group of youths stood against the wall. Their gazes traveled up and down him, and then they leaned closer to one another, not even trying to hide the fact they were gossiping about him.

Heat filled Dierk's ears, and he turned away. Sunland's law provided for worthy youth to observe and learn the customs of court, preparing to take the role when they grew old enough. Dierk had held that place himself many times.

Never had he dreamed to stand, a supposed criminal, the center of their undivided interest. What a blow to his pride.

Which didn't matter. His pride could perish in the depths of the Abyss if that gave him a chance to aid Fredrik.

"My lords and honorable men." A scribe, who sat at his own tiny table in the corner, raised his hands. Instant quiet blanketed the room. "I present to you the case of Torben of Sun City, peddler." He paused, and Torben bowed to the men at the table. "Versus Kik Holtzer, woodcutter, son of Henrik Holtzer, woodcutter."

Dierk put all his noble training into making his bow flawless.

The scribe read the case summary, and his slightly nasal voice grated on Dierk's tense nerves. "This court shall determine the truth, as clearly as human wisdom may do. May the Almighty God aid our endeavors."

Dierk bowed his head while Brother Marwin prayed aloud that justice might be achieved. Dierk had always ignored this part of the court. Today he entered into it with his whole soul.

Then followed the arguments. Because he was the elder party, Torben spoke first, accusing Dierk of the crime. Dierk tamped down his indignation until his turn. Then he held his head high and presented as clear and correct a charge as he could. He took care to avoid the common speech he'd used for weeks now; he spoke as he would with his tutors at Duke Ebner's.

The council then required both of them to give rebuttals and include any other details they could remember. Customary process, but Dierk wanted to hit something.

Instead, he must maintain calm patience. Heaven help him if this dragged on through the afternoon. At least they needed no extra witnesses since half the council members had witnessed the fire.

At last, Lord Moritzburg stood. "The council is satisfied. Let all others withdraw for discussion of the verdict."

Finally. Dierk drew a long breath. He'd done his best. Now he must wait for God to prove him innocent.

Wait for God. When he'd much rather duel with Torben for insulting his honor. Not that peasants dueled in any event.

The gaoler's assistant escorted Dierk out the door into the Great Hall. The servants busy with their various duties eyed the two potential criminals. The boys who'd observed the court gathered in a knot, whispering. They couldn't speak to others until after the verdict.

Dierk caught several glances his way, several pointing fingers and raised eyebrows. He tried to ignore the foolish pangs of his wounded pride. He was accustomed to preeminence among the squires. How the mighty had fallen.

But it didn't matter, as long as his innocence came to light.

DIERK'S PULSE THUDDED WITH painful rapidity as he stood erect at the foot of the council table, awaiting the verdict. In a few moments, he would either walk out of here free, or ... what would he do if they found him guilty? He'd have to appeal to the throne and face who knew how long in the dungeon before he could be transported to Sun City. Wonderful.

And what would become of Fredrik, wherever he was?

Lord Moritzburg met Dierk's gaze, a slight smile touching his lips. "We find Kik Holtzer and his father innocent."

An invisible weight disappeared from Dierk's shoulders, bringing a moment of lightheadedness in its wake. He touched the cool, silk-smooth wood of the table to steady himself.

"We find Torben of Sun City and his comrade Ottmar of Sun City guilty of setting fire to the church of Moritzburg."

Torben exploded in a curse. The gaoler boxed his ears so hard Dierk almost cringed for him.

"Our reasons for the verdict are as follows." Lord Moritzburg read from the parchment the scribe had prepared. "We do not see sufficient reason for Kik Holtzer to have set a fire, then changed his mind and aided the efforts to put it out."

At last. He'd tried to tell them so the whole time.

"The peddlers' belongings at the scene of the fire suggest to us a plan to flee when the crime had been committed."

These same townsmen had seemed none so sure of that last night.

"If Kik Holtzer were guilty, it seems to us he would have slain Torben of Sun City and fled with his father, Henrik

Holtzer, despite the chance that Ottmar of Sun City might later bring a charge against them."

Broad daylight must improve men's reasoning.

Lord Moritzburg cleared his throat. "Therefore, inasmuch as Torben of Sun City has been found guilty of setting fire to a church of our Lord Jesus Christ, and inasmuch as a valuable portion of the Holy Scripture was housed in this church, this court hereby sentences Torben and Ottmar of Sun City to branding on the forehead and seven years of forced labor, to be served at Moritzburg. Court is concluded."

Dierk closed his eyes for a moment. *Thank You, Lord.* He didn't want to ask for more now. Not when God had done so much for him. But for Fredrik's sake, he dared not rely on his own skill. *If it be Your will, let me find Fredrik. Let him be well.*

A hand clasped Dierk's shoulder, and he turned.

The innkeeper smiled. "You spoke well, Kik Holtzer."

Dierk smiled back. "Thank you."

"What are your plans now?"

Find Fredrik. "I'll retrieve my knife and axe from the inn. Then I must search for my father."

"Come, I'm bound for the inn myself."

Head up, Dierk walked beside the innkeeper out of the castle. An hour or more past noon, judging by the sun. He'd best lose no time.

HAVING SWALLOWED A HASTY midday meal at the inn, Dierk took his axe and set out for the blacksmith's shop. The blade needed sharpening, and he wanted to get a feel for the town.

The blacksmith took the axe with a grunt. "'Tis good iron."

"Aye." Father had seen to that.

The man carried it to the whetstone, and the grinding of metal on stone filled the shop. A townsman approached, and Dierk gave him a nod. But the man only watched him from the corners of his eyes, his mouth a flat line, as he walked by.

Seemed some of the people didn't trust the council's ruling.

In a few moments the blacksmith returned, testing the edge of the axe. Dierk took it and thumbed the blade. Perfect. "How much?"

The blacksmith named a price. Twice what Fredrik had paid last time for sharpening both axes.

"Too high." Dierk handed him half the amount.

"You better pay, boy." The blacksmith leaned closer. "'Tisn't too late to bring you up on charges that will stick."

So, that's how it was. Dierk kept his teeth tight together to keep from mouthing off as he paid the rest of the money. This left his purse lighter than he'd planned. But he could do nothing about it now.

He slid the axe into the strap on his back and turned on his heel. Now, to start at the woods where Fredrik had run after the peddler Ottmar.

CROUCHING TO STUDY THE ground, Dierk sighed. If only he were a woodcutter's son in truth. Then he might know a thing or two about tracking through the woods. He'd never hunted without hounds, nor tried to follow a fugitive. Every now and then he found what might be a footprint where the leaf-strewn ground was soft, or a squashed ground-plant that may have been flattened by a wolf or some other animal for all he knew.

He stood from examining a depression in the soil. Useless. If it *was* a footprint, which he doubted, it pointed north of his route. But he had nothing better to go on. He adjusted his course and pressed on. Why had Fredrik tried to pursue the man? In the dark, Ottmar had every advantage. He might have waited and ambushed Fredrik.

Something caught Dierk's eye. Blue. Dark, vibrant blue snagged on a branch. He dashed forward and snatched the wisp of cloth.

Fredrik's cloak.

Thank God. He'd finally stumbled across the right trail.

He slowed his pace. A few more minutes turned up nothing new. Perhaps he should turn back to where he'd found the blue scrap, try a different direction. He shoved a sapling aside and halted.

Torn-up ground fairly screamed of a struggle. Leaves scattered, shrubs broken, dirt gouged. He squatted, trying to decipher the outcome of the damage.

His chest seized. He picked up a torn green leaf, curling at the edges. The brownish-red stain in the center set his pulse to throbbing in his head.

Blood.

He raked the ground with his gaze. There, another spot. And there, and there.

Oh, God, no. He jammed his fingers into his hair. Fredrik had found the peddler. But who had come out victorious?

Drawing long, audible breaths, he stood. He had to keep searching. Had to find the truth.

Off to his left, a sort of trail led into the underbrush. Dead leaves were crushed and black soil exposed, as if someone had dragged something away. Or someone.

40

The Message

Hand on his knife hilt, Dierk followed the track. He had to duck under tree limbs a few times, but the trail kept a straight course, more or less. Until it met the road.

He studied the road's packed surface. No distinguishable track. Just ruts and hoof prints and water-etched grooves.

Dierk sat down on the roadside, sinking his head in his hands. "God, show me what to do. I'm terrified Fredrik is dead. Help me, in Jesus' name I pray."

He rubbed his face. Maybe Fredrik had bested the peddler, not the other way around. If so, perhaps Fredrik took shelter for the night in a nearby house or barn.

Which still didn't explain why he hadn't returned. Maybe he had a severe wound. But someone might have seen him.

Dierk planted a palm on the grass and pushed to his feet. He could ask around for Fredrik.

After careful consideration, Dierk selected the direction that led toward Moritzburg. It stood to reason Fredrik would want to return there.

THE SUNLIGHT GLOWED DEEP gold by the time Dierk gave up his search. He'd asked at every house on the way to town with no success. He'd checked the inn to see if Fredrik had turned up, and then he retraced his steps and pestered every man and woman working in the fields, every child herding sheep or geese in the meadows. Some were sympathetic, some scowled at the interruption. But no one had seen anything of Fredrik.

Tired with worry, walking, and sleeplessness, Dierk made his way back to Moritzburg, scouring the roadsides for anything amiss. Nothing so far as he could tell.

People milled about in the town streets, greeting one another, laughing over jests. No one spoke to Dierk. In fact, everyone seemed to look at him askance. Well, let them. He was too weary to care.

At the inn, he stuck his head inside on the chance Fredrik had come. He hadn't.

Unable to rest, Dierk paced the dirty streets. People didn't evaporate like puddles in sunshine. Fredrik must be somewhere—close. *God, please show me what to do.* He'd probably prayed that a thousand times today, but what else could he do?

He needed to send word to Sunset Castle. Father would probably remain there a few days. But how could he pay to send a swift message? Fredrik kept most of their money on his person. After the blacksmith's extortion earlier, Dierk had enough for one more night's lodging. He'd have to chop wood for someone tomorrow just to provide for himself.

The count might send word if Dierk took him in confidence. But could he trust the man for sure? Relatively few nobles qualified for the League, or desired to join, according to Fredrik. Would Father approve Lord Moritzburg's learning of the Crown Prince's secret journey?

Besides, Dierk couldn't prove his identity. Lord Moritzburg would be more apt to take him in custody for an impostor scheming who-knew-what, than to believe such a tale as Dierk's.

If only Dierk had joined the League. Maybe then he could find someone to help him. Someone to send word of Fredrik's disappearance. Someone to advise him on the next step.

Dierk skirted around two boys chatting by a shop, buckets in hand.

"Have you seen Nik Nagel today?"

Dierk halted as the name registered in his brain. Careful to hide his surprise, he turned toward the boys. Neither of them looked his way.

One of them shrugged. "No, have you?"

The other boy shook his head. "Saw his uncle in town earlier, but not Nik."

Veit Nagel in town? Today? Dierk sauntered to the next-door shop, leaned against its corner post, and let his gaze drift over the passersby.

"Funny. Nik always comes with him."

"Aye. Maybe Nik's out at Baldur's place. I'd run out to see, if I had time."

"Maybe he'll come in tomorrow." A dark frown contracted

the second boy's face. "Hope Veit didn't beat him bad again."

"Me, too." The first speaker sighed. "Better take this water home to mother. See you later."

The boy carrying his full bucket continued down the street, and the second boy passed Dierk without a glance.

Dierk couldn't let this information slip away. He followed him.

The boy stopped at a well where two streets intersected. He grabbed the windlass and ran the pail into the well, cranked it back up, and emptied it into his bucket.

How to get him to talk. Dierk had no idea. But he'd made friends with Niklas—eventually. Ah, well, he'd just have to try his best. With three strides, he reached the boy's side and grasped the windlass. "Let me run it down for you."

The boy frowned under tousled brown hair. "I can do it."

Dierk smiled as he took the wooden pail and hung it on the hook. "No doubt. But I have a question for you." He eyed the boy as he cranked the windlass.

The kid widened his stance and crossed his arms. "Who are you?"

"Kik Holtzer." He offered a deep bow. "At your service."

The boy didn't look impressed. "I heard about you."

Apparently, nothing he'd heard commended Dierk. Well, what was new? "I overheard you talking about Nik Nagel. Is he a friend of yours?"

"Maybe he is. Maybe he isn't."

"I met Nik a couple days ago. He was running an errand for his uncle."

The kid didn't comment, didn't change his calculating, narrow-eyed expression.

Dierk reversed his cranking and pressed on. "Nik decided to run away from his uncle. My father and I helped him." His real father, not Fredrik, had promised to find Niklas a good apprenticeship. "Can you tell me where Veit is staying so I can inform him Nik's not coming back?"

"Are you stupid or something?"

A dry smile tugged at Dierk's mouth as he handed over the dripping pail. "Why do you ask?"

"Veit'd beat you silly." Water splashed as the boy upturned the well's pail over his bucket. "I've seen what he did to Nik."

The picture of a powerful man pounding on Niklas's narrow frame heated Dierk's blood. With effort, he played nonchalance. "I'm a bit bigger than Nik, don't you think?"

"Don't matter."

Dierk sent the pail down the well shaft for one more filling. "I still want to know where Veit Nagel is staying."

The boy eyed Dierk a moment longer, then shrugged. "Your neck to break. Go that way out of town about a mile." He pointed. "Turn left. The first farm on the right belongs to a man named Baldur. If Veit is in town, that's where he's staying."

"Thanks. What's your name?"

"Markus."

"I appreciate your help, Markus."

"You won't when Veit gets his hands on you."

Dierk almost smiled at the boy's tone—Markus clearly thought him a fool. The windlass squeaked as he hauled the pail up. While Markus emptied the water, filling his bucket almost to the brim, Dierk fished in his purse until he found his last two coins. He couldn't spare the silver moon. He probably shouldn't spare the copper farthing. But he drew it out anyway. "Thanks again," he said, handing it to Markus.

The boy stared at the coin in his palm, then lifted his eyes to Dierk's face. "You're welcome." For a kid, he had a penetrating stare.

Dierk nodded, and Markus turned back the way he'd come, staggering a bit under the weight of the full bucket. Dierk leaned against the stone rim of the well. So, he had directions to one of Veit Nagel's haunts. Should he go investigate? Or wait until he'd found Fredrik? As if that would happen any time soon.

Dierk's hands itched to whittle something. Instead, he dug a larch cone from his purse and picked off the tiny scales. That house where Veit stayed ... Dierk must have stopped there asking for Fredrik today.

Not the place with the squalling twins. No, 'twas the place where a man answered his knock, growled about the interruption, and all but slammed the door in Dierk's face. Dierk half-smiled. Supposing he went back to this farm and had a look around—without knocking first. Couldn't hurt. Aye, he'd do it.

He dropped the larch cone's core and turned. His toe met a bucket and kicked it over. He grabbed it before it could roll away, and only then looked for the owner.

A young woman with a child clinging to her skirts pointed to the bucket. "Excuse me. I was about to fill that."

"Forgive me." Dierk set the bucket down, grasped the windlass, and lowered the pail again. "Allow me."

"Why, thank you." A soft smile graced her tired face. "Are you Kik Holtzer?"

"Aye, frau."

"I thought I recognized you from last night, when we fought the fire."

Her tone brought a dry smile to Dierk's face. *Kik Holtzer, the lad tried for setting the church afire.* What a reputation. The woman didn't eye him like he had leprosy, though. A pleasant change.

She tugged at one sleeve of her kirtle. "So, you like larch cones?"

Dierk followed her gaze to the dismembered cone at his feet.

"Have you ever made a wreath of them?"

Dierk had to stop himself from flinching. A larch wreath. What had Fredrik and Heike said? *Lord, help me remember.* Reversing the crank, he turned it slowly. "I've seen them, never made one." He rehearsed the next line in his head before he spoke. "It takes all of twoscore cones to make the best larch wreaths."

"An exhibition of patience and cunning skill." The woman reached for the pail, but her eyes met Dierk's, full of meaning.

A woman in the League. He couldn't lie to her, not to a League member. "Forgive me. My father is in the League, not I."

She nodded and replaced the pail on the hook. "Your father is missing, is he not?"

"Aye."

"May I help you in any way?"

Dierk frowned as he wound the windlass. "You would trust me?"

"I would trust the passwords." Her voice was barely more

than a whisper. "No League member, even your father, would allow you to steal the passwords if you were not trustworthy."

Fredrik had mentioned something about that. Though Dierk didn't fully understand this League business, he'd take all the help he could get.

Yet, if he didn't know all the signs himself, how could he trust this woman? *Lord, what do I do?*

"Can I send a message for you?" she offered.

He had to have help from somewhere. *Lord, stop me if I shouldn't do this.* He waited, sliding the pail from the hook. He hadn't much practice listening to God.

But this seemed the best thing to do. He faced the woman. "Send to Sunset Castle. Say that Henrik and Kik Holtzer are in need of immediate reinforcement. Use those exact names. They'll send help." Father himself would probably come if he were still there.

She eyed him. "I need not know more, lad. The message will be sent with all haste tonight."

"Thank you." He emptied the pail into her bucket. If the message went tonight, help might come within two or three days. A pleasant thought, but useless for the present.

Because if Dierk had not found Fredrik in two days ...

He dare not dwell on the possibility.

41

Footstep in the Shadows

SINCE HE PLANNED TO spy around for Veit—and Fredrik—until well past dark, Dierk stopped at the inn for supper first. He wolfed down the mutton pottage, blocking out the noisy talk and laughter around him.

The innkeeper slid into the empty seat across from him. "How heavy is your purse, lad?"

Dierk looked up and blinked. "I beg your pardon?"

"Now don't take offense." The man leaned his forearm on the table. "Have you enough coin to let your mind rest easy?"

Dierk glanced toward the man on his right, who had left a considerable distance between them on the bench. Not that it mattered if someone overheard. He stuck his spoon in his bowl and met the innkeeper's gaze. "I will need work tomorrow."

The innkeeper smiled. "I have wood in need of splitting. Keep this." He slid his palm across the table and lifted it. Dierk's last silver coin shone against the dark, stained wood of the table.

Dierk straightened. "'Tis my payment for tonight's lodging. I cannot take it back."

"Aye, you can. Your work tomorrow will cover what you owe. Take it, and don't say another word about it."

"Take nothing without paying," Father had said, but work would pay. And Dierk appreciated the innkeeper's generosity. He picked up the moon and tucked it into his purse. "I thank you."

The innkeeper dipped his chin. "No sign of your father, I take it?"

"No." Dierk spooned another bite of pottage, and his tongue savored the saltiness. "I'll search more tonight. Don't expect me until after dark."

"Very well." The innkeeper splayed his fingers on the tabletop and pushed to his feet. "God grant you find him."

Amen. "Thank you, sir."

The innkeeper rounded the table and clapped Dierk's shoulder. "Your father will be proud of you, lad." With that, the man moved off toward another table.

The man's friendliness was an unexpected comfort. He spoke as if finding Fredrik were a sure thing. With a half smile, Dierk dug into his meal again. He hoped Fredrik would be pleased with him, as the innkeeper said. But was it too much to hope his real father might be proud of him?

Dierk shook his head. He had no business pining for something so trivial when Fredrik was missing.

ONCE OUT OF TOWN, Dierk met no one on the road. It didn't take long to reach the place he sought. A neat cottage and a dilapidated barn cast long shadows in the setting sun. Behind them, a wide, low-roofed building stretched beside a meadow. The occasional bleat of a sheep drifted through the quiet air.

Dierk wanted complete darkness before he attempted his spying. So he slipped into the woods across the way and sat beneath a pine tree where he could watch the door. His favorite pastime—waiting with nothing to do. He picked up a pinecone and peeled off the scales with his knife.

After a while, someone came out and hung shutters on the front windows. Dierk hadn't bargained on that. But perhaps 'twas only for privacy from the road. Maybe the man would leave the rear windows uncovered for fresh air. A flimsy enough chance.

He needed to see inside that cottage. Dierk slashed viciously at the pinecone in his hand. Never had the sun's light lingered with such interminable persistence.

He had destroyed several pinecones by the time he could barely distinguish the shadows from the surroundings. Finally. Time to move. He scrubbed his sticky hand on his breeches, sheathed his knife, and stood.

A short hedge fenced the meadow and its cottage, but earlier Dierk had passed a stile a little distance down the road. He found the place with no difficulty and stepped up the planks and over the fence. He kept the distance between himself and the house, creeping from tree to haystack to rubbish pile until he could see the back of the cottage.

One of the small rear windows glowed, its lattice a black crisscross against the mellow light. Dimmer light faintly outlined the other window. Dierk smiled. No shutters, just as he'd hoped.

Nothing stirred in the yard. Dierk crouched and moved forward to the low woodshed. He slipped around it and pressed his back against the wattle-and-daub wall. The house stood only a few yards away.

Two men sat in the brighter room, absorbed in something, perhaps a game. Their faces in profile didn't match Veit's description. But perhaps another man sat out of sight, or even in the other room.

Now or never. Dierk dropped on all fours and crawled to the nearest window.

Turning his back to the wall, he rose and leaned just far enough to his right to peer inside. The two men sat on a wooden chest, playing dice. Through the doorway into the other room, Dierk glimpsed a trestle table.

He ducked beneath the windowsill, then stood so he could view the other side of the room. A man sat on the floor, feet bound together, arms apparently tied behind him. He rested his head against the wall, eyes closed. A black eye and swollen lips marred his face.

Dierk's heart imploded, stealing his breath. The man looked like Fredrik: tawny hair graying at the temples, about the same size. Dierk forced air into his lungs. He'd prayed to find Fredrik, but he didn't want to believe this was him. Yet those were Fredrik's clothes.

The bound man bent his head to the right, let it roll forward, around to the left, and back. Slowly, he repeated the process.

Horror clawed at Dierk's stomach. How many times had

he seen Fredrik make that exact movement when he woke in the morning? *O Lord, what is he doing here?* How had Fredrik become a prisoner of Veit Nagel and his cronies? Where was Veit anyway?

Dropping to the ground again, Dierk crawled past the back door to the other window. This larger room took up the rest of the cottage. Coals smoldered amongst a few licks of flame on the cooking hearth. Dierk needed no lamp to spot the stash of weapons: swords, knives, bows. No farmer had so many.

Dierk held his breath to listen for a sign of someone in the corners he couldn't see. His ears detected no one.

So Veit wasn't here, after all. But Fredrik was.

No telling how long these men had held Fredrik prisoner. But Dierk must free him. Now. He couldn't spare the time until aid arrived. Not with these men beating Fredrik, likely starving him.

Dierk snuck back to the other window and peered through the lattice at Fredrik's captors. One of them had answered Dierk's knock this afternoon and declared he'd seen nothing of Henrik Holtzer. The liar. The other man looked famil—

The peddler. Ottmar. What on earth was he doing here? Surely those men hadn't conspired with Veit. But then again ...

No matter. He must act now, while he had only two to contend with, before Veit and any others returned. He needed to get them out of the house, somehow.

Some noise for them to investigate? No, they'd be sure to leave one to guard Fredrik.

How about a fire? In the ramshackle barn behind him. They'd need all available hands to put it out. A grim smile touched the corners of Dierk's mouth. Fitting, to use the peddler's trick against him. He slid his hand into his purse, feeling for the chunk of quartz and his iron fire-striker. Straw piled against the building would ignite beautifully.

If Fredrik had enough strength to flee, this plan would work. The villains' capture could wait until Father came with help.

A footstep padded behind Dierk. He whirled.

A man crashed on top of him, pinning him. Dierk's axe-handle dug into his back, and the man's weight stole his breath.

He went for his attacker's throat. Stout neck muscles met his fingers. He squeezed hard with his thumbs.

Something slammed Dierk's chin. His head jerked to one side. He tried to hold his grip, but the man's neck was dissolving in his grasp. The window light blurred. And went black.

42

A True Knight

FREDRIK BROUGHT HIS MIND into focus, trying to guess the cause of the scuffling outside. His captors' dice quit rattling, and they looked toward the rear window.

Baldur, the house's owner, stood and picked up a lamp. He stepped into the other room, grabbed a short sword, and disappeared from Fredrik's view in the direction of the back door.

A couple of wooden thumps followed, as if someone kicked the door. "Open, 'tis I."

Must be Veit returning from town. He'd bring word of the fire's outcome. Maybe word of Dierk. Gossip about the woodcutter's son who'd raised the alarm would travel fast.

Poor Dierk. How had he occupied himself today, waiting for Fredrik's return?

Fredrik drew a long breath and exhaled, the movement awakening every bruise on his ribs. He ought not to have pursued the other peddler. But he'd been certain he could capture him. Aye, he caught Ottmar. And lamed his left shoulder in the process. Which led to—

Cease, Fredrik. The thing was done now, and it did no good to dwell on it.

Baldur returned, and Veit stomped behind him with something slung over his shoulder.

Not something. Someone. A sick feeling welled in Fredrik's belly. Who was this—an innocent Sunlander to be used as leverage against him?

Veit slid the limp body to the floor. The head lolled, turning the face toward Fredrik.

Dierk. *O God, no.*

"That's the boy who came seeking his missing father this afternoon," Baldur said.

Fredrik didn't remember that. Must have been unconscious.

"You should have taken him then." Veit beckoned to the peddler. "Friend Ottmar, come look at this lad."

Ottmar, the peddler, came and scrutinized Dierk's face. "I've seen him. At the Faust Sisters' cottage." The man spat on the floor. "He called himself the son of this woodcutter-palace-guard you hold captive."

Veit nodded, his lips curved into a satisfied smile. "Caught him peering in the back window. Figured he must be connected to Sir Fredrik. Look at the axe he carries."

Why under the sun had Dierk come to spy? Here, of all places? As if Fredrik hadn't trouble enough, now he had to get Dierk to safety. If such a thing were possible.

Veit looked up and met Fredrik's gaze. "You'll open your

mouth quick enough when the lad starts screaming for mercy."

Fredrik's stomach twisted but had nothing in it to heave. Appalling possibilities whirled through his head. *O Lord, please have mercy. Please spare Dierk.*

Veit nudged Dierk with his toe, but the lad didn't stir. "As soon as we get the map, we'll send for the others."

Others? Other vile men who would help Veit infiltrate the fortress? How many?

Veit seated himself on a stool against the wall as Baldur and Ottmar returned to their dicebox. "I have news of the fire."

Ottmar raised his head. "What news?"

"Little damage. They saved the Bible. The count held court to determine the culprit. Your partner, Torben I believe they call him, declared you had caught this lad"—Veit tipped his head toward Dierk—"and his father trying to burn the church."

Ottmar let out a growling laugh as he shook the dicebox.

"But the council ruled in favor of the woodcutters." Veit pointed to Dierk. "The lad must have a silver tongue. You and Torben get a branding and seven years forced labor."

At least one culprit had received justice. Though Fredrik couldn't appreciate it properly while Dierk lay here unconscious.

Ottmar muttered a curse. "Twice, then, the lad and his father have thwarted our work. Now I must devise a scheme to free Torben."

"The lad's appearance here makes that easier." Veit brought one ankle up and rested it on his opposite knee. "Go to town. They'll arrest you, but you can protest your innocence. I'll help you spin a tale to match your partner's. And with the lad and his father both missing ..."

Ottmar gestured to his black eye. "What about this gift from Sir Fredrik?"

Veit shrugged. "You fled through dark woods. You tripped and hit something."

Ach. Fredrik almost groaned aloud. If Ottmar spun his tale well, it could sound convincing. A new council might be called. The verdict might change.

Which, truth be told, mattered but little in light of their current situation—the Crown Prince held captive by a ruthless knave. Fredrik's whole body could attest to Veit's cruelty.

Fredrik never had a son. But the son of his king came close. Veit was right. 'Twould be very hard to hold his tongue and watch Dierk suffer.

A DULL ACHE THROBBED in the back of Dierk's head. The smells of stale dirt and lamp-grease smoke filled his nostrils. He tried to move his arms from behind his back, but they didn't obey. Cords dug into his wrists. He was bound.

His eyes popped open as energy born of fear flowed through his veins. Flat on his stomach, cheek against the dirt, he glimpsed the inside of a dimly lit cottage.

Cottage. Where—?

The cottage. He'd gone looking for Veit and found Fredrik. Then that unknown attacker must have knocked him cold.

He turned his head a little more to assess his

surroundings. A yard away, someone's worn boot-soles pointed toward him. He followed them to their owner's bruised face. Gray-blue eyes watched him. "Fredrik." His whisper came out scratchy.

"So, the lad awakens," said a strange man's voice behind him. "A lad who knows Sir Fredrik's true name."

Boots appeared beside Dierk a moment before a hand grasped his arm and hauled him to his knees. Dierk looked up at the man. Fredrik's features—with a broken nose. *Veit Nagel.*

That's who pounced on him. How many enemies did he face now? The peddler was nowhere in sight. The other man he'd seen throwing dice now leaned against the wall, sneering. Fredrik sat bound, worry etched on his face.

Veit struck Dierk a back-handed blow on the cheek.

Dierk blinked against dizziness. He focused on the smarting pain, trying to clear his head.

"Now we will be honest with one another," Veit said. "Fredrik, I want that map. I shall beat this lad—your son, squire, whoever he may be—until you yield."

Another back-handed strike hit Dierk's mouth. He tasted blood. He must bear this. Whatever map Veit wanted, Dierk must help guard it, no matter what. *Merciful God, give me strength.* He swallowed. "Don't speak, Father."

Veit threw Dierk to the floor. Hands bound, he couldn't catch himself, and his cheekbone slammed the dirt. Strong fingers grasped his arm again, yanked him up, and flipped him.

Dierk landed face up across Veit's knee. Veit's powerful hand on Dierk's chin forced his head back so he viewed the room upside down.

"'Twould not be hard to cripple him." Veit's knee dug into Dierk's spine. "Such a handsome, promising lad. 'Twould be a pity—would it not?—for him to never walk again. Come, I demand so little."

The man's smooth voice sickened him. This utterly vulnerable position—maddening. Veit pushed harder on Dierk's throat. Dierk choked on his own breath, and a cough battered his windpipe.

Veit might well cripple him. He'd prefer death. But if Fredrik could endure, so could he. "Don't speak," he croaked.

Veit jumped up, hauling Dierk to his feet. Veit's knuckles smashed Dierk's jaw, and he hit the floor.

FREDRIK SHIFTED AGAINST THE wall behind him, trying to ease the pressure on his swollen left shoulder. Dierk lay beside him, unconscious from that last blow, his chest rising and falling at even intervals. He was young and strong. Given a day or two, he'd recover. If he lived a day or two.

Veit would eventually kill them if Fredrik refused to yield. But if Veit got the map he wanted, he would still kill them. Only a fool would let them live knowing what they did, and Veit was no fool.

Dierk's breath hitched, and he drew his knees toward his chest. In a moment, he turned his face toward Fredrik, blinking. "Am I dreaming?" he whispered.

"I wish you were, lad."

"My head's full of wool, I think." Dierk's words came slow, as if his brain hadn't fully wakened. "Not the first time

A smile touched Dierk's lips above the bruises darkening his jaw. "I should have liked to wear the crown, but Anselm will make a good king."

Anselm. Dierk's thirteen-year-old brother. Sudden tears burned Fredrik's eyes. Phil had accomplished his goal. His son had grown into a man willing to sacrifice anything for his duty. A man to make a compassionate, wise, and valiant king.

Yet Phil would never know.

He *must* know. Dierk must not die. Fredrik clenched his fists behind his back. He must free Dierk though he died himself in the process. Phil had entrusted his son to him. He couldn't—and wouldn't—fail. *O Lord, let me not fail in this. Please. If it be Your will.*

What if God willed that Dierk die? *Ach, no.* Fredrik tamped down the turmoil in his soul. He would trust God, whatever happened.

"If I had not been so rebellious, Father would never have commissioned you to take me on this journey."

Fredrik tried to smile at the unspoken apology, though his battered face protested. "It was—it is an honor. If I was your father, I would be proud."

"I thank you. I ..." Dierk paused. "I have come to respect you, and ... it has been my honor to journey with you." He stretched his legs out. "Difficult to be comfortable with your arms behind your back."

"Enough!" Veit's shout cracked through the quiet. "Cease whispering in that devil's tongue."

By his tone, Veit was ready to enforce his orders this time. But at least his anger proved he hadn't understood their conversation. Fredrik raised his voice as he said in French, "I have hope, Kik. He will make a mistake. I will be ready."

Veit jumped to his feet. "I said enough." He stalked toward them. "But since the lad's awake, we might return to our *discussion*."

Fredrik glanced at Dierk, whose throat bobbed. But his eyes held determination. *A man of courage.*

His only hope of protecting Dierk was to draw Veit's fury on himself. A temporary solution at best.

But if Fredrik were rendered incapable of divulging the information Veit sought ... then Veit would have no reason to beat Dierk. Fredrik could feign severe weakness until Veit had to ease up on them lest Fredrik die too soon. Aye, 'twas worth a try. Could buy some time.

"What say you, Fredrik?" Veit kicked Dierk's ribs. Dierk gasped and curled reflexively. "Ready to negotiate?"

Fredrik gathered what saliva he could in his parched mouth. Then he held Veit's gaze and spat.

Deep red flooded Veit's face. He grabbed Fredrik's collar and threw him face down on the floor.

Fredrik's nose struck the dirt, bringing tears into his eyes. *If Veit breaks my nose, 'twill be easier than ever to mistake us for twins.* Strange thing to pass through his mind at such a time.

Veit's right fist slammed Fredrik's back, near the base of his ribs. Excruciating pain speared through his body and robbed him of breath.

Unconsciousness coming. A bit of relief. *Lord, grant this succeeds.*

DIERK STARED AT FREDRIK'S still form, horror and fury swelling within him.

Veit turned and kicked Dierk's shoulder, knocking him to his back. "Your turn will come. As soon as your father awakens." He sneered and headed toward Baldur.

Dierk let his eyelids slide shut. *O God, help us.*

43

A Fist and a Bargain

Though no direct sunlight penetrated the front shutters, the rear windows set the cottage awash with silvery morning light. Dierk had slept little, rolling and squirming for a more comfortable position on the floor, wrists and ankles bound. 'Twould be a mercy if he could move his fingers after this.

The shallow movement of Fredrik's ribs proved he still breathed, but he hadn't stirred since Veit punched him. Hadn't even snored all night. He'd probably had no food, maybe no water, since his capture.

And Dierk couldn't do a thing about it. Maddening.

He shifted his weight again. *O Lord, I know nothing is too hard for You. You hold the stars. Veit Nagel and his schemes are nothing to Your power.* He sighed. *But I also know Your ways are not man's ways.* Mother and Father often reminded their children of that. *If You will that I die, I am honored to obey*

You. But if it may bring You glory that we come out of this alive, then protect us, strengthen us, and show me what to do to help Fredrik. I pray in Jesus' name.

Someone stomped through the back door. Baldur appeared in the doorway between the rooms, a leather pail dangling from his fingers. "Veit!"

The bed behind Dierk creaked. "What."

"Just wondered if we should feed them this morning." Baldur tipped his head toward Dierk and Fredrik.

Feet hit the floor behind Dierk. "Aye. Don't want Fredrik dead yet," said Veit's voice.

Of course. Couldn't get information from a dead man.

"Well, I don't want to spoon-feed 'em." Baldur turned back to the main room.

"So, we'll bind their hands in front of them."

Footsteps approached Dierk, and something kicked his shoulder blade. He got the idea and rolled to his stomach.

What felt like a knee landed on Dierk's back, bearing down. "Don't try anything, boy. I swear you'll regret it."

Dierk forced himself to nod. He wouldn't "try anything" with Fredrik so vulnerable. He had to keep his wits about him and watch for a valuable opportunity, not spring at the first chance.

The cords about his wrists loosened, and Dierk's hands slid to his sides. He tried to flex his fingers. They might have been dead for all the response they gave.

Veit rolled Dierk to his back and knelt over him. Hot hatred seethed through Dierk's gut as he looked up at that face, familiar in its features yet strange in its cruelty. Veit sneered as he bound Dierk's wrists together again.

Love your enemies.

Dierk drew a sharp breath. Veit laughed and cinched the cord tighter. Dierk turned his face away. Love his enemies. Ha. No one could love Veit Nagel.

But that wasn't true. Dierk hadn't listened to sermons and Bible reading all his life to be ignorant of God's love for all mankind, including the most wretched sinners. And Jesus expected the same of His followers.

Dierk almost groaned aloud. *Lord God, I cannot love Veit.* He could face pain and death for his country and His God, but he could not love his enemy. Didn't that sound pathetic? *Lord, Father delights to quote, "I can do all things through Christ who strengthens me." You must strengthen me if I'm to love my enemy.*

He asked for strength because he was supposed to, not because he wanted to.

Veit kicked Dierk's leg. "Sit up, out of the way."

Easier said than done with hands and feet bound. By the time he managed to comply, painful tingles sizzled through his arms all the way to his fingertips.

Veit rolled Fredrik to his stomach and performed the same process on him. Fredrik didn't rouse. Didn't control his head. Didn't open his eyes. Didn't make a sound.

Veit strode into the other room, and still Fredrik didn't move. Dierk's heart squeezed into a hard, pulsing knot. Fredrik mustn't die. Escape would lose its joy if Fredrik didn't come with him. Fredrik, so self-sacrificing, Father's brother in all but blood.

His movements awkward, Dierk dragged himself to Fredrik. He touched Fredrik's face, prodded a tender-looking bruise. A slight pucker of the brows rewarded him. "Father, awaken. 'Tis morning."

Nothing.

He switched to French. "Father, they plan to give you some food." Dierk's split lip hurt as he spoke. "You must waken and eat to regain your strength."

Nothing.

He tried German. "Father, please. I need your help."

Still nothing. Ach. Dierk had little knowledge of healing. Fredrik might have fallen into one of those deep sleeps so like death—and oft enough death's forerunner.

Veit returned and set a cup of water and a hunk of bread beside him. "Ah, poor Sir Fredrik. He takes it hard, does he?"

Dierk gritted his teeth until the pressure threatened to drive them into his jawbone. *Love your enemies.* Ha. Ignoring them instead of striking out was the best he could offer.

Veit stalked out, and Dierk turned his mind to rousing Fredrik. He couldn't lift Fredrik's head and give him water at the same time. So he maneuvered his legs to support Fredrik's head. With utmost care, he pressed the wooden cup to Fredrik's lips.

'Twas too full. He dared not risk spilling the water, so he drank some himself. Two or three swallows ignited furious thirst. Dierk pulled the cup away with a stern mental rebuke.

This time he parted Fredrik's lips and tipped a trickle of water into his mouth. *Lord, please let him not choke.* "Father, drink. Wake up. Drink." He spoke Sunman. Let Veit eavesdrop if he wished.

Fredrik swallowed. Thank God. Dierk eased another sip into his mouth. Though Fredrik's eyes didn't open, he drank until he emptied the cup.

Dierk set it aside. "Can you hear me?"

Fredrik drew a long breath. "Aye." His voice was barely audible.

"Will you take some bread?"

The faintest nod.

Dierk pinched off a bit and poked it between Fredrik's lips. Then he tore off a bite for himself. Good bread for peasants' fare, but dry.

Fredrik's jaws moved, but without purpose. After a moment, they halted.

"Fredrik, you must eat," Dierk whispered.

Fredrik opened his eyes, clear blue-gray in the midst of dark purplish bruising. "Lad, I can't." His eyes drifted shut.

Ach. Dierk couldn't chew for him. "Could you take more water?"

"Perhaps."

It cut against the grain to request something from Veit. Like trying to chop straight through a tree trunk with a dull axe. But for Fredrik, he'd do it.

"Ho, can we have more water in here?" He didn't have to sound humble about it.

"If you'll say please like a good lad." Veit mimicked a mother's tone in a most disgusting way.

Dierk said it before his pride could argue. "Please."

Thumping footsteps approached, and Veit set down a bucket. The water sloshed about halfway down the inside. Veit stood there with his arms crossed, but Dierk pretended the man didn't exist, filled the cup, and helped Fredrik drink it.

Water was good, but Fredrik needed nourishment. Dierk could play on Veit's need to keep Fredrik alive. "Have you any milk?" he asked, not looking at Veit. "He's too weak to eat the bread. If he dies of starvation, you'll never get your map."

Veit boxed his ears. A high-pitched bell chimed in Dierk's head.

Veit stomped out and returned with a bowl of milk, goat's milk by the smell, and left them to themselves. The bowl proved awkward to manage with bound hands, and Dierk spilled a little down Fredrik's cheek.

Still, Fredrik drank it sip by sip until he turned his face from the bowl toward Dierk. "No more, lad."

"There is but little left. Try."

"No. You drink it."

"Father, I won't take special treatment. I don't care if you're in charge, and I don't care if—" He switched to French. "If I am Crown Prince." Back to Sunman. "Drink it."

A hint of a smile touched one corner of Fredrik's mouth. "I cannot. Truly."

"Please?" Veit might give them nothing more all day. Fredrik needed every drop.

"No." His Adam's apple bobbed. "But I thank you."

Dierk sighed. "Try some bread?"

"No. Nor water," he added before Dierk could suggest it. "You're ... worse than a woman."

An involuntary smile died when it stung Dierk's split lip. He licked the spot, finding it swollen.

"Let me rest."

Dierk ate most of the bread, though he tucked a chunk into his pocket in case Fredrik awakened hungry later. Dierk was young. Well-trained. He could do without when necessary.

Fredrik was by no means weak. But anyone might have difficulty recovering from such abuse.

For the tenth time, Dierk bathed Fredrik's face with water and a strip of cloth he'd torn from the hem of his tunic. As if it would actually help Fredrik somehow. The helplessness was frustrating, but at least Veit wasn't beating them. During the hour since Baldur went outside to work, Veit had mended tools and burnished knives in the main room of the cottage. Twice he came to smirk and slap Dierk and prod Fredrik with his toe.

Dierk wanted to tear Veit's foot off for it.

As the cool water touched his skin, Fredrik blinked and turned his head toward Dierk. "Praying, lad?"

"Aye." God was probably tired of hearing from him by now.

"Good." Fredrik smiled as his eyes closed. "So am I."

Veit came to the doorway between the rooms and leaned his shoulder against the jamb. "Fredrik, I've changed my mind about that map to the fortress. I want a guide instead. Someone the guards won't suspect."

Dierk stared. Veit wanted Fredrik to *guide* him through the maze? As if twin Fredriks wouldn't look suspicious. It could work out to their advantage, though. Fredrik would manage to alert the guards, and they'd catch Veit in his own trap.

Fredrik snorted, though his eyes didn't open. "You're

walking in a drunkard's dream if you think I'll consent to that."

Why would he not consent? They had a much better chance with one of them free, even though Veit would doubtless hold Dierk here to keep Fredrik cooperative.

Ach. Dierk's swelling hope collapsed. Fredrik would never leave him a hostage.

Veit grinned. "Ah, but your son is the one I want. I have the signet to prove I'm Fredrik. What could be more natural than the Chief of Palace Guard inspecting the fortress with his son?"

Dierk's mouth fell open. Veit couldn't know how *unnatural* Fredrik's visiting that place was. This could be the perfect opportunity. Except … Dierk did not understand the maze. Perhaps he could fake it long enough to reach the guards. They would recognize him as Crown Prince, he could get them to capture Veit, and they would send to Sunset Castle for men to rescue Fredrik.

Fredrik. Dierk looked at the man lying beside him. What would happen if he left Fredrik alone?

Fredrik opened his eyes and tried to raise his head. Dierk slid his bound hands underneath to help. Fredrik held Veit's gaze. "My son does not yet know all of the maze."

Understatement.

Veit shrugged. "He'll know enough. And he completes the disguise."

Fredrik's gaze shifted to Dierk, and determination lined his face. "Go, lad."

"Aha!" Veit straightened and crossed his arms. "Fredrik has sense between his ears after all." He stepped forward and

44

The Choice

DIERK TWISTED HIS WRISTS, trying to find a gap, a loose strand, anything to work with. Nothing.

If this was Veit's idea of satisfactory bindings, 'twas quite effective.

Veit had gone to town to purchase food for the journey tonight. He had crossed Dierk's wrists behind his back, bound them, and tied him to the heavy wooden bracket which held the front door's bolt. A rope wound around Dierk's ankles. A sour, gritty rag stretched between his teeth, knotted behind his head. He tried to ignore the taste. Not easy.

But Veit couldn't have him shouting at passersby. As if anyone would travel this path.

At least Veit hadn't bound Fredrik the same way. He'd left him lying on the floor in the bedroom, taking the precaution of binding his hands behind him. And gagging him.

Fredrik tried to smile. "You are not a fool. You are ... a brave man. You will yet outwit Veit."

"As I did just now?" Dierk snorted and tossed the cup into the bucket.

"Pray." Fredrik opened his eyes fully and met Dierk's. "God will guide you." His eyelids drifted shut.

Weariness washed over Dierk. He lay back on the floor, Fredrik's head still pillowed on his thigh. He covered his face with his hands, and his throat tightened. This helplessness was maddening.

He ought to devise a way to trap Veit at the fortress. But the possibilities were too varied to plan for.

Dierk's mouth tasted bitter. That worthless dog deserved to die. Arrest and imprisonment weren't enough. If Dierk got the chance, he'd kill Veit.

Love your enemies.

No. Dierk didn't even want to.

Yet he'd vowed to follow Jesus. He curled his fingers into tight fists. *Lord, I want to obey You, but this I cannot do.*

Why did it matter if he loved Veit anyway? He needed to free Fredrik, and whatever it took, he would do it.

now. Right in front of him.

"For God's sake, stop!" he shouted. "I'll guide you!"

Veit released Fredrik, who slid down the wall and toppled into a pitiful heap.

O God, he's going to die anyway. He might be dead now.

Veit rubbed the knuckles of his right hand. "I thought perhaps that would change your mind. We leave tonight." He strode out of the room.

Dierk scooted across the floor toward Fredrik. *O God.* He had no words. He rolled Fredrik onto his back and tugged his legs into a relaxed position. Fredrik still breathed, though every breath hitched as if it pained him. New bruises were gathering over the old ones on his face.

Tears burned behind Dierk's nose. "Fredrik, I'm sorry," he whispered. "I shouldn't have defied him."

How could he have been so stupid? He'd wanted to stay with Fredrik, to endure everything with him. Instead, he'd managed to add another beating to Fredrik's agony.

Dierk, you dolt. Always thinking he knew best. His stupid pride. "God, forgive me."

Fredrik's eyelids fluttered. "Water?"

Dierk stretched across the floor to reach the water bucket and dragged it to them. He picked up the cup inside, propped his leg under Fredrik's head, and helped Fredrik sip. Fredrik coughed, and Dierk jerked the cup away, spilling water down Fredrik's neck.

"I'm sorry." Dierk wiped at the droplets.

"No matter." Fredrik coughed again. "Don't ... fret, lad." He drew a breath and winced.

"I'm a fool. I should've obeyed you."

pinned Dierk with his gaze. "But lest you think of tricking me, *lad,* your father will remain here and eat nothing until I return safely."

Dierk lifted his chin. "Then I will not guide you."

Veit lunged forward and slapped him. Dierk's head whipped around so fast his brain seemed to bang against his skull.

"Lad, you must go." Fredrik's quiet voice rang with authority. "I bid you."

Veit laughed. "Your father has sense, at least, if you do not."

Dierk swallowed. Fredrik, trying to protect him by sending him away. Fully prepared to die for him.

This new scheme of Veit's didn't change the ultimate plan—get into the fortress, then kill both Fredrik and Dierk. If Dierk managed to arrange Veit's arrest, he could save his own life, but he had no way of guaranteeing Fredrik's safety. He would not let Fredrik die alone.

Dierk eased Fredrik's head back to the floor and squared his shoulders. "I will not leave my father."

"Kik—"

"Then you will both die here!" Veit shouted.

Dierk braced himself for a blow.

Veit turned and kicked Fredrik's ribs. Fredrik gasped. Veit grabbed Fredrik's tunic, hauled him to his feet, and shoved him against the wall. Fredrik's head drooped forward. Veit's fist hit Fredrik's chin, and his head smacked the wall.

Again and again, Veit punched Fredrik in the face, in the gut, in the ribs. Blood trickled into Fredrik's mustache.

Horror tore at Dierk's insides. Fredrik would die. Right

Now, with Baldur busy in the field, they were unguarded. Dierk *had* to find a way out before their captors returned.

If he rubbed his rope against the edge of the wooden bracket, maybe he could tear the cord in two. He tugged his arms up, then shoved them down, keeping tension on the bindings. They bit his wrists, but he tried again.

The notch in the bracket gave so little room to work. The rope clung tight to the wood, resisting his efforts to slide it. But until he thought of a better plan, he'd keep this up.

Something shuffled in the other room. Fredrik must have wakened. A good sign, Dierk hoped. He dragged his wrists upward and thrust them down.

Great thunder, was that Fredrik's head poking in from the other room? In a moment, Fredrik's shoulders appeared, his right arm scraping the dirt floor.

Dierk froze. Not an hour ago, the man could hardly move. Now he pushed with his bound feet, one shove after another, writhing his way forward. Slow progress, but steady. How in the world?

Fredrik sank to his belly, turned his head, and caught Dierk's gaze. He offered a quick nod before levering back to his right side. He inched onward, little push after little push. He rounded the table in the room's center and paused, his chest heaving, breath loud. Then he bent his knees, dug his toes into the floor, and pushed on. Taut muscles in his neck betrayed the strain.

He passed in front of Dierk, by all appearances aiming for the weapons piled on the far side of the front window.

Dierk's heart hammered inside his chest. *If* Fredrik reached a weapon, how could he cut himself loose? *O Lord, please let him make it.*

Sweat trickled down Dierk's neck by the time Fredrik reached the weapons. Fredrik lay on his stomach, eyeing the assortment of knives and swords. He rolled onto his right shoulder, and edged himself against the pile of blades. With his bound hands, he reached out. His fingers fumbled a moment before they closed around a knife hilt.

Dierk exhaled a long-held breath. Fredrik had gotten his weapon.

Fredrik rolled to his stomach and bent his knees, pulling his feet toward the knife in his hands.

He intended to cut his feet loose. Dierk watched, willing it to work. Willing Fredrik's muscles, undoubtedly stiff and numbed, to stretch enough.

Fredrik's feet drew closer to the knife. The blade groped until its tip hit Fredrik's boot heel. He shifted the blade and arched his body tighter.

Dierk caught himself biting hard on the gag and forced his jaw to relax. *Lord, please let him succeed. Please.*

The knife slid between Fredrik's legs, its edge against the topmost coil of rope. Fredrik froze. The knuckles of his right hand whitened as he gripped the hilt, pointing the blade almost straight up. Then he pulled his feet down, a steady, inexorable movement.

The rope split. Fredrik spread his feet apart, unwinding the rope.

Dierk sagged against his bindings, even as his pulse thrummed with eagerness. *Thank God.*

Fredrik flexed his legs before rolling to his knees. He pushed to his feet, wobbled a little, then staggered to Dierk.

He turned around and for a moment leaned his right shoulder against the doorframe, his breaths heavy. Then he backed up and thrust the knife behind Dierk.

Unable to see what Fredrik was doing, Dierk twisted away to give the best possible access. The narrow rope pinched his wrists. Fredrik's fingertips tapped Dierk's hands and wrists, exploring the knot perhaps. Cool metal brushed his fingers once or twice.

Then the bonds tightened, as if something pulled a strand. It grew tighter until, with a jerk, it broke loose.

With the sudden loss of support, Dierk pitched forward. The rope unwound, burning his wrists, as he fell to his knees. Before the momentum threw him on his face, he rotated his body and landed on his left shoulder.

Exultation coursing through him, he sat up. His shoulder throbbed, but who cared? Fingers tingling, he went for the knot at the back of his head and looked up at Fredrik.

With a nod, Fredrik dropped the knife.

The knot came loose, and Dierk flung the dirty rag to the floor. He snatched the knife and slashed his feet free. They stung with a thousand needle-pricks as he stood.

"Fredrik, I thought you were near dead." He made short work of Fredrik's wrist ropes.

Fredrik shook the bindings off, exposing what he'd mentioned last night about laming his shoulder. His left arm hung limp at his side.

With the pain of a dislocated shoulder, Fredrik had still managed to free Dierk. He was a man to reckon with.

Dierk tossed the knife toward the weapon pile and moved behind Fredrik to untie his gag. In a moment, he picked the knot loose.

Fredrik tore the gag from his mouth and turned around. "Good to have that out."

Dierk grinned.

Fredrik wavered, and Dierk stuffed his shoulder under Fredrik's good arm. "Fredrik, are you well or not?"

"Well enough, lad." A wry grin twitched his stubbled face. "Choose a sword for yourself. I need some water."

"Here, lean on the table. I'll get the water." Leaving Fredrik propped on the age-worn wood, Dierk strode to the water bucket and returned with a dripping cup.

That done, Dierk turned to the weapons. Deep within him, a flame of joy leaped to life at the thought of carrying a sword after all these weeks. He picked up a leather scabbard about three spans long and drew out the blade: broad, double-edged, perfectly balanced. The hilt burrowed into his palm as if it belonged.

He tipped the blade so the window's light gleamed along the bluish silver metal. Fine steel, blended and tempered. He thumbed the edges. Flawless. Some wealthy noble lost a valuable piece when Veit stole this.

Dierk sheathed the sword and slung its leather baldric over his right shoulder so it crossed his chest. The familiar weight of a good sword, its slap against his left leg, brought a satisfied smile to his face. He tied the sheath-thongs to his belt, binding the baldric in place. "Fredrik, do you want a sword?"

"No, lad." Fredrik stumbled to the water bucket and dipped another cupful. "I'm not coming. You go, bring help if you can." He handed Dierk the cup. "I'll give you my signet.

Veit hid it somewhere when he searched me."

Jaw loose, Dierk could only stare as Fredrik walked past him. He gathered his senses and quaffed the water. Then he plunked the cup on the table. "What do you mean you're not coming?"

Fredrik poked in the dirt around the hearth. "Lad, I'm not dead, but neither am I well. I haven't the strength to flee."

"But you just freed us both." Apparently, Fredrik needed reminding. "I don't understand how you go from near dead, to cutting us loose, to having no strength to escape."

"To deceive Veit, I feigned some of my weakness. Not all of it." Fredrik knelt and scratched at the sandy dirt under a hearthstone.

Dierk snapped his teeth together. "We can go slowly, through the woods."

"Ah, here 'tis." Fredrik brushed off his signet. "Dierk, I am too weak for even that."

Dierk took the ring Fredrik handed him and stashed it in his pocket. The man *did* look terrible. Bruised, blood-smeared, dirt-stained. One arm useless.

"Very well." Dierk squared his shoulders. "I'll stay with you." Nothing could induce him to let Fredrik face Veit alone.

"No. Your father bade you obey me." Fredrik's iron tone rivaled Sir Wilhelm's. "You must go."

Dierk's heartbeat sped, pulsed through the veins in his neck, and pounded in his temples. This morning he'd disobeyed Fredrik with the best of intentions, and only brought his friend more pain. He wouldn't flout Fredrik's orders again.

Yet Fredrik would surely die if Dierk did not return

before Veit. "Please, Fredrik. Don't force me to leave you."

Fredrik sighed as he looked up. "Dierk—"

"I beg you." Dierk sank to his knees, bringing himself eye-to-eye with Fredrik. "Don't order me to disgrace my rank by deserting a comrade in danger."

Fredrik turned his face away. "Dierk, in many ways you are a man."

"Then let me stay."

"But." Fredrik looked at him again. "You must consider your duty. You are Crown Prince, destined to be king. For the sake of your people, you should leave me." Fredrik smiled ever so slightly. "You will make a good king, lad."

Dierk swallowed and shifted his gaze to the cut ropes sprawled on the floor. He could escape now and live to rule Sunland. That's what he'd always wanted. What he had been born to do. If he stayed with Fredrik, they might both end up dead. No one would even know how they died.

But if he left Fredrik now, he'd never return with help in time. Veit would kill Fredrik, then he and Baldur would flee to heaven knew where. The only thing gained would be Dierk's own life.

Unacceptable.

He lifted his gaze to meet Fredrik's unrelenting gray eyes. "If you command me to leave, I will obey you. But my choice is to stay. Were I an only son, perhaps my duty would be different, but I have a brother well-able to rule." Chest aching of a sudden, he clenched his left fist around the sword hilt. "Let me stay. My duty is to you, my comrade and friend. Father wouldn't want me to leave."

Dierk waited, but Fredrik said nothing. A verse of

Scripture emerged in Dierk's memory. "'Two are better than one ... Woe to him who is alone when he falls, for he has no one to help him up.'" 'Twas a marvel he recalled that.

A suspicious twitching convulsed Fredrik's mouth. "You would quote Scripture at me like a priest? Or like your father." His tone was stern—mostly.

Dierk dared to smile. "Please, may I stay?"

"Aye." Fredrik let out a soft groan. "May God help us both." His eyes slid closed and he toppled forward into Dierk's arms.

DIERK PEERED OUT THE rear window of the bedchamber. Sheep dotted the meadow, but Baldur was nowhere in sight. Veit should return soon unless he'd stopped for a few drinks. Dierk turned away to look at Fredrik.

Dierk had dragged him to the bed as soon as he assured himself Fredrik still breathed. He'd taken advantage of the man's unconsciousness to reset his shoulder. The relaxed muscles allowed Dierk to guide the joint almost effortlessly back into place.

Now he waited for Fredrik to wake. Perhaps after some rest, Fredrik could flee.

A faint whistled tune floated into the silence. *Veit!*

Dierk shook Fredrik's shoulder. "Veit's coming," he hissed.

Fredrik didn't move.

Well, this was why Dierk had stayed. To defend Fredrik. He slid his sword free, enjoying the feel of it in his grasp. Swordplay was his territory. He could do it. *Lord, I must win* offense and defense.

Metal rang against metal, and the blows vibrated up Dierk's sword arm. Dierk fought to wound. Veit fought to kill. More than once Dierk blocked a thrust at his throat. He caught each strike, focused on Veit's blade—and his eyes. Sir Wilhelm said reading your opponent, while remaining unread, would win the battle.

Veit shifted a quarter turn, and Dierk shifted to match. His sword hit another beam, and he lunged aside to compensate. But Veit's blade grazed his left ribs.

He must keep his position parallel to the beams. He stepped back. The table brushed his empty shield-arm. He met Veit's knife as hard as he could, driving the blade wide. Side-stepping, Dierk pierced Veit's left underarm, then jumped back to avoid Veit's retaliation.

Red liquid soaked the side of Veit's tunic. He dodged around the table and faced Dierk, pain tight around the corners of his mouth.

Dierk paused, on guard, and drew a long breath. "Yield, Veit. You cannot win."

Veit smiled, and Dierk leaped aside just in time to avoid the table Veit sent crashing toward him.

Sir Wilhelm was right about watching your opponent's eyes.

Veit's blade slashed back and forth in a furious onslaught. Not so furious he lost his skill. Dierk countered, strike after strike, mindful of two things: the beams' position and the need to end this soon.

He couldn't fight forever, not after the past day. Next time he wounded Veit, it must cripple him, preclude any chance of retaliation. Dierk used every one of Sir Wilhelm's tricks to achieve the perfect stance. If this failed, 'twould be difficult to recover.

The world narrowed to Veit and his long knife, the jarring clash of steel blades, the subtle movements to hold the advantage. Veit gave ground a bit. Dierk took his chance. He swung over his head, between the beams, and straight down, adding the strength of his shield arm at the last second. The sword sliced Veit's right wrist straight through.

Veit screamed to wake the dead. He fell, blood pooling on the dirt floor.

Dierk's stomach wrenched, and he swallowed the bile burning his throat.

"Kill me, will you?" Veit snapped, his voice like a too-tight harp string. "You know you want to."

Dierk's chest heaved. Part of him did want to kill Veit. The man deserved it. But the Lord had given Dierk this victory, and he had no plans to retract his vow.

"Well done, lad," Fredrik said behind him.

Sword in hand, Dierk turned.

Fredrik leaned against the doorjamb into the other room. "You might find clean cloths in that chest under the rear window. Press it firm against his wrist. We'll heat a knife and sear the wound to stop the blood."

Dierk raked his gaze over Fredrik. *Good to see him standing up.* "When did you wake?"

"When the table crashed over."

"And you are well?"

"Better than I was. Now fetch that cloth."

Dierk headed for the chest Fredrik indicated, leaned his

sword against the wall, and lifted the heavy lid. Sure enough, a stack of clean, stained cloths nestled in one corner. He grabbed a few and approached Veit, who kicked his leg.

Dierk kicked Veit, hard, in the thigh. "I haven't time for this. Lie still and keep quiet. Pretend you're dead if it suits you." He knelt and crammed the wad of cloth against Veit's arm where his hand used to be.

Veit sucked in air, but to his credit, he didn't cry out. Sweat shimmered on his ghost-pale face, and his good hand kept fisting and relaxing with a jerk.

Fredrik picked up one of the cloths and ripped it into strips. "Baldur will come to investigate Veit's scream, if he was near enough to hear."

Of course. Dierk hadn't had time to think that far ahead. "Hope he doesn't fight as well as Veit."

Fredrik grunted as he squatted at Veit's other side. "I'll get him with the bullwhip." Fredrik punched Veit's jaw. Veit went limp.

Dierk raised his head and stared at the man across from him. Fredrik's temper had showed at Lady Melankardja's fortress, hot beneath the surface. But he'd controlled it. *Guess Veit's treatment was too much.*

Fredrik shrugged. "Don't have any other way to put him out. No sense in him suffering unduly. He'll come to soon enough."

Dierk nodded and bent his attention to the blood-soaked bandage. Of course Fredrik hadn't struck a helpless enemy for revenge. He'd never violate the knight's creed.

Instead, Fredrik had just shown Dierk how to love his enemies.

"Tie the bandage as tight as you can." Fredrik stood. "I'll see to the fire."

Dierk fought with the strips, trying different positions to bind the clumsy dressing in place.

Wooden thuds near the fireplace came to an abrupt halt.

Dierk glanced over his shoulder. Fredrik stood by the rear window, gazing through the lattice. "Here comes Baldur."

Dierk cinched a knot around the bandage. "This should hold for now."

"Bind his feet." Fredrik grabbed a coiled bullwhip hanging from a rafter. "I'll take Baldur." The back door creaked open, shedding more light in the cottage. The whip hissed. Something thumped. Baldur cursed.

Dierk hastened to tie Fredrik's cut leg rope around Veit's ankles. Then he jumped up and hurried outside. In the sunshine, he squinted. Baldur lay on the ground, the bullwhip coiled around his right arm, a knife under his empty hand.

"Grab a rope and get him tied for me, Kik."

Dierk looked at Fredrik. "Father made no jest that you are skilled with a whip."

"Aye, well. I've used it in less noble causes before. Make haste."

Dierk ducked inside, found a couple lengths of rope, and returned.

Fredrik flicked the whip free. "Bind his hands in front. If he makes trouble, it goes the other way."

The whip left a spiraling red cut on Baldur's arm. Dierk tore off the man's short sleeve and wrapped it around the wound before he tied the rope. No sense in him suffering unduly, as Fredrik said. He hauled Baldur to his feet. "Come inside."

Baldur didn't resist, which showed good sense, what with Fredrik's whip ready to yank him down at the first sign of defiance. When Baldur was seated against the wall, feet safely bound, Fredrik leaned against the wall and coiled the whip.

"Kik, stick a knife in the coals and tell me when you think it's hot. I must rest. Again. Better tie Veit's good hand to his belt, too. And wrap up his shoulder." Fredrik paused, his smile apologetic in his bruised face. "Can you handle it?"

Half a smile stretched Dierk's split lip. "Rest. I'll shout if anything goes awry."

"Might want to look to that scratch on your side, too."

Dierk looked down at the bloodstained rent in his tunic. He'd forgotten it, although, now that he remembered, it had hurt for a little while. He grinned, regardless of his bruised lip. "I'll see to it."

Fredrik gestured something like a salute and shuffled into the bedroom. The bed creaked a moment after.

Fredrik was a remarkable man. Dierk poked through the assortment of knives until he found the dullest one. Intense heat could damage a blade. Dierk grabbed a couple logs, their roughness familiar, and placed them on the coals, crushing a charred stick to ashes.

To think an hour ago he'd held no real hope of escape. Of course, with Fredrik's weakness and two prisoners, something could still go wrong. Wouldn't pay to nap on duty.

Dierk thrust the knife into the coals and turned to gather more rags for Veit's wound. When he finished that, perhaps he'd try to find something to eat. He was no cook, but he hoped his stomach would cease its complaints if he put *something* in it.

'Twould distract his mind from the exhaustion creeping into his body.

46

At This Hour

THE LAMP ON THE table cast velvety brown shadows all over the cottage. Dierk leaned against the back-door frame because if he sat down, he was sure he'd go to sleep. He'd offered to take first watch since Fredrik needed rest.

Veit let out a soft groan, and Dierk straightened. He lifted the water bucket off the table and knelt beside the huge man lying on a blanket. When Fredrik had cauterized his wrist hours ago, Veit had shrieked once and passed out. He still hadn't regained his senses in full.

Dierk touched Veit's forehead. Warm. Fredrik had said Veit might run a fever. Dierk dipped a rag in the cool water, wrung it out, and bathed Veit's neck and forehead.

Strange. This afternoon, he could have killed Veit with pleasure. Now the craving to hurt him had disappeared. He almost pitied the man. His obsession with robbing an empty fortress cost him his right hand and his freedom; soon enough, 'twould cost his life. And if he died now, estranged from God, he would face hell.

Aye, the man was worthy of pity. Dierk soaked the cloth again and dribbled water into Veit's hair. Then he laid the rag aside and stood.

"Why do you do that?"

Dierk looked at Baldur, tied hand and foot, sitting against the wall. "Do what?"

"Tend him as if you care. Why not kill us both?"

Because the Crown Prince shouldn't go around killing his father's subjects. Though these particular subjects would likely die for their treason. Father wouldn't have reproved him if the fight ended with Veit and Baldur dead; Dierk would gamble on that. The true reason ran deeper. "Because God would not have it so."

"Hm." Baldur looked away, and the lamplight illumined his profile. The face of an ordinary man.

Dierk leaned against the table and rested his palms on the smooth-worn edge. "Why do you aid Veit in his schemes to rob Lady Melankardja's fortress?"

Baldur shrugged. "Why shouldn't I? He does the hardest work, and I'll get—I was to get—an equal share of the treasure."

Dierk glanced down, scuffing streaks in the dirt with his toe. "What gave Veit the idea the Crown stores treasure in the fortress?"

"What makes you think they don't? 'Tis a good place."

True. And the guards made it look more suspicious. "How many of you are part of this scheme?"

"Why should I tell you?"

Dierk crossed his arms and looked at Baldur with a weary smile. "No reason. In fact, you probably shouldn't."

Baldur lifted his bound hands to scratch his chin. "Why did you and your father travel here in disguise?"

Dierk half-smiled. "Private business for the Crown."

"The Crown." Baldur snorted.

The scorn in those two words took Dierk by surprise. He'd assumed pure greed led Veit and Baldur to weave their schemes. Not animosity toward the Royal House. "Tell me something, Baldur. What has the Crown ever done to you that you would scheme to rob the fortress even if you had to kill two innocent people to do it?"

"They cheated us."

Fine falsehood. "Cheated you?"

"You're a nobleman. You wouldn't understand."

Dierk pushed himself to a seat on the tabletop. "Try me."

Baldur lifted his chin. "Three, almost four years ago, we had a poor harvest. Too poor to pay the nobles their normal share. But the nobles demanded it anyway. So we appealed to the King. Traveled all the way to Sunland Castle. Veit was among the delegation. But—"

"Veit went to Sun City?" Must be where he saw Fredrik, noticed their resemblance.

Baldur bent his knees toward his chest and said nothing.

"Sorry. You were saying?"

"I was saying His Most Gracious Majesty ruled in favor of his own rank. We should've known he would."

That didn't sound like Father. "You mean the King bade you pay the full amount?"

"He lowered the rate a little. But we had nothing to spare. Nothing."

Dierk gave a meditative nod. He recalled nothing of it. Must have happened after he moved to Duke Ebner's. "Did anyone starve to death?"

"No." Baldur's face morphed into scorn. "You nobles. When no one dies, you think we peasants ought to be content. Never mind you have wealth and comforts, more food and clothes than you could ever need."

"You might be glad we're not part of the Holy Roman Empire. Their serfs fare worse than Sunland's peasants."

"So you would have us believe."

Dierk sighed. Those words ought to anger him. But he scarce cared, for a tempting wave of sleepiness rolled over him. He yawned as he slid off the table and knelt to sponge Veit's face again. Anything to stay awake.

"You say God wouldn't want you to kill us. Yet you accept He gave you nobles power over us. Why would He do so?"

Dierk stroked the cloth down Veit's cheek. "I don't know." He remembered Gertrude's words. "'Will the thing formed say to him who formed it, why have you made me like this?'"

"I might have expected such an answer from a noble."

Dierk looked up, piercing Baldur with his gaze. "Have you any idea of the responsibility a noble bears? How he must guard the welfare of his people, yet be prepared to provide an army for the king at a moment's notice? How he must discern justice in delicate matters? How the peace of his people must always be foremost in his plans, though he never knows when an enemy may come to war against him? If a man is any noble at all, it weighs on him."

"You have some fancy arguments, noble boy."

Dierk returned his attention to Veit. Deep lines creased the man's face. Dierk tossed down the rag. "It matters not. There are many things in life I don't understand. Probably never will. 'Tis my business to follow the Lord wholeheartedly. Even when I don't wish to."

Baldur barked a rough laugh. "Perhaps you are in school to become a priest."

The idea. Dierk tipped his head back in silent laughter. "Not I. But, God willing, I'll become a better Christian than I have been." He sobered. "Do you know God wants to save *all* people, Baldur?"

"I might have heard the priests say something of that nature." His tone was dry.

Dierk shrugged. "That is why I did not kill you." He pushed his fingertips against the dirt as he stood. "Want some water?"

Baldur nodded. "Boy, I don't know whether you're a religious fanatic or a madman."

Who would have thought anyone could suspect *him* of religious fanaticism? Dierk smiled as he dipped the water. His fellow squires would mock a little when he returned home. No matter. He'd changed on this journey.

The very thing he'd promised himself he wouldn't do.

He shook his head, handing the water to Baldur. As it turned out, he liked his new self better.

KING PHILLIP SAT DEEP in the saddle, urging his steed up the steep incline. The stars were fading. Dawn would break soon. Moritzburg couldn't be far.

"Your Majesty, the horses would appreciate a rest after this climb." The voice of one of his knights drifted through the darkness behind him.

Phillip looked over his shoulder so his words would carry. "Very well. We shall let the beasts walk." He faced frontward again. It had gone thus for hours now, ever since the urgent message arrived yesterday afternoon from a League member in Moritzburg: *"Henrik and Kik Holtzer require immediate reinforcements."* No horse could achieve the pace Phillip craved. So he pushed on, trying to be reasonable, resting when his companions reminded him.

Phillip crested the rise and reined his mount to a walk. Hoofbeats clopped behind him, slowing to match his pace. The path sloped down and eased into level ground. The air smelled of damp soil and dead leaves. Shadowy trees slipped by as the horses trudged on. Would they never reach Moritzburg?

What trouble had forced Fredrik to send for aid? Why had he not specified more in the message, hinted at how best Phillip could help?

By now, the trouble could have already come to its crisis. And with no help, Fredrik and Dierk might have lost. Perhaps they were—

No! He would not think that way. He couldn't. He must keep going, trusting God. *O Lord, let me find my son safe. Please. In Jesus' name I ask it. Be with him, and with Fredrik.*

The deeper darkness of the woods ended abruptly, replaced by what looked like meadows. Phillip kicked his horse's flanks. The well-bred animal responded as if it hadn't traveled all night with only an hour's break. Hooves cantered behind him, their rhythm filling the night's silence.

A breeze brought the faint smell of wood smoke and animal dung. Phillip clamped his knees tighter.

THE CASTLE WATCHMAN'S TRUMPET blared warning of their approach, but Phillip didn't slacken his speed. When he reached the stone walls, he leapt from his horse and pounded on the door set in the castle's huge gate. "Open, in the name of the King!" He slammed his mailed fist against the iron-plated door until a voice cut through the racket.

"Who calls at this hour?"

"Our Majesty, King Phillip Lichtensitz, to speak with Lord Moritzburg!"

Silence. Phillip waited. No doubt the gatekeeper wondered what business the King had here, if he even believed Phillip's claim to be king.

"Get back," the voice called. "We're lowering the portcullis."

Phillip and his men backed up. Chains creaked, and the iron grate grumbled down its grooves. It halted with a shudder.

A bolt screeched and the door in the gate creaked ajar, throwing torchlight in Phillip's face. He squinted at the man who held it and the armed guards flanking him. Draping his reins over his arm, Phillip slid off his right glove and thrust his signet hand through the bars. In case the emblem on his jerkin and the crest on his armor weren't enough.

The gatekeeper's sleepy eyes opened wide, showing the whites. "Your Majesty." He bowed low, then spun around. "Raise the portcullis. Open the gates."

The door slammed. Chains groaned as they hauled the portcullis up. Thuds filtered through the gate until one half cracked open and swung back slowly.

The gatekeeper appeared, bowing again. "All courtesy to you. Enter with the warmest welcome of Lord Moritzburg."

Phillip led his mount inside the huge courtyard, followed by the eighteen knights from Sunset Castle who had accompanied him.

As several men set to shutting the gate, the gatekeeper turned once more to Phillip. "How may I serve Your Majesty?"

"I understand 'tis early yet. But I must see Lord Moritzburg immediately." He'd intended to keep his business private until he spoke with the count, but urgency disregarded caution. "I am seeking Henrik and Kik Holtzer, woodcutters. Have you heard anything of them?"

"Kik Holtzer? A woodcutter's son of that name was tried for setting the church afire two days ago. The council found him innocent."

Church afire? Dierk on trial? "Where is he now?"

"He disappeared the day he was released. No one's seen him since." The man paused. "Unless he returned to the inn last night and I have yet to hear of it."

"And his father?"

"Disappeared the night of the fire, Your Majesty."

Great thunder. Phillip's mind reeled, struggling to make sense of this news. No use. "Send to this inn you speak of to discern whether he has returned. I must meet with the count."

"And you did not think it necessary to aid Kik Holtzer in his search for his father?" Frustration crept into Phillip's tone in spite of his effort for calm.

"Ah, no, Your Majesty." Lord Moritzburg spun the wine cup in his hands. "That is, I do not think my aid would have helped him find his father any sooner."

Ach. He must not rage at his vassal. He *must not*. The man had judged the case well. A supposed woodcutter's son deserved no special treatment. But couldn't he have taken pity on a lad stranded in his town?

"And now, since the other peddler Ottmar has returned with his story, it seems I was mistaken in my judgment." Lord Moritzburg sighed. "I believed the lad. But it seems he cleverly pled his case, intending to rejoin his guilty father, as the peddler Torben told us. I suppose—"

Phillip smashed his fist on the table. Plates and cups rattled. "Did it never enter your mind that the peddler Ottmar might have slain Henrik the night of the fire, then caught Kik later and killed him, too?"

Stunned silence filled the chamber.

Unable to remain still, Phillip stood and paced to the dark window at the room's far end. Here in this very room his son had stood trial two days ago. He had acquitted himself well, according to the count. *Dierk, my son, where are you?*

Phillip turned to the assembled men—Lord Moritzburg; the castle scribe; the steward; an old squire, never knighted, who had sat on the council; and the knights who had accompanied him. "I crave your pardon. I am in turmoil. Kik Holtzer is, in fact, my son, Crown Prince Dierk."

Mouths dropped open. Even his companions had not known the true identity of the "woodcutters" Phillip sought.

"Your Majesty," Lord Moritzburg gasped. "I did not know."

"Of course you did not." Phillip waved his hand. "It is not for that I fault you. You judged aright, and you tended it at once. I commend you. I could only wish you had shown more compassion for the stranger in your gates."

The count bowed his head briefly. "I acknowledge the justice of Your Majesty's rebuke. None shall have cause to charge me with such neglect again."

"The principal concern now is to find my son and his companion." Phillip crossed his arms. "I offer a reward of ten gold suns for any useful information leading to their whereabouts. Only, let Dierk's rank not be known. Let the people think of him as Kik the woodcutter until he is found." He must be found. Phillip dared not let his mind dwell on any other possibility.

The castle steward drummed his fingers on the table. "'Tis well thought of. The minute dawn breaks, send word to the inn. News will travel."

Phillip glanced at the window. Faint light suffused the thin horn panes. "'Tis near enough to dawn. Send word now."

"I'll see to it immediately," the steward said.

"And question this peddler Ottmar you speak of." Likely the man would not speak, but they could try. "See if he knows anything of use."

"Yes, Your Majesty." Lord Moritzburg beckoned to one of his men-at-arms, who nodded and followed the steward out of the room.

Phillip turned and braced his forearm against the cold stone window frame near his head. He needed Fredrik to clap his shoulder, assure him all would come right, and remind him to pray. Or Zorena to take his hand in hers and pray with him. *O Lord, help me. I have not been so undone in years. Be with my son and my brother. Your will be done. In the name of Jesus.*

Someone gently touched Phillip's shoulder. He turned, and the knight behind him gave the Royal Salute, bowing deep as if ashamed of his boldness.

"Your Majesty, we will pray. Our God is not weak that He cannot save."

Phillip extended his hand, and they clasped forearms. "Thank you, my friend."

47

The Coin

"Your Majesty, a young boy named Markus wishes to speak to you about the matter of Kik Holtzer."

Phillip jumped up so fast he upset the chessboard in front of him. "Send him at once."

The servant bowed, retreating, and Phillip turned to Lord Moritzburg. "Forgive me. I think you had won in any case."

The count smiled faintly. "Your Majesty's mind is engaged elsewhere. This game was a vain hope of distraction."

Phillip nodded for politeness's sake. More than three hours since dawn. Ottmar insisted he knew nothing of the woodcutters' whereabouts. The six men sent searching had not returned. No villager had come to the castle bringing word, not even the League member who must have sent the message.

The servant reentered with a boy of perhaps twelve

standing straight and proud beside him. The boy advanced and knelt on one knee at Phillip's feet. "Your Majesty, Markus of Moritzburg at your service."

"Rise, Markus."

The boy rose and met Phillip's gaze. "I bring you word of Kik Holtzer. I met him the evening he disappeared, and he asked if I knew where Veit Nagel stayed."

"Veit Nagel?" God help them if Dierk had attempted to capture that knave on his own.

"Aye, Your Majesty. I gave Kik directions, and he didn't say for certain if he planned to visit there, but 'tis possible he did. Veit may know more. Although ..." Markus's voice dropped to a mumble. "You'd probably have to beat the information out of him. He's like that."

Panic rose in Phillip's throat. He tamped it down with a painful swallow. "Let us go and visit this Veit Nagel. Will you accompany us, Markus, to show the way?"

The boy's brown eyes rounded. "I would be honored, Your Majesty."

Phillip smiled, clapping his shoulder. "We ride in ten minutes."

DIERK SWALLOWED THE LAST bite of the warm oat porridge Fredrik had cooked for breakfast and licked his fingers. "'Tis good food."

"Better than the scorched kraut we enjoyed last night?"

Dierk grinned wryly as he stood. "Sorry. I know nothing of cookery." Nothing of milking goats, either, although he'd tried it this morning for the sake of the milk. The poor animal.

Fredrik grinned back, a bit lopsided to accommodate his

swollen face. "We'd best be getting to town soon. Veit will need a healer, and your cut ought to be looked at."

"That." Dierk flicked his hand. "'Tis you who needs to be looked at." Sleep and food had done wonders for Fredrik, but a healer's treatment would ease Dierk's mind. "I'll hitch up the pony, and then we'll see about loading Veit."

The fresh morning air was delicious. Dierk couldn't get his fill of sunshine and breezes after spending most of yesterday bound inside. Breathing deep, he tipped his face toward the cloudless blue sky. "O Lord, I must thank You. First You sent Markus who directed me to Fredrik. Then You freed us both from Veit Nagel and let us capture *him*. Fredrik is safe. I'm alive. I couldn't ask for more. Thank You for Your protection and care. You are good, and righteous, and merciful."

Faint thunder rumbled from the direction of the road. It grew louder and became rhythmic, like the hoofbeats of cantering horses. Dierk strode to the front of the cottage.

Where Baldur's field adjoined the main road, a group of superb steeds turned down the path toward the cottage. Their riders' mail armor glinted in the sunlight. Lord Moritzburg's men?

Dierk rapped on the front door. "Father, armed men approaching. Come see."

In a moment, the bolt grated back, and Fredrik stepped outside. Dierk had his eyes on the riders, trying to identify them by their heraldry, but sunlight flashing on their shields obscured the images. They didn't slow as they turned into the yard. The lead rider's jerkin was blocked by the boy sharing his saddle.

Markus?

And the face above him—*Father?* Impossible.

The horse skidded to a halt. Its rider all but flattened the boy into the horse's mane as he leapt down. "Dierk!" The man rushed forward. "Son!"

Strong arms encircled him and crushed him close to a mail-clad chest. Thrown off balance, Dierk returned the embrace as best he could. Great thunder. Father hadn't hugged him since ... he didn't know when. "Father, what are you doing here?"

Father didn't answer. Finally, he released Dierk and stepped back, but his fingers lingered on Dierk's shoulders. "Let me look at you."

"I'm hale and hearty, Father, except for a little scrape on my side." He cupped his hand over the spot as he studied Father's eyes, framed by shadows and deep lines. "Are you—well?"

Father let out a laugh. "Now I am. When I received Fredrik's message, I nearly flew to pieces. I have had no rest since."

"You needn't have worried, Phil," Fredrik said. "Dierk's the one who sent the message. He took better care of me than I did of him."

Father turned to Fredrik and extended his hand. "Fredrik. Thank God you're safe." Father's gaze darted to Fredrik's sling, then perused his face mottled with purple and green. "You look terrible. What happened?"

Fredrik chuckled dryly as he grasped Father's forearm. "Thanks, Phil. 'Tis a long story. Come inside. We have Veit and one of his fellow conspirators held captive."

Eyebrows raised, Father slid his gaze to Dierk.

A smile tugged at Dierk's mouth. "'Tis quite a tale. Let Fredrik begin. I wish to speak to Markus, if you don't mind, sir."

"Certainly. Had it not been for him, I would not be here now. He deserves his reward if ever a man did." Father squeezed Dierk's shoulder before he followed Fredrik.

Dierk spun on his heel and took in the twelve mounted guards—knights, judging by their gold spurs. A regal sight, and most welcome. In almost perfect unison, they delivered the Royal Salute. Grinning, Dierk returned a crisp military one. Then he stepped up to his father's horse where Markus sat astride it. "Markus, your information proved more helpful than I expected. I found Veit, as well as the other man I sought."

Markus flung his leg over the horse's withers and slid down. A bit of his former skepticism lurked in his eyes. "Did you really catch Veit?"

"We did. Although he did knock me cold, as you warned."

Markus's eyes widened.

"But we survived."

Markus kicked a tuft of grass. "He used to beat Nik, you know. Once I thought Nik might die, and I swore I'd kill Veit when I got big enough. Guess I won't have to now."

Dierk ran a hand through his hair. Who would've thought? "Veit won't be harming Nik or anyone else after this. The Crown wants him for something, besides what he did to Fredrik and me. He won't leave prison until he dies—or is executed."

Markus pulled something from his pocket and handed it

to Dierk. "I don't want to be paid for helping you catch Veit. I just want to know I helped."

The small copper coin he'd given Markus two nights ago nestled in Dierk's palm.

Markus picked up a pebble and hurled it at some distant target. "I don't want the gold suns His Majesty offered as reward for finding you, either."

"You should take the reward. You could give it to whoever you think needs it if you don't want it yourself."

"Maybe." Markus squinted up at him. "You're the Crown Prince, aren't you?"

"Aye." Dierk looked again at the farthing in his hand, then tipped his head toward the cottage. "Come here."

Markus followed him the few paces to the window. Dierk had to remove a shutter to expose the windowsill. He dropped the farthing back into his purse, pulled out his silver moon, and laid it on the window sill. He drew his knife, and with hard, steady force, he split the coin in two. Half-moons were common enough currency, so he notched the flat edges with the tip of the blade.

He dropped one half in Markus's hand. "Keep it for remembrance of the time you aided the Crown Prince to capture a treasonous criminal. Remember that justice is better than revenge, and God's power can conquer any darkness if we but do our best to serve Him."

Markus studied the broken moon as if committing Dierk's words to memory. Then he raised his head, and a grin exposed his even teeth. "Thanks, Your Highness."

"Just Dierk." He clapped Marcus's shoulder. "Thank you again for your help."

Markus shrugged. "Greet Nik for me if you see him again."

"That I will. Now I'd best go inside and help Fredrik explain so we can get back to town." Dierk stifled an urge to yawn. Father's coming had ended the crisis, relieving Dierk of the stimulation to keep alert. His body told him he could sleep all day. Maybe he would, once they'd delivered Veit to prison.

Dierk tucked the other half-moon into his own pocket and entered the cottage.

DIERK WOKE TO THE golden glow of afternoon sunlight. He rubbed his face and rolled to his back, luxuriating in the soft, deep mattress and the silken coverlets. The healer who had ruthlessly cleansed and bound his wound had ordered a few hours of undisturbed rest.

Dierk hadn't argued. He'd bathed first, and never had he so enjoyed washing off the grime and filth. Then he'd tumbled into the bed and slept, not interrupted by even a dream.

He hoped Fredrik had fared as well in his chamber.

Sitting up, Dierk took in the surroundings. The colorful tapestries, the thick fur rugs, the glass window. A chair stood beside the bed with clean clothing, silk and velvet, draped across it.

As he crawled out of bed and dressed, stabs of pain came from his wound. If that healer had let it alone, it wouldn't have hurt so. On the table at the bed's foot, he found an ivory comb and a polished-silver mirror. In the blue tunic and red dress-cloak, he looked like himself—Prince Dierk, squire of Duke Ebner. Yet so much had changed inside him. He ran the comb through his hair, which had lengthened over the weeks.

Someone knocked on the oaken door.

"Enter." Dierk turned. A grin stretched his face when he saw it wasn't just a servant with a message. "Father. Fredrik." They both looked much better than they had this morning. "Did you rest well?"

"Aye, lad," Fredrik said. "As did you, I see."

"I won't deny the bed is more comfortable than Baldur's."

Father chuckled. "In a couple hours, Lord Moritzburg plans to feast us, unless you would rather dine in private."

His mouth watered at the thought of roasted meats. "I'm not *that* ill."

Father smiled. "In that case, I have something I wish to discuss with you. Let us sit."

Dierk took a seat on the edge of the bed. Father's tone implied something grave. Which, in the past few years, meant an uncomfortable conversation for Dierk. He couldn't think of anything he'd done wrong since they'd left Lady Melankardja's fortress. Except for the dreadful moment of disobedience that resulted in Fredrik's being beaten half to death. His stomach clenched at the recollection.

The mattress shifted as Fredrik sat beside Dierk.

Father took the chair beside the bed. His brown eyes were serious as he met Dierk's gaze, one side of his face swathed in golden sunlight. "You have done well, my son. In aiding Fredrik. In your conduct toward the villagers. In capturing Veit and Baldur without killing them, although I would not have faulted you if you had."

Dierk waited for a "but."

"Sending for help shows wisdom. I doubt you found it easy to control your temper, yet from all accounts you succeeded. Fredrik told me how you conducted yourself as a prince should. A servant of his people. I want you to know I take pride in your conduct, Dierk."

Not a single word of disapproval. 'Twas easier to take Father's scoldings, unflinching, than to hold his gaze now. But Dierk did it, swallowing the emotion swirling inside him. "Thank you, Father. I am honored."

"Are you ready to take the Vow of the Royal League?"

Dierk sat up straighter. He hadn't expected that. "I needn't wait until I'm nineteen?"

"The age matters not with royalty. Only your readiness."

Dierk glanced down at the wolf skin rug. "I think I am ready, sir. As best I know how to be." He looked up. "If you think I am, 'twould be my joy to become a member."

A smile relaxed Father's expression. "Proceedings shall begin as soon as we reach Duke Ebner's castle."

"Yes, sir. I shall be honored." And thrilled. And proud. "Wait, what do you mean, 'we'? Will you travel with us?"

"Dierk, I shall barely let you out of my sight until we reach his castle. Notwithstanding your competence, my mind will rest easier if I accompany you." Father winked, and Dierk laughed. "Besides, I must be there for your vow. Would you mind if I sent for your mother?"

Mother. Maybe she would take pride in his conduct, too. 'Twould be a pleasant change. "I shall be glad if she can come."

"Good." Father slapped his knees. "That settled, I should go and dress for dinner."

"I should like to walk about the castle and courtyards. If you will permit me." Dierk shot Father a teasing grin.

"Of course." Father stood. "But take Fredrik with you. For my peace of mind."

"Aye." Dierk smirked, slanting his eyes toward Fredrik. "Wouldn't want him running off again. He gets himself hurt that way."

Father's laughter filled the room.

Fredrik stood, eyebrows soaring in mock-incredulity. "I beg your pardon?"

Dierk shrugged. "Look at that sling you're wearing."

"Impertinent lad." Fredrik cuffed Dierk's shoulder. "But I, too, am proud of you."

Dierk sobered. "I thank you, Fredrik." He stood, extending his hand. Fredrik appeared in Dierk's earliest memories, the nearest he had to an uncle. Yet he'd known little of him. This journey had instilled a deep, new respect for the man who had once served Satan but now followed God so whole-heartedly. If ever there lived a true servant of Christ, 'twas Fredrik.

His grip firm, Fredrik clasped Dierk's forearm. Dierk squeezed back, hard. They needed no other words.

48

Bound with This Vow

DIERK RODE UNDER THE gate at Duke Ebner's, astride a splendid black steed. Notwithstanding his new proficiency at traveling by foot, he much preferred these last few days riding the well-bred courser borrowed from Sunset Castle.

The familiar cacophony of people at work filled the vast courtyard. Dierk raised his voice to speak to his father riding beside him. "If I may, I should like to take my horse to the stables myself."

"As you wish. Only hasten to the Hall to greet Duke Ebner."

"I will." Dierk guided his mount to the right while Father, Fredrik, and their six escorts continued across the courtyard toward the castle's entrance. At the stables, Dierk halted. With a final pat on the horse's neck, he leapt from the saddle.

"Ho, if it isn't Prince Dierk himself. Welcome back."

Dierk turned at the stable-master's voice. "Thanks, Timo. How were things in my absence?"

"Quiet." Timo reached for the bridle. "I hope your visit home was pleasant?"

Ha. Everyone knew he'd left in disgrace. "I wouldn't call it pleasant, but very beneficial. How's Bastian?"

Timo turned the horse toward the barn. "His arm mends."

Something Dierk hadn't known was tight relaxed in his chest. "Where is he today?"

"Here in the stables, tending saddles."

Tending saddles. Aye, that pricked. "Thanks. I wish to speak with him." Dierk jogged around Timo into the stable. He passed horses crunching feed and servants whistling as they mucked stalls.

Quiet filled the saddle room except for the swish of one young man polishing a bridle. A young man with his right forearm ever so slightly misshapen. Or did Dierk only imagine that?

He stepped inside, clearing his throat. "Bastian?"

Bastian raised his head. His eyes widened, and he bent his attention to his work. "Prince Dierk."

Lord, help me do this right. "How's the arm?"

"It mends." *No thanks to you,* his tone added.

"I am glad of it." Dierk ambled to the wall. In silence, he fingered the saddle that had thrown Bastian. Its repaired stitching suggested no such disaster. Drawing a deep breath, he turned around. "I ask your forgiveness, Bastian."

His fellow squire lifted his head.

Dierk hurried on before Bastian could speak. "I can blame no one but myself for your injury, and I deeply regret my behavior. You have a right to be angry with me. I can only beg your forgiveness and assure you I will endeavor to make it right in any way I can." He stopped, looked at the floor, and kicked at a stray straw. "I wish the horse had thrown me."

For a long time, Bastian didn't answer. Dierk waited, but perhaps he ought to let Bastian alone for a time. Prove the sincerity of his apology with his actions.

"You're serious, aren't you?"

Dierk met Bastian's gaze. "I am."

"I expected you to act as if nothing happened."

Aye. 'Twould have been much easier. "I was careless, Bastian. I want to make it right insofar as I can."

Bastian tipped his head back a little. "You can't un-break my arm."

"That is true." Dierk refused to look down.

"Ah, forget it, Dierk." Bastian rubbed his cloth along the bridle again. "I should have seen the torn stitches myself."

Dierk exhaled. They had a truce. "Look, I have to get up to the Hall. See you tonight." He headed for the door.

"What's with the axe?"

Dierk turned, sliding the tool free of its strap. Its handle fit his palm as well as a sword hilt. One day, it would hang in a place of honor in his bedchamber at home. "'Tis a remembrance from my adventures these past weeks."

Bastian smiled for the first time. "A good story for tonight, then?"

Dierk returned his smile. "A story for many nights."

Bastian stood and carried the bridle to its peg. Then he

whirled and flung his polishing rag at Dierk. "Good to have you back, Your Highness."

Dierk caught the rag before it smacked his face. He grinned. Bastian had forgiven him. "Thanks, Bastian."

AT HIGH NOON THREE days later, Dierk knocked on the carved oaken door of Duke Ebner's private chambers. He'd spent a good deal of the past two days being questioned by several men he'd never met before, a council for admittance to the League.

They posed questions on topics ranging from the Bible to politics to the subjects he studied in school. They proposed all manner of difficult circumstances, asking how he would handle them. After he answered, they wished to know *why* he gave that answer, until his head ached with the effort of concentration.

Their faces never indicated whether they found his replies satisfactory or not. But here he stood. He'd fasted since yesterday at noon. Now he would take the Vow of the Royal League.

The heavy door swung open to reveal his father, smiling encouragement. "Ready, son?"

"Ready, sir."

They passed through a high-ceilinged room, a smaller version of the Great Hall, into a little chamber lit by a tall, narrow window. Fredrik stood inside, along with Duke Ebner, the castle steward, a priest of Sunland's Church, and Mother.

Dierk hadn't seen her when she arrived this morning. She glided across the stone floor and embraced him. He wrapped his arms around her slender, silk-clad shoulders.

"I am so proud of you, Dierk." She pulled back, her eyes teary.

He smiled, surprised at his lack of embarrassment at her emotion. "I thank you, Mother."

Father cleared his throat. "Inasmuch as this man has come today to be joined to the Royal League, let us commence. Dierk Lichtensitz, come stand here, before the cross."

An ornate golden cross hung on the wall opposite the window. Beneath it stood an intricately carved table holding a Bible, two lighted candles, and a cup of wine. Dierk stepped forward, and the others gathered around him.

Father nodded to the priest. "Brother Andreas."

The man bowed his head. "O Lord, we thank You for this man and his willingness to serve You and to serve his country. We ask Your Spirit upon him to guide him all the days of his life. May he be wise, courageous, and righteous. In the holy name of Jesus, Your Son, we pray."

Dierk lifted his head.

"Place your right hand upon the Bible," Father said.

Dierk obeyed. Soft leather surrounded the jeweled design embedded in the cover. He fixed his eyes on the gold cross before him.

"Do you, Dierk Lichtensitz, Crown Prince of Sunland, take this vow upon you willingly and freely?"

Dierk gave the prescribed reply. "I do."

"Do you vow to uphold all the laws of Sunland?"

"I vow."

"Do you vow to hold the security of Sunland second only to your devotion to God, superior to your love for family, friends, prosperity, and your life?"

This aspect of the vow discouraged some members from matrimony, Fredrik had said. The League demanded undivided loyalty. "I vow."

"Do you vow to adhere to the Code of the Royal League, which you will hereafter commit to memory?"

"I vow."

"Do you vow to guard all secrets of the Royal League with utmost care, with your life if necessary?"

A tiny smile touched his lips. He'd already practiced this part. "I vow."

"Do you vow to protect and defend all Sunlanders, regardless of rank, when it is in your power to do so?"

"I vow."

"Do you accept that this day you take a lifelong vow, even if you should choose to withdraw from active duty?"

The king never had the option to withdraw from active duty. "I do."

"Do you understand that failure to keep these vows, through either willfulness or neglect, is a crime which shall be punished by death?"

"I do."

Father laid his hand on Dierk's shoulder. "In the presence of these witnesses, Dierk Lichtensitz has taken the Vow of the Royal League. Let us commend him to God." This time Father bowed his head and led them in a prayer that was no rote petition, but a heartfelt blessing. Then each person in the room added a short prayer. Even Mother. Tears pressed hard on Dierk's eyelids as he listened, but they didn't escape.

At the end, Father picked up the fragile earthen cup on

the table.

Following Father's earlier instruction, Dierk sipped the sweet wine it held to make the cup his own. Then he poured the rest of it on the floor, as if he poured out his life for the sake of Sunland.

Which, as Sunland's Crown Prince, was only right he should do.

"Before the Almighty God, and in the presence of these witnesses, I, Dierk Lichtensitz, Crown Prince of Sunland, do now bind myself with this vow." He hurled the cup to the stone floor, smashing it to tiny pieces that skidded far and wide.

The ceremony was finished.

Fredrik slapped his back. "Welcome, lad."

Dierk smiled so wide it almost hurt. "Thanks, Fredrik."

The others in turn extended their hands, and Dierk grasped their forearms, accepting their words of welcome. Except for Mother. She kissed his cheek instead.

Father drew something from his pocket. "Give me your left hand, son."

Dierk complied, and Father clicked a gold armband onto Dierk's wrist. Its clasp lay cool and heavy against his skin. Vibrant, colorful jewels set in the gold depicted the Royal Crest, a rising sun. A copy of Father's armband.

"'Tis time you had one. For now, keep it for special occasions." Father winked and pulled Dierk into a hard embrace.

Dierk clamped his eyes shut as those absurd tears clamored for escape again. Could be the fasting that had his eyes playing at waterfalls. Sufficient excuse.

"Now." Father stepped back and clapped his hands. "Let you break your fast at table with us."

The group moved toward the door, still congratulating Dierk and reminiscing about their own vows.

At last he had joined the Royal League. *Lord, grant I may serve my people well all the days of my life.*

Epilogue

In a guest chamber of Lord Sonnenburg's castle, Dierk fastened his ring-brooch at the shoulder of his purple cloak. Tonight was his first official royal visit. His parents, especially Father, visited a few of their higher-ranking vassals every year, but Dierk had always been occupied at Duke Ebner's.

In the past two years, the language of the Royal League had become as familiar to him as Sunman. He had even completed a few assignments for the League. He'd reached the highest rank of squire—bachelor—and Father spoke of knighting him next year. Meantime, his political studies had intensified. Hence this visit.

Of course, this journey might have something to do with Lord Sonnenburg's daughter. Dierk dropped onto a stool to buckle on his tall black leather dress boots. Father had more than hinted 'twas time to be thinking of a bride for Dierk.

Ah, the ways of royalty. One must always have an heir in mind. At least Father hadn't forged an agreement with some foreign noble and wed Dierk to a girl he'd meet the week of the wedding. Dierk wanted a girl like Gertrude if such a nobleman's daughter existed. Sweet, kind, spicy, and strong in her faith. If she had blue eyes, he wouldn't complain.

But enough of this. He tugged his tunic hem straight and arranged the drape of his cloak. Satisfied his appearance wouldn't disgrace his position, he left the room to join Father and Mother.

IN THE COUNT'S CHAMBERS, Dierk waited behind his parents to greet his hosts. Lord Sonnenburg had met them the moment they arrived, but now they would meet his wife and daughter before the evening's feast began.

Dierk's turn came to greet the count with a bow and the customary formalities. He seemed a pleasant man. Dierk took the countess's hand, bent and kissed it, exchanged the usual phrases.

Last in line stood Lord Sonnenburg's eldest daughter, Lady Crescentia. Dierk took the hand she extended, bowing to kiss it between her sapphire ring and intricate gold bracelet.

When he raised his head to look her in the face, deep blue eyes caught his. His heart leaped up to meet them.

A sound like a suppressed gasp escaped her lips.

Dierk blinked, but still couldn't tear his attention from her face. How could this happen again? Had he not grown mature in these two years? "Forgive me," he stammered. "I—You remind me of someone I knew once."

EPILOGUE

She stared back, her wide-open eyes mirroring his surprise. "I have sometimes been called Gertrude."

Gertrude. Then she must be ... But it made no sense.

The room's quiet struck him. He broke free of her gaze and glanced toward his father, only to discover smiles playing with the lips of both his own parents and Crescentia's.

Dierk looked again at the lovely maiden before him. "Did you ever meet a lad called Kik Holtzer?"

"'Tis you," she breathed. "I feared—that is, I did not wish to insult you if I was mistaken."

It was her. And he was still holding her hand. He gave it a gentle squeeze before releasing it. "'Tis good to see you again, Lady Crescentia." He smiled. "Perhaps in the course of this evening you will find time to tell me how you came to dwell with the Sisters at Spatzberg."

Crescentia smiled back, the same smile he'd seen so often during his stay with the Sisters. "I will gladly do so, if you will be so kind as to explain how the Crown Prince came to visit them as a woodcutter's son."

Ach. He'd have the less pleasant story. Yet, he'd like Crescentia to know the truth. "'Twill be a pleasure."

"Then let us proceed to the Hall for dinner," Lord Sonnenburg said, offering his arm to Mother.

As the hostess, the countess took Father's arm, and the two couples turned toward the door. By all rules of etiquette, Dierk must offer Crescentia his arm. So he did.

She took it, pink creeping into her cheeks. Her fingers cupped his arm, their warm pressure stealing his thoughts. She was more beautiful, more womanly, than he remembered.

As they followed Lord Sonnenburg, Father glanced over

his shoulder and winked at Dierk.

He knew the whole time.

A little brindled hound came from nowhere, leaping at Crescentia's hand.

She turned her palm to it. "Down, Inga."

"Inga?" Dierk looked at the sleek hound who settled into a trot beside her mistress. "She grew up more handsome than I imagined."

Crescentia smiled, glancing at him without turning her head. "Yes, I have reason to rejoice that I did not follow certain advice to do away with her."

"The man who advised you was obviously a fool."

That won a soft laugh from her. "Not a fool. Only a jesting lad."

Unable to contain his smile, he met her gaze again. His focus drifted down to her well-sculpted lips. Great thunder, he wanted to kiss her. He snapped his attention back to her eyes.

Her expression changed, and she looked away before he could read it. *Steady, Dierk.* He turned his attention to the couples preceding them down a staircase to the Great Hall.

Lady Crescentia, daughter of Theodore, Count of Sonnenburg. He liked the name. His own Gertrude, a noble lady, kept step beside him, her head reaching only to his shoulder. The last time they walked side by side, a storm had raged in the woods around them.

God willing, that rain-drenched trek was the start of a lifetime walking together.

𝔉𝔦𝔫𝔦𝔰.

Glossary

Baldric—leather strap worn over the shoulder (often cross-body style) to support a knife or sword

Brom bread—coarse bread made of leftover wheat bran and wheat germ, which was sifted out of whole wheat flour to make lighter, whiter flour for fine bread

Courser—swift, well-conditioned horse used for hunting or in battle

Cur—disreputable dog

Destrier—warhorse used in formal competition, but not usually on a battlefield

Fortnight—two weeks (fourteen nights)

Frau—(as used in this book) Mrs. or ma'am

Fraulein—(as used in this book) Miss

Furlong—unit of measurement equal to the length of a plowed furrow; in modern usage, 220 yards

Gauntlet—glove with cuffs that extended up the forearm for protection

Great Hall—main room of a castle, used for eating, feasting, working, and sometimes sleeping

Handbreadth—unit of measurement equal to the width of a man's hand; commonly approximated at 3-4 inches

Herr—(as used in this book) Mr.

Hist—a word commanding silence

Kirtle—long, loose dress worn by women in the Middle Ages

Knave—dishonest or wicked man

Liebchen—sweetheart, dear

Lief—gladly, willingly; also used like "soon" in the modern phrase "I'd just as soon"

Mace—weapon with a long handle and a spherical, spike-covered head

Page—boy of noble birth preparing to be a squire

Quintain—mechanical "knight" used as an opponent when practicing the use of a lance

Score—twenty

Span—unit of measurement equal to the distance from the tip of a man's thumb to the tip of his little finger when his fingers are spread wide; approximately 9 inches

Squire—young man not yet knighted who serves another noble; in some cases, men remained squires all their lives

Tiltyard—yard for practicing with a quintain

Trencher—slab of bread used as a plate, then given to the poor; in this book, also used to refer to a dish that's something between a bowl and a plate

Yeoman—commoner who owned and worked his own land

Author's Note

I hope you've enjoyed your time in Sunland! With all the good books out there, I'm honored you spent time on mine. I hope it's blessed you in some small way.

Sunland is so real to me that when I look at a map of Medieval Europe, part of me cries, "This map is a fake! It's missing Sunland!" But, though I've based the country on a particular piece of land in Europe, Sunland is entirely fictitious. I've tried to stay true to the medieval life and times, but I allowed myself a few liberties. It's my country, after all.

Because my characters speak Sunman (a fictitious Germanic dialect), I chose, for ease of reading, not to bother with strict older English in the dialogue. All languages have a formal version and a casual one, so I've tried to reflect that in modern English—translating from Sunman, if you will. Also, I'm aware that my use of the titles *sir*, *herr*, *frau*, and *fraülein* is not strictly consistent with modern or historical usage; my intention was only to create the "feel" of a Germanic language to enhance the setting without distracting the reader.

Along the same lines, I decided not to quote the King James Version of the Bible. My characters are quoting a Sunman version (from before 1611), so I could pick any English version for the translation. To make it easy for today's readers, but not to sound *too* modern, I went with the New

King James Version.

Sources for medieval history sometimes contradict themselves about details for the time period. I crave your indulgence for any historical errors and beg you would attribute it to Sunland's unconventional practices.

If you enjoyed this story the least little bit, I'd love for you to leave a review on Amazon or Goodreads (or anywhere, really). Just a line or two about what you liked, and maybe even what you didn't like. It's truly one of the best ways to support any author.

If you'd like to keep up with my writing (there are two more Sunland novels in the works), please visit my website, **darcyfornier.com**, and subscribe to my newsletter. As a thank-you for signing up, you can download my free novelette, *Blade-Caster*, and spend a little more time in Sunland. And if you're already a subscriber, thank you so much for supporting me on this wild writing journey!

Shalom!

-*Darcy Fornier*

Acknowledgements

A heartful of thanks ...

To my Lord: for calling me out of the kingdom of darkness and into the Kingdom of Your Son; and for this story—it isn't perfect, but You gave it to *me*, and I am overwhelmed with the joy of it!

To Mama: for planting a love of books in me; for all the English you made me study; for always supporting me; for reading this book again and again; and for always pointing me to the most important Book of all.

To Daddy: for encouraging me to write without fretting over others' opinions; for helping me get inside a guy's head; for sharing just enough of the darkness in your past to make me love the Light; and for always pointing me to Jesus.

To Molly: for loving Dierk from the first time you met him; for reading my roughest drafts; for keeping me from getting carried away with the conflict; for the chapter titles; for all the long walks where I rambled on and on about this story; for the mermaid joke; for the gorgeous cover; and for being my best friend.

To Leah: for reading the dialogue aloud to me; for brainstorming fixes for plot holes; for the chapter titles; for helping me find names; for Dierk's costume; for the axe graphic; for saying, "There needs to be a swordfight"; and for being my best friend.

To Hannah Miller: for liking every Facebook post; for sharing my excitement at milestones; and for being best friends with this slightly crazy writer.

To Courtney Cooper: for saying I'd have my picture on the back of a book one day.

To Stephanie Ridge, Amber Brooks, and Regina Prewitt: for asking me to tell you about my book.

To my faithful critique partners—Pam Green, Esther Bandy, Linda Strawn, Kyleann Hawkins, Sharon K. Connell, Patrice Doten: for loving Dierk's story and pushing me to make it the best I could. This book wouldn't be near as good without you.

To my beta readers—Kyleannn Hawkins and Christie Kern; for making sure things made sense.

To my proofreaders—Kathy McKinsey and Lori Southern: for catching all those horrid little errors that I couldn't see after reading the text twenty times.

To my friends in the North Alabama Writers' Group—Ginger Solomon, Bonita Y. McCoy, Janie Winsell, Betty Boyd, Jennifer Hallmark: for helping me find my footing as a writer; for your encouragement and prayers; for being fellow Bohemians.

To Mark Lewis: for providing Dierk's axe.

To Greg Bearden: for providing Sunland's forest.

To Tyler Adams: for being my cover model.

To every friend and family member who asked about my book: you can't know how much you encouraged me.

To the reader: May you ever walk forward in the Light.

Scriptures Referenced

Chapter 4: 1 Corinthians 15:55

Chapter 19: Romans 9:20

Chapter 31:   Psalm 91:1;   Psalm 139:8:   1 John 1:9; Hebrews 8:12; Romans 8:15-17

Chapter 33:   Philippians 4:13;   Romans 8:18;   1 John 5:4; Psalm 93:1; Psalm 46:1-2; Ephesians 6:13

Chapter 34:   Psalm 136:1;   Acts 2:21;   Hebrews 6:4-6; Luke 17:4; Matthew 8:22

Chapter 35: 2 Peter 3:9

Chapter 43: Matthew 5:44; Philippians 4:13

Chapter 44: Ecclesiastes 4:9-10

Chapter 46: Romans 9:20

Made in United States
Orlando, FL
05 January 2025